Scandal Above Stairs

Center Point
Large Print

Also by Jennifer Ashley and available from Center Point Large Print:

Death Below Stairs

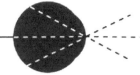

Scandal Above Stairs

Jennifer Ashley

CENTER POINT LARGE PRINT
THORNDIKE, MAINE

This Center Point Large Print edition
is published in the year 2018 by arrangement
with The Berkley Publishing Group, an imprint of
Penguin Publishing Group, a division of
Penguin Random House LLC.

The text of this Large Print edition is unabridged.
In other aspects, this book may vary
from the original edition.
Printed in the United States of America
on permanent paper.
Set in 16-point Times New Roman type.

ISBN: 978-1-68324-923-8

Library of Congress Cataloging-in-Publication Data

Names: Ashley, Jennifer, author.
Title: Scandal above stairs / Jennifer Ashley.
Description: Center Point Large Print edition. | Thorndike, Maine :
    Center Point Large Print, 2018. | Series: A below stairs mystery
Identifiers: LCCN 2018024046 | ISBN 9781683249238
    (hardcover : alk. paper)
Subjects: LCSH: Large type books. | BISAC: FICTION /
    Mystery & Detective / Historical. | FICTION / Mystery & Detective /
    Women Sleuths. | GSAFD: Mystery fiction.
Classification: LCC PS3601.S547 S29 2018b | DDC 813/.6—dc23
LC record available at https://lccn.loc.gov/2018024046

1

The clatter of crockery on the flagstone floor broke my heart. I knew without turning that it was my platter of whole roast pig, the crowning glory of the vast meal I'd spent days creating for the supper party above stairs in this grand Mayfair house.

A less capable cook would have buried her face in her apron and sunk down into wailing, or perhaps run out through the scullery and shrieking into the night. I had a better head on my shoulders than that, even if I was not quite thirty years old, and so I stayed upright and calm, though *stoic* might be the more appropriate adjective.

"Leave it," I snapped at the footmen who were scampering after the clove-studded onions rolling about the floor. "I'll send up the fowl, and they'll have mutton to follow. Elsie, cease your shrieking and scrub those parsnips for me. A dice of them will have to do, but I must be quick."

The scullery maid, who'd screamed and then leveled obscenities at the footmen after being splashed with the juices in which the pig had been roasting, closed her mouth, snatched up the bowl of parsnips, and scurried back to the sink.

I ought to be mortified to serve a joint of mutton with sautéed parsnips at Lady Cynthia's aunt's supper party in their elegant abode in Mount Street. But I was too worn down from the work that had gone into this night, too exasperated by the incompetence of the staff to worry at the moment. If I got the sack—well, I needed a rest.

But first to finish this meal. There was no use crying over spilled . . . pork.

My task was made more difficult by the fact that my kitchen assistant, Mary, whom I'd painstakingly trained all spring, had left a few days before—to get married, if you please.

I'd tried to tell the silly girl that looking after a husband was far more difficult than being in service ever would be. Husbands didn't pay wages, for one thing, and you never got any days out. Asking for extra pin money or an hour to oneself could send a husband into a towering rage and earn a wife a trip to the doctor, both to have her bruises seen to and so the doctor could assess whether there was something wrong with the woman's mind. A true wife was a sacrificing angel who asked nothing for herself.

I had taken time to explain this to Mary, but nothing had penetrated the haze of love into which she'd lapsed. Her young man seemed personable enough, at least upon first assessment. Some married couples rubbed along quite well,

6

I'd heard, which definitely had not been the case for me.

I hadn't exactly given Mary my blessing, but I hadn't hindered her from going either. Lady Cynthia, at my behest, gave Mary a parting gift of a few guineas—or at least, Cynthia borrowed the sum from her uncle to give, as she hasn't a penny to her name.

However generous I'd been to Mary, her going left me shorthanded. The agency had not yet sent a satisfactory replacement, and the other maids in the house had too many chores of their own to be of much use to me. We had no housekeeper, as the woman previously in that position, Mrs. Bowen, had retired in March after a bereavement. None of the potential housekeepers Lady Cynthia's aunt had interviewed had taken the post, so many now that I feared the agencies would stop sending them altogether.

Therefore, the butler, Mr. Davis, and I struggled to do the housekeeping duties as well as our own. So of course Mary chose this very time to run away and leave us.

But I could not worry about that at present. At *this* moment, I had to save the feast.

I at last convinced the footmen to cease trying to put the roast-blackened pig back onto the platter, and to run up to the dining room to receive the two capons laden with carrots and greens I lifted into the dumbwaiter. The downstairs maid cranked the lift upward while I got on with chopping the parsnips Elsie had scrubbed and thrusting them into already boiling water. A quarter of an hour in and they'd be soft enough to brown with onions and carrots and adorn the mutton. A sauce of mint and lemon would accompany the meat, and the meal would finish with various sweet treats.

Those at least I'd made well in advance, and they already waited upstairs on a sideboard—a raspberry tart with chocolate film on its crust, a lemon and blueberry custard, ices in bright fruit flavors, a platter of fine cheeses, a chocolate gâteau piled with cream, and a syllabub. Syllabub was a rather old-fashioned dish, but as it was full of sherry and brandy, I could not wonder that ladies and gentlemen of London still enjoyed it.

I was halfway through preparing the mutton, perspiration dripping down my neck and soaking my collar, when Mr. Davis appeared in the kitchen doorway.

Mr. Davis had been butler to Lady Cynthia's brother-in-law, Lord Rankin, for years, and could be haughty as you please above stairs. Below stairs, he dropped his toffee-nosed accent, sat about in his shirtsleeves, and gossiped like an old biddy. This evening he was in his full butler's kit, his eyes wide with consternation, the hairpiece he wore to cover his thinning hair on top askew.

"Mrs. Holloway." His horrified gaze took in the skinless pig on the floor in a spreading puddle of spiced sauce, and two maids at the table chopping vegetables as though their lives depended upon it. One was the downstairs maid who'd helped send up the capons, the other the upstairs maid, Sara. I'd laid my hands on *her* and dragged her in to help when she'd been unwise enough to come down to the kitchen in search of something to eat.

"What the devil has happened?" Mr. Davis demanded. "I announced the pièce de résistance to Mr. and Mrs. Bywater and Lady Cynthia and all their guests—which include His Grace of Guildford and the Bishop of Dorset, I might add—and I uncover two chickens. The same as their Saturday lunch at home."

I did not bother to look up after one hasty and irritated glance at him. "It is perfectly obvious what happened. Your footmen are clumsy fools. And I'll thank you *not* to compare my *blanquette de poulet à l'estragon* to a Saturday lunch. They will find them tender and declare the fowl the best they've had in years. Now, unless you wish to don an apron and peel carrots, you may leave my kitchen." When he only stood in the middle of the floor, his mouth open, I took up the paring knife that lay next to me. "At once, Mr. Davis."

I'd only intended to hand him the knife and tell him to get on with the carrots if he continued to stare at me, but Mr. Davis eyed the blade, took

9

a hasty step back, and then scuttled away, nearly tripping over the mountain of pig in his haste.

How we finished the meal, I have little recollection. Somehow, the two maids and I had the vegetables peeled, chopped, sautéed, and seasoned, the mutton sauced and presented quite prettily, and everything hauled upstairs via the dumb-waiter.

Sara, who had at first resented mightily that I'd recruited her for kitchen duty, beamed as the last of the food went up, and impulsively hugged the downstairs maid. Sara looked as though she wished to embrace *me,* but I stepped out of her reach before she could give in to the impulse.

"I'll never doubt you again, Mrs. Holloway," Sara said. "You worked a miracle. Like a general, you are."

I abandoned the kitchen, letting the footmen clean up the remains of the roasted pig—which I knew they'd devour or rush it home to their families as soon as I was out of sight. If I wasn't in the room to see it go, I couldn't stop them, could I?

I'd eaten little tonight, but I crossed the passage to sink down at the table in the servants' hall, thoroughly tired of food. I slumped in my chair a moment until my shaking ceased, and then I drew my notebook from my apron pocket and began to jot my thoughts on the meal.

I did this most nights, especially after I'd prepared a large repast. The notes were for my own guidance or perhaps would be used to train my assistant, if I ever found another one.

Sara brought me a cup of tea, for which I thanked her warmly. She looked upon me with admiration—at last, after my three months of employment in this house in Mount Street, she had found respect for me.

I wrote in relative peace for a time—jotting down what had turned out well in the meal, and what needed more polish. I did my best to ignore the noises across the hall—I heard more broken dishes and made a note to ask for funds to replace them.

Mr. Davis found me there an hour later. I'd longed ceased to write, my pen idle on the paper, my thoughts far from the meal and the noises around me.

Earlier this week, on my half day out, I'd gone to a lane near St. Paul's Churchyard to spend the time with my daughter. She'd grown an inch since I'd taken this post, becoming more of a young lady every time I saw her. One day, I vowed, I'd take what I'd saved of my wages, and Grace and I would live in a house together, looking after each other.

My daughter and I always made a special outing when I visited, and that day we'd gone to look at exhibits in the British Museum. Quite a few antiquities had been flowing back to London these days from archaeological digs in Egypt, Greece, Rome, and the Near East, and ladies and gentlemen flocked to see them—mummies, sarcophagi, and little dolls that had accompanied the ancient Egyptians into their tombs; as well as more cheerful things like vases, jewelry, jars, and combs from the civilizations of Greece and Rome, and tablets of writing only scholars could read.

While we'd stood waiting to enter the building, I'd sworn I'd seen the face of a man I knew. His name was Daniel McAdam, a gentleman I'd come to look upon as a friend—a very close friend.

Of late, though, I'd revised that opinion. I'd seen much of Daniel in the early spring, and then nothing at all in the last two months. Not a sign of him, not a glimpse of him, not a dickey bird, as I would have said in my youth. As I'd lectured Mary about marriage, in the back of my mind was a promise that I'd not make a fool of myself over a man ever again. I vowed I'd put Daniel straight out of my head.

However, when I'd glimpsed a gentleman in a plain suit coming out of another door in the museum, his dark hair barely tamed under a black bowler hat, every ounce of my resolve fled. I'd found myself stepping out of the queue, craning to see him, turning away to follow him when he walked off toward Bedford Square, blast it.

Only Grace's puzzled query—"Where are you going, Mum?"—had brought me to my senses.

Mr. Davis cleared his throat, and I jumped, opening my eyes. I seemed to have dozed off.

"Lady Cynthia wishes to see you," Mr. Davis announced, looking too smug about that. "You're in for it now, Mrs. H."

I gave him a prim stare. "I am quite busy, Mr. Davis. I must prepare for tomorrow."

A cook's work is never done. While the rest of the household sits back and pats their full stomachs, I am in my kitchen starting dough for tomorrow's bread, making lists of what I'll need for the next day's meals, prepping any ingredients I can, and making sure the scullery maid has finished the washing up.

Mr. Davis had shed his coat, and damp patches adorned his shirtsleeves beneath his arms. His brows climbed. "You expect me to go upstairs and tell her ladyship you're too busy to speak to her?"

"She will understand." I liked Lady Cynthia, for all her eccentricities, but at the moment, I did not wish to have a conversation with anyone at all.

Mr. Davis eyed me closely, but I turned a page of my notebook and pointedly took up my pen.

As I bent over my notes, he heaved a great sigh, and then his footsteps receded. He stepped into his pantry—probably to fetch his coat—then I heard him start up the stairs. He was gone, and blissful quiet descended.

The peace was shattered not many minutes later by heels clicking sharply on the slate floor and an impatient rustle of taffeta. A breeze burst over me as a lady stormed into the servants' hall and leaned her fists on the tabletop in a very unladylike manner.

She had a fine-boned face and very fair hair, lovely if one enjoys the pale-skinned, aristocratic version of beauty. Her high-necked and long-sleeved gown was deep gray with black soutache trim—she wore mourning for her sister, recently deceased.

I jumped to my feet. She straightened as I did so, a frown slanting her brows, her light blue eyes filled with agitation.

"It is important, Mrs. H.," Lady Cynthia said. "I need your help. Clementina's going out of her head with worry."

I had no idea who Clementina was—I assumed one of Lady Cynthia's vast acquaintances.

"I beg your pardon, my lady. What has happened?"

"She was here tonight, very upset." Cynthia waved impatiently at the chairs. "Oh, do let us sit down. Davis, bring me tea to steady my nerves, there's a good chap."

Davis, who'd followed Lady Cynthia down,

stuck his nose in the air at being ordered about like a footman and said a haughty, "Yes, my lady." He glided out to shout into the kitchen for someone to make a pot of tea for her ladyship and be quick about it.

I had not seen much of Lady Cynthia since Lord Rankin had retreated to his country estate to console himself. He'd allowed Lady Cynthia to remain living in his London house, which revealed a kindness in him that surprised me. Lady Cynthia had no money of her own, as I've mentioned, and not much choice of where to go. Her parents, the Earl and Countess of Clifford, lived in impoverished isolation in Hertfordshire, and I knew Cynthia had no desire to return to them.

An unmarried lady could not live alone without scandal, however, so Cynthia's aunt and uncle—the respectable Mr. Neville Bywater, younger brother to Cynthia's mother, and his wife, Isobel—had moved into Lord Rankin's house to look after her. Her aunt was content to put her feet up and enjoy the luxurious house in Mount Street while her husband went off to work in the City. The Bywaters were not poor, but they were careful, willing to save money by taking Lord Rankin's free room and board.

"Clemmie's married to a baronet," Cynthia said as soon as she and I sat down. "He is appallingly rich and has priceless artwork hanging on his walls. That is, he *did*—that artwork has started to go missing, whole pictures gone. Sir Evan Bloody Godfrey is blaming Clemmie."

I blinked. "Why should he? It seems a bizarre assumption to make."

"Because Clemmie is always up to her ears in debt. She plays cards—badly—and wagers too much, and she likes the occasional flutter on the horses. As a result, creditors visit her husband. Before this, he'd pay up like a lamb, but a few months ago, he suddenly announced that enough was enough. He forbade Clemmie to wager ever again, but of course, Clemmie couldn't help herself."

"Her husband believes she sold the paintings to pay the debts," I finished as Sara scurried in with tea on a tray and set it carefully on the table. She curtsied, waited for any further instruction from Cynthia, then faded away when Cynthia dismissed her.

I reached for the teapot and poured out a steaming cup of fragrant tea for Lady Cynthia then topped up my empty teacup. The scent of oolong, my favorite, came to me.

"Exactly, Mrs. H. But Clemmie swears it isn't true. She says she has no idea how she'd sell the paintings even if she did take them, and I believe her. Clemmie is an innocent soul." Cynthia sighed, running her finger around the rim of her teacup. "She says there's been no sign of a break-in or burglary. The paintings are simply there in the evening, gone the next morning."

Interesting. The problem piqued my exhausted brain. However, I did not allow myself to speculate too deeply. Simple explanations are usually the wisest ones—a person can complicate a straightforward situation with unnecessary dramatics and end up in a complete mess.

"Perhaps an enterprising butler is having the paintings cleaned," I suggested. "I understand old paintings can acquire quite a bit of grime, especially in London."

Cynthia waved her long-fingered hand. "I thought of that, but Clemmie swears she's questioned the staff and none have touched them. They rather dote on her, so I'm sure they would tell if they knew anything."

"Hm." Either one of the servants was lying quite fervently, or someone had managed to creep into the baronet's house in the middle of the night and silently rob it. I tried to picture a man walking in, taking a painting from the wall, and walking out again with it under his arm, frame and all, but I could not. London houses had servants roaming them all hours of the day and night, and he'd be spotted.

"You are intrigued," Cynthia said in triumph. "I see the sparkle in your eyes."

"I admit, it is odd," I answered with caution. Lady Cynthia was apt to throw herself into things rather recklessly. "Though I am certain there will be a clear explanation."

"Clemmie will be happy with *any* explanation. The silly cow is devastated her husband doesn't believe her, terrified he'll cut her off without a shilling. She wants to find the culprit and present him to the baronet on a platter."

"If she finds the culprit, she should summon the police," I said severely. "Does she mean to catch the burglar herself, tie him up, and wait for her husband to come home?"

"Ha. Sir Evan is a high-handed, dried-up stick, but I don't want him putting it about that Clemmie is stealing from him. The only reason he doesn't have her up before a magistrate is that he'd die of shame." Lady Cynthia clattered down her teacup and leaned to me. "Say you'll help, Mrs. H. I'd bribe you with extra wages, but Rankin holds the purse strings and my aunt and uncle are parsimonious." She brightened. "But Clemmie can reward you. Her husband might embrace you and give you a heady remuneration if you found his precious paintings. He is oozing with wealth. Has a roomful of art and antiquities from all over the world—can't think why this burglar is not touching *that*."

Even more interesting.

I was comfortable with my salary, as Lord Rankin paid what was fair for a cook of my abilities and experience. The thought of extra was always welcome, of course—something to put by for my daughter—but that was not why I nodded in agreement. The puzzle did make me curious. Besides, looking for missing paintings seemed far less dangerous than hunting murderers or chasing Fenians.

Sometimes I can be a foolishly confident woman.

Cynthia fixed our date to meet with Clementina the day after tomorrow. Not *tomorrow,* I said firmly, as it was Thursday, my day out. No one, not even a wealthy baron with missing paintings —not the Queen herself—would sway me from taking my day.

Cynthia looked annoyed she'd have to wait, but she knew I was immovable. We'd go Friday after breakfast, we agreed, then she left me. She was going out, Cynthia said as she went, sending me a dark look.

I smothered a sigh. She meant she would be donning gentleman's attire and meeting her lady friends who enjoyed dressing thus. They'd lark about and try to gain admission to seedy clubs where gentlemen slummed. I worried when Cynthia did this, certain one night her uncle would have to retrieve her from some filthy jail, her complete ruin ensured.

I knew Cynthia would not be dissuaded—I had tried to reason with her before. The look she gave me also meant I should see that the scullery door was kept unbolted for her. She had a key to the house's doors, but we drew a bar across the back and front ones after midnight if no one was out, which meant she'd be unable to get in without rousing the house and revealing her truancy to her aunt and uncle. They were amiable people but uncomfortable with Cynthia's wild streak.

Cynthia's mother and father—especially her father—had been wild in their day as well. Still were, from all accounts, though Cynthia's mother had become a near recluse after Cynthia's brother had shot himself years ago.

Mr. Bywater, Cynthia's uncle, seemed to have inherited everything staid in the family. He believed Cynthia should find a husband who would settle her down—his idea was that having a child or two would calm her even more. Mr. Bywater enjoyed inviting eligible young gentlemen to the house, hoping Cynthia would fall madly in love with one of them and accept his inevitable proposal.

Hence the supper party tonight, and Cynthia's rebellion of the moment.

I promised to aid in her deception, and we parted ways.

Cynthia returned safely in the wee hours and crept off to bed. Or so Sara assured me in the morning.

I fixed a full breakfast for the household, then put aside enough food for a luncheon for the staff and family. I would be back in time to make supper.

As I prepared the repast I'd leave behind, Mr. Davis, as usual, found time to sit in his shirtsleeves at my table and read bits out of his newspaper to me.

Today it was the French foray into the lands of the Bey of Tunis. Apparently, Tunisian tribesmen there had been crossing into Algeria, a French colony, and pillaging as they saw fit, and the French were retaliating. Mr. Davis read along through the details of the French attack, when he paused and looked up.

"Oh, by the bye, I saw that chap who worked here a few months ago—what was his name? Daniel—that was it. Daniel McAdam. In a pawnbrokers on the Strand, of all places." He shook his head. "Dear, dear, how the mighty have fallen."

2

My knife slipped from the mushrooms I was chopping. I caught myself and continued slicing, only missing one stroke. "Oh?" I asked as nonchalantly as I could.

"Yes, indeed," Mr. Davis said. "I glanced in when I walked past, and there he was behind the counter, cool as you please, selling things to punters. I am glad he found employment, but in a run-down pawnbrokers? The gentlemen inside were not the most salubrious customers, I must say."

I swallowed and made myself shove the mushrooms aside, moving an onion into their place. "We all have to make a living, Mr. Davis."

Mr. Davis moved the paper to peer at me. "Didn't he used to be sweet on you, Mrs. Holloway? As I said at the time, you can do much better."

"I do not wish to do better, Mr. Davis." I sliced the onion in half with vigor. "That is, I am not looking for a man to marry." I made quick slices in the half onion up to its root end, then turned my knife horizontally and slid it through what I already cut. I turned the onion around again and chopped at right angles to my first cuts. Pieces of onion fell away in a small, perfect dice, and my eyes began to water.

"Oh no? So every Thursday, you are not slipping out to meet a beau?" Mr. Davis's eyes twinkled, his curiosity alight.

I had no intention of telling the biggest gossip in London where I went on my days out. I gave him a frosty look. "Indeed no. I visit friends, have a healthy walk, take in sights, and try to improve my mind."

"I take your meaning, Mrs. H." Mr. Davis returned to his paper without offense. "None of my business."

He thought I lied. I did, but only a little.

As Mr. Davis continued to read, I finished my chopping, sautéed the mushrooms and onions, and poured plenty of hot stock into the pan on top of them along with a chunk of ham. "That will simmer nicely all morning and be a hearty soup for your dinner," I said to Mr. Davis. "Tell Sara to put the greens in at the very last moment, or they'll be bitter. I have them washed and crisped in the larder."

"Sara don't want to be a kitchen maid, you know," Mr. Davis said, turning a page.

"Then we had better hope the agency sends us another one. Good morning, Mr. Davis."

I removed my pinafore and cap and climbed the back stairs to my chamber, where I donned my best dress and hat, setting the black straw with dark feathers and ribbon on my brown hair.

Taking up my gloves, I marched down the six

flights of stairs and out of the house, determinedly not speaking to any of the staff I passed
on my way—I refused to miss a moment of my
precious day with my daughter. I walked through
the kitchen, noting that Mr. Davis had removed
himself, and out the scullery door and up the
steps to the street.

May had crept into the city, turning it gloriously
warm without being too hot. The sticky heat
would come later, when the social season was
over, and the fortunate retreated to the country.
Lady Cynthia had not yet revealed her plans for
the warmer months, and I had no idea whether I'd
stay on in the town house or follow her and the
Bywaters to a summer home. Or perhaps I'd have
to find a new place altogether. I hoped not, as I was
well set up in the Mount Street house and had no
wish to move. But domestics cannot always count
on their ladies and gentlemen to be dependable.

I pushed that worry aside as I traveled out of
Mayfair on a crowded omnibus, rolling slowly
along Piccadilly past the houses of the very
rich, then changed to another omnibus to travel
the Haymarket and pass Trafalgar Square to the
Strand.

I peered out the window as we went along the
Strand, wondering about Mr. Davis's story of
Daniel. Had he been mistaken? What on earth
would Daniel be doing working at a pawnbrokers?

Perhaps Daniel had simply needed the post. He arbitrarily seemed to have much money or none at all, and he changed his guise and his employment on a whim.

I knew there must be more to it. Daniel had something to do with the police, but I did not know what—and he had not chosen to share the details of his life with me. When last we'd spoken, he softening me with a kiss or two, he promised one day he'd tell me all. That day had not yet manifested, and as I say, I'd not seen him for some time.

I ought to forget about him. No woman needs a gentleman who pops in and out like a jackrabbit, and transforms himself from deliveryman to City gent to pawnbroker's assistant to commander of a troop of constables at the drop of a hat. My existence had been calm until Mr. McAdam had walked into it.

That was rubbish, and I knew it. I'd had plenty of drama in my life before I'd met Daniel. One reason I guarded my days out like a lion is that it gave me time to visit the person who'd been the product of the drama. Grace was the one constant in my world, the goodness that had come of grief.

No one in the Mount Street house, not even Lady Cynthia or Mr. Davis, knew I had a daughter, who was now ten years old. I had not exactly been married at the time I'd borne her—a fact unknown to me until too late—and an unmarried woman with a child can hardly hope to work in a respectable household. *Holloway* was my maiden name, which I'd resumed when I'd learned my so-called husband had already been married to someone else before he'd beguiled me into a church. I was *Mrs.* Holloway because all cooks and housekeepers were "Mrs." regardless of whether they were married. It was a mark of respect, just as all butlers and valets were "Mr." to the other servants.

Respectable Mrs. Holloway now rode through Fleet Street and Ludgate Hill and around the majestic bulk of St. Paul's. It was a beautiful cathedral, so reverent I knew it would stand forever. I descended not far from there, and in a small lane off Cheapside, I knocked on the door of a modest house where my friends Joanna and Sam Millburn lived. They were dear, kind people, and had the keeping of my daughter. Though they had four children themselves, they had brought her into their fold, embracing her as they would one of their own. Grace had grown up with their children and looked upon them as true brothers and sisters.

I heard Grace's voice rise in excitement, and I went weak with the joy of it. Once my arms were around her, and we were hugging as though we hadn't seen each other in months, my troubles fell away. They always did, which was why I'd fight tooth and nail to guard my time with her. My Grace, my daughter, my haven.

Today Grace and I visited the Tower of London, paying our fee and gawping at the medieval rooms and beauty of the crown jewels, and listening to a lecturer talk about the ghosts. Grace shrank close to me, and we kept a sharp eye out for ghosts in the shadows, but we saw none. I never do.

We stopped on the way home for tea, always our treat. We had too many cakes, which would make Joanna unhappy, but Grace deserved a bit of naughtiness. We crammed the sweet tea cakes and scones into our mouths, giggling like mad.

It was four in the afternoon when I returned Grace to the Millburns and said good-bye. My heart was heavy, as always at the end of our day. I woke every Thursday with a lightness in my limbs and ended it already wishing away the days until Monday, when I could see her again.

My savings were meager but growing, put aside for the time I'd retire from service and have Grace live with me. Perhaps I'd open a tea shop, where I'd make the very best pastries in London, and Grace would do her lessons in the back room while I worked.

The vision was so heady, and so real, that I nearly walked in front of a tram heading its way down the Strand.

I jumped out of its path, surprised I was next to

the little church of St. Clement Danes—I'd come that far without noticing, my mind in the clouds.

I brought my thoughts firmly to earth and walked briskly along, keeping well away from the wheeled traffic. I studied the shop fronts as I went—which of these was the pawnbrokers where Mr. Davis had seen Daniel?

Whenever I spotted the sign of three golden balls dangling above a door, I'd enter the shop, my heart thumping. I pretended to browse the goods for sale while I glanced about for Daniel, but I saw him in none of them.

Not until I was on the far west end of the Strand, just before Charing Cross Station, did I find the correct shop. This one was seedy indeed, its small windows covered with grime, the three balls above its door tarnished and blackened with soot.

The door creaked as I entered, and silence met me within. This pawnbrokers was set up like many others, with a long counter against one wall, behind which was secured the more expensive items—jewelry, musical instruments, small paintings, silver pieces. In a place like this, however, I'd wonder about the silver content in the candlesticks and the provenance of the paintings.

On my side of the counter, a few tables held cheaper items—small books with whole signatures of pages missing, plaster-cast knickknacks, small wooden boxes, tarnished pewter candle-sticks and scratched wooden ones, and empty and chipped picture frames.

The man behind the high counter sat on a chair tipped back against the wall, so that only his hair and forehead showed. When I peered over the counter, I saw that he had his feet propped on a wooden crate while he read a magazine, the drawing of a large-bosomed lady cheekily advertising cigars on its back. The man's dark suit was dusty and had a rent or two on its sleeves, and his boots, crossed at his ankles, were caked with mud. A greasy cap lay on a table by his side, leaving his hair, thick and wayward, exposed to my gaze. A more disreputable character I do not think I'd seen in many a day.

He had obviously heard me enter, because he turned a page of the magazine without looking up and said, "You see something you like, missus, I'll wrap it up for you."

I kept my hands folded over my reticule, not liking to touch the dirty counter. "If the books are missing bits, is the price for them less?"

I had the pleasure of seeing Daniel McAdam give a violent start. I so rarely caught him unawares that I smiled in triumph.

He quickly tossed the magazine under the counter and stood up to his full height, staring at me wide-eyed across the counter.

"Bloody hell, woman. Is there nowhere in this

29

city I cannot turn and see you before me?"

I regarded him primly, not letting on how glad I was to have found him. "I very much doubt it," I said. "I travel along the Strand on my days out, as you know, unless I go along High Holborn. Is it so odd that I should pass this shop and see you in it?"

Daniel's look turned skeptical. "You happened to glance into an unsavory pawnbrokers and decided to browse its wares? Or are you selling something?"

"Don't be silly. Mr. Davis spied you here, and he cannot keep anything to himself. As I was walking along this street this afternoon, I thought I'd look for you."

Daniel relaxed, and his lips twitched. "Good—I would hate to think of you dirtying your shoes in a place like this for any other reason. It is a fine thing to see you, Kat." For one moment, Daniel regarded me in a manner that made his shabby clothes and this dusty place fall away. I saw only his blue eyes, his charming smile, the handsome man hiding behind the scruffy clothes.

Then his glad look vanished. "I enjoy your company, as I have told you, Kat, but you do know how to choose exactly the wrong time for a friendly chat. I need you to go—I can meet with you later if you like."

His impatience was unfeigned. Daniel might truly wish to talk with me after he conducted

30

whatever business he wanted me out of the way for, but I sensed he had no intention whatsoever of telling me what he was up to.

"I can hardly step out of the house and have a chin-wag with you whenever you ask," I said in a lofty tone. "This is the end of my day out. I must return and prepare supper."

"Yes, yes, of course." His smile returned as did the charming Daniel. "Another time, then."

"Do not patronize me, Mr. McAdam," I said. "I am wise to your ways. Good afternoon."

I saw the dismay on his face, and I nearly apologized for my brusqueness, but then again, the man drove me to distraction. He must be here for intriguing reasons, and I admitted I was annoyed because he would not satisfy my curiosity.

However, I then reasoned I ought not leave in a huff, because Daniel would be an excellent person with which to discuss the problem Lady Cynthia had laid before me.

I began to offer to visit him at a more opportune time, when Daniel jerked from the counter and bolted out through the door in the wall that separated the counter from the shop. He grabbed me by the arm and without explanation fairly dragged me into the back, shoving me through another door that led to a dingy storage room.

"Stay there," he said. "Don't make a sound."

3

Daniel's sharp tone alarmed me. I did not demand, like a ninny, to know what he thought he was playing at or grow outraged that he told me what to do. I knew Daniel well enough to understand that when he spoke like that, it meant danger was not far behind.

I gave him a nod to show I understood, and he closed me into the room in silence. The latch did not catch, the door swinging the slightest bit ajar, but its creak was drowned out by the sounds of a man coming noisily into the shop.

The storage room was filled with dusty shelves piled high with objects of every sort, from broken toys to fine clocks to sets of porcelain dishes to much-dented tin cups and plates. Some of the things in this dim interior looked as though they'd sat here for a very long time.

I pressed my hands to my skirts and moved to the crack in the door, peering through. I was disappointed in that I could see very little, but I could hear quite well.

A lone man had entered, but hardly furtively. He sang out a greeting, calling Daniel "Tom."

"Plenty of tickers," the man said. "And wipes, beautiful linen ones. Cost a fair penny, I'd wager."

"Mmm." Daniel made an impatient rumble. "Anything else?"

"Statues—marble. Well, look like marble anyway."

"Nah." Daniel's chair creaked; I imagined him leaning back in it. "Not worth me time, mate."

"What you want then?" the other man growled in irritation.

"Something with a bit more class. Something a punter ain't going to flick with his nail and tell me it's fake. Something real, know what I mean?"

The man's voice went low. "What you're talking about ain't easy. Not for the likes of me, anyway."

I heard Daniel flap open the pages of his magazine. "You'll do fine. You said you had mates, didn't ya?"

"Oh, I know plenty. But they don't know *you.* They're used to the last bloke."

"Look, old son," Daniel said with exaggerated patience. "I'm not asking you to upset the applecart. I'm only asking for a little business to come me way. I want to move up in the world. And you can tell 'em no one's more discreet than me. Old Tommy will never steer 'em wrong." The magazine rustled, and the chair creaked. "Come back when you've got something better for me."

The other man went silent for a time. "Right,"

33

he said in resignation. "I'll have a chat with me friends. They're not the most trusting sorts."

"I understand. They don't know me. But when we get acquainted, they'll see it as a beneficial cooperation, eh?" Daniel pronounced the long words carefully, as though unused to speaking more than a syllable or two at a time. "Old Tom can make them a few bob. You too."

"Yeah." The man sounded more cheerful. "Don't mind if I do. Be back when I can, all right, guv?"

"Don't hurry yourself. Now be off with you. I've got hordes of customers to tend to here." Daniel chortled.

The man laughed, sounding happy to be let in on the joke. "Good evening to ye, Tom."

"Right you are. Mind how ye go."

The man chortled again, his footsteps light as he crossed the gritty floor and let himself out. The shop bell clanged, then all was silent.

"Stay there a moment," Daniel said before I could move. "Mr. Varley is fickle-minded and might come back to tell me something he left out."

I spoke through the crack. "If I stay in here much longer, I might have a fit of the sneezes."

"Soon, I promise."

I moved so I could see Daniel through the slit. He remained with his chair tilted back, his feet up, the magazine in front of him as though it enthralled him. The room I stood in was not only dusty but dank, chilly on this warm May afternoon.

Daniel had an uncanny way of being right. Sure enough, the door banged open in a few minutes, and Mr. Varley's step sounded.

"Fing is," Varley began.

"Eh?" Daniel asked. "Forget something, did ya?"

"Fing is, there might be a bit of luck coming your way soon. Can't say more than that."

I couldn't see Varley from my angle, but I watched Daniel toss down the magazine and give Mr. Varley a stern look. "I don't deal in *mights,* me old china. I like actual things I can put my hands on, right?"

"You will, you will," Varley said hastily. "But I can't tell ya anything else. More than me life's worth. But when it's done, I'll cut you in. You're a fair-minded man, Tommy. Ya won't regret it."

"*You* won't, ye mean. Ye wouldn't bring me nuffink if ye didn't stand to get paid, would ye?" Daniel chuckled. "It's all right; I like a man what knows his mind. We wouldn't be in business at all if we didn't want the blunt, would we?"

"Huh, right you are, guv. As long as the coin is spread to me, I'm your man."

More laughter. They were very happy with their little joke. "It's getting late, Tom," Varley went on. "Pub?"

"Naw," Daniel said. "Need to finish up here

then I'm off home. Missus don't like it when I'm late."

Varley found this hilarious. "Henpecked, are ye?"

"Ain't it the troof," Daniel said. "Ye married?"

"Naw, I never."

"*Trouble* ain't an exaggeration," Daniel said. "Why d'ye fink I need the money?"

More guffawing, then Varley, sounding a bit superior that he could go along to a pub anytime he wished, said a final good night and disappeared again.

Trouble was rhyming slang. *Trouble and strife—wife.* Quite unjust, I'd always thought. Husbands could be just as much of a bother, if not more.

"May I emerge now?" I called once Varley's footsteps had faded into the traffic outside.

"Of course." Daniel was up, his working-class accent falling away as he opened the door for me. "My apologies, Kat, but for all his groveling, Varley is a dangerous man. I did not wish him to see you or know you have any connection to me."

"I quite understand." I did not, not entirely. But I concluded that Varley was a criminal, and he'd likely not be too happy that a woman had heard him and Daniel discuss what sounded like a shady deal.

"Stay a bit longer," Daniel said as I brushed

off my skirts. "I want to make certain he's well away."

"I do have supper to cook," I reminded him. The sun was shining mightily, and would for some hours—as we approached summer, the days were growing longer. However, the clocks continued at their same steady pace, and Lady Cynthia's aunt and uncle expected their meals on time.

"Rest yourself a quarter of an hour at most." Daniel's tone told me this was not an offer of comfort, or even a request. Daniel did not want me to move one step out of that shop until fifteen minutes had elapsed.

"All right, then," I said. "That will give you time to tell me exactly what you are doing, and why you have set yourself up to be a receiver of stolen goods."

One of Daniel's pleasing traits was that he did not look surprised when I understood something. No shock that I, a mere woman and a domestic, could grasp a situation. He only nodded thoughtfully.

"You are indeed correct. Not much excitement in it, I am afraid. It's a sordid business, one I seem to be suited for."

His nonchalance and little smile made me give him a sharp look. "No excitement, you say, but at the same time, you do not want Mr. Varley to see me?"

"These men have no honor, Kat. I do not want

them to grow angry with me and use you to punish me."

I regarded him in surprise. "Would it punish you?"

His voice softened. "Indeed, it would."

I refused to let him know that my heart squeezed at this declaration. "Funny way you have of showing it, Mr. McAdam. Not a word from you in weeks and weeks, not a sign until Mr. Davis spies you in a pawnbrokers."

"I had to go to Scotland," Daniel answered without apology. "Unexpectedly and discreetly."

"I see." I looked him up and down, from his unwashed hair to his dirty boots. "What were you there? A Highland laird?"

Daniel leaned against the counter and folded his arms. "I promised I'd tell you all my adventures one day, remember?"

"Yes, indeed. I have decided we will both be quite elderly when that day comes."

"This current business truly is uninteresting, Kat. Thieves are stealing items for the money they will make and taking them to pawnbrokers to sell. Therefore, I am now a pawnbroker."

"Funny, that." I pretended to examine the clasp of my reticule. "Lady Cynthia told me last evening that one of her friends has had paintings go missing from her house. I will visit with this friend tomorrow and listen to her tale of woe."

Daniel did not look surprised or concerned.

"It is a sad fact that theft is rampant in London. From pickpockets to wellborn art thieves stealing paintings from the walls of a fine house, there is an amazing abundance of burglary. I'm looking in particular for items coming out of museums. Antiquities long forgotten."

I looked up with a start. "I was at a museum earlier this week. Showing Grace bits from Egyptian tombs. Have those things been going missing?"

"Nothing from the public exhibits. The items in question have been stored away—bits from digs in the Greek isles and Egypt that haven't been cleaned or displayed. Things that wouldn't be noticed right away."

"Clever," I said.

"Easier," Daniel amended. "Unlike in magazine stories, museum pieces are not locked away or protected by armed men and guard dogs. Sometimes they are left on shelves in unlocked rooms or tossed into boxes. Lately, they have been turning up at pawnbrokers—small pieces at a time, not a lot of them at once."

"Possibly nothing to do with Lady Cynthia's friend's troubles, then," I said.

"Likely not." Daniel unfolded his arms. "Still, I'd like to hear about her burglary."

"Well, it will be quite the task for me to find time to tell you," I said, my vexation returning. "The house is at sixes and sevens with no housekeeper and no assistant for me in the kitchen." I waved my hand. "My apologies. You have no need to hear my domestic troubles. They must seem trivial compared to chasing thieves who run about London stealing what they please."

Daniel shook his head. "Not trivial. I do know what it's like to work in a place that's short-handed."

He had done all sorts of jobs and held all sorts of posts even in the year or so since I'd met him. A veritable jack-of-all-trades was Daniel.

Clocks hanging on the walls and on the shelves began to chime. "I see that my quarter of an hour is up," I said. "If you wish to hear what Lady Cynthia's friend tells me, you will have to seek me out. Call after supper tomorrow or after breakfast on Saturday. Good evening, Mr. McAdam."

The grin he flashed at me was his own—the Daniel I knew, if I knew him at all.

"Good evening, Mrs. Holloway. Save me back something, eh? I haven't had a decent meal in donkey's years."

Tonight's supper was not as difficult to assemble as last night's had been. I had prepared well before I'd gone out, and only two people dined tonight— Lady Cynthia and her aunt. Her uncle had gone to his club, and Lady Cynthia and Mrs. Bywater would leave for the theatre after their meal.

I did not even have Sara's help tonight, because she was in a bother trying to make certain Lady Cynthia's theatre clothes were in good order. Truth to tell, in spite of her praise for me last night, she'd jumped at the excuse to take herself from the kitchen. I was certain Lady Cynthia's gowns were all quite pristine, as she seldom wore them—the Bywaters tolerated her lounging about the house in breeches and frock coat, as long as there were no guests.

I sent up a simple repast of beef and roasted potatoes dressed with a sauce of the roast's juice flavored with herbs and onions. I served pieces from the remains of last night's tarts on small plates, and jumbled the rest of those leftovers onto a platter for the servants to enjoy.

Though the meal was fairly easily put together, I was glad to sit down with a cup of tea and a small meal for myself and Mr. Davis, with a footman to wait on us in the housekeeper's parlor.

I liked this room, with its books, worn furniture, and comfortable respectability. In the absence of a housekeeper, I had been using it as my own retreat. Whenever Mrs. Bywater got around to hiring a new housekeeper, I'd have to give up my haven.

Mr. Davis chattered about anything and everything, never minding that I only nodded or said, "Oh really?" at intervals. I was thinking of my lovely day with my daughter, and after that,

Daniel in the dingy shop waiting for dangerous criminals to offer him stolen goods.

What would he do when they came? Arrest them himself? Men like Mr. Varley would fight, I was certain, and there Daniel was, all alone. Or did he have policemen lurking outside awaiting his signal? Either way, what he did was perilous, though he seemed used to such things.

I worried for Daniel, but at the same time, the man made me fume. Surely, he could trust me enough to share his exploits with me.

He certainly knew about mine. Daniel had told *me,* if you please, that he was aware of my bigamous marriage and that my daughter had been its result. And yet I did not know where he'd been born and under what circumstances—although his tones of South London weren't false. Only someone raised there could speak so.

I'd been born in a lane off Cheapside, not far from where the Millburns lived, so close to St. Mary-le-Bow that I couldn't escape being a Cockney. I'd trained myself to speak clearly and properly, but Cockneys could ensure an outsider couldn't understand a word they said if they so wished. That was the case in South London as well; such things weren't easily feigned.

Daniel could also take on a cultured accent, that of an educated man. I had taught myself to throw off my lower-class pronunciations, a slow and painful process, but no one would mistake me for a highborn lady. Well-bred and polished young women spoke differently, another cant if you will, that was difficult to fake.

Daniel slid back and forth between sounding like a lordling who'd attended university with his chums to a man who'd never left the gutters of Bermondsey. Whenever Daniel spoke in what I considered his "normal" voice, he was somewhere in between. He'd learned long ago to be a chameleon, but where he'd learned this and why, I had no idea.

Mr. Davis set aside his last cup of tea and declared he'd see the house was secure and then retire. I returned to my kitchen, which was happily deserted, measured out flour and water, yeast, salt, and on a whim, a pinch of dried herbs, and mixed it into a dough, which I left to rise in the larder. I paused on the larder's doorstep, a frisson of pain and memory touching me, before I resolutely turned away and went upstairs to bed.

The next morning, as I was putting the same dough into the bread pans for its final rise, Daniel's son, James, came tripping into the kitchen.

James looked much like his father, only younger and lankier. His eyes were brown rather than blue, and his face, when clean, was full of freckles. He was coming up on his sixteenth summer, I believed, and he'd sprung up another five inches, I swore, this spring.

Unlike his father, James had visited me several times since our last adventure, so much so that the footmen and scullery maid greeted him without surprise as he walked tamely in through the back door. James shared Daniel's friendliness to those of every walk of life, and everyone below stairs perked up whenever James sailed in.

Today he was followed by a cynical-looking young woman who gave the kitchen and all in it a dubious once-over. This lady wore a respectable-looking gray frock, a matching bonnet, and brown leather gloves that were clean and neat.

She was a few years older than James, but not many—I put her at eighteen at the most. She had dark hair and brown eyes, but her skin was very fair, the porcelain white that upper-class ladies hid themselves under shawls and veils to achieve. A turned-up nose and too-wide mouth gave her face a good-humored rather than elegant air, making her pleasant-looking instead of a great beauty. Or would, I thought, if she dropped her sneer and smiled.

James marched her straight up to me and then nudged her with his elbow. The young woman went down in a stiff curtsy, and said, "Morning, missus."

"This here's Tess," James said without preliminary. "Tess Parsons. She heard ye might have need for a kitchen maid, and she's looking for a place."

44

"Oh?" I looked Tess up and down, noting the stubborn light in her eye, one that boded no good. She lifted her chin and stared right back at me, no submissiveness in this one. "It's not up to me who works in the kitchen, James. Mrs. Bywater and Lady Cynthia hire the staff."

Tess's frown deepened while James sent me a pleading look. "You can put in a good word for her though, can't you Mrs. H.?"

I wondered. James was a few years younger than Tess, but he might be sweet on her. Tess had a sour look, however, and James was not a fool. But then again, the heart does not always let the head lead it, especially when one is very young.

"What can you do, Tess?" I asked. "Have you done kitchen work before?"

Tess shrugged one shoulder. "Don't know, missus. Haven't tried, 'ave I?"

I hid a sigh. Inexperienced, untaught—I could not possibly run a kitchen, take the duties of a housekeeper, *and* train a bad-tempered girl at the same time.

Tess caught on to my disapprobation and swung to James. "See? I knew she wouldn't want me. Your dad's gone soft."

"Your father?" I asked James with a start. "What has he got to do with it?"

James sent me an ingenuous look. "He heard you was shorthanded. So he sent Tess around. Thought she could do well for ye."

4

I studied Tess more closely, and she returned a defiant stare. Daniel must have had some reason to choose Miss Tess Parsons, ill-humored London girl, to assist me in the kitchen. I'd have been better pleased if Daniel had consulted with me, warned me, at least sent a note along with her, but Daniel did things in his own time for his own purposes.

"I see," I said coolly, which made Tess's spark of defiance burn brighter. "You haven't told me what skills you have, Tess. What sort of work have you done in the past?"

"Scrubbed floors, didn't I?" Her dark eyes held determination. "But I ain't doing that no more. You can teach me how to cook, and I'll get a better place."

Daniel *had* gone soft. What he thought I could do with this prickly creature, I did not know.

I gave her a narrow look. "I will have to be clear about one thing, my girl. This is *my* kitchen. Doesn't matter that Lord Rankin owns the house or his late wife's aunt runs it for the moment. In the kitchen, I reign. You will do what I say when I say it, without argument or sullenness. There's no time or place for those. Do you understand me?"

The scorn flared, a young woman who'd decided she would dare the world to thwart her. I could admire her attitude, as I had much of that in myself, but it would not help when we were rushed to get a meal on the table.

James gave her another poke with his elbow, and Tess sent me a reluctant nod. "I understand, missus."

"Mrs. Holloway," I corrected her. "I will let you help me get breakfast, and if all goes well, I'll ask the mistress if she will consider hiring you. That is all."

Tess's brows came together, and I thought she'd turn around and march out, her nose in the air. James cleared his throat, and Tess went down in another awkward curtsy. "Yes, Mrs. Holloway."

"Good. On the table is a bowl of eggs. You will crack them into another bowl. I don't want to see any bits of shells among them, or any bad eggs dumped into the good. Bad eggs go into a separate bowl to be discarded into the slop pail. First, hang up your hat and coat, and go into the linen room and find a clean apron. Do not touch anything else. And wash your hands in the scullery before you begin."

Tess curtsied once more, the movement more like a slap in the face. "Yes, Mrs. Holloway," she said with all the haughtiness she could muster. She unbuttoned and slid off her coat, stuffing her gloves into its pocket and hanging it on the peg

47

with her bonnet at the scullery's door. Then she looked about. "What's a linen room?"

I let out a heavy sigh. "James, show her."

James shot me a grin, impudent thing, as he guided Tess through the kitchen to the passage that led to the rest of the belowstairs rooms. I pulled him back after he'd pointed Tess the way.

"Is he certain?" I asked in a low voice.

"Dad don't do nothing without a reason, Mrs. H."

No, he did not. Yesterday I had mentioned my frustration in the kitchen and Daniel had sent me Tess. I wondered how he'd been able to put his hands on her in such a short time, and whether he had people in reserve all over London for whatever he might need them for. I also wondered whether he considered *me* one of those people.

Tess strode out of the linen room, shaking out a pinafore. She stopped when she saw James and me in the doorway.

"All right?" she demanded as she draped the pinafore over her shoulders and tied its strings behind her. "I'll need to get at them eggs."

James's smile beamed out, his mission accomplished. He touched his hat. "Good luck, Mrs. H.," he said then rushed through the kitchen to the scullery and out.

"Cheeky bugger, ain't he?" Tess said, watching him go. "His dad ain't much better."

It took all my strength *not* to ask how she knew Daniel, and I gave her a frown.

"You will have to cease using such language while you are under this roof," I said. "Mr. Davis—he's butler here—would sling you right out. This is a respectable household."

"Ooh, pardon me, I'm sure." Tess gave me a lofty look. "You really is the Queen of England, ain't ye?"

"In my kitchen, I am," I said. "Now see to the eggs. I need breakfast to go upstairs right quick."

By the time I had the covered dishes sent up via the dumbwaiter to the dining room above us, I had to concede that Tess was a quick study. She had the eggs in the bowl fairly rapidly, no shells with them, and had found only a single bad one that she'd smelled before she cracked it.

I whipped the eggs into a froth and made a large batch of omelets, each flavored slightly differently—some with fresh herbs, a few with crumbled bacon and a bite of cheese, and three with fruit and cream. Those upstairs would have their choice. The Bywaters had hearty appetites, for which I was grateful, and I knew all the omelets would be gone.

To these I added bacon broiled over a hot flame and took from the baking oven a dish of mushrooms with butter and pepper, pouring them onto the platter Tess held out for me. To her credit, she held the plate steadily, even though I splashed her hands with a bit of the hot butter. She did let out a swear word, but I chose to ignore it as a reward for not dropping the plate of mushrooms.

Tess helped me load the dishes onto the dumbwaiter, and I showed her how to work the mechanism to crank it upstairs.

Tess let out her breath and wiped her brow when it was gone. "Whew. Well *that's* done. Cookin's a fair bit of work, ain't it?"

"We're not finished, my girl," I said, unable to keep the smugness from my voice. "Now we make breakfast for the staff and start preparing lunch."

Tess groaned, but she turned back with me.

I showed her how the stove operated, with its five plates for cooking plus one in the back for warming, and two ovens, one on either side of the firebox. I was rather proud of my stove, though I'd had nothing to do with choosing it; I could bake a loaf of bread and broil a roast at the same time, and sauté several dishes at once.

Tess watched without much interest, but she took it in, then cracked more eggs for the staff's breakfast. I mixed the eggs with bacon and mushrooms, adding a dice of potatoes to make it a hash. I chopped the potatoes myself—I was not about to give over my good knives to a girl I'd known an hour—but Tess tore apart the mushrooms and whipped up the eggs as I showed her without too much trouble.

Once the hash was finished, I carried a platter of it to the table in the servants' hall and set a pile of plates next to it. There was always so much to do in the morning, especially these days, that the staff did not always sit down to a breakfast but came in and ate as they could.

I carried another covered dish of the hash and one of toast down the passage to the house-keeper's parlor, bidding Tess to follow me with plates and flatware. I deposited the dish on the table in the parlor and sat down, ready to get off my feet, and instructed Tess to serve me a portion of the food. She plunked a spoonful of hot eggs, bacon, mushrooms, and potatoes onto a plate and shoved it at me, then served herself without waiting for permission.

I decided not to admonish her, as she'd already done much work without promise of pay or even a position. I could at least allow her a hot breakfast.

Tess scooped a dollop of hash onto a fork and touched it to her lips as though dubious about eating it. Her tongue came out to flick the smallest bit of the eggs and potatoes into her mouth. She played that around a moment, then her face changed, and she plunged the entire forkful inside. She'd hardly swallowed that bite down before she was scraping in another.

I stopped to watch her. Tess lowered her head to the plate, eating rapidly, like a dog who expected the food to be snatched away at any moment.

"Easy, my dear," I said gently. "You'll make yourself ill."

Tess looked up, shoving a bit of potato that had slopped onto her lips back into her mouth. "This is good, missus," she said around the food. She swallowed and sat upright, a flush spreading across her face as though realizing how desperately she'd been shoveling things in. "I mean, Mrs. Holloway."

"Thank you," I said with my usual modesty. "It's only a bit of plain cooking."

Tess nodded and went back to eating. Her hand shot out and snatched up the top piece of buttered toast on its platter, that following the last of her eggs down her throat.

I realized the girl must have been starved. She was quite thin, bony even. I could imagine her on the street, stuffing scraps into her mouth as she could get them, head down to fend off those who wanted to take them from her.

Pity moved me. Her defiance came from pride, I realized, and fear. A sharp young woman, I could see, but one who'd been in very bad circumstances. Not an uncommon story for London, I am sad to say. I would have to wring her history from Daniel.

Her rough edges could be smoothed, I decided. I would have a word with Lady Cynthia, and ask her to let me take Tess on as my assistant.

∙ ∙ ∙

Lady Cynthia had said we'd visit her friend Clementina—Lady Godfrey—after breakfast this morning, but as it turned out we did not go until after luncheon. Lady Cynthia had not factored into our plans that while *she* enjoyed rising at eight and taking a ride after breakfast, most of her friends lay in bed until afternoon. Mrs. Bywater made a habit of joining her husband at the breakfast table instead of having a tray sent to her room, but she was not the usual Mayfair lady.

We at last made ready at two o'clock, but this put me in a bother, because I needed to be home soon to prepare the evening meal. I told Tess what ingredients to assemble and which vegetables to peel and chop—not all of them, because the flavor of certain produce is enhanced by not cutting it until the last minute. Tess frowned in perplexity when I explained this, but I couldn't linger to make certain she understood.

Sir Evan Godfrey and his wife, Clementina, lived in Park Lane, just past Upper Grosvenor Street and near the bastion of Grosvenor House, one of the most lavish abodes in London. While Sir Evan's home lacked the grand colonnaded entrance of Grosvenor House, the drive bent around a stand of trees that hid it from the well-trafficked Park Lane, a piece of country estate in the heart of the city.

The house itself stood alone and was more

modern than the usual side-by-side townhomes in Mayfair's squares. It had been built in what I thought of as the Indian style, which meant pointed archways and onionlike domes, I suppose in attempt to make it look like the famous Taj Mahal.

Cynthia gathered her skirts—she'd donned a frock for this outing—and hopped straight out of the carriage when it halted, to the consternation of the Godfrey footman who'd placed a cushioned stool at the carriage's door and reached to hand Lady Cynthia down.

The footman was even more nonplussed to see me in my gray working gown and plain gray bonnet. I gave the lad a fierce look, which restored his respectfulness in a trice, and let him help me down—I did need the stool and a steady hand. Lady Cynthia, with her slim build and the robustness of a boy, was already striding for the door.

I was not used to entering great houses through the front, but Cynthia sailed inside without hesitation. I came behind her, my hands folded over my reticule, trying not to look as though I was doing anything unusual.

The Indian style continued inside the house. The vestibule had a lofty ceiling tiled in bright blue, red, and orange, from which hung a large slitted lantern that would have been at home in a seraglio. A pointed arch led into the main hall, which was decorated with tall urns, swaths of silk drapery, peacock feathers pinned to the walls, and an enormous arrangement of flowers. The flowers were tropical, from bright orange blooms that looked like birds to giant scarlet poppylike blossoms, to blue and yellow flowers I did not know. The cost to have that refreshed every few days from a hothouse must be immense. Even if Sir Evan grew his own flowers in the back of his house, he would have to go to much expense to cultivate plants used to the heat of the subcontinent.

The staircase had a balustrade that looked like marble, but I imagined it was only painted plaster, as marble would be much too heavy. A stately and elderly butler waited at the foot of the stairs, greeting Lady Cynthia, commanding the maid who'd appeared to take our wraps.

Lady Cynthia, after handing over her shawl and hat, skimmed up the stairs, knowing the way. I chose to keep my small jacket and my bonnet, not wanting to appear too much at home in a nabob's house. I did not belong here, and so I would maintain my outdoor garb, to signal I would stay only temporarily.

I gave the butler a dignified nod and thanked him by name—Mr. Brampton. I did not know him, but Mr. Davis did, and I knew the cook of this house. I said nothing more to Mr. Brampton, as that would not be fitting of me as a guest of his mistress. He nodded back, his rheumy eyes holding disapproval but understanding.

Lady Godfrey—Clementina—met us in a parlor that was free of the Indian decor of the rest of the house. A square-backed sofa occupied the carpeted floor, paired with a Morris chair—one of those newer kinds of chairs whose back could be adjusted. It looked well used, as the velvet upholstery was shiny and a slight tear showed in the seat cushion, though an attempt had been made to tuck the torn part behind the spindles. An upright secretary in burnished oak with a stubby, scrolled top was open to reveal nooks and crannies stuffed with papers.

The pictures on the walls were photographs showing wide-eyed children, a gathering of about a dozen people who looked as though they wished to be doing anything other than standing for a photograph, and one of Clementina herself in an artful pose. The photographer had seated her in a chair half turned from the camera and curved her gracefully over a bouquet of flowers she held in her arms. A lovely picture, but I imagined holding the pose until the camera made the exposure must have been excruciating.

"Clemmie." Lady Cynthia stretched out her hands as Clementina came to us.

Lady Godfrey was Cynthia's age, in her late twenties, slim of build as was the fashion in the upper classes. Her light brown hair was dressed in complicated braids and ringlets coiled and pinned around her head, a much more formal style than the relaxed one of her portrait, where her hair was in a loose knot, a curl draping to her shoulder. That picture must have been taken several years ago, perhaps just after Lady Godfrey's debut, because the fresh softness depicted in the photo had gone from her face.

Lady Godfrey was still very pretty, with high cheekbones and blue eyes, but those eyes had lines feathered about them now. They also held the look of a woman who'd been through harrowing times. I wondered what had happened to a wealthy, pampered woman living in luxury to etch such an expression onto her, but I had learned, working in the houses of the privileged, that their existence was not always a happy one. Money did much to alleviate basic needs—ensuring food to eat and a warm place to sleep—but wealth and power could cause as much pain and sorrow as it alleviated.

Clemmie had dressed in an airy frock of pale blue, which was frothy with lace and ribbon. Cynthia, in contrast, wore a more tailored gown of dark gray, its close-fitting bodice, stiff placket, small round buttons, and upright white collar mannish in style. Cynthia's gown's bustle was small, in contrast to the broad platform of Lady Godfrey's, which was piled high with lace and bows.

I thought Lady Cynthia the more comely of the pair, with her simple knot of hair contrasting Lady Godfrey's fussy coiffure. Lady Cynthia's sister had been rather colorless, but Cynthia's cheeks could flush a becoming pink, her eyes sparkling with animation when she grew interested in a thing.

Cynthia and Clementina kissed each other's cheeks, professing great delight to see each other, although Clementina had been to supper only two evenings ago. Nonetheless, they held hands and exclaimed over each other until they finished with their greeting ritual.

"I've brought Mrs. Holloway," Cynthia said, waving a hand at me. "I told you about her, remember? She is marvelously clever."

I curtsied to Clementina and tried to look respectable rather than clever. Lady Cynthia was prone to exaggeration.

Cynthia plopped herself down on the Morris chair while Clementina lowered herself more gracefully to the sofa. I decided to take the plainest seat in the room, a balloon-back side chair, its seat a pleasant blue pattern of embroidery.

"Tell her," Lady Cynthia said to Clementina. "I regaled her with a few of the details, but I don't know them all myself. Do not worry, you may speak freely to Mrs. Holloway. She is frightfully discreet."

"My husband is certain what happened," Clementina said, anger in her voice. "He believes that I took his old paintings from the wall and sold them to pay my debts. It is true I owe money, but I would hardly lift down a painting, frame and all, and sell it out the back door, would I?"

"Exactly," Lady Cynthia said. "Why would you do something so obvious and then not make it look as though there'd been a burglary? And you still owe the debts, do you not?"

Clementina flushed a dull red. She was not a woman for whom more color in her face was attractive. She went blotchy, her eyes moistening.

"As a matter of fact, the debt has been paid."

Lady Cynthia sat back with a thump. "Good Lord. Who by? Never your husband."

"No." Clementina rose swiftly and nearly ran to the bellpull. "Where is that wretched girl with the tea?"

Since I hadn't heard Lady Godfrey ask for tea, she could hardly call the maid wretched for not bringing it. I knew, however, that her movement was to cover her sudden confusion.

Lady Cynthia drew a breath to ask a puzzled question, but I shook my head ever so slightly behind Clementina's back. Lady Cynthia was not a fool—her brows climbed and she closed her mouth.

Clementina yanked on the bellpull as though she intended to summon a fire brigade. I'm certain it jangled horrendously in the servants' hall. She remained at the bellpull for a moment as though to compose herself, and when she turned back, her scarlet cheeks had cooled. By the time she sat down, sending Cynthia a smile, she was sanguine again, and the maid appeared with the tea.

Clementina graciously poured out, which seemed to further compose her. She asked me how I liked my tea—sugar, no cream—and handed me the cup as though I were a highborn guest.

I took a sip and then cleared my throat. "I beg your pardon, my lady, but have any other items gone missing?"

Clementina jumped. "No. That is, not since the last painting."

Lady Cynthia took a long swallow of tea and returned her cup to the delicate-legged table between us. One leaf of the table bore a scar across its surface. That leaf had been turned toward an empty chair in an attempt to hide the flaw, but my eyes caught it.

"Tell her all about it, Clemmie," Lady Cynthia said. "It's why I brought her."

Clementina cast me another doubtful look, but it was clear she trusted Cynthia, because she set down her tea, clasped her hands, and launched into her tale.

"Three paintings have gone missing in all.

Quite valuable ones. I don't know much about art, but I do know famous names. A Gainsborough that has been in Sir Evan's family for a century, a Rembrandt, and one from an Italian-sounding name I can't remember. I know they must be worth thousands and thousands of guineas. They've gone. One in January, right after New Year's. One in March. This last a week ago."

One every two months, as though the thieves stole to a schedule. "Lady Cynthia said there was no indication that someone had broken in," I said. "Are you certain? That is, there might not be an obvious sign, such as a broken window or door latch. Nothing was amiss below stairs? The scullery door left unlocked by mistake? A window in the attic open? The thieves may have also picked the locks."

"Our front door is bolted," Clementina said decidedly. "With quite a heavy bolt, drawn across it every night by Mr. Brampton, our butler. He has been serving my husband and his family for decades and wouldn't dream of leaving the door unbolted at night. Nor do I think he's been stealing the things himself. He's growing decrepit, poor man, and could hardly lift a heavy painting from a wall."

I nodded in agreement. I hadn't suspected the butler in any case. I hadn't imagined the distress I'd seen in his eyes, and it was true, he was quite bent with rheumatism. Not that he could not hire

61

others to do the physical labor for him, but Mr. Davis spoke highly of him, which counted a long way toward his character.

"Is the scullery door bolted as well?" I asked.

"Good heavens, I have no idea," Clementina said. "I will have to inquire."

I would do that myself, but I held my tongue. "Would it be possible, my lady, for me to see the space where the paintings hung? I might be able to discern more about the thefts."

"Well, I don't see how that will help." Clementina looked to Cynthia for confirmation.

Cynthia sprang to her feet, kicking the hem of her skirt out of her way. "Of course it will help. Your husband wants to find the damned things, doesn't he?"

"Yes, all right." Clementina flushed as she rose. "Don't swear in front of Evan, please, Cynthia. He'll never let you into the house again."

Cynthia's brows shot up. "Evan is here? I thought he couldn't be dragged from the City for any reason, not while the Exchange is open."

"He had an appointment with the prime minister and decided not to go farther than Whitehall today. He came home for luncheon and hasn't left since." Clementina's distress was apparent.

I remembered the day I'd realized I loathed my husband. I had been out shopping with our meager funds, and when I'd returned to the tiny rooms we shared, he'd been there instead of out laboring as he should have. I remembered my heart sinking, knowing I'd have to go inside and be with him the rest of the day and into the night.

I'd understood in that instant that I didn't love him, didn't even like him. My head had been turned by romantic nonsense and excitement, sinking me into a fog that had hidden the true man he was.

Clementina's expression was similar to what mine must have been when I'd returned home with the shopping that day—dismay, unhappiness, resignation.

Clementina led the way out of her chamber in a rush, Lady Cynthia on her heels. I walked swiftly after them.

We went down the stairs under its pointed arches and tiles. The wallpaper above rich wooden wainscoting was a deep blue and crimson pattern, quite lovely, if twenty years out of date. We emerged on the first floor—one above the ground floor—and into a lofty room lit by high windows that gave on to the street.

Our hostess marched to the fireplace and flung up her hand at the wall above it. "The Gainsborough was *here*. I had this photo moved here to cover the gap once it was gone."

The photograph was a portrait of a man in an officer's uniform standing stiffly near an arch that resembled the ones in this house. A palm tree curved over him, and his foot rested on the head of a tiger who'd ended up a rug, poor thing.

"A bit grim," Lady Cynthia said, studying it. "Very pukka sahib."

"Sir Evan when he was in India," Clementina said. "He was in the Punjab. It was dreadful, I've been given to understand."

I had thought tigers were found in Bengal but I wasn't certain, so I said nothing. I gazed up at Sir Evan with his fair hair, thick mustache, and side whiskers, his eyes hard as diamonds. Though I could not be certain about the eyes—the harsh lights used for photographed portraits, especially twenty years ago, might have given them that appearance. The tiger's eyes had the same glitter.

The frame was heavy, gilded, befitting the portrait of the man of the house. Older than the photo, I thought. It must have been taken off another picture and given a second duty here.

"The Rembrandt was there." Clementina pointed to a rectangle on the wall where the wallpaper, the same blue and crimson, was a crisper color. "A biblical scene. I never liked it, but it was my husband's pride and joy. He won't let me move anything there, because he lives in hope we can hang it again. The Italian—I wish I could remember the artist's name—was there." She pointed at a place high above the window where there was another rectangle, this one horizontal. "Again, Sir Evan hopes for its return. His friend Mr. Harmon—Sir Evan's man of business—says we might get insurance to pay out for it, but he's not certain."

I walked to stand under both empty spaces in turn and looked them over. They told me little but that the wallpaper around the paintings had faded a great deal, which was not surprising. London grime destroyed all.

"Canaletto," came a stern voice from the doorway. "A painting of Westminster Bridge."

"Was it, darling?" Clementina's voice changed in an instant from uncertain and worried to bright and cheerful, with a brittle edge. "I never paid it much attention."

Sir Evan gave his wife a look of scorn but a slightly more respectful one to Cynthia. "Lady Cynthia," he said with a stiff nod.

His gaze went to me, puzzlement on his sharp face. I hadn't been wrong about Sir Evan's eyes—cutting, intelligent, penetrating, and not in a comfortable way. I could understand Clementina's unhappiness that he was home.

Clementina flushed as Sir Evan looked me over, opening her mouth to explain me, but Lady Cynthia broke in.

"I brought my cook," she said, as though daring him to wonder what mad thing she'd do next. "She'd come to confab with yours, but then Clemmie told me you'd had a burglar, and we had to see what he'd stolen. How frightfully thrilling."

"Not so much thrilling as a damned nuisance," Sir Evan snapped. "Clementina, I'm sure Lady Cynthia will want tea. And the kitchen is below stairs, not in my front sitting room."

"Well, *we* know that," Lady Cynthia said, unfazed. "I dragged the poor woman in here—don't blame her." She looked past Sir Evan. "You there—yes *you,* in the hall." She imperiously beckoned a footman. "Show Cook the way to the kitchens, will you? I imagine she's had enough of the upstairs."

I curtsied with all the humbleness required of me and walked unhurriedly out of the room. I did not look Sir Evan in the eye as he stepped back so I could go around him, but one does not have to stare at someone directly to see all.

I perceived several things as I observed Sir Evan from the corner of my eye. The first was that he did not blame *me* for being in his parlor, nor did he blame Lady Cynthia. He blamed his wife. The second thing I saw was that he was not angry with Lady Cynthia and her outrageous behavior. I saw admiration in his glance at her, liking, and something even more than that.

Dear, dear. Not that I believed Lady Cynthia would reciprocate. I'd come to learn she was determinedly loyal to her friends, plus I could see that Lady Cynthia had little use for Sir Evan.

I followed the footman through a door and down the back stairs. The footman was jolly curious about why I was here, but my severe look kept him quiet.

I did wish to speak to the cook, Mrs. Martin, whom I'd known for some years, but only to confirm my suspicions. I believed I knew who had stolen Sir Evan's paintings, and why.

5

Mrs. Martin was in her fifties and the very picture of what was expected of a cook—plump and white-haired, her cap starched and pinned on straight, her apron dusted with flour.

I'd known her for some years, as she'd been a friend of the woman who had trained me, though we'd gone our separate ways.

Mrs. Martin was at the moment putting a light meal together for upstairs, and I automatically began to help her, patting out dough for scones and cutting them. I did not feel right to sit with my hands idle while another cook bustled about.

"Oh aye, they're good enough, the master and mistress," Mrs. Martin said in answer to my questions. "Never tell me you're looking for another place, Mrs. Holloway. Ye can't have mine, anyway. It's comfortable here, though the master can be mean with money. The mistress wants oysters and truffles, but the master tells me I'd better buy skate and plain mushrooms. And then the mistress runs off with her friends, and the master mostly dines alone in any case."

"He was upset about the thefts?" I asked. "The paintings that were stolen are worth a fortune, I gather."

"So I've been told." Mrs. Martin diced carrots,

and I shoved the scones into the oven and sat down at the table to shell peas. "I'm sure he feels it dreadfully. He spends what little he has on his bits and bobs he collects and shows to his cronies. More important to him than his wife's frocks or new furniture."

"Anything else taken?" I asked.

"Not that we found. Butler and I went through the silver so carefully, and the wine too, but all was there. But I don't feel safe in my bed. He's been all over Mayfair, hasn't he, this thief? Other houses have been burgled."

"Have they?" I'd not heard this. Daniel had mentioned that thievery was rampant in London, but he'd been speaking generally.

Mrs. Martin gave me an ominous nod. "The Smoke is a dangerous place, I've always said. I don't feel easy, you living in that house in Mount Street. Lord Rankin is off his head somewhere down in Surrey, they say, and young Lady Cynthia is a wild sort. Her aunt and uncle ought to take her in hand."

I was not surprised Mrs. Martin knew all this, as Mayfair was a veritable pool of gossip, but I did not like to hear Lady Cynthia disparaged. "Her lady-ship is high-spirited," I said, "but a good soul."

"That's as may be." Mrs. Martin looked unconvinced. "Are you done with those peas yet, dear? The master is home early and will be shouting for his dinner soon."

I gave over the peas, and at about the same time, the footman who'd shown me downstairs returned and told me Lady Cynthia was ready to depart. I gave Mrs. Martin a polite good-bye and a promise to deliver her my recipe for stewed mushrooms, which she'd always admired.

Lady Cynthia was in the landau by the time the footman trundled me into it. "Well?" she said the moment the footman slammed the door and the carriage jerked forward. "Can you help poor Clemmie?"

"I'm not certain if I can *help*," I said. "But the answer to the puzzle is perfectly simple. Sir Evan Godfrey stole his own paintings and sold them himself."

Lady Cynthia stared at me. "*Evan?* Good God, are you sure?"

I rested my hands on my lap, my feet perfectly in line with each other. "It is my belief that Sir Evan has been losing money steadily and recently has felt the pinch. The furnishings in that house are old and need repair. It is likely they were all put in when he returned from the Punjab, if that is indeed where he'd been, twenty years ago. You say he married Lady Godfrey a few Seasons ago, yet he has not allowed her to redecorate his house in any way, and only her sitting room has furnishings to her taste—I would guess from their wear either brought with her from her father's house or purchased secondhand."

Lady Cynthia's quick mind darted through my reasoning. "Yes, yes, I see. You are right, she did bring things she liked from her father's attic. But Evan—or rather Mr. Harmon, his man of business—had been paying up Clemmie's losses at cards without fuss until this year."

"He'd have found the money, so the debts wouldn't embarrass him," I said. "But something must have happened at the end of last year, something for which he needed much money quickly. He sold the paintings, one every two months. I wonder which one he'll sell in July."

Cynthia curled her gloved fists. "The blackguard. He's making Clemmie miserable. I suppose Mr. Harmon advised him to sell the paintings to keep himself solvent. But why should Evan accuse Clemmie of stealing the blasted things? No, don't answer. I know why. To deflect suspicion from himself, to keep others from realizing he's going skint. When it seemed ludicrous to try to pretend the house had been burgled, he shouted accusations at Clemmie, who I am sorry to say is a lovely creature but not gifted with reams of cleverness. She will only weep and ask for her friends' opinions. I hope Evan won't be hard on her for showing me the drawing room. But from the looks of things, she's found consolation elsewhere, eh?"

"The person who paid the debt for her, you mean," I said. "A man, I am guessing. She might not have taken it further than that, you know."

Cynthia barked a laugh. "Her blush told me it has already gone *much* further. Oh well. Good for Clemmie. Godfrey is a stick, as I said. She married him because it was assumed he had blunt—which he no longer does—and many important connections. She'd be a great hostess and invited to all the best dos in Town. This is precisely why I am never for the noose, Mrs. H. Who knows what imbecilic creature one will be stuck with for life?"

I could not blame her for thinking so. "I would have a care, if you forgive me saying it, about Sir Evan," I said. "I did not like the way he looked at you."

Cynthia gave me a nod, unsurprised. "Yes, I caught that. But he is only fascinated by me because he knows I put on trousers. Many gentlemen look at me like that, including your Mr. Thanos."

I thought about Elgin Thanos, the friend to Daniel who was a genius at accounts and mathematics. He was also one of the most amiable young men I'd ever met.

"He is not *my* Mr. Thanos," I said stiffly. "And he is quite a different sort of person from Sir Evan Godfrey. You know this. Mr. Thanos is a kind man, if a bit featherheaded about ordinary life."

Cynthia waved this away, though her cheeks grew pink. "Oh, he's all right. Don't take offense.

But men do become titillated at the thought of females in gentlemen's clothing—do not tell me they do not."

"I grant you that. But it does make me wonder, in that case, why you do it."

Cynthia flashed me a sudden grin. "That is because you have no idea what it is like to stride around in perfect freedom, able to go where you please, purchase what you wish, and speak as you wish, because people believe you are a man. I'll get you into a pair of trousers yet, Mrs. H."

I could not think of anything more appalling. "Indeed no, my lady. I'd look like someone's portly uncle."

Lady Cynthia went into peals of laughter. She had a lovely laugh, and she gave herself over to mirth without inhibition. "You're a fine woman, Mrs. H. Thank you for being so candid about Clemmie and her husband." She sighed, her amusement dying. "I'll tell her. Maybe this will give her the nerve to confront Evan. He ought to have told her about his financial troubles—she *is* his wife."

I had the feeling Sir Evan was not the sort of man to include his wife in any of his private matters. No gentleman should have implicated a lady in the disappearance of the paintings, and Sir Evan had done so too readily. I hoped Clemmie put him in his place.

Lady Cynthia and I parted after the carriage

let us out at the front door. I hurried down the scullery steps, yanking off my gloves as I went inside, anxious as to how Tess had got on in my absence. The sidelong looks the scullery maid and Paul the footman slanted me in passing did nothing to ease my trepidation.

I found Tess lounging on a chair at the kitchen table, her feet propped on a second chair, though she was peeling the onions as I'd told her to, a basket of them at her elbow.

"Oh, there you are," Tess said without getting up. "Ye showed me how to *start* peeling an onion." She tapped the one she held with her paring knife. "But how do you *stop* peeling it? It just goes on and on, don't it?"

"For heaven's sake." I hung up my hat and coat, quickly put on my apron, and took knife and onion away from her. "Remove your feet from that chair and watch me. You cease when the papery skin is gone, and definitely when you're down to the white. Now to chop."

I put a larger knife in her hand, and stood over her, explaining the technique for slicing, until the first onion was in a rather lopsided dice. Tess sniffled as the onion's potent fumes worked their power.

"Gracious, I've never cried so much in me life," she said, wiping her eyes on her sleeve. "You want me to do *all* of these?" she asked in incredulity, looking into the full basket.

"I do indeed." I was already at the stove, ladling stock I'd kept warm on a back burner into a pot. I'd do a nice sauté of vegetables to put over the roast.

"I won't have enough water left in me after I'm done," Tess complained. "Did you have a fine time out in the carriage with her ladyship?"

"We were visiting one of her friends who was not well." Not much of an exaggeration. "But never you mind."

"I hear her ladyship gets up to all kinds of larks," Tess went on as she peeled the next onion. "Goes to secret clubs where ladies prance around and kiss one another. She take you to one of those?"

I turned from the stove and pinned her with a freezing stare. "Certainly not. And you keep a respectful tongue in your head about Lady Cynthia. Or I'll speak to Mr. McAdam and tell him there is no place for you here."

Tess stared at me in shock, as though amazed I'd defend a member of the upstairs. "Well, excuse me, I'm sure," she said, but her tone was more subdued. "It's just what I hear, missus."

"Mrs. Holloway," I said firmly. "Now get on with those onions."

Tess, to her credit, did close her mouth and work. She soon had the onions sliced rapidly and competently, which told me why Daniel had sent her to me.

I guided her onward, and we got the roast braised and into the oven then filled pans with butter, throwing in the onions, garlic, new carrots, and asparagus, to let them sizzle. For fish, I ladled a sauce of dill, butter, and cream over cold cooked sole and followed that with clear beef broth with fresh buns. Once the roast was sent upstairs and the scraped plates came down, the footmen helped carry the food for the staff into the servants' hall. I chose to eat my supper there instead of retiring to the housekeeper's parlor, because I wanted to introduce Tess, and make sure she curtailed her sharp observations.

As it was her first evening, I did not make Tess serve, but told her she'd be expected to wait on me and Mr. Davis most nights. Tess rolled her eyes, but when she dug into the food—not quite as savagely as she had at breakfast—she ate with enjoyment and without comment.

The other servants asked where she came from. Tess was evasive and only told them "London," but she said it in a cheery manner, and laughed, which put them at their ease. I had worried she'd be sullen, but Tess was friendly and open, not standoffish. I relaxed. If she continued this way, she'd fit in well. Strife below stairs was not a situation to be wished.

After supper, Tess and I prepared for the next morning's meal, and then I showed her where she was to sleep.

The attic hall was chilly and stark, my candle throwing strange shadows onto the ceiling. The only place available to house Tess was a tiny cubbyhole at the end of the hall, and she'd have to share a bed with Emma, one of the downstairs maids. When I stopped in front of the chamber door, gesturing that this was hers, Tess flung her arms around me, nearly making me drop the candle.

"Good gracious, girl," I said, staggering under her onslaught.

"Thank you, missus—Mrs. Holloway." Tess's voice was clogged with tears. "Thank you for not slinging me out into the street. He said you'd be good to me, and you are. I ain't been this warm and full in a long time, and now I get a bed with only one other girl. Don't send me away, all right? Please, Mrs. H. I'll do me best, I promise."

"Now, now." I patted her with one hand while I held the candle well away from us. "Don't be going on so."

Tess released me as abruptly as she'd embraced me and wiped her streaming eyes. "You don't know, missus—Mrs. Holloway. You don't know." She scrubbed her eyes with the heel of her hand. "Look at me weeping like a fool. I might be chopping the onions again."

I patted her shoulder once more. "Make sure you go to sleep. I'll need you fresh in the morning."

"I'll try, Mrs. Holloway. 'Course I'm so excited, I might just piss meself."

"Without language like that, young lady." I sent her a frown, but my eyes were stinging—no doubt the smoke from the candle. "Good night, Tess."

"Night, Mrs. Holloway." Tess banged into the room, singing out, "Hiya," to Emma. She slammed the door, making the thin partitions shake.

"I do hope you know what you're about, Daniel McAdam," I muttered as I made my way to my own bedchamber and inside. "I do hope."

Tess appeared in the kitchen at sunrise the next morning, her frock, apron, and cap neat, which I put down to Emma's help more than Tess's eagerness to please. I had to send Tess to the scullery to scrub her face and hands, which puzzled her, but she obeyed. I surmised that she'd had no one to tell her to wash herself before.

I hadn't had the chance to speak to Lady Cynthia or Mrs. Bywater about taking her on, but I would today. Tess was learning quickly, her help had already made a difference, and Sara was far happier waiting on the ladies upstairs than assisting me in the kitchen.

I showed Tess how to boil a quantity of eggs to exact doneness without letting any of them crack, while I shoved bacon into the oven to grill.

Mr. Bywater was very much an Englishman who liked eggs, bacon, and a mountain of buttered toast for his breakfast. Let his colleagues enjoy thin slices of beefsteak or a pile of sweet fruit, but for Mr. Bywater, it was eggs and bacon and buttered toast, in some form or other, like the omelets and mushrooms I'd served the day before.

Because of Mr. Bywater's fondness for toasted bread, I had convinced Mr. Davis to purchase a rack that could toast a half dozen slices in the fire at once. I buttered the bread before I shoved the rack into the oven, using an iron bar that clamped around it to guide it, and let the flames do their work. I'd keep one pile of finished toast warm on the stove while the next seared.

I always used leftover bread from the day before for this task—no need to waste fresh baked on something that would become a butter-soaked crust. For the day's bread, I showed Tess how to punch down the dough I'd left to rise overnight, knead it a bit, and set it aside for another rise.

"Good Lord." Davis was at the kitchen table, coatless, his face hidden behind his newspaper. I'd put one stack of toast out for the staff to enjoy as they went about their morning duties, and a loud crunching came from behind the paper, his exclamation muffled.

"What is it now, Mr. Davis?" I asked. "Do we have a new prime minister? Or did your astronomers discover yet another planet circling the sun?"

Tess darted me a look of inquiry, but I shook my head. Mr. Davis liked to bombard me with all sorts of information, from the important to the trivial.

"There's been a murder," Davis said, incredulity in his voice.

I leaned down to clamp my bar around the toast rack and withdraw the next batch. The slices were golden, just beginning to char. Perfect.

"There's a murder every night in London," I observed. "Or seems like. Men will drink and men will fight. Knives come out, and there's blood on the taproom floor. One can only pity them."

"That's true," Tess said from where she cut rashers of bacon. "Sometimes wives off their husbands for beating them, or husbands off their wives for having lovers. Sometimes the man offs the lover too, for good measure."

Davis flapped the paper down and stared at us. "Listen to you going on. Never knew ladies were so violent. No, this caught my eye because of our Mr. McAdam."

I froze, my clamp missing the toast rack's bar.

Tess squeaked. "Mr. McAdam?" She voiced the questions that stuck in my throat. "What about him? Never tell me 'e's been murdered!"

Davis scowled at her. "Well, I don't know, do

I? Remember the pawnbrokers I told you I saw him working in, Mrs. Holloway? There was a dead body found there this morning. A man's body—he was wearing a brown wool suit and had dark hair, but his face was all smashed in. He was lying in the middle of the floor, the only man there. Tut-tut. I hope that's not our Mr. McAdam. 'Twould be a shame. He could tell a good story."

My iron bar fell with a clatter, bouncing against the oven door and hitting my foot as it landed on the floor. I never felt it. Nor did I feel the heat of the oven, or the searing on my outstretched hand as the master's breakfast toast caught fire and went up in flames.

6

The next thing I knew, a strong arm caught me around the waist and hauled me from the oven door. I came to myself sitting hard on a chair, Tess unwinding herself from me and peering into my face.

"You all right, Mrs. H.? You had your hand right in the fire!"

I looked down at my palm, which was indeed reddening, but Tess must have exaggerated. I was well acquainted with burned flesh, and this was but a light searing.

The scullery maid rushed in with a cloth, dripping water all over the freshly scrubbed floor. She and Tess, both exclaiming and fussing, wrapped my hand in the cold cloth, which, in the back of my mind, I admitted was soothing. Tess rescued the toast rack, but the toast was a charred mess. I must rise and make more.

But I could not move. I pictured Daniel lying facedown on the dirty floor of the pawnbrokers in a congealing pool of blood. Dead, dead, killed by whomever he'd been awaiting to offer him antiquities stolen from museums.

It could not be Daniel, I told myself, not the man with the warm smile and blue eyes that lit when he saw me. Not the man who had kissed me under the bridge in Cornwall, such a kiss I'd never experienced in my life. Not Daniel with the voice that could make even the worst day better, a laugh that cut through all my troubles.

Tess's brown eyes were wide in a pale face, her freckles standing out like specks of cinnamon on cream. "It can't be him, Mrs. H. Not our Mr. McAdam. He's too cunning to get himself killed, inn't he?"

She spoke stoutly, with the air of one trying to convince herself. We shared a look of worry.

Mr. Davis came to hover over me, his false hairpiece askew. The paper hung in his hands, and the cords with which he tied his shirtsleeves trembled.

"Read it to me," I said. "Quickly. The entire article."

"Not much of an article," Mr. Davis said, his blue eyes troubled. "But it's a touch gruesome."

"Please, Mr. Davis."

Mr. Davis spread open the newspaper and scanned until he found the right place.

BODY IN THE STRAND

A boy making deliveries late on the night of the seventeenth observed a door to a shop ajar, and alerted a constable. The constable, upon his arrival, found, to his horror, that a gentleman lay stretched out on the floor below the counter, with musical instruments, books, and weapons leftover from Crimea dangling above him. The man wore a brown wool suit and heavy boots, worn gloves, and had thick brown hair. His face was too crushed to be identified. The constabulary encourage anyone who might know who this poor fellow is to report to a constable or inquire at the Metropolitan Police.

My heart beat in little bangs. The words could describe Daniel—or they could describe one of his customers, or the man who'd visited him that night—Varley. I'd only caught a glimpse of him, but he'd been dressed so. Daniel was expert at blending in with his fellows in whatever guise he took that I could not be certain it was he until I saw the body.

I rose to my feet . . . and found myself in the chair again. "Steady, Mrs. H.," Mr. Davis said in concern.

Tess had my hands, including the one covered in the damp cloth. "We'll go, Mrs. Holloway. We'll find out."

"Yes." My voice was barely a whisper. "Yes. We must not let him be unidentified, buried anonymously, without a name, friends . . ."

"I can't understand what you're saying." Tess regarded me with consternation. "Come on, then. We're off to Scotland Yard."

"Hang about," Mr. Davis said. "You can't *both* go. What about the master's breakfast?"

Tess had me out of the chair, steadying me on my feet. "She can't go alone," she said to Mr. Davis. "Can't you see she's in a state? I'll have to make sure she gets on all right. The breakfast is done—there's already one pile of toast finished. Surely, you can carry it upstairs to his worship? You're a butler, ain't ye? You too lofty to both serve at table *and* get the food there?"

Tess had me moving to the back door as she spoke, plucking down my everyday bonnet and coat from their hooks, while Mr. Davis spluttered behind us.

"You watch your tongue, girl," Mr. Davis called to Tess. "I'll box your ears, wretched creature."

"Ya have to catch me first!" Tess yelled behind her, and then she had me out the door, herding me up the stairs.

Mount Street was its usual bustling self for a Saturday morning. The aristocrats might be lying abed, but the working class were scrambling to provide them fuel, food, drink, and every device known to man to make their lives run smoothly. Add to this the usual London traffic moving through the street to elsewhere, and there was a nice crowd.

We'd have to find a hansom, because I would not have the patience to wait for an omnibus. I headed for South Audley Street, a wider artery where hansoms might abound.

I heard a cry, shrill and hoarse, my name on the wind. I turned in a daze to see young James dodging and ducking his way toward us, his elbows jerking as he tried to shove his way through the crowd without earning a blow.

"Mrs. Holloway!" he yelled as he ran for us. "Mrs. H., wait!"

I halted as the son of the man I feared dead raced toward me. My heart sank when I saw the same desperate hope on his face that I felt on mine.

"Is he well, James?" I cried, at the same time James nearly fell upon me and asked, "Have you seen him, Mrs. H.?"

"We ain't," Tess answered for me. "Oh Lord, do ye think someone's killed 'im?"

James's wide eyes were moist. "He never came home last night. I waited then I went back to me own boardinghouse. This morning, the landlady shows me in the paper a man's been killed. We don't know what to think. It can't be him, can it?"

"I don't know," I had to say. "James, find a hansom. We'll go to the pawnbrokers and see what we can see."

"I already been there. They took the body away, and wouldn't let me in. I went back to Da's rooms in Southampton Street, but he never come home, *his* landlady says."

Mrs. Williams, who was housekeeper in the house where Daniel sometimes let rooms, was a keen observer. She'd have known if Daniel returned in the night and left again early, and would have said so. If she hadn't seen him, then he hadn't come home.

My thoughts whirled. The pawnbrokers wasn't far from the main Metropolitan Police's headquarters at Great Scotland Yard, near where Charing Cross Road became Whitehall. I reasoned that the man's body would have been taken to the morgue there, but even if it hadn't, the police might direct me to the correct station.

"All right, then, we'll go to the police. James— the hansom. Hurry!"

James scampered off, but Tess dug her fingers into my arm. "The police! I can't be going there, missus."

I turned to her, too agitated to be gentle. "Why not? Are you a wanted criminal?"

I would not be stunned if she were. Daniel knew some very odd people.

Tess shook her head. "Last time the coppers got hold of me, I was almost hanged, wasn't I? I'll not let them near me again."

Her words cut through some of my terror. "Hanged for what, child? What are you talking about?"

Tess's fingers on my arm dug harder. "Thieving. There, now you know. I'm a tea leaf, ain't I?"

I looked her up and down. "Have you come to Lady Cynthia's house to rob it?"

"No. I never." Tess's wide eyes held fear. "I came to give you a bit of help, like Mr. McAdam told me to. He's the one what got me off and made them let me go."

I could not be surprised, but it was a small detail I wish James had told me. "They can't arrest you for a crime you've been acquitted of," I said. "That's the law."

"Yeah, but they might fit me up for something else."

I had no inclination to argue with her about it in the middle of the street. James waved his arm from where he stood on the step of a waiting hansom.

"Stay, or come with me," I told her. "It's up to you." I lifted my skirts and hurried to the cab, gabbling the direction to the cabbie before I scrambled inside.

James held out his hand to Tess, who'd followed me more slowly, but she hung back, uncertain.

"Tess," I called sharply. "Make up your mind. I won't let them take you, I promise."

Tess drew a long breath. She was afraid, I could see, with a dark fear I well understood. The police had swept *me* up and shoved me into Newgate once upon a time, and only Daniel's arguments had let me out again.

"Blast." Tess snarled the word, gathered her skirts, and bowled headlong into the cab, barely touching James's hand as he boosted her in. "Bleedin' 'ell, I must be mad."

James swung himself inside, the three of us squashing into the small hansom as the driver started the horse. James sent Tess an appealing look. "Mrs. Holloway don't like strong language, Tess. You'll be out on your ear."

Tess only straightened her frock. "This is a special circumstance. We're per—per—aw, something beginning with *per*."

"Perturbed," I finished. "Now both of you, hush. I am already distracted as it is."

Thankfully, James and Tess fell silent as we careened through the press down South Audley Street. I had hoped the cabbie would have been one of Daniel's friends, perhaps able to tell us whether he was all right, but I did not recognize the man.

The cabbie trundled us down to Piccadilly and then east to Haymarket, down that busy thoroughfare to Cockspur Street and Charing Cross, past Trafalgar Square and the very tall column with Lord Nelson on the top. I'd laughed only a week ago with Grace that I'd never recognize Lord Nelson if I traveled back in time and met him in the flesh, because he wouldn't have any pigeons on him.

Grace had giggled, and I'd meant to tell Daniel my quip, to see if he would laugh too. My heart burned.

The cabbie let us off in front of the Admiralty building. I paid him with the few coins I had in my pocket, vaguely wondering how we would afford to get home.

I led the way across the mad crush of vehicles to the lane that was Great Scotland Yard, and so to the building that housed the Metropolitan Police.

I remembered Mr. Davis reading in one of his newspapers that the police had outgrown its original building and would soon move to new digs nearby on the Embankment. *This* building looked plenty large enough to me for now. Floor upon floor of brown brick rose to the sky, grim in the gloom of the overcast day.

An archway gave on to the front door. Constables lurked outside this, perhaps to keep criminals from rushing in and causing havoc. I walked past the constables, pretending I knew what I was about, James behind me.

Tess lingered outside the door, but when a constable in a blue uniform, his brass buttons shiny, began to approach her, she turned her face from him and scuttled after me.

Inside we found an echoing hall with a staircase, a desk at the far end. Men moved to and fro behind this desk and up and down the stairs, paying no attention to us. Some of the men wore uniforms, some were in plain suits, some carried sheaves of papers, and some were empty-handed, but all seemed to be in a great hurry.

I approached the desk, holding my head high.

James came a step behind me, with Tess, keeping her face averted, behind him.

I was as wary as Tess of the constabulary. They had arrested me without a second thought when a man had pointed at me and accused me of no less than murder. I'd been shoved through a ridiculous trial presided over by a magistrate who'd thought himself a wit, and I'd been banged up in a trice. I owed Daniel my life.

I stood at the counter for a good five minutes without anyone taking any notice of me. The constables and clerks glanced at me, but each apparently hoped another would ask me what I wanted.

Finally, I rapped on the counter with my knuckles, fixing a uniformed sergeant sitting at a desk with a sharp stare. "Excuse me, young man."

Anger and impatience had returned the vigor to my voice, and the sergeant reluctantly dragged his attention from the papers before him and answered in a bored tone. "Yes? What is it, love?"

"We have heard that a man was killed in the Strand." I swallowed as the words threatened to choke me. "In a pawnbrokers. We might know him."

The sergeant rose to his feet and slicked down his dark hair with his palm. "The murder in the pawnbrokers?" He moved a few sheets on the desk, then nodded. "He's here all right—coroner's looking him over." He pursed his lips as though about to whistle. "He's a popular gent, is our pawnbroker. You're not the first to come to claim him. He ought to have sold tickets."

Another wit in London's constabulary. "He might be the lad's father," I said in freezing tones. "Have some pity."

The sergeant peered at James, who had pulled off his hat and now bunched it in his rawboned hands, and his look softened.

"Sorry, love—I mean, missus. Now then, if ye want to see the poor beggar, you sign your name in this book, and follow me."

He lifted a ledger and turned it to me, laying a pen and a pot of ink next to it. I dipped the pen into the ink and then carefully wrote my name beneath the illegible scrawls of the previous visitors.

The sergeant did not ask for James or Tess to sign—I saw Tess's body go slack with relief that he did not. The sergeant simply wrote the number three next to my name, slid the ledger out of sight, and beckoned us to follow him.

The only police station I had ever been to was Bow Street, which had been an old house converted through the centuries to the magistrate's court and jail. Stories of the Bow Street Runners pervaded, brave thieftakers of the past.

This building stood in what had been part of Whitehall Palace, back in the days it had been an actual palace, not simply government offices. Scotland Yard had been so called because ambassadors from Scotland had stayed in the buildings around it. Now this cold edifice, which opened from the street of Great Scotland Yard, held the noise and chaos of the police as they rushed about dragging criminals to jail. Most ordinary people no longer referred to our constabulary as the Metropolitan Police but thought of it chiefly by its location, Scotland Yard. I wondered, when the police moved to their larger offices down the river, if we would begin to call them "the Embankment."

The sergeant led us through a door in the back, along another hall, and down a flight of stairs. The air grew colder as we descended, leaving the softness of May behind. The basement was more like November, I decided as we hurried after our guide and tried not to dwell on what I'd find at the end of our journey.

The odor of the morgue struck me before we reached it. They did their best, I suppose, keeping bodies cold and whisking them away for burial as quickly as possible, but the lingering scent of death and decay permeated the very walls.

I halted outside the door to which the sergeant led us, the small sign next to it identifying it as the morgue.

"James, you should wait here," I said. I certainly did not want James, no matter how gutter-smart he was, distressed by the gruesome sights within. If the dead man proved to be Daniel, I would be looking after James from now on. I'd start by keeping him free of the sight of his father's battered body.

James gave a stubborn shake of his head. "I want to know."

"He'll need to identify him," the sergeant said without concern. "Best if it comes from the next of kin."

Both James and the sergeant looked at me, united in male obdurateness. I clenched my hands. "Very well, but, James, you stay well back until I look first. You too," I said to Tess.

Tess only nodded, her volubility gone. My respect for her courage rose. She was quite frightened to be here, but she'd come anyway out of concern for Daniel, James, and me.

"Come on, then," I said to the sergeant. "Let's get on with it."

The sergeant ushered us into a dark room lit by windows high in the outside walls, the smell of death sharper here. On one wall was a large, thick door with a massive handle, chained shut. I did not like to think about what was behind it.

The morgue was not as frightening as I imagined it—in spite of the darkness, it was quite clean and neat. A high table ran the length of one wall, its surface littered with glass vials and vessels, some empty, others filled with various colored liquids. Flat tables were lined up in the middle of the room between the pillars that held up the ceiling. All but the one table was empty—the body on that one, at the far end of the row, was covered with a sheet. My heart lurched when I beheld the man-shape under the cloth then dropped off into tiny beats I could scarcely feel.

Did Daniel lie there? Daniel, whose laugh could warm a winter's day, who had the knack of making the impossible happen, who knew people up and down the heart of London from magistrates to cabbies to outright thieves. Who was equally at home delivering crates of potatoes down the stairs to a kitchen as visiting a marquess in his home.

I remembered Daniel keeping me out of sight at the pawnbrokers, making me wait until the man, Mr. Varley, had gone for certain before he'd let me out. He'd feared for me, not himself, the daft man. Had Mr. Varley returned last night, found out Daniel was working for the law, and dispatched him?

Tess and James hung back as I followed the sergeant, my boot heels ringing, down the row of tables. As we rounded the pillar next to the last table, I saw that another man stood there, his head bowed as he contemplated the covered body.

This man had very dark hair, the sunlight filtering through the high windows giving it a gloss. He dressed well, but his suit was rumpled, his coat awry. Large gloved hands curled and flexed, as though their owner did not know quite what to do with them.

The stance, the hands, the hair were familiar. I walked quickly around the pillar and looked up at him. The man peered back at me nearsightedly a moment before he recognized me, then he jerked upright with a start.

"Good Lord," Mr. Thanos said. "*You.* That is to say—oh dear, if you are here, Mrs. H., it really must be him under this sheet."

7

My spirits, which had held a tiny bit of hope, plummeted as Mr. Thanos spoke. I'd hoped, upon seeing Mr. Thanos, that he would tell me all was well, that Daniel was safe elsewhere and simply playing another part.

Elgin Thanos was a dear friend of Daniel's and a genius, at least as far as mathematics and calculations were concerned. He could take a jumble of numbers, turn them around in his head, and come up with amazing conclusions.

Toward the rest of life, he was always a bit muddled. Today his coat was misbuttoned, and his cravat was half twisted around his neck, as though he'd dressed hurriedly and not bothered to look into a mirror. He appeared as though he hadn't slept in some time or eaten properly either.

"Mr. Thanos," I greeted him. "I am sorry to see you under such circumstances."

"So am I, dear lady." Elgin cleared his throat. "He was supposed to have met with me yesterday and never turned up. *I* am bad at keeping appointments, but our friend? Not in the least. Then what do I see in my morning newspaper? I raced out to the shop where he'd planted himself like a spider in a web, to see it crawling with constables. They shoved me in the direction of the Yard, and here

I am." Elgin glanced at the body. "Not a sight for ladies, I think. You wait over there, and I'll have a look."

Elgin's skin held the darkness of his grand-father's Greece, but at the moment, his face wore a sickly pallor. I raised my chin.

"Nonsense, Mr. Thanos. I am made of stern stuff." I did not feel so stern at the moment, but needs must. "Come along, sergeant. We'd better get it over with."

The sergeant stepped to the end of the table. "I won't show you his face. It's pretty much gone and a gruesome sight. It was the blows to his head what killed him, coroner says."

So speaking, he folded back the sheet from one side of the body, exposing the man's shoulder, arm, and chest.

The poor fellow was naked, a thick red scar running down the center of his body where I suppose the coroner had opened him up. His flesh was gray with death, the black hair on his chest and arms all the more stark. He had quite large hands, almost square, with blunt fingers covered with calluses and scars, the nails uneven and broken. The hands were outsize in comparison with the rest of his body, which was of ordinary height, no taller than the sergeant beside me.

Watery relief coursed through me. I looked up in elation at Elgin, who was squinting hard. "Use your spectacles, Mr. Thanos. This is not him."

Elgin blinked as though he'd forgotten his eyesight was poor, and pulled out the silk bag that held his spectacles. He looped them on, then bent forward and peered at the dead man's exposed flesh.

"You're right, by Jove." Elgin hooked his finger around the man's thumb and carefully lifted the hand. "Our friend has the hands of a working-class man, yes, but this fellow has done some hard labor. As in the quarries of Dartmoor." He gently lowered the man's arm, his voice more matter-of-fact. "Wouldn't you say, sergeant?"

The sergeant gave the body a quick glance. "Most like. He's got the look of a prisoner. Question is, what's he doing in London? You saying you don't know him, missus? Sir?"

"No," I said, trying to keep the joy out of my voice. "He's a stranger to me." I wondered if he was the man called Varley, but I could not be certain. I hadn't seen enough of him through the crack in the doorway.

"A stranger to me as well," Elgin said. "I wonder who the devil he is?"

Now that his worry was gone, Elgin's curiosity returned.

I felt a rush of air at my side, and James was there, gazing avidly at the body. "That's not my dad." He turned to me, his eyes shining. "It's not my dad."

I put my arm around his shoulders and gave him a squeeze. "No, it is not. Let us thank God."

James nodded fervently, tears on his lashes. He hastily wiped his nose, his cheeks reddening.

Tess cocked her head to study the man's wan flesh before the sergeant dropped the sheet over him again. "The thing is," she said, her voice regaining its robustness, "if *that's* not James's dad under there—where the bloody hell is he?"

An excellent question. The sergeant thought so too, as shown by the way he moved to block our way out of the room.

"Well now," the sergeant said. "If this bloke ain't who you thought he was, then maybe *your* bloke killed him. I'd like to lay my hands on him—what was his name again?"

None of us had mentioned Daniel by name. Elgin flushed and contrived to look blank.

The sergeant scowled at us. "I can have the detective upstairs ask you, if you like."

Tess went a bad color, but I lifted my chin. "Ridiculous. Our friend is no murderer. It is perfectly obvious what happened—this man and a partner in crime went into the pawnbrokers to rob the place. They had a quarrel, and the second man killed the first. He was a criminal, at some time sent to Dartmoor or a like place. No doubt he escaped, or if he finished his sentence, then he went right back to thieving, as he had no other means of making a living. Depend on it, Sergeant. This is most likely what happened."

"That's as may be." The sergeant slid his gaze from me to Elgin, as though uncertain what to make of him. "Even so, you'll come upstairs and talk to the detective inspector in charge of the case. You can put your theories to him. You seem to have believed this lad's dad was the one killed in the shop, so you need to tell the detective just why you thought so. This way, please."

Elgin didn't move. "Now, Sergeant, why don't you let my friends go home. I'll speak to your inspector if you like, but the lady, the lad, and the girl don't need to remain in a police station."

The gesture was kind, but I was not quite sure what Elgin would say when he was taxed, and I wanted to be present to find out. "I will stay," I said quickly. "But Mr. Thanos is correct. The boy and my servant should go."

The sergeant considered, his lips and brow scrunching up as he debated with himself. "They can wait in the foyer," he concluded. "You, missus, and you, sir, will tell your tale. The inspector might want to speak to the lad though. You do want to find your dad, don't you?"

James only nodded in silence, which told me of his deep concern. He usually did not hesitate to make his opinions known. Tess pressed her lips firmly together and moved closer to James.

We trooped upstairs, thankfully leaving the odor of death behind, though the scent seemed to linger as we ascended to the main hall.

The sergeant escorted Elgin and me to a room with wooden paneling, a barred window giving onto the back of the building, and a table and four chairs. Elgin and I were directed to sit on one side of the table, while a man in a dark brown suit, his waistcoat buttoned to his chin, which wreaked havoc with his cravat, walked in and dropped a sheaf of papers on the table.

This man had a thick yellow mustache with sideburns that grew into it, making a half circle on his face. The hazel eyes above a curved nose were impatient, distrustful, and watchful.

"I'm Detective Inspector McGregor," he said without so much as a *good morning.* "I'll need your names and the name of the man you are looking for. And then you tell me why you thought the dead man was him, and why the sergeant says *you* have already solved the crime." He pointed a thick-ended finger at me.

I wondered whether the detective was married. I thought not, from the state of his waistcoat and lack of a wedding ring—though not everyone wore their wedding rings for every day. A wife would make sure he was properly dressed and had better manners. If he *was* married, I pitied the woman.

"Of course," Elgin said in his cultured voice. "My name is Mr. Elgin Thanos. We are—"

The door opened abruptly, and another man walked inside. He had graying hair and an equally graying mustache, and blue eyes in a weathered face that had looked upon many terrible things. A soldier, I thought. A former one, anyway. He was better dressed than the inspector, the knot in his tie correct, and he wore an air of authority that had the inspector rising to his feet after an angry glance at me.

"Sir," Inspector McGregor said in grudging deference.

"McGregor, may I have a moment?" The man beckoned McGregor out the door, leaving it open. Elgin and I exchanged a glance then watched as the new man began whispering at McGregor in the hallway. Inspector McGregor listened, his mouth turning down, his expression growing sourer by the moment.

Finally, Inspector McGregor gave a surly nod and strode away. The other man returned to the room, not closing the door.

"I am Chief Inspector Moss," he said. "I apologize for the trouble." His tone was anything but apologetic. "Go, please, and cease asking about Mr. McAdam."

I got to my feet, hiding my start that Chief Inspector Moss had called Daniel by name. "Do *you* know where he is?" I asked him.

"No." Moss sounded angry, both that I'd asked and that he didn't know. "Good morning, madam, sir."

That seemed to be that. Chief Inspector Moss indicated the open door, in a hurry to see us go.

Mr. Thanos gave him a cordial nod and escorted me out of the room.

We made our way downstairs and back to the foyer where we collected James and Tess, James sending me an appealing look. I kept my silence, not wishing to discuss the matter within earshot of the milling constables, and heaved a sigh when we emerged onto the street, at liberty once more.

Elgin had a hired coach waiting for him, which he kindly offered for our use. In ordinary circumstances, I would have thanked him politely and asked him to find a hansom for me, or I'd have walked to an omnibus or all the way home. I was not a frail creature.

But James was wilting, though trying manfully not to show it, and Tess did not look much better. For their sake, I accepted Elgin's offer.

Tess refused to ride inside. "I've never ridden in a coach with a toff in me life," she declared. "And I ain't about to start now." Before I or Elgin could argue, she scrambled up to sit beside the coachman, giving him a cheery, "Hiya!" as she plumped down on the seat.

James hesitated, uncertain, but I caught him by the arm as he helped me in, and more or less dragged him inside. James landed next to me on the seat, leaning back into the corner like a frightened dog.

Elgin pulled the carriage's door closed once he was settled opposite us, and the coach moved forward. "Who the devil is that creature?" he asked, pointing to the roof, more or less in the direction of the coachman's box.

"Tess? She's another of Daniel's—I mean, Mr. McAdam's—strays," I explained. "I suppose we all are."

Elgin gave a laugh. "A good way of putting it, Mrs. Holloway." He'd forgotten to remove his spectacles and gazed at me without squinting. Daniel said he ought to wear them all the time but was embarrassed by them.

I told James what had happened in the interrogation room, which had been very little. Inspector McGregor had been less informed than we had. Chief Inspector Moss seemed to know Daniel—which meant he likely was aware Daniel had been pretending to be the pawnbroker. Had we just met Daniel's employer? But if Daniel was working for the police, why didn't Inspector McGregor know anything about it?

James looked morose. "So, where's me dad got to? If there was a fight, and that bloke was killed—was my dad there? Or did he run after the killer? Or . . ."

He trailed off, but an alarming number of possibilities presented themselves. Daniel could have been captured by the murderer and taken away, perhaps killed elsewhere, his body at the bottom of the Thames. I did not like to think so.

I had to acknowledge the fact that Daniel

himself might have killed the man who lay in the morgue. If so, he could be anywhere by now, in any guise.

I hoped he *had* fled. I would rather have him turn up in Paris, right as rain, than be deceased in the Thames, even if I could not be near him to scold him for giving us a fright.

"We ought to go to the pawnbrokers," I said. "Daniel might have left some indication of what happened."

Elgin shook his head. "Constables were all over it when I was there, not many hours ago. Guards were stationed in the street to not let anyone inside. I suppose they worry about looters."

Indeed, a deserted and unguarded shop would be a target. While each bit of the jumble of things had not been worth much by itself, a thief could make himself quite a bit of money selling the whole lot.

"Well, I will have to investigate later, in any case," I declared. "The family will want their midday meal, and I am already behind. Drat Mr. McAdam. He'll lose me my place."

My light tone made the other two grin but did not assuage my fear. I could only pray that Daniel was alive and well and would turn up with his usual energy when I least expected it.

I had to say that riding in Mr. Thanos's hired coach was a comfortable way to travel through the metropolis. My backside was far less bumped than it would have been on an omnibus or even a hansom. Plus, this coach smelled as though it had been cleaned a time or two—some of the cabs I'd ridden in had been quite disgusting.

The coachman halted in front of number 43 Mount Street, and Elgin politely stepped out to hand me down. One reason I liked Mr. Thanos was that he treated all people with equal respect and friendliness, whether one was a cook or an earl's daughter or a youth who'd grown up on the streets. He saw no difference between us—indeed, I don't believe he was aware there was any.

James scrambled down then reached up to help Tess descend. She put her hands on James's big shoulders and braced herself to leap from the wheel, landing lightly on her feet. "Ta, then," she called up to the coachman, who looked less annoyed than he had when she'd first climbed to him. Tess seemed to have a way with her.

I thanked Mr. Thanos and began to follow Tess to the stairs, but Elgin put his hand on my shoulder. "I say, Mrs. Holloway." He cleared his throat. "Will you convey my regards to Lady Cynthia? She is well?" His tone was anxious.

Ah. I paused to give the question the attention it was due. "She is much better," I assured him. "She did feel the pall of grief, but she is a hearty soul and has been recovering rapidly. I will certainly tell her you asked after her."

"Good. Good." Elgin tried to straighten his

cravat. "And is she . . . does she . . ." He gave a resigned sigh. "Oh, drat it all. I suppose it is no good to think I will encounter her again. Unless she darkens the library archives at the British Museum, or the pub near Bedford Square— scholars like myself meet there." He sent me a hopeful look.

"I do not know about that," I said. "But there is a gentleman's club in Leicester Square that she and her friends try to, as she puts it, *crash*. You will likely find her there on Wednesday nights."

Elgin gave the house above us an admiring look. "The cheek of the girl." Then his face fell. "If it's a members-only club, they might not let *me* inside."

"Ask her to accompany you," I suggested. "Good morning, Mr. Thanos, and thank you for your kindness."

"Eh? Oh. Right." Elgin tipped his hat to me, brushed his spectacles on the way down, realized he still had them on, and yanked them from his face, his cheeks reddening. "Good day, Mrs. H. That is—Mrs. Holloway. James, lad, don't dash away. We'll put our heads together and see if we can't find your wayward father."

James came to him, animation in his step. "Right you are, Mr. Thanos. Be back soon, Mrs. H." He hurried to the coach, leaping inside with Elgin behind him. Elgin raised his hand in farewell to me, and the carriage moved off.

Tess waited for me at the door to the scullery. I ducked inside and hung my bonnet on its peg, realizing I still had my cook's cap on—now slightly squashed beneath. A sight I must have looked. My coat, a lighter one for spring, went next to the bonnet.

I plucked my apron from its hook, unpinned my cap and fluffed it out, and moved to the mirror on the scullery wall to set it back on. The mirror's backing was coming off, making dark spots in the silver.

The reflection showed Tess right behind me, almost on my heels. "So who's he when he's at home?" she asked. "Gent with the specs? A good friend of Mr. McAdam, is he?"

"Mr. Thanos," I said. "Yes, they are quite good friends. Mr. Thanos is very bright. He did well at Cambridge, I believe." Daniel had told me Elgin had baffled his professors, who could not keep up with his quick mind.

"Mr. McAdam likes all kinds, don't he?" Tess observed with a shake of her head.

"He does indeed." I put a stern note in my voice. "Such as you and me."

Tess's eyes widened. "No offense, I'm sure. Want me to peel more onions?"

She swung away in her energetic fashion and sailed into the kitchen. I followed once I had my cap and apron adjusted to my satisfaction, but stopped short inside the doorway.

Lady Cynthia sat at the kitchen table, dressed in a man's suit, reading a copy of the *Sporting Times*. The footmen and maids went about their business around her, used to Lady Cynthia running downstairs to avoid what she called the stifling atmosphere above stairs.

As soon as Cynthia spied me, she threw down the paper and came to her feet. "I saw you rush off in a hansom, Mrs. H. Where did you go, and what the devil has happened?"

8

"Errands," I extemporized, mindful of the scullery maid who washed dishes; Charlie, the boy who kept the fire high sitting in his favorite corner; and Mr. Davis, who leaned to watch us from the servants' hall as he vigorously rubbed a cloth over a silver tureen. "Now there is much to do. I have tarts to make and greens to buy. Tess, we need to go to the market."

"You've only just returned." Mr. Davis crossed to the kitchen doorway, tureen in hand. I could smell the washing soda, vinegar, and lemon juice in his polish that he made himself. He refused to buy polish from a shop, he said, because who knew what sort of chemicals were put into such concoctions? I agreed. Every day we read of scientists who pour beakers of liquid together and create some substance with an unpronounceable name that we have done just fine without for centuries.

"Elsie," I called to the scullery maid. "When you're done with the dishes, bring out the soup pot and make sure it's clean. I'll do a vermicelli soup today with clear stock, fry some sole in butter, and have veal cutlets for meat. And I need to make tarts—break up the loaf of sugar in the larder and put it into a large bowl for me. Charlie, make sure the fire is stoked high, as I'll have to cook everything quickly. Mr. Davis, I imagine you'll have that tureen clean for me by the time I need it. Tess, you must learn to buy the food we are to eat, so off we go."

Tess, who'd just hung up her hat, blinked at me a moment, then caught on, yanked down the hat, and jammed it back on her head. "Right you are, Mrs. Holloway."

"I beg your pardon, your ladyship," I said to Cynthia, who had sunk back into the chair, watching as the staff scrambled to obey me. "We must go at once, or the best produce will be gone."

I hesitated, waiting for her to dismiss me, because of course I could not simply turn around and rush out when a lady of the house was present.

Cynthia raised her brows, her slim chest in her man's waistcoat rising. She seemed to understand, because she came to her feet again and waved a long-fingered hand. "Yes, yes, go on." She moved her gaze about the kitchen, taking in the servants who had frozen as soon as she'd risen. "Carry on, you lot."

Folding her paper under her arm, Cynthia marched to the stairs and started up them. In a few moments, the door above clicked closed, and she was gone. The servants let out their breaths and returned to their duties, the scullery maid taking up the singing she liked to do as she washed.

I reflected, as Tess and I made our way out of doors again, that poor Lady Cynthia was out of place in both worlds. She'd never be servant class—she couldn't help her birth—but she was uncomfortable in the world of upper-class ladies and gentlemen. They didn't like her reading the racing news and riding horses hell-for-leather, and driving rigs, and *she* didn't like to put on lacy frocks and discuss the difficulty of finding a good lady's maid. The chemical-making professors at the lofty universities could devise new forms of fuel for our lamps every year, but they could not formulate a way for a person who feels herself outside of things to have a happy place in the world.

"Are we really going to the market?" Tess asked as we reached the street. The day had turned cool, clouds obliterating the sunshine.

"Of course we are," I said. "I had intended to all along, except we were distracted."

"By a dead body? Oh aye, missus, I'd say that was distracting. What we going to do about Mr. McAdam?"

"Everything we can." I shivered, and not because of the wind. I wanted to find Daniel, make certain he was all right. "But if we wish to keep our places, we will get the master and mistress their midday meal."

So saying, I walked briskly to South Audley Street and turned north this time, heading to Grosvenor Square and Oxford Street beyond it.

The best place to go to market was Covent Garden for produce and many other wares, Smithfield for meat. But that was only if one rose early and hastened through the wakening city to choose the best foodstuffs before every other housewife, cook, kitchen maid, chef, and restaurant staff got there too.

When I could not go to the main markets or send someone in my stead, I made do with shops and greengrocers—after all, that is what they are for. A number of shops have sprung up in and around Mayfair to cater to the wealthy households.

"You must cultivate a good rapport with the grocers and butchers in your neighborhood," I told Tess as we walked. "If they like you, they'll save the best bits for you and knock a few pence off the price. Now, if they *don't* like you, they'll try to sell you spoiled meat, sugar that's half full of sand, and flour that's mostly powder. You have to watch them, my girl, so look sharp but be ever so polite."

"Are you saying they try to swindle you?" Tess asked in indignation. "Huh. And people call me a bad 'un."

"It is a sad fact that many people will try to take advantage of anyone they can," I said. "That is why you must be sharp-eyed but not foul-tongued. Best you say nothing at all on this first visit."

Tess shook her head. "My, my, the things that go on in the posh world."

"It's a dangerous world," I warned. "You must be very careful. You can do well here, if you obey their rules, or at least appear to."

Tess broke into a grin. "Become a sort of swindler too, ya mean? It's all a game, ain't it?"

"A serious game," I said. "One you play for keeps. Remember that. This world can ruin you in a trice, so mind your manners."

Tess blew out her breath. "Cor blimey, I'm learning something new every day. Oi—ain't that her ladyship in trousers?"

Lady Cynthia lounged by the railings at the corner of Grosvenor Square. She'd learned the stance of a man, and with her hat pulled down and a scarf hiding her bun of hair, she looked very much like a young man-about-town who had nothing to do but accost a cook on her way to market.

As we passed, she turned and fell into step with us. "Tell me about it *now,* Mrs. H.," she commanded. "What has happened?"

In the relative calm of the street as we walked along, I related the tale of Mr. Davis reading about Daniel, and me rushing headlong to Scotland Yard to find out whether the dead man was he. I told her about Chief Inspector Moss and

Inspector McGregor, and finished with our worry about Daniel, and how Mr. Thanos and James had hurried off to look for him.

"Jove," Cynthia said as I finished. "I do hope McAdam's all right. He was working in a pawnbrokers, you say?"

"Yes." I was uncertain how much Daniel wanted revealed of his activities there, but Cynthia was well aware of Daniel's strange ventures. "He was doing something for the police, I believe. Looking for stolen wares."

"Ah, I see. And maybe this chap came in to murder Mr. McAdam for pretending to be on their side."

"I wish I knew. Finding Daniel is key to the puzzle, I am certain."

Cynthia's booted feet skipped on the pavement. "Is that where you're going now? To look for him?"

Tess gave me an eager look, but I shook my head. "No, we are truly out to shop for foodstuffs. I am a cook, not a police detective."

"Ha. Scotland Yard would be lucky to have you, Mrs. H." Cynthia grinned. "Tell you what, you fix my staid old uncle his boiled mutton and I'll have a look 'round for poor Mr. McAdam. Have you any idea where I should start?"

"Goodness, I don't know much more than you. He frequents insalubrious places, I am afraid." I thought a moment. "A pub on the Edgware Road called the Dog and Bell. Probably every pub and boardinghouse in between here and there. I really have no idea."

I heard my voice rise as I said the last, my worry coming through. Cynthia put a kind hand on my arm. "Steady, Mrs. H. You say Mr. Thanos is already looking for him? He'll know where to search, won't he?"

"Yes," I admitted. "And James." I took a handkerchief from my pocket and dabbed my eyes.

"I'll fetch my rig and drive about to likely places," Cynthia said. "Old Rankin forbade me touching the phaeton, but he isn't here, and Uncle Neville doesn't care what I do. He believes me positively tame compared to the rest of our family." She laughed, but the laugh was hollow.

"Even so, there is a dangerous person running about London bashing men to death," I reminded her.

Cynthia gave me a nod, but I could see she was not as alarmed as she ought to be. "Another reason I rushed down into the hinterlands of the kitchen was that I wanted to tell you about Clemmie. I pulled her aside last night at the theatre and explained to her what you concluded, that her husband has been selling the paintings. Needless to say, she is furious. The worm has turned, I think. She is about to pounce on him with the news"—Cynthia pulled out a heavy pocket watch and opened it—"right about now. Good thing too—maybe old Godfrey will stop treating her like dirt. No wonder she had to find herself a Casanova."

"We can hope they will mend their fences," I said, but I was not optimistic. Once a husband and wife lose respect for each other, in my experience, the marriage is doomed.

Cynthia snorted a laugh. "I hope he buys her something pretty or sends her to Paris or some such place and leaves the poor girl alone. Well, I'm off to scour the metropolis." Cynthia gave us a cheerful salute, ready to dash home for her phaeton.

"By the bye," I said before she could depart, "Mr. Thanos sends his regards."

Cynthia's blush broke through. "Does he? Well . . . that was kind of him."

She looked away, studying the trees inside the fence around Grosvenor Square's park. I thought she'd say more, but she only turned around and strode back down the street toward home, her shoulders level and her hands bunched into fists.

Tess gave me a shrewd look. "Is she sweet on him, then? The Greek bloke?"

"Mr. Thanos is not Greek," I corrected her. "That is, not anymore. His grandfather was, but he married an Englishwoman. Mr. Thanos is as English as you or I."

"He ain't," Tess said with conviction. "Never

seen a man with hair that black. Eyes neither. He's handsome enough, I suppose. If he takes her ladyship walking, will she wear her trousers? Toffs are passing strange, ain't they?"

"Keep a civil tongue," I said, moving briskly along to North Audley Street. "You are not to say one word about Lady Cynthia or Mr. Thanos, or anyone else above stairs, for that matter."

Tess made a show of turning a key over her lips. "I don't tell tales. Half me friends would be in the dock if I did, wouldn't they? Ye learn young not to peach, where I come from."

Not exactly what I'd meant—not telling the police the identity of a thief or housebreaker and practicing discretion were two different things. I had much to teach her.

"Quite," I said, and led her onward.

At the greengrocers in a lane off Oxford Street, Tess gaped at the sight of all the food. Piles of shining cucumbers were jumbled next to heads of cabbage, and asparagus lay in ordered lines. I checked the asparagus for tightness of the bud and also for insects before I signaled to the greengrocer which I wanted.

"A cucumber should be heavy for its size and dark green," I explained to Tess. "Cabbage tight without too many blackened leaves. Do pay attention, please—you will be required to purchase these things on your own before long."

Tess was staring in rapture at bunches of

light green, veiny berries. "Can we have gooseberries?" she asked in excitement. "I love gooseberries. I've only ever had them once."

I needed to do a tart, so I conceded. "Pick some out. Make sure they're firm but not hard. Not squashed and not too dirty. Come along. We still have to go to the fishmongers."

The greengrocer totted up our purchases, which included spring onions and new potatoes, and wrote them in the book that contained Lord Rankin's account. Lord Rankin might remain in Surrey, and Mrs. Bywater ran the household in his absence, but the foodstuffs were paid for by Lord Rankin. A good thing too, as Mrs. Bywater was a bit of a pinchpenny. We'd never eat so well if she were in charge of the larder.

I dug into my reticule. "And here are some ha'pennies for the gooseberries Tess has already eaten," I said, handing the coins to the greengrocer. "I am still training her. She will do no such thing hereafter."

The greengrocer, who was of amiable disposition, took the ha'pennies and dropped them into his pocket. "Never mind, Mrs. Holloway. She looks hungry. But I'll watch her sharp whenever she comes back without you." He tapped the side of his nose.

"So you should." I herded Tess out. She was speechless, but only because her cheeks were full of gooseberries.

We were almost to the fishmongers before she could mumble, "Sorry, Mrs. H."

"Good heavens, Tess, I always save food back for the staff. You never have to worry about having a meal when you work for me."

Tess shifted the full basket to her other arm so she could rub my shoulder. "You're too good to me. Aw, look, you're going to make me cry again."

"Well, do not," I said. "We are on a public road. But no matter. Your eyes will water much at the fishmongers. It can be rather smelly."

"Better than the morgue," Tess said cheerfully. "Any day, I imagine."

It is almost impossible to find good fish if you are not at the stall very soon after the catch comes off the boat. However, I was able to spy a decent piece of salmon, kept cold in sawdust, and took it home.

"I had planned on sole," I told Tess as we walked back. A few beggars near the post office held their hands out hopefully, and I gave the poor creatures a farthing each. "But you have to keep an open mind about what you will cook. You might find something that is much nicer than what you planned, and you change accordingly."

Tess nodded, as though trying very hard to remember all I was imparting.

Back in the kitchen, Elsie cleaned the fish, and

I cut it into several hefty slices. I made a sauce with butter, wine, shallots, parsley, and capers and poached the salmon in this for a time, while I boiled the thin noodles called vermicelli. I showed Tess how to slice a cucumber paper-thin, and then we dressed it with some tasty oil, vinegar, and ground pepper and salt.

I had not been able to find any decent veal cutlets, so I made do with leftover pork ones instead. I pounded these thin, covered them with breadcrumbs, and fried them in butter, which rendered them as tender and tasty as any veal.

All this went with the gooseberry tart I was able to throw together quickly. Tess washed the fruit while I made a quick crust, and I had the pie baking while the salmon and pork cooked.

A fine repast, if I said so myself once we'd finished and sent it up.

On a normal day, I would have been pleased, and tucked into the portions I'd kept back for the staff, but I was too worried about Daniel to eat much. The relief that he had *not* been the man in the morgue had only left a gnawing concern about his welfare. James and Elgin, and now Lady Cynthia, were out searching—Lady Cynthia had not returned for the meal—but did they have a chance of finding him? And would he be alive or dead? Daniel might have fled town, boarding a train for who knew where, perhaps back to Scotland, where he'd said he'd disappeared to earlier this spring. We might not see him for months.

Cold shivers went through me, and I could not enjoy a bite of my fine meal.

The rest of the day was taken up with cooking and showing Tess what I expected from an assistant. I needed my ingredients ready for me so I could make each dish quickly, and if I called for extra salt or sugar or some such, she should be on hand to give it to me immediately. Playing a game of dice with Charlie, the kitchen boy, in the corner *and* explaining to him how to cheat was *not* one of her duties, as I had to coldly tell them both.

Tess's spirits could not be abated. She only grinned at my scolding and promised to do better, giving Charlie a wink when she thought I wasn't looking.

I admired her energy and her verve for life and was glad Daniel had saved her from hanging, however he'd done it. When I found him—and I made myself believe I would—I'd make him tell me the tale.

I finally found a moment to gain Mrs. Bywater's permission to take Tess on, though we were so busy I had to send a message up through Mr. Davis. Mrs. Bywater, Mr. Davis reported, said that if Mr. Davis and I vouched for the girl, she'd add her as part of the staff.

Mr. Davis looked doubtful, but I glared at him

until he sighed. "Very well, Mrs. Holloway," he said in his lofty butler tone. "But keep her away from the silver and the wine. I know a little tea leaf when I see one."

I hoped Mr. Davis was wrong, but I knew better than to trust without knowledge. "I will keep an eye on her," I promised. Mr. Davis only shook his head but said no more about it.

We muddled through supper and finished for the night, Tess mixing up the dough for the morning's bread while I observed. She did well, except for over-flouring, but a bit of water compensated, and the dough came together.

I put it in its place to rise, and Tess and I climbed the stairs to the attic story. Lady Cynthia, if she'd returned, had not sent for me or tried to come to the kitchen. Lady Cynthia often kept very late hours, so I concluded I'd not see her until the next day.

In the morning, I cooked the Bywaters their plain English breakfast, and fried up potatoes, bacon, peppers, and onions for the staff and served them along with leftover boiled eggs.

After breakfast, I put on my best hat and told Tess I was off to chapel, it being Sunday. A handful of the staff went, or at least we had since Cynthia's aunt and uncle had come to live here. I hadn't been much of a churchgoer before then. But Mrs. Bywater had said we were welcome to accompany her to Grosvenor Chapel, a small, pleasant edifice in South Audley Street, built in the last century.

Accordingly, this morning, I walked out with Sara and Elsie and one of the footmen, following Mrs. Bywater at a discreet distance like ducklings after their mother.

Tess had refused to come. "Me, in a church?" she'd gasped. "Not bloody likely. Wouldn't be let in, would I?"

"All are welcome in church, Tess," I said as I drove a pin through my hat to my thick coil of hair. "We are all the same under the eyes of the Lord."

"Well, *I* ain't the same. Born in the gutter, weren't I? And I weren't no angel, believe me. I can't be going into a posh church."

The child hadn't an idea of what Christian charity was all about, but I did see her point. The pomp and extravagance of some church interiors and the superiority of the clergy in their finery could be off-putting, though I'd found Grosvenor Chapel to have a subdued elegance.

"The meek shall inherit the Earth, Tess," I tried.

Tess returned to cutting butter into flour to begin a pie dough. "Well, I ain't meek," she said decidedly. "And anyway, what would I do with the Earth?"

I couldn't argue with her. I left her under the charge of Mr. Davis, who said he had far too much to do to run off to a Sunday service.

Considering he was in his shirtsleeves in the servants' hall perusing a newspaper as he said this, I did not give his statement much credit, but I left him to it.

I fell behind the others as we walked, the two young maids and Paul the footman setting a rapid pace. The streets were not as crowded this morning, but plenty of traffic milled about, coaches heading for the chapel and other places, people walking or riding, out to enjoy the sunshine after the rain.

As they had in Oxford Street yesterday, a few beggars lingered around the side of the chapel, I suppose hoping people emerging after the service would feel charitable.

Beggars were always a nag on my conscience. On the one hand, I was moved to pity and a need to help those less fortunate than myself. On the other hand, many of these sorry specimens take the money they are given and squander it on gin instead of good nourishment and a safe place to sleep. They grow drunk, are arrested, and then are turned out to the street again once they sleep it off, where they go right back to begging for money. Workhouses are too full to accept all the impoverished in London, though I wouldn't wish a workhouse on anyone.

I chose the path of appeasing my conscience and hung back to open my reticule and give each of the beggars a coin.

"Now, you use that for food," I admonished a man who was so foul smelling I had to breathe through my mouth to drop the coin into his hand. "Some good grub, understand?"

The wretch mumbled something, closed his hand over the coin, and bowed his head.

I turned to the man next to him, who mercifully didn't have a cloud of odor wafting from him, and placed a farthing in his outstretched palm. "You too," I told him. "If you use it for gin, your lot will never improve."

The man nodded, his shaggy hair dirty, the cap that covered it full of so many holes it could scarcely have done him any good.

He darted a glance up at me as I began to turn away. The man's face was filthy and covered with sores, pitiable. But his eyes . . . I saw for the fleeting moment they connected with mine that his eyes were a dark shade of blue, the whites around them clear and not bloodshot like those of his fellows.

The moment our gazes met, he was up and away. With a speed his hunkered body belied, the beggar dashed down the shadowy passage beside the chapel, leaving me staring in his wake.

"Oh, no," I said, snapping my reticule shut. "You'll not get away from me *that* easily."

I gathered my skirts and charged after him.

9

I scurried down the lane that flanked the long side of the chapel, passing its plain windows in a brown brick facade. The heels of my best shoes skidded beneath me, and my hat loosened, threatening to slide from my head.

Wind followed me down the passage, which ended at a gate that led to a green beyond, the trees there thick with spring foliage. The strengthening breeze blew away the stench that had surrounded the beggars, and stirred the coal smoke and clouds overhead.

The gate was closed when I reached it, but I saw no one, not the beggar, not any living soul. The man had vanished.

I tried the gate, finding it unlocked. The hinges creaked, a sound I hadn't heard, but the wind in the trees hissed like an ocean wave, covering all other noise. I hadn't heard the gate clang closed either, but this must have been the way the man escaped.

I stepped to the green on the other side of the gate, adjusting my hat and looking every which way. The path, which was uneven and petered out soon after the gate, looked to at one time have led to the churchyard behind the shut-down workhouse that faced Mount Street. Trees closed in around me, untrimmed, the churchyard no longer used. The bulk of the workhouse could be seen in the distance, at the end of a row of houses that had sprung up around it. Backing onto it was another church, which, if I had my bearings correct, was a Catholic one that faced a quiet lane. All was still.

I stood uncertainly as the trees creaked overhead. I could chase through the small wood after the man I would swear was Daniel, or I could let him be. I wanted to put my hands on him to reassure myself that he was alive and well, but if that pathetic soul was not Daniel, I'd terrify him or possibly provoke him to violence.

If he *was* Daniel, then he'd dressed in rags and painted on the sores for a reason, though why he'd hide near a chapel in the heart of Mayfair I had no idea. But then Daniel had a purpose in everything he did, no matter what mad thing it might be.

I did not know how he'd disappeared so quickly but assumed he must still be nearby.

"I am quite angry with you," I told the empty air. Then I strode back through the gate and along the passage to the street, scuttling into the chapel to take a breathless seat at the end of the last pew, just as the service began.

By the time I reached home, I'd convinced myself I'd been imagining things. I'd wanted to see Daniel alive and well, so I'd decided that the first man with eyes his color must be him. I'd probably frightened the wretch, and he'd run off to whatever hole he chose to hide himself in.

I would never know until Daniel turned up and explained all to me. Short of rushing about the Mayfair streets hoping to spy him, I could do nothing.

After luncheon, I sat in the housekeeper's parlor, going over the accounts for the week and making lists of staples to stock in the pantry. I was running low on flour and sugar, and I needed to make certain Mr. Davis told Mr. Bywater to purchase more robust red wines for my sauces.

By rights this was the housekeeper's job— to make certain the larder was stocked and the expenses of the kitchen were kept in order, and that the cook wasn't being too lavish in her use of ingredients. Because we had no housekeeper, I had to do both.

The lady of the house decides on the menus, or at least she should, but I usually convinced my ladies within a few days of working for them to leave the menus to me. Mrs. Bywater had, with the exception of Mr. Bywater's breakfast, and Lady Cynthia had told me to do what I liked.

As I tallied up numbers in my painstaking way, Tess opened the door without knocking. Her eyes were wide, dark in her pale face.

"The police have come for ya," she announced.

For a moment, panic washed over me, as I

remembered the horrible day I'd been led away to Newgate. I calmed that fear, telling myself this was a peaceful Sunday afternoon with no murders upstairs, and Lady Cynthia would hardly let a constable drag me out without ceremony.

As the first worry fell away, a second one rose. Police visited for other reasons—to announce the death of a loved one, for instance.

Grace. I was on my feet, spots dancing before my eyes.

I made myself speak in a level voice. "Do not be silly, Tess. Tell me who has come and what they want."

"It's that detective inspector. The one you and Mr. Thanos spoke to in the police station. He wants to talk to you."

She must mean Inspector McGregor, the man with the blond mustache who'd started to question us before he was interrupted by his superior. A third fear nudged out the first two—had he found Daniel? Arrested him? Or had he come to shake information about Daniel from me?

"Where is he?" I asked. "Was he let in upstairs?" My question rang with doubt. Mr. Bywater believed policemen to be a lower form of life, and I had difficulty believing he'd admit the man in through the front door. I'd observed Mr. Bywater scolding a constable who lingered too long near the house, when the lad had only been walking his beat.

Tess shook her head. "He came to the back door. Said he didn't want to bother the upstairs. He ain't even dressed like a policeman. Wearing a gent's suit, more like."

I hesitated. The only reason Inspector McGregor had spoken somewhat civilly to me had been because I'd been with Mr. Thanos, who was a gentleman, in spite of his befuddled manner. How would he behave to me if he cornered me alone?

On the other hand, I was quite curious as to why he'd come. Perhaps he *did* have news about Daniel.

"Very well," I said. "He may speak to me here in the housekeeper's parlor. But I wish Lady Cynthia to attend, if she is at home. If she is not, this detective will have to fix a later appointment with me."

Tess stared, certain I'd run mad. "He'll arrest you if you don't want to talk. Bang you up. You'll have to piss in a common bucket in front of everyone—"

"Tess, what have I told you about language?" I frowned at her to hide my nervousness. "Now, inquire about Lady Cynthia—no, ask Sara or Mr. Davis to do it. You stay below stairs. I will let you know when you may send the detective in."

Tess looked impressed at my courage, and she hurried away, calling for Mr. Davis.

I tried to return to the accounts, telling myself

132

I might as well finish while I waited, but the numbers jumbled, my pen scratched, and a blot of ink marred the ledger's page.

As I wiped it clean, Lady Cynthia came in, eyes alight. At least one person was excited about the visit of a policeman.

She wore a gown today—Mrs. Bywater insisted on it for Sunday meals—a very dark gray trimmed with black.

"Send him in, Tess," Lady Cynthia called out and then turned to me. "What's it all about, Mrs. Holloway?"

"I have no idea," I answered, pretending composure. "We shall have to wait and see what he says."

Cynthia remained standing as Detective Inspector McGregor entered the room. He strode in with arrogance, as though prepared to browbeat a young cook until she gave him all he wanted to know, but he pulled up short when he saw Lady Cynthia. He took her in, quickly assessing that she was a lady of the house and no servant.

I put McGregor in about his mid-thirties, old enough for experience, young enough for exuberant energy. I renewed my conviction that he was not married as I viewed his rumpled frock coat and noted a missing button on his waistcoat. No wife would let her husband be seen like that unless she severely disliked him and no longer had interest in how the world perceived him.

Inspector McGregor gave Cynthia a bow. "I beg your pardon, ma'am." His hazel eyes flickered as he rearranged his thoughts. "I am afraid I must speak to your cook on an important matter."

If he expected Lady Cynthia to leave me to it, or be shocked and grieved that a policeman had come to see one of her domestics, he did not know Lady Cynthia. She sat down on a chair in a swirl of skirts. "Speak away. What is this important matter?"

The inspector remained stiffly standing. "I'd hoped to do so in private."

"Not a bit of it." Cynthia waved to a chair. "Close the door and sit down, man. This is as private as you will find."

McGregor shot her a look of dislike. I assumed he did not appreciate being ordered about by women.

However, he closed the door without argument and seated himself on a hard wooden chair, as Cynthia and I had taken the only comfortable ones in the room.

"I am Detective Inspector McGregor," he began, speaking to Lady Cynthia. "Mrs. Holloway came to Scotland Yard yesterday to identify the body of a murdered man."

"Yes, she told me," Lady Cynthia said. "And she did not know who it was. I am aware of all this. What do you need to ask her?"

"I want to know who she came to the morgue

to find. If the man she's searching for isn't the dead man, who is he?"

I did so hate when people spoke of me as though I weren't in a room. It was something that happened frequently when one was in service, however.

"You put this question to me at the police headquarters," I said. "I remember that your chief inspector—Moss is his name?—told you not to. At least, that is what I assume he said to you in the corridor. I could not hear the precise words."

McGregor's eyes went cold. He might be a handsome man, I thought, if he didn't let his features become so pinched with anger. And if he shaved off his mustache and brushed his hair back from his forehead. Some men looked fine in whiskers, but McGregor's weighed heavily on his face.

"That is why I am here," McGregor snapped. "The chief inspector had no business interfering in the matter. This is *my* case."

Before I could answer, Lady Cynthia broke in. "You mean you're here without leave? To question Mrs. Holloway on your own? Isn't that not done?"

McGregor leaned forward, elbows on his thighs, his eyes taking on a determined light. "Only a few years ago, my lady, a number of chief inspectors were tried and sentenced to hard labor for colluding with known criminals.

Taking money to tell confidence tricksters when they'd be investigated, giving them time to get away, even steering customers to them. These were high-ranking officers of the Yard, men who'd given years of service, who ought to have been honorable and trusted. Instead, they were paid to look the other way while these criminals swindled people out of thousands and thousands of pounds." He tapped his chest. "*I* do not intend to let that happen again." His eyes glinted and his lips drew back in a snarl.

"What are you saying?" Lady Cynthia asked. "That this Chief Inspector Moss is corrupt? What has that to do with Mrs. Holloway?"

McGregor shook his head with impatience. "Not Chief Inspector Moss. That is, I don't know. I don't know *what* he's up to." He returned his hard gaze to me. "He told me outside the interview room that *Mrs. Holloway* was not to be questioned. He knew you by name, though I had never seen you before, never heard anything about you. I want to know why, and what you have to do with Chief Inspector Moss and the dead man in the pawnbrokers." His words rang in the small room.

"I have nothing to do with Chief Inspector Moss," I said. "I'd never met him before—never seen him until yesterday."

McGregor's hands balled as he leaned to me. "Then why the devil did he call you by name?"

136

"Please do not swear at her," Lady Cynthia said coolly. "I am certain there is some reasonable explanation."

There was. *Daniel.* I did not know what position Daniel held with the police, if he held any official position at all, but there was no dispute that he at least worked with them. I was certain now that Chief Inspector Moss had put him up to sitting in the pawnbrokers, and Daniel had probably told him about me. Why the chief inspector had come to my rescue at the police station I could only speculate—either he or Daniel had not wanted me to impart information to Inspector McGregor.

That left me now trying to decide what to tell McGregor. On the one hand, Daniel likely wanted me saying nothing about his mission. On the other, a zealous man like McGregor might poke and pry where he should not if I left him too curious and perhaps bring danger to Daniel.

I drew a breath. "I advise you to speak to your chief inspector, Detective. If you are adamant about keeping corruption out of the police, perhaps he can set your mind at rest."

"Or appease me with what I want to hear," McGregor growled. "You know something, Mrs. Holloway. As do *you.*" He turned a sharp look on Lady Cynthia. "Withholding knowledge of a criminal or criminal activity is a crime itself, your ladyship. I should not like to see a young woman such as yourself having to go before a magistrate. It would not be pleasant."

"Sounds like it would be jolly amusing," Lady Cynthia drawled. "Especially when I told the magistrate what rot this all is. Mrs. Holloway is a respectable woman who would never have dealings with criminals. You have my word on that. She's worked for the best families in England and has no stain on her character. Suffice it to say that Mrs. Holloway was relieved she did not know the identity of the dead man and has no more to do with it."

McGregor listened, scowling, not at all mollified. But he must have realized Lady Cynthia and I would tell him nothing more. Unless he arrested us and dragged us off with him, he was powerless here.

"I can assure you, Detective," I said in a reasonable tone, "that my errand to the morgue had nothing to do with corrupting the police or committing criminal acts. I read of the death in the newspaper and worried that it might be a friend I'd seen in that pawnbrokers. That is all."

Near enough to the truth without betraying Daniel. McGregor's frown deepened. "The pawnbroker there is a known receiver. Is *he* your friend? Where is he now?"

"The man I sought is hardly a criminal," I said coolly, but I could not stop my face growing warm. Daniel might be the best criminal of all, working with the police and having us all fooled. That did not seem quite right, but I did not *know,* and this unnerved me.

"You did not answer my question," McGregor said sharply. "Where is this man?"

I spread my hands. "That I do not know."

He must have read the truth in my eyes, because he looked disappointed.

"There, she's told you," Lady Cynthia said, getting to her feet. McGregor rose hastily, at least having enough manners not to remain seated while a lady stood. "Be off with you now. If you wish to speak to Mrs. Holloway further, I suggest you send a note and fix an appointment instead of barging in. Yes?"

McGregor gave her a stiff nod. His keen stare made me uneasy, but at the same time, I could not help feeling sorry for the man. I understood his worry that the corruption high up in Scotland Yard, which had been shouted from every newspaper three or so years ago, might happen again. Not long after this sensation, the Metropolitan Police had been reorganized, with a new division of detectives in plain clothes installed, of which McGregor must be a member.

I wondered whether Daniel was also a part of this Criminal Investigation Division, but if so, McGregor would know that, wouldn't he? McGregor had no idea what was going on, however, and this frustrated him. I found I could sympathize with him in a small way.

I gave him a nod as I rose. "I promise that if I discover anything helpful, I will send word to you. I too have no wish to see the police compromised. Then where would we be?"

McGregor's look could have cut glass. He let out a sound like a snarl then made a curt bow and left the room. I heard Mr. Davis in the passage—where he'd no doubt lingered to listen—tell McGregor he would show him the way out.

Cynthia turned to me, eyes alight. "Well, that was exciting. What is McAdam up to that the police don't know about, eh?"

"I'm certain they *do* know," I answered. "Or at least some of them might. Which is more than I do." I sighed. "I thought I saw Daniel this morning skulking around the churchyard, but I cannot be certain."

"Truly? Perhaps we should have another look for him, then." Lady Cynthia headed for the door as though ready to charge around Mayfair on the moment.

"I must prepare the evening meal," I said unhappily. "Mrs. Bywater has invited six guests, Mr. Davis told me."

Cynthia grimaced. "Yes, Aunt Isobel and Uncle Neville are at it again. Bringing bachelors around to have a look at me. They plant these eligible gentlemen among their happily married friends and parade me before them like a prized dog. A hound getting on in years, so they need to snap her up quick."

She flung herself into a chair, her energy sending it skittering a few inches backward. "Can't you do something, Mrs. Holloway?" she pleaded. "I helped you with this officious policeman. I implore you to get me out of this supper with the not-so-Honorable Harcourt Plimpton and the horrible Ferdinand Marchand. Imagine having to write *Mrs. Harcourt B. Plimpton* on all your correspondence."

"You do not have to accept their proposals," I pointed out. "You have free will. This is not the England of the past—forced marriages are no longer legal." I took in her unhappy face and relented. "Let me think on it."

"Please think quickly," Cynthia said as she sprang up again and strode for the door. "Davis!" she called as she moved down the passage. "Have Sara bring me tea, and for God's sake, put a dollop of brandy in it for me."

I sighed and returned to the table. I had work to do, interruptions by policemen notwithstanding. I called out to a passing footman and told him to send Tess to me, while I opened the account books again, and took up my pen.

Tess looked perplexed when I gave her new instructions, but as I explained, her quick mind took it in, and she began to grin.

"Right you are, Mrs. H. I'm off." She tore her apron from her and flung it down, its ties fluttering on the floor even as her footsteps faded.

I finished my menus, put the cookery books away, picked up Tess's discarded apron, and went to the kitchen.

"Where did *she* run off to?" Davis asked with a frown as I hung up Tess's apron. "She can't work here if she dashes about as she pleases."

"She's conducting an errand for me, Mr. Davis," I said. I moved to the kitchen table to tear up the lettuce Tess had competently washed. "I would not have sent her off were it not important."

"Well, pardon me." Davis put his hands on his hips a moment before reaching up and delicately straightening the hairpiece on the crown of his head. "I'm only looking out for you, Mrs. H."

"Of course." I sent him a forgiving look. "You will have to set one more place. There will be an additional guest."

Mr. Davis stopped fiddling with his hair and gave me a surprised look. "I beg your pardon? I was not informed."

"A last-minute addition," I said. "A man called Mr. Thanos. A friend of Lady Cynthia's. He might be a bit late. Do go up and add the place setting, or it might be awkward when he arrives."

Davis stared at me another moment before he heaved a sigh that came from the bottom of his boots. "She should inform *me*," he said, aggrieved. "Lady Cynthia is a dear young woman, but really she has no idea how to run a household."

I said nothing, letting him fume.

Of course, Lady Cynthia hadn't told Mr. Davis because she did not know herself yet. I'd sent Tess out to look for James, and then both of them were to find Mr. Thanos and bring him here, dressed for supper, no misbuttoned coats and no arguments.

I went back to preparing the salmon à la Genévése and apricot tart so all would be ready, trusting James and Tess and their youthful exuberance to complete the task to satisfaction.

10

The evening meal was elaborate, this being Sunday. When Tess returned, buoyant, an hour later, I put her to work with a vengeance.

"James is with 'im," Tess told me as she chopped the mountain of mushrooms I shoved at her. "Mr. Thanos looks like a rich cove, don't he, but he lives in a little flat in Bloomsbury with a dragon of a landlady. She didn't want to let me in, I can tell ya, but James made her. Seems James comes and goes as he pleases." Her small knife flew, as did bits of mushrooms, the blade tap-tapping on the cutting board. "Lady Cynthia fancies him, does she? Mr. Thanos, I mean."

She sounded interested. I stirred my Genévése sauce as it slowly cooked on the stove top— carrots, cloves, herbs, butter, sherry, and stock. It would be rich when it reduced, and then I'd thicken it with butter and flour.

"I have no idea whether she does or not," I said, though I had my private opinion on the matter. "She does like him, and I thought she'd enjoy someone with intelligent conversation at the meal."

Tess only laughed. She continued to chop until I told her to cease, then I showed her how to melt butter and stir flour into it to form a paste called a roux, which could be used to thicken all manner of sauces, from white sauce to velouté.

"A roo?" Tess asked, wrinkling her nose. "Like those beasts in Australia?"

"No, you silly creature. R-O-U-X. It's French."

"Well, I don't know French, do I? I was born right here in London."

"You barely know English," Davis said as he came through, heading for the servants' hall to don his coat. "Best let Mrs. Holloway teach you a thing or two, my girl."

Tess waited until Mr. Davis had turned around, and she put out her tongue at him. "How do you stick it here, Mrs. H.? With all these people what get above themselves?"

"Mr. Davis is not above himself," I said. "He's butler, which means you answer to him as much as to me. Though me first, naturally."

Tess flashed me a merry look. "Of course. Mr. McAdam said I was to obey you better than I would me own mum—which I wouldn't. Me mum was drunk from gin all the time before she fell on the road and was killed." She peeked into the pan, stirring the lump of roux as it started to brown. "What do we do with this now?"

I had to blink at the matter-of-fact way she spoke of her mother's death, but I realized it wasn't matter-of-fact to her at all. She kept her gaze on the pot, her cheeks flushed, and my pity for her stirred.

We put the cooked roux in the Genévése sauce

to thicken it up, and ladled the sauce over the salmon that came bubbling out of the oven. I sent this up with the salad of greens and mushrooms, and then turned to getting out the second course— ham and asparagus, and chicken vol-au-vent. I'd already baked the small cases of dough for the vol-au-vent, and now Tess quickly scooped out the interiors, helping me fill them with a heap of minced chicken and mushrooms in a white sauce.

Those went up next, and we set about finishing the apricot jam tart, gooseberry fool from the leftover gooseberries Tess and I had bought, and a sponge cake I'd baked yesterday.

After that, as the scullery maid rushed back and forth from kitchen to sink, I loaded a plate with vol-au-vent, a bit of salmon, and gooseberry fool, and Tess and I shared it.

"This ain't bad, is it?" Tess said as she shoved a whole ball of vol-au-vent into her mouth. She chewed and swallowed before she spoke again, pride in her voice. "Look what we did, eh?"

"Indeed." I gave her a modest nod. "You were of great help, Tess. If you can learn to cook this food, you'll be able to find a place anywhere."

"*If* I want to sweat in a kitchen all me days." Her brows came down. "You been ever so kind to me, Mrs. H., but I ain't fit to work in a lady's house."

"Nonsense. My mother was a charwoman, and I assumed I would be myself. But I worked hard and studied and bettered myself. You can too."

"But I talk like a gutter tart. And I am a tea leaf, like I told you, and Mr. Davis thinks. You know what that means?"

"I do," I answered. *Tea leaf—thief.* "But Mr. McAdam believes in you. If you behave yourself, you will do fine. No need to scrub any more floors."

"All I'm fit for, some say. Or worse." She took a large forkful of sponge cake. "But the eatin's good when you're a cook, ain't it?"

"It can be. But you have to learn to be choosy about your places. Some ladies in the finest houses can be quite parsimonious and yet expect you to prepare exquisite meals."

Tess stared at me as she licked crumbs from her fork. "How do ya know how to talk so nice? I don't know what *parsi-thingee* or *exquiseet* means."

"I learned by listening and by learning to read and pronounce." I was quite proud of myself for mastering my letters, and I saw no reason to be modest about it.

"Well, that's all right for some. I'm gutter London to the core, ain't I? Ain't no one going to raise me high."

"My dear, I was born in Watling Street, within a few feet of Bow Lane," I said. "I told you, my mother was a char. We lived in two tiny rooms with one tiny stove and had to scrounge up every meal ourselves."

Tess's mouth hung open, showing crooked

teeth that managed to look charming on her. "You never. You ain't no Cockney, Mrs. H."

"Ain't I just?" I said, falling into the tones of my youth. In my opinion, no person had a more musical lilt to their voice than a true Londoner, but in this world, one is judged by one's accent and manner of speech—a person is placed instantly as soon as he or she opens his or her mouth. I had learned to speak rather neutrally, neither posh nor working-class. I suppose I could say I now had the accent of a domestic trying to get on with things. "Me mum's friends said I'd be good for nothing but kicking me heels to the ceiling, but me mum wasn't having that." I cleared my throat and returned to my usual voice. "So you see, Tess, being born in the gutter does not mean you have to remain there."

"Well, ain't you full of surprises." Tess grinned at me, her freckles spreading. "All right, then, you teach me to cook, and if you can make me into something like you, I'll give you a guinea. If I ever get me hands on one, that is."

"A bargain." I held out my hand, and Tess shook it, at first doubtfully, then with strength.

Mr. Davis strolled into the kitchen, his coat over his arm, which was a signal that service was done for the night.

"Wherever did Lady Cynthia find that Mr. Thanos?" he asked. He hung his coat carefully on a peg then dropped into a chair and reached for a vol-au-vent. "Bizarre fellow, but fascinating. Who the devil is he?"

"A learned man, I believe." I spoke offhandedly, but I was agog to hear how his visit had gone.

Davis rose and found a plate and a fork, returned, and speared a bit of salmon in sauce for himself. "Those two twits who came to woo Lady Cynthia were put in their places, all right," he said admiringly. "Lady Cynthia got Mr. Thanos to talking about antiquities, and Mr. Plimpton and Mr. Marchand only looked bewildered and out of their depth. They tried to turn the conversation to sport, but Lady Cynthia, who adores sport, for heaven's sake, steered it right back to the ancient world. Then she and Mr. Thanos began quoting things in Latin, throwing lines at each other, and laughing. I had no idea what they were saying, but it was comical, bless her. Even the master looked confused, and him a Cambridge man as much as Mr. Thanos."

I smiled in satisfaction. "Well, it serves Lady Cynthia's aunt and uncle right to bring addlepates to court her. Lady Cynthia is an intelligent young woman and should marry a man with some book learning."

Mr. Davis huffed. "Good gracious, I knew more than those sprigs of aristocracy did, and that only from reading the newspapers every day. Mr. Bywater and Mr. Thanos started talking of how Athens is still crying out for the return of the

Parthenon friezes and statuary that Lord Elgin purloined almost a hundred years ago now. Even Lord Byron thought they shouldn't have been taken. Those lads at the supper table had never heard of Lord Elgin and had to be told that the marbles he sold to the British Museum aren't British at all. They couldn't understand why the Greek people would want British statues when they have plenty of statues of their own." Mr. Davis rolled his eyes. "I don't think they'd ever heard of Lord Byron either."

"*I* don't know who any of those blokes are," Tess said brightly.

Mr. Davis sent her a patient look. "You didn't spend years in university either, did you? Mr. Thanos calmly explained it all to them. I thought Lady Cynthia was going to kiss him, right there at the table."

"Oh?" I asked with eagerness. "Truly?"

"Subdue your matchmaking instincts, Mrs. H." Mr. Davis gave me a disapproving look. "Why do women always insist on marrying fellows off?"

"We only want to see our friends happy," I said. I'd had a bad marriage, it was true, but that did not mean I was against marriage entirely. My friends the Millburns were quite peacefully married, doves in a nest.

"Well, leave me out of your sights, Mrs. H., thank you very much." Mr. Davis busied himself chewing through the salmon, and then reached for a large hunk of cake. "Make sure you bolt the doors and windows tonight. Apparently, more houses on Park Lane have been burgled. Lady Cynthia's friend again, and others too. It wasn't in the newspapers, but Mr. Bywater said so. He told me to make sure the silver was locked up tight." He shook his head. "We aren't safe in our beds anymore, are we?"

I listened in surprise and trepidation. I knew I was right about Clementina's husband selling off his paintings to pay his debts, but he'd been stealing to an exact schedule—I hadn't expected another attempt until July, if there would be another at all, as Clemmie had already cornered Sir Evan about it.

In disquiet, I wondered if I'd been too hasty to believe the matter closed—perhaps there was much more going on than I'd previously believed.

"What sort of things were taken?" I asked. "More paintings?"

"No, no. Statuary and curiosities—antiquities. That's what had Mr. Thanos and Lady Cynthia going on about them. Things like hair combs from ancient Rome, pots from ancient Greece. Other things from collections. One fellow, who lives next door to Lady Cynthia's friend Lady Godfrey, inherited a large collection from his grandfather and is a collector himself. Apparently, he lost some fine bronzes and boxes made of silver and precious gems. Some gold pieces as well. A terrible pity, Mr. Thanos said. Sad when things are lost forever."

I assumed those to be Mr. Thanos's words, because Mr. Davis looked quite cheerful with his mouth full of cake.

"Well, there aren't any antiquities in this house," I said and then hesitated. "Are there?"

I caught sight of Tess, who had her hand over her mouth, trying not to laugh. I glared her quiet, but Mr. Davis hadn't noticed.

"Lord Rankin doesn't collect," Mr. Davis said. "Too frivolous for him. But he bought this house and everything in it from its last owner. Don't think there's ever been a proper inventory, except for the silver. That I know down to the last pepper pot."

"Hmm," I said, and then we spoke no more about it.

Once Mr. Davis had eaten and gone and the house began to settle for the night, I asked Tess what she'd been laughing about.

"When you said there weren't no antiquities in this house," Tess said as she brought a clean bowl from the scullery for my bread dough. "I wanted to say *except you, Mr. Davis*. But I didn't say it, did I?" She looked proud. "Am keeping guard on my tongue, like you said to. And like Mr. McAdam said." Her expression changed to worry. "Do you think Mr. McAdam's all right? James said he still hasn't seen him."

"I *believe* he is." I thought of the beggar with Daniel's eyes, wondering anew if I'd decided he was Daniel because I needed him to be. "But I'd feel better if I could lay hands on the man."

"Me too," Tess said, downcast. "He's been good to me."

I would have to pry the entire story of how she'd met Daniel and why he'd decided to save her, but we still had much to do tonight, and no more time for talk.

I had hoped Mr. Thanos or Cynthia would come down to speak to me, but neither did. It was not uncommon for guests to seek out the cook and give her thanks for a meal or a coin as a gift. Tonight, however, none of them appeared, the guests departing quickly.

Mr. Thanos stayed longest of all, I was gratified to see. I knew who was coming and going, because I stationed Charlie, the boy who looked after the stove and fires, on the stairs leading to the street, and he reported to me.

When Charlie came down and yelled to me that Mr. Thanos was leaving—*the black-haired gent with specs,* he called him—I dusted off my hands and hastened up the outside stairs, the rain-soaked night air curling the hair on my forehead.

Mr. Thanos walked out from the main house to a cab, Mr. Bywater with him. Lady Cynthia, to my disappointment, was nowhere in sight.

Mr. Bywater, a medium-height man, slightly

portly in the stomach with gray hair and a salt-and-pepper mustache, shook Mr. Thanos's hand. "Very pleased to meet you, sir. Quite lively conversation. I look forward to our outing at the museum."

I kept to the shadows, far enough down the stairs that they wouldn't see me unless they looked hard past the railings. This meant I had to rise on tiptoe, straining to hear them over the rumbling of passing coaches and carts.

Mr. Thanos put on his hat and started to turn to the cab, and then realized he still wore his spectacles. He took off his hat and removed his specs, sliding them into his coat pocket. He dropped his hat in the process, and when he bent to retrieve it, his spectacles fell from his pocket and clattered to the street. Mr. Bywater quickly helped restore both hat and spectacles. Mr. Thanos laughed at himself, and then climbed aboard the hansom.

As Mr. Thanos settled in, Mr. Bywater waved good-bye and retreated into the house. The cab started. I saw Mr. Thanos peer out, start as though he caught sight of me, and fumble in his pocket for his spectacles to make certain, but the cab lurched around a large cart and Mr. Thanos was lost to sight.

"He has one of the most brilliant minds of the age," a man's voice said from the deep shadows under the staircase. "And is a fine and loyal gentleman. I could not ask for a better friend."

11

I stifled a shriek as I scurried down the stairs and into the damp darkness beneath them. "Daniel McAdam," I scolded in whisper. "What the devil do you think you are about?"

I could barely make out the man huddled in the darkness, but I saw the flash of white teeth.

"Don't give me away, Mrs. H. There's constables about." His voice was that of deliveryman Daniel, a bloke just trying to make a living.

My heart beat wildly in relief, which I let surge to anger, but I glanced furtively about and kept my voice down. "You can't skulk out here. Come inside at once."

"I can and I will. Dangerous men about, as well as constables looking for the pawnbroker what killed a gent."

Something cold stole around me. "*Did* you kill him?"

"No." The word was firm. "But the police think I did, and the true killer would be happy to see me arrested for the crime."

"Do you know who killed him, then? Is the man in the morgue Varley? The one who came into the shop?"

"No, it isn't Varley. I don't know the cove who's dead—he was a go-between, a deliveryman, and

I have no idea why anyone would want to kill him. I don't know what he was doing in the shop, but I walked in and nearly tripped over him. I knew the constables would fit me up for it, so I scarpered."

"Why would they?" I asked. "The chief inspector—Moss—knows you're innocent. He'd make the constables let you go at once."

"Not necessarily." Daniel's voice became calmer, his accent less broad. "Moss had a hand in setting me up in the pawnbrokers—the previous pawnbroker has been charged with receiving and is tucked away in a cell where he can't talk to any of his cronies—but Moss doesn't know me well. He might believe I killed the man and think it his duty to lock me up. And how the devil do you know about Moss? I don't remember mentioning him to you."

"That is because you have mentioned *nothing* to me. I met him when I went to Scotland Yard, to find out whether you were dead."

I heard the catch in my voice, and the next instant, Daniel's hand was on mine. "Kat—good Lord, you thought the man was *me?*"

I nodded, realized it was too dark for him to see me, and said, "Yes."

I squeezed his hand in its frayed glove, unable to express my jubilation that he was whole, alive, unhurt.

"I'm so sorry," Daniel said in a low voice. "I

would have sent word, but I had to vanish. I didn't dare even speak to my son. Is James all right?"

"He is." I released Daniel's hand to dab at my eyes. "He's resilient, and he believes in you. Mr. Thanos was at the morgue as well, quite worried about you. You certainly owe an explanation to all your friends."

"And you shall have one, when I decide it's safe to come out from the shadows."

"I see." My chest was tight, my eyes stinging, and I could scarcely catch my breath. My reaction to finding him alive and well made me a bit sharper than necessary. "Why not don one of your many disguises and walk about without worry, as you usually do?"

"I *have* donned a disguise," Daniel said. "As you saw in the churchyard. I ought to have known I couldn't fool you."

"Only because I saw your eyes. If you wish to stay hidden, I advise you not to look straight into anyone's face."

"I couldn't help myself." Daniel's voice went soft.

I folded my arms, though my heart thumped. "Base flattery. It was foolish. What are you doing for food?"

"Not much. I was waiting for the rest of the staff to retire before I approached you. I know you are usually the last one to go upstairs."

"And how did you expect to get inside? Pick

the locks? Saw through the bolt? Or had you planned to tap on the door and scare the wits out of me?"

"None of that matters now." Daniel grinned as he slid into his South London persona. "Spare me a crust, missus? I'm powerful hungry."

He wouldn't tell me what he'd planned, drat the man. I had no doubt that Daniel was a skilled housebreaker on top of his other areas of expertise.

"Very well. Stay there. I'll bring out what I was saving for the beggars. Which, tonight, I suppose is you."

"I'm ever so grateful, Kat." Sincerity rang in his voice. I supposed that if he'd been hiding since yesterday morning, he'd have missed several meals and be truly hungry.

"*What* am I to do with you?" I muttered as I swung around and entered the kitchen.

Mr. Davis had gone into his pantry, door closed, to finish his duties for the night—I suspected part of those duties was to polish off the wine that would only go to waste. But the footmen were still rushing about, shouting jovially at one another as they wound down from serving or answered bells from upstairs. Tess was nowhere in sight, but I could hear her voice coming from the linen room as she chatted cheerfully with whoever was there with her.

I laid the remains of the vol-au-vents and cake

into a basket, covered the food with a cloth, and walked outside again, snatching up a lit candle in a chamber stick along the way. I did not slip out furtively, because that would have drawn far more attention than me walking outside with a purposeful step. The footmen and Charlie would see me going out to give food to the beggars as I did every night.

Daniel screwed up his eyes at the candle flame. Sudden light can be painful when one has been in darkness for a long time. He seized the basket as I handed it to him, tearing back the cloth to get to the food inside.

"It's a lucky beggar what gets your leavings," he said, reaching for one of tasty balls of pastry and chicken.

"The cloth is for wiping your hands first," I said. "I imagine they are quite grimy."

"You are right, as usual." Daniel cheerfully shook out the cloth and scrubbed his hands. "London streets are full of dirt."

"And all manner of other things." I shook my head as he stuffed a vol-au-vent into his mouth much as Tess had. My candle's flame lit the fierce red pustules on his cheeks. "You look dreadful."

"That is the idea," Daniel said, chewing. "No one wants to be near a man with sores on his face."

"They are very realistic." I bent to examine them in horrified fascination.

"Flour and water with a little red dye," Daniel

said cheerfully. "Learned it from an actor."

"Of course you did." I realized I was shaking and closed my hand more firmly around the chamber stick. "Where have you been sleeping? On the streets?"

"Kindness of strangers." Daniel gave a low laugh around a mouthful of vol-au-vent. "Don't worry about me, Kat. I learned resilience at a very young age."

He'd told me, more or less, that he'd grown up in the gutter. I was not quite sure what he meant by that, except that he'd learned how to survive in a brutal world.

"What about James? How can you take care of him when you're hiding from the law?"

Daniel shook his head. "James is living well in his boardinghouse, looked after by his landlady, a woman I chose for her kindness. I tell no one I work with where it is. There is a reason James does not live with me. This way, I always know he's safe."

"Does he know *you* are safe?" I snapped. "You must give up this life you lead and do right by him. Cease the intrigues and become the deliveryman you know how to be. It's an honest job for an honest wage."

Daniel listened, but unfortunately, I only made him smile. "Such an idyllic life is not for the likes of me, Kat. I'm paying off debts. One day, when I've paid them . . ."

"I know, I know. You'll tell me all. I hope I have the patience to wait that long."

Daniel sobered. "So do I."

I flushed. "Well, see that you pay them quickly." The words were foolish, but they were all I could think of. "You should not sleep out here. You'll catch a chill, and besides, someone will see you sooner or later. If you wait, I can smuggle you upstairs to the storage room—there's a bed there for those who are doing poorly, and everyone is in robust health at the moment."

"No need." Daniel broke through my babbling. "The parish vicar is being very kind to me. I only came here to see you."

He'd melt my heart, this one. I clenched my hand at my side, trying not to let warmth dance around my chest. "Because you knew I'd feed you."

Daniel's laughter made the warmth expand. "I'd have come even if you couldn't stir up a decent gruel. But as it is . . ." He shrugged and made an *Mmm* noise as he popped a large piece of cake into his mouth. "You're a treasure, Mrs. Holloway."

I huffed. "Go on with you. Take the basket if you like—if you leave it back here from time to time, I'll fill it up. But if Mr. Bywater catches you, he'll fetch a constable. He's wary of burglars. You have heard that there have been thefts up and down Park Lane, haven't you?"

"So I gather." Daniel finished the last chunk of cake and very properly dabbed at his mouth with the napkin, a vagrant with fine manners. "An advantage of this guise is that I can speak to the gentlemen of the road who drift about London. They carry a surprising wealth of information."

As did servants in large households. I had already made a plan in my head to find out about the Mayfair thefts as I introduced Tess to my acquaintances.

"By *gentlemen of the road,* you mean tramps," I said. "What do they have to say?"

"That it's not the usual housebreakers and thugs robbing the places. Or tramps, as you call them, finding an opportune door or window left open. Most of them would steal food or clothing or something small to sell—but in these cases they swear they haven't. They also say doors *haven't* been left open, or windows broken."

"Mr. Bywater says it's antiquities that have gone missing," I said. "So Mr. Davis heard as he was serving tonight. Bronzes, silver boxes, Greek and Roman things, objects from Egyptian tombs."

Daniel sat so still I feared he'd been taken with apoplexy. I crouched down, risking my skirts, to flash the candle at his face.

He looked awful, as I'd said, with the very real-looking sores, his eyes lined with exhaustion, his face dirty with beard. He wasn't ill—he was deep in thought. I could tell by the sparkle in his eyes, though that might have been the reflection of the candle.

"Conclusion," Daniel said in a quiet voice. "The thefts are done by someone who is welcomed into the houses, someone who understands exactly what he is taking. Or she. A houseguest."

"Or a servant," I pointed out. "We visit one another, run errands between houses."

"A servant would have to get upstairs and know what they are looking for." Daniel rubbed at his face, some of the flour and dye flaking away. "Damn and blast. If I wasn't a hunted man at the moment, I'd don my suit and get myself invited into one of these homes and have a look around."

"Mr. Thanos could do that," I said. "He could claim to be an expert at antiquities and ask to see collections. I'm certain he'd be happy to do so."

Daniel nodded but hesitantly. "I have no doubt Thanos would enjoy it, but he is not always discreet."

"You mean he'll blunder about? He's very intelligent—he and Lady Cynthia had a lively discussion about antiquities at supper, Mr. Davis told me."

"His expertise is mathematics. History and antiquities is more of a hobby. A true fanatic collector would know far more than even Elgin. Although, if we put it to him, I'm certain he could read up faster than lightning."

"Lady Cynthia could go with him," I went on, growing animated. "She can make certain he doesn't say the wrong things. You'd have to take her into your confidence, but she can be trusted. I could go as well, though of course, I'd stay downstairs, but I can certainly make the staff talk to me."

Daniel scowled. "Is it any use for me to tell you to leave it alone? Remember Saltash? There is as much danger in this."

"I do remember." I thought of the cold darkness, explosions lighting the night, my terror when Daniel was nowhere to be seen. "You are fortunate I was with you, and you know it. A warm kitchen will be a much safer place for me to sit while information comes to my ears. I will speak to Lady Cynthia and Mr. Thanos." I met his angry gaze. "Meanwhile, what will you do?"

"Decide who murdered the man in the pawnbrokers. There is a very good chance he meant to murder *me* and struck down the other man by mistake. This is why I say there is danger." Daniel let out a breath. "We had word that those stealing antiquities from the museums would contact that particular pawnbroker. The pawnbroker was quietly arrested and removed, as I said, and I was installed in his place as his trusted confederate. I'd developed a rapport with the man, Varley, who was on the verge of bringing me what I was looking for, or at least

164

putting me in contact with those who could get them for me. And then the thug is killed. I have no idea if Varley killed him, or if the thug was one of Varley's and another thief killed him for his own reason, or whether the target was me. No matter what, someone wants people involved in this to die, and me to be arrested for it." He growled in frustration, hands balling in his gloves.

"Why doesn't everyone in the police know what you are doing?" I asked. "I had an Inspector McGregor here today, trying to pry information out of me. He was very angry that he had no idea what was happening. Shouldn't your Chief Inspector Moss have told him?"

Daniel was already shaking his head. "Very few at Scotland Yard know about me. That must remain so." He gave me a sharp look.

"Well, I certainly didn't betray you to Inspector McGregor. But I am very puzzled. This spring, you commanded constables, and they obeyed you without question."

"Oh, there were questions." Daniel's teeth flashed in the darkness. "The men in Cornwall were obeying their chief constable, not *me*."

"And then you were sitting in a pawnshop waiting for men to offer you stolen antiquities, so you could haul those thieves off to a magistrate. What is your rank in the police? Sergeant? Inspector?"

His grin widened. "I never said I was a policeman, Kat."

I longed to grab him and shake him until he told me *everything.* "You don't look much like a copper, I will concede. But what other man would lay traps for criminals, or have the power to release an innocent woman from prison, or dress up like a gentleman to catch swindlers?"

Daniel shook his head. "I can only give you my word I am no policeman." His looked wistful. "At one time, I wanted to be, but they turned me away."

This was a piece of information wholly new to me, and I clutched at it. "Did they? Why? You are obviously good at catching villains."

He shrugged, as though nonchalant, but I saw a flicker of old anger in his eyes. "Because they saw a young man who would be disobedient and insubordinate, who would never be able to follow rules or even be bothered to polish the buttons of his coat. I was furious and disappointed, but they were right."

"So you decided to go after evil men on your own." I had no idea if this was true, but I hungered to know more about him.

"Not quite. Much of what I've done would have landed me in Newgate by now if I'd struck out on my own." Daniel lifted a hand as I opened my mouth. "No more questions. The reason I don't tell you is I gave my word, a solemn and binding oath."

166

Drat him. He knew I highly valued a person keeping his word.

"I can only ask that you trust me," Daniel went on. "I know I have not earned that trust, but I hope for it."

"I haven't much choice, do I?" I straightened up, the candle wavering. "I will speak to Mr. Thanos and Lady Cynthia regarding attending gatherings in Park Lane. I will also make my visits to the servants and see what I can discover. How are we to find you to tell you the results of our busybodying? Send a carrier pigeon with a message on its leg?"

Daniel's true laughter burst around me. "One reason I treasure you is that I never know what you will say. No need to round up pigeons. Two evenings from now, have Thanos meet me at the pub near Bedford Square. He'll know the one."

"Where the scholars go?" I asked.

I had the satisfaction of seeing Daniel start in surprise. "Yes—how did you know that?"

I knew because Mr. Thanos had mentioned it. "I have secret informants myself, Mr. McAdam."

Daniel peered at me as though assessing whether I joked. "I see. Well, use your informants to tell him to meet me there. We will discuss what he finds. I should be able, by that time, to transform myself into a man who'd be let into a pub."

I sobered. "Do take care, Daniel. If something happened to you, how would I know?"

"I'd cease arriving to badger food from you," he said in a light tone.

"It is not funny. You tell Chief Inspector Moss to take better care of you. And to tell me if you are hurt or—or worse. I'd need to break the news to James, wouldn't I? And arrange to adopt him."

Daniel gave a start. "Adopt him? Kat . . ."

"I couldn't let a fatherless boy run about the streets, could I? He has been of great help to me, and I feel responsible for him." I took a step back, the wobbling candle spattering wax on my fingers. "You keep yourself well and such a thing will not be necessary, will it? Good night, Mr. McAdam."

I spun on my heel and strode off, not wanting my trembling to be put down to anything more than a chill in the air.

Daniel said not a word as I hurried to the scullery door and let myself inside. I glanced back before I shut the door, but I could not see Daniel—the darkness under the stairs was too complete. Whether he remained there or had already fled, I could not see.

I shut the door, contemplated keeping the bolt drawn back in case he did need to come in to keep warm, then I decided against it. Daniel would not come in, but a burglar could, and I could not let the vagabonds of London run off with Lord Rankin's silver.

I closed my eyes, whispered a prayer for Daniel, and shoved the bolt home.

· · ·

I remained in the kitchen very late that night, sending Tess up to bed. She went readily—"So nice to sleep in a soft bed with covers over ya and a girl who don't kick too much, innit?"

I didn't know how Emma felt about sharing a bed with Tess, but Emma had not complained. I envied Tess for finding such comfort in the simple things in life, but perhaps she was right. Nothing wrong with enjoying warmth and a good night's sleep when it was available.

For me, I knew sleep would not come, so I busied myself in the kitchen and larder as I did many nights, making notes and planning recipes, looking things up in the cookbooks, my treasured two and the ones that had been in the house when I arrived.

I was surprised this household had so few cookbooks, and those years out of date—one of the first ladies I was cook for had a mania for collecting them. Plenty were produced each year, here and in America, giving not only recipes collected and tested but instructions on how to do everything from basting and braising to planning a large supper party to making paper boxes for delicate confectionaries. I was of the opinion that more people had a passion for reading cookbooks than actually cooking or I would not see so many new books advertised.

I wondered, as I debated the work involved in

making a gâteau St. Honoré—a lovely combination of choux pastry, cream, and caramelized sugar—if I remained awake in case Daniel should knock on the door and ask for more sustenance or take up my offer of the bed for the night. I told myself I was only doing my job and preparing future menus, and went back to the instructions for the gâteau. It would be quite an undertaking, plus I'd need ice in which to chill the cake so that it did not melt into a puddle on the sideboard. Daniel would like the confection—he'd close his eyes in enjoyment as he savored the sticky caramel and the cold cream, the soft bite of the choux pastry . . .

"Are you awake, Mrs. H.?"

I blinked open my eyes as Lady Cynthia sat down in front of me at the kitchen table. I saw that I'd broken the end of my pencil by pressing it too hard against my notebook, and hastily set the pencil down.

Cynthia wore a tailored black frock coat, watered silk waistcoat and white cravat, black gloves, and black trousers over elegant leather boots that she crossed as she stretched out her legs. Even in her gentleman's attire, she didn't wear color. She felt the death of her sister more keenly than others realized.

"I beg your pardon, your ladyship," I said, closing my book. "I did not hear you."

"It's two in the morning. I'd think you'd want

170

to toddle off to bed, but since you're awake . . ."

Cynthia sprang from her chair. I struggled up, my training not letting me remain seated while my employer stood. Cynthia surged forward and caught me in an exuberant hug. "You're a genius, Mrs. Holloway. You saved my sanity tonight, no mistake."

12

Cynthia released me as effusively, and I stepped back, struggling to keep my cap from sliding from my head.

"Mr. Thanos was a success?" I asked when I'd regained my balance.

"You know he was. Those two simpletons Uncle Neville invited to woo me were complete asses. Mr. Thanos did not have to say much to make them look like idiots; he just blinked behind those specs of his, surprised they'd never heard of the Elgin Marbles. He even made a jest of it because his Christian name is Elgin, but the joke not only sailed over the two gentlemen's heads but bounced from the wall and careened into the backs of their skulls. Even Uncle Neville was trying not to laugh."

I smiled in appreciation. "I have the impression that Mr. Bywater and Mr. Thanos have planned a museum outing?" I asked, recalling what I'd heard Mr. Bywater say when Elgin was departing.

"Indeed, Mr. Thanos and Uncle Neville became quite chummy. We will meet at the British Museum three days hence, and Mr. Thanos will tell us more about the antiquities there than the museum curators know. He didn't exactly say that, but it's what he meant." Cynthia paused, rocking back on her heels in a mannish fashion. "I say, come with us."

My curiosity was such that an acceptance was on my lips. Daniel had spoken of pieces going missing from the museum—what better excuse to poke around than a planned outing with the family?

I shook my head regretfully. "It is hardly my place, my lady . . ."

"Pish," Cynthia said, waving her hand. "Anyone is allowed in the museum as long as one pays the fee. You'd enjoy it, and Mr. Thanos likes you. If you can't bear to be seen with us, you may walk at a distance. But I'd prefer to have you at our side."

Her expression remained neutral, but I saw the pleading in her eyes. Why she wanted me to accompany her on this outing, I couldn't say, but I found myself nodding.

"Good, then." Cynthia danced away, her boots scraping on the flagstone floor. "Keep the scullery door unbolted for me, will you, Mrs. H.? I'm off. Meeting Bobby."

I'd been introduced to the woman she called Bobby—Lady Roberta Perry, who was a daughter of the Earl of Lockwood. She, like Cynthia, enjoyed dressing in male attire and smoking cigars, but Bobby apparently took things further, by preferring the company of women in all aspects. Cynthia had been uncomfortable being the object of Bobby's desires, telling me she in no way reciprocated them. I wondered if the two had come to some agreement to remain friends.

Cynthia must have noted my look, because she sighed. "Bobby believes I will see her way in the end, but she's ceased badgering me at least. We grew up together, Bobby and me." She shrugged her slim shoulders then made for the scullery and outside with her usual energy.

I hurried after her to close the door she'd flung back. I stepped out into the stairwell as Cynthia rushed up the steps, and peered into the small space under the stairs, which smelled of the dust-bins.

I saw no one there—Daniel had gone, probably long ago. I let out a breath, returned to the scullery, and closed the door. I left the bolt drawn back so Cynthia could slip in before dawn, her uncle and aunt none the wiser, and went to bed.

In the morning, I entered the kitchen to find Charlie blacking the stove. He rubbed the blacking stick into the metal with vigor, then polished it with a brush until it gleamed.

"Excellent, Charlie," I told him. "Wash up your hands, and I'll give you a scone."

Charlie, who was far too young and thin for such labor, grinned at me and ran into the scullery.

He came dashing back a moment later, his hands still filthy. "Back door's open, missus!" he yelled. "It weren't me. Weren't no one but me here when I came down, but I didn't open that door, I swear to ya."

"Yes, all right," I said as I stepped past him, alarm rising. "I believe you. Do cease shouting and wash your hands as I told you to."

Charlie snapped his mouth shut, climbed onto an upturned box by the sink, and turned the tap to let in water from the pumps below the house. Absolved of blame, he completely ignored me and the open door.

I stepped outside, finding nothing out of place but a stray cat who only stared at me in the imperious way of felines. I wished it could talk and tell me who had burst into the house and left the door wide open. Lady Cynthia returning in the night? A housebreaker? Someone looking for Daniel, knowing he'd come here for a meal?

"Go on," I said impatiently to the cat. "I have nothing for you this morning."

The cat only sat on its haunches and continued to gaze at me. It knew that I sometimes brought a scrap or two of bacon outside after breakfast for it. Not being a fool, it was going to wait and see if I'd do the same today.

I closed the door and turned around to find Mr. Davis directly behind me. I jumped and pressed my hand to my chest.

"Good heavens, Mr. Davis, you should not creep up on me so."

"I wasn't creeping." Mr. Davis looked offended. "I heard Charlie yelling that the door was open. Have we been burgled?"

"I've found nothing amiss so far," I said, trying to remain calm. "A footman or maid on an errand might have left the door ajar and the wind caught it." I did not truly believe that, as I was usually one of the first downstairs in the morning, except for Charlie.

"No, ma'am," Charlie said loudly. "No one went past me. Everyone's still upstairs. Or was, until you came down."

More of the staff poured into the kitchen, the maids, footmen, Tess, all accounted for, ready to begin their morning duties.

"You were down here late last night, Mrs. Holloway," Mr. Davis pointed out. Oh so helpful was Mr. Davis. "Did you see whether the door was bolted before you went to bed?"

I struggled with my answer. I was glad he hadn't asked point-blank whether I'd left it unbolted, because I'd have to lie, and I was not happy with lies. The way he posed the question, I could waffle around it, but before I could answer, I was saved from my dilemma by Tess.

" 'Course she bolted it," Tess said stoutly. "I saw her do it."

She had, when I'd come in from giving Daniel the leavings of supper. She had no way of knowing I'd left the door unbolted for Cynthia after that, so she did not lie either. Tess had her chin up, triumphant that she could look Mr. Davis squarely in the eye and tell him the truth.

Sara was the last to join us, her eyes wide with worry. "Lady Cynthia isn't in her bed," she announced. "I mean, in her rooms at all. I went in to wake her, but the bed hasn't been slept in. She's gone."

"Good Lord," Mr. Davis said, his consternation rising.

Elsie, the scullery maid, let out a shriek. "Robbers came in and carried away Lady Cynthia!"

I opened my mouth to deny this, but I was drowned by a chorus of voices that began to babble about the burglaries on Park Lane, conviction they'd seen someone lurking, white slavers who carried off innocent ladies, and then accusations about who'd left the door unlocked followed by stout denials from those accused.

"Cease!" I shouted over the noise. Amazingly, they all fell silent and looked at me. "It is no good speculating until we know whether we have in fact been burgled. We might be shouting when it was only the wind blowing down the stairs."

"I'll check the silver." Mr. Davis rushed away, touching the top of his head to make certain his hair stayed in place. The rest of the staff began to race for the stairs, oblivious to my admonishments, until I was left in the kitchen alone.

"Bloody hell," I whispered.

177

A thief could very well have waltzed into the house and made off with valuables, and it would be my fault for not bolting the door. I ought to have tried to make Cynthia stay put instead of condoning her running about London and leaving the door unfastened for her. But I'd wanted to make certain she could return safely without rousing the house. Cynthia's key would not help her once the doors were bolted, because the bolts on the front and back doors were solid affairs that slid into iron straps affixed to the wall. No one could move them from outside.

The sounds of the staff shouting at one another floated down the stairs. The Bywaters would wake and emerge to see what was the matter. They'd find Lady Cynthia not in her room and demand Sara to tell them where she was. I should go upstairs, be there to claim I'd seen Cynthia leave the house early—to go riding perhaps.

The moment I made up my mind to do so, Lady Cynthia herself came down from the street and in through the scullery. She found me in the middle of the kitchen, ready to dash off as the shouting escalated above.

"Good God, what's all the fuss?" she demanded.

I swung around to her, agonized. "Sara knows you're gone. Better take yourself up the back stairs, try to slip into your chamber before you're seen. *Go.*"

Worry flickered in Cynthia's eyes, but she

nodded and hastened toward the staircase. Before she could reach it, Mr. Davis came down, alone, thank heavens.

"Lady Cynthia!" he said in surprise.

Cynthia paused as though she'd explain, but I pushed at her to go on. "Not a word to her uncle and aunt," I said to Mr. Davis. "Don't you dare."

Mr. Davis took in Cynthia's paling face and my adamant expression, and his lips parted, but then he closed his mouth and stepped out of the way. Bless him. I shot him a grateful look as I hurried up the stairs after Cynthia.

She'd have to go out the green baize door at the top, which led into the main hall, and then duck around the corner through another door to the servants' stairs, hopefully without anyone seeing her. This house had once been two before it had been made into one—the staircases of each house had run side by side. The second staircase had been walled off for the servants, but one had to walk a few feet through the main hall to reach it.

"Mrs. Holloway," Mr. Davis called behind me. "Mrs. Bywater has sent for us. She wants to see us immediately."

Botheration. I did not turn back but gathered my skirts and continued up the stairs. At the top, I moved past Cynthia and made her wait until I glanced out of the green baize door. Once I found the main hall clear, I beckoned her to follow me the few steps through the hall and around the corner. Then I more or less shoved her through the door of the next staircase.

"If any of the staff see you, tell them to hold their tongues," I said in hushed tones. "Or they will answer to me. Now, hurry."

"You're a peach, Mrs. H.," Cynthia whispered. "I've always said so."

She gave me a parting smile and ran lightly up the stairs. I closed the door to the staircase, letting out a breath of relief.

Mr. Davis was behind me again—the man could move like a cat. "Upstairs, Mrs. Holloway. In the mistress's morning room."

I let out another sigh, heavier this time. Nothing for it. I followed Mr. Davis up the front stairs and to the sunny sitting room on the first floor, where Mrs. Bywater took her morning tea before joining her husband and Cynthia for breakfast.

Mrs. Bywater, a thin, almost bony woman, was seated on a soft chair drawn up to a table on which newspapers lay. She had no tea yet, as no one had had the opportunity to bring it. Mrs. Bywater had graying dark hair that she kept neatly in a bun, eschewing the excessive braids, padding, false hairpieces, or little curls painstakingly put into place with a crimping iron. She wore a simple gown of a rich chocolate color, again neat and not excessive, but I could tell that the material was well woven and expensive.

"Mrs. Holloway," she greeted me, pinning me

with a dark-eyed stare. "It appears we are at sixes and sevens this morning."

She'd had time to rise from her bed and don a gown, however, and have her hair dressed, even as simple as it was. That meant she'd been awake at least an hour before Sara had come flying down to tell us Lady Cynthia was not in her room.

"I'm certain everything will sort itself out, madam," I said, as she was clearly waiting for an answer.

"Sara came tearing in, shrieking about burglars," she said. "And that we'd been robbed. What has been stolen, Davis?"

"Nothing, madam," Mr. Davis answered with confidence. "I checked all the silver, both in my pantry and the dining room. All seems to be accounted for. I've set the maids and footmen to go through the other rooms, but so far, everything seems in order."

I relaxed a fraction. "I'm sure the wind opened the door," I said. "The draft down the scullery stairs can be unmerciful."

Mrs. Bywater gave me another sharp look then shrugged. "I will have a workman come and repair it. Now—how is your new kitchen maid getting on, Mrs. Holloway? Tess, her name is?"

"Quite well, indeed," I said, pleased to report it. "I believe I can train her to be an excellent help to me."

"Good," Mrs. Bywater said briskly. "If she can

be trained to do many of the things you do in the kitchen, Mrs. Holloway, you will have more time for the housekeeping duties, which you and Mr. Davis are managing nicely. I am certain you understand that having no housekeeper for the moment is a savings. Tess's wages will be far less than a housekeeper's, of course."

I recalled even Lady Cynthia telling me her aunt and uncle were penny-pinching. Lord Rankin paid our salaries, but Mrs. Bywater prided herself on frugality, and the hiring of the staff had been left to her.

Mr. Davis's face was as blank as I'd ever seen it. He said politely, "Yes, madam."

"I'll leave Tess's training to you, Mrs. Holloway. And I will send someone to look at the back door. It is probably, as you say, a faulty latch." She lifted a magazine from her side. "Now, go about your business. Mr. Bywater will be wanting his breakfast soon—he's cross as an old bear when he doesn't get it." Her thin mouth bent into a smile.

Davis bowed, I gave Mrs. Bywater my best deferential curtsy, and we made to depart.

"Oh, Mrs. Holloway," Mrs. Bywater called behind me. When I turned, she beckoned me to her then waved Mr. Davis to go on. With a worried glance at me, Mr. Davis left us.

I curtsied again. My knees would begin to ache with all my ups and downs if I kept on.

"My niece is quite fond of you," Mrs. Bywater said, fixing me with a patient look. "She praises you often."

I made myself remain rigidly upright. "Her ladyship is too kind."

"She had a miserable life at home. I would not gossip to servants about my husband's family, of course, but I believe you should know. Her parents are not the wisest of people, and you will have heard of her brother and his sad end, as well as her poor sister's."

Indeed, I had, and I'd never forget it. I said, "Yes, madam."

"It has made Lady Cynthia a bit . . . odd. I do not simply mean her enjoyment of wearing gentlemen's suits. Ladies' clothing I admit is restricting, especially the ridiculous fashions nowadays. Lady Cynthia goes too far, but I imagine she will tire of it one day." Mrs. Bywater spoke with condescending surety. "But she does not always choose her friends wisely. Lady Roberta, for instance, was sent to a quiet house for a bit of rest a few years ago—so her family said, but we all know it was an asylum for the insane. A very expensive one." She sent me a pointed look. "Lady Cynthia also has the habit of becoming too familiar with the staff."

I stiffened. "I assure you, madam, she has shown me kindness only."

"You are a very good cook," Mrs. Bywater

said. "I have no fault with anything you have prepared. But a friendship between a lady of the house and a servant can never come to any good. We have to be very careful with Lady Cynthia if she is to have a chance. If we all remember our place in this world, Mrs. Holloway, we will find happiness."

I nodded. "I agree, madam. I would never dream of *not* keeping to mine."

Mrs. Bywater looked me up and down as though trying to decide whether I meant to be insolent. I only stood still, as blank faced as Mr. Davis.

Mrs. Bywater must have decided I meant well, because she gave me a nod and dismissed me. I bent my knees in yet another curtsy and scurried away, taking myself safely below stairs.

"Bloody miserly woman," Mr. Davis snarled as I passed him on the way to the kitchen. "Having Tess instead of a housekeeper will be a savings? I ask you. *We* do extra work beyond our duties, and she rejoices in the economy. It's enough to make me want to give notice."

"Please do not, Mr. Davis," I said in alarm. "Then I will be expected to cook *and* be butler at the dinner table as well. I'll not fit into your kit."

I was attempting to make him laugh, but unfortunately, my statement likely wasn't far from the truth. Butlers, especially experienced ones like Davis, commanded a high salary. Mrs. Bywater might try to make do without one, or else hire an incompetent man for lesser pay.

Mr. Davis only growled. "I work for Lord Rankin," he said. "And Lady Cynthia. I'll stay for their sakes. And yours, Mrs. Holloway."

I was surprised and touched by the compliment. Mr. Davis was not one to heap praise on a person, so the offhand comment warmed me.

"Thank you, Mr. Davis," I said. "Perhaps there will be a few extra scones for you this morning."

"That would be most welcome, Mrs. Holloway."

His tone remained haughty, Mr. Davis not liking to be caught out in a kindness. I continued past him, saying no more, but as I did so, Tess came dashing out of the kitchen.

"Please don't turn me out, Mrs. H.," she babbled. "It ain't my fault. I didn't mean it, and I'll never do it again."

13

Tess's brown eyes were wide with anguish, her hands going to my sleeves to clutch at me.

"Do what, child?" I asked in astonishment and no little trepidation.

"Whatever it is you say I did. I don't want Mr. Davis to give notice. Not because of the likes of me. I'll scrub out the privy, wear the butler's kit at table, anything ye want, only don't send me away."

Her fingers clamped down, her eyes wide and filled with terror. Whatever she feared going back to if she was turned out frightened her immeasurably.

Mr. Davis rolled his eyes. "Don't be ridiculous, girl." He turned his back on us and stalked away into his butler's pantry, slamming the door behind him.

I took Tess by the hand and led her into the kitchen. "Stop your crying at once," I said sternly. A firm tone was best for cutting through hysterics, I've always found. "I need you to help me get breakfast ready. No one is sending you away. I won't let them. In fact, I need you more than ever now."

Tess gulped on a sob, her red-rimmed eyes overflowing tears to stain her too-white cheeks. "Truly?"

"Truly. Now rinse off your face and get water boiling. I must have the eggs ready, and I'm behindhand."

Tess dragged in a breath, her chest rising sharply. "Right you are," she said with a croak and tore from me into the scullery. A moment later, I heard the banging of a kettle and water crash into the sink.

As I brought out bacon from the larder and sliced it up to lay in an iron skillet, I wondered why Tess had been so afraid we thought she'd been up to mischief. Or perhaps she simply knew she had nothing in her life outside this house and dreaded returning to the streets. She'd been dubious when she'd arrived, but now she was adamant about staying. I would have to mull this over and also discuss her history with Daniel.

Meanwhile, I filled the pot of water Tess had brought to boil with a dozen eggs. I told her how to watch the eggs and time them to be boiled to perfection. If the yolk got too hard, it was dry and tasteless. Too soft, and it was a mess of raw egg when opened.

I let her brood over the eggs while I sautéed potatoes I'd parboiled the evening before, and thought about what Mrs. Bywater had said to me about Lady Cynthia.

Mrs. Bywater had implied that Cynthia and I had struck up a friendship, one that might curtail Cynthia's chances . . . On the marriage mart, I knew she meant. A lady who was more at home lounging about with her cook in the kitchen than receiving visitors in the parlor likely would not attract a gentleman who wanted a wife, Mrs. Bywater might as well have shouted. Also, a cook who thought the lady of the house would indulge her because of that friendship might get above herself and stop working as hard as she ought.

All very convenient for Mrs. Bywater to say that keeping to our place in life brought happiness. Indeed, if that place had money, a large house, plenty of leisure time, and the respect of society, I had no doubt it was true. The rest of us had to grub for everything we got.

I decided to take no notice of Mrs. Bywater's warning. If Lady Cynthia counted me as a friend, I was honored. If she was happier sitting at my kitchen table watching me cook than arranging flowers in the drawing room, that was her family's fault for not making her feel more accepted and wanted above stairs.

My mind settled on this matter, I returned to musing on the open back door.

I'd first feared, upon Charlie pointing it out, that Lady Cynthia had left it open in her haste upon her return, but her bewilderment when she'd arrived told me she'd had nothing to do with it. She'd not known about the door until she'd entered the scullery and asked me what had happened.

My next thought was that Daniel had come inside through the unbolted door for his own reasons. But I knew Daniel would never have made his entrance obvious. He might have picked the lock to let himself in, but when he left, he'd be certain to pick it closed again.

Also, I would not be surprised if Daniel had his own keys to this house. When he'd worked here in March, he might have seized the opportunity either to purloin a key or have one copied. The more I came to know Daniel, the more I believed him capable of.

But I believed one thing—if Daniel had come through that door, we would never know about it.

That left me with no ideas. Either someone had come in from the outside and left in a hurry, without making certain the door was properly closed, or someone from inside the house had gone out, again not fastening the door completely.

Charlie had seen no one and had been genuinely alarmed. But anyone could have come downstairs in the night and left through the scullery. One of the maids might have been slipping off to meet a man, or one of the footmen, a paramour.

Or, we *had* been robbed, but the thief had been very subtle. But why make a secret of what had been stolen and then leave the back door open?

I knew I fretted about the question because I'd been the one to leave the bolt undone. If I hadn't, I'd be quizzing the staff right and left until I found out who'd been so daft as to not shoot the bolt home. My guilt must be shouting itself in my silence.

Tess and I finished the breakfast. Once she'd ceased her panic, she'd worked hard and helped me have everything done and sent upstairs for the footmen to lay out on the sideboards exactly on time. Mr. Davis stepped into the kitchen to report that none of the staff had found anything missing or out of place upstairs, and every piece of silver and bottle of wine were accounted for. We hadn't, it seemed, been burgled at all.

I saw nothing of Lady Cynthia that morning and heard of no sort of row above stairs, so I assumed that she'd been able to slip into her room, don a frock, and go down for breakfast as usual.

Daniel likewise did not reappear. I found no sign of him when I went out the scullery door, and checked the area behind the stairs. No Daniel, not even any crumbs from the supper I'd given him the night before. If anything, the area was a little neater than usual.

As this was Monday, my half day, I quickly swept aside the remains of breakfast and prepared a midday dinner of beef cutlets in a sauce of mushrooms, onions, and deep red wine along with new potatoes and the last of the asparagus I'd bought with Tess at the greengrocers. The asparagus stalks were starting to shrivel, so I chopped them and sautéed the pieces in butter and pepper. I'd made a batch of buns after breakfast and sent half of them upstairs as well.

Once dinner was sent up I began the tarts that would finish supper, then I fetched my hat and my spring coat. The weather had turned, warming a bit.

Tess looked absolutely terrified that I was going.

"I'll return by six," I said, rather impatient with her histrionics. "Put the bread into the oven once it has risen an inch over the top of the pan. Chop some onions into a fine dice and then some carrots. Keep them in separate bowls, covered, and store them in the larder. Wash the lettuce and dry it, then put it into the larder as well. Make a show of working all afternoon, because if you do not, I'm certain Mr. Davis will find something for you to do. If he tries to coerce you into polishing silver, tell him absolutely not. I do not want silver polish working its way into my food. Have a bun if you get hungry. Leave the plate of them on the table for the others, but I advise you to pick the choice ones first, or they'll be gone."

So speaking, I pinned on my hat and checked in the mirror that my hair was unruffled. Tess nodded at all my instructions, her face wan.

"I'll try, Mrs. H."

"You will do more than try," I said briskly. "You will be fine, Tess. If I had no confidence in you, I'd not go."

191

That wasn't strictly true—I'd never miss a chance to be with Grace. But if I'd worried about Tess, I'd set someone else in charge of her. Tess was bright, however, and she'd caught on very quickly to any task I'd set her to thus far.

I never felt happier than when I walked away from the kitchen on my days out. Today I had hours of freedom before me, and at the end of my ride across London was my daughter.

For our outing, Grace and I walked down Cannon Street to the hotel at Cannon Street Station to take tea like grand ladies. We pretended to be very rich without a care in the world, while we watched ladies and gentlemen come and go. We admired gowns or whispered our disparagement of them, smiled at married couples who were obviously in love, laughed at young gentlemen who were trying too eagerly to please ladies they wanted to woo.

The tea was not all it could have been—the seedcakes were too dry, for instance, the lemon curd heavy and too runny—but sharing all with Grace made everything ambrosia.

We walked back as slowly as we could, so we might savor every second together. A day and a half out for a cook was generous, but to me, it was far too little time to spend with the girl I loved with all my heart.

I held Grace tightly when we hugged good-bye, and she kissed my cheek.

"Don't cry, Mum," she said, ever cheerful. "It will be Thursday before we know it. Only two days away."

Two long days and three nights, in which I would work my fingers to the bone to feed a family more than they could eat while beggar children roamed the streets happy for the crumbs I gave them. Those children were reminders of why I stayed in service, hid my shameful past, and collected my pay. Grace would never be one of those children, never know poverty and want.

I decided to travel back to Mayfair after I left her, by way of Fleet Street and the Strand. I left the omnibus at Charing Cross and strolled nonchalantly to the pawnbrokers where Daniel had waited for stolen antiquities to come his way.

All was dark within the shop, and a blind had been pulled halfway down the door's long window. Pretending curiosity, I bent and peered through the lower half of the dusty window at the same time I tried the door handle.

"It's shut," said a gravelly voice at my elbow.

I straightened up with a gasp. The man standing next to me was the one called Varley, who'd come into the shop the afternoon I'd cornered Daniel there. I hadn't had a clear view of Mr. Varley, try as I might, but I remembered his voice.

"I see that," I said, taking on the tone of an annoyed customer. "Any notion why?"

"No," he snarled.

I pretended his large size and suspicious stare didn't unnerve me. I was simply a passerby, a woman wondering why she could not enter a shop and purchase what she wished.

"Ah well," I said, shrugging. "I'll pop back another day."

Varley stepped in front of me as I turned away. I understood Daniel's concern about the man as he loomed over me. He was quite tall and very broad of body, his hands not as large as the ones of the man who'd lain in the morgue, but not far off. He had blue eyes that regarded me with more intelligence than I'd thought he'd possess, and a shock of black hair that was greasy under his flat cap.

Varley studied me, trying to decide whether I was a fellow criminal, a person who would run to the police, or simply a curious woman vexed she could not enter a pawnbrokers.

I assumed a virtuous stance and gave him an irritated frown, as would a lady who had no idea who this man was and why he was standing before her.

"The shop'll be shut for a long while, missus."

"Oh?" I lifted my brows. "You work here, do you?"

"No." The word was abrupt. "You'd best be getting on, woman."

"I intend to if you will move out of my way,

194

sir," I said, my haughty best. "And do not call me *woman.* It is quite rude."

His eyes sparkled as he took me in again. "Well, pardon me, I'm sure."

Varley stepped aside with a sweep of his arm, gesturing me onward. As I passed him, he called me a name far ruder than *woman,* but I chose to walk on, my back straight, marching toward Charing Cross as though only irked by a boorish man.

In truth, my knees were quivering—I knew he was dangerous. Daniel had told me so, and Daniel did not fear many. I felt Varley's gaze on my back, scrutinizing me, and I did not cease shaking until I'd passed through the corner of Trafalgar Square.

I paused under Nelson's monument, pondering. Charing Cross railway station was steps away. From there I could take one of the underground trains straight north, disembarking in Bloomsbury near Bedford Square, and find the pub Daniel and Mr. Thanos had mentioned. I told myself I was only curious to see a pub where scholars met, and I had a little time before I was expected home.

I found myself walking toward the station, feeling in my reticule for a coin to purchase a ticket. Perhaps I simply wanted to know where the place was in case I had to run Daniel or Mr. Thanos to ground in the future.

But the idea that Daniel might be there, out of

his beggar's clothing and enjoying a decent meal, took hold of me, and there was nothing for it but that I had to look.

I did not like underground trains, though some of London's did travel aboveground part of the time. How a train managed to get through the long tunnels without us all suffocating from the smoke, or the sparks from the engines setting the beams that held up the tunnels on fire, I did not know. Best not to think about it.

I emerged from the train in Tottenham Court Road and walked to Bedford Square. How I supposed I'd find the correct pub in the side streets without poking my head into each one, I could not say. I had to hope that there were not many taverns in the vicinity, but this was London and perilously near St. Giles. In spite of the vigorous temperance movement and the Salvation Army, Londoners could find a drink on every corner of the metropolis.

A respectable public house wasn't the same thing as a gin hall, I frequently argued with the temperance women who attempted to hand me pamphlets. While I did not much like ale, finding it too sour for my taste, there was no harm in it, provided one did not drink it to excess. Wine, likewise, was produced to delight the palate, not dull the senses. I also enjoyed a drop of brandy in my tea for medicinal purposes from time to time. The hard drinks like gin, which ruined all who touched them, I agreed ought to be purged.

I chose a lane and prepared to dive down it. Before I could, a coach halted behind me, and I was hailed by a voice I knew.

"I thought I spied you, Mrs. H.," Lady Cynthia called out. "I see you were curious too. Excellent. I believe Providence sent you to keep me respectable."

14

Lady Cynthia leaned out the window of a carriage halted on the east side of Bedford Square. The line of fine houses behind her hid the bulk of the British Museum.

I recognized the landau Lord Rankin left to be the Bywaters' town coach. As I approached it, Paul the footman leapt from a perch on the back and opened the door so Lady Cynthia could step out.

She wore a gown of dove gray trimmed with black, her pillbox hat a creation of light and dark grays adorned with feathers that swirled elegantly around the hat's crown. A net that covered her forehead and eyes, and her coil of blond hair neatly offset the millinery concoction. Lady Cynthia looked this afternoon like the aristocratic daughter she was.

"Ladies can't stir a step out of doors without their maid, aunty, or a male relative to guard their reputations," she said as she let Paul help her down—no leaping out on her own today. "Thought I'd be contrite this morning and dress to Aunt Isobel's taste *and* agree to take the town coach instead of striding about on my own. But as you're here, you can be my chaperone."

So speaking, Cynthia landed beside me,

shaking out her skirts and brushing soot from the sleeves of her short-waisted jacket. She noticed me staring at her head and frowned. "What is it? Is my hair falling down?"

"I am admiring your hat. It's quite lovely." I owned only two hats that I kept as well as I could, but they were aging and soon would be too far out of fashion to wear. I always admired a good hat and wished I could indulge in buying them when I pleased.

Cynthia yanked up the veil. "It's ridiculous. Makes me see spots in front of my eyes. But mourning bonnets are even more ridiculous. Don't know how the Queen, God save her, can stick them. Your hat is plenty nice," she finished generously.

"Thank you," I said, flattered. I always wore my best black straw while visiting Grace or going to church. "Shall we see if we can locate this pub for scholars? I suppose they will let two ladies into its snug?"

"I know exactly where it is." Cynthia pointed down Gower Street in the direction opposite the one I'd chosen. "Mr. Thanos told me. He should be there, by the way. That's why I need a chaperone. Paul." Cynthia pulled a coin from her pocket and flipped it to the footman. "Find yourself some grub. *Don't* wander too far or get into any trouble."

Paul snatched the coin from midair, flashed a

smile, and said, "Yes, my lady," before sprinting away.

"You might as well have some dinner too," Cynthia called up to the coachman, who was new, as Lord Rankin had taken the last coachman to the country with him. "No drink, mind."

"He can hardly leave the coach and horses," I pointed out.

" 'S'all right," the coachman said affably. "Paul will see me well. I'll wait here, my lady." He nodded down at me. "Mrs. Holloway."

I returned the nod. The coachman had a florid face, red hair, and blue eyes under a broad forehead. He looked Scots, but his name was Henry and his speech told me he'd lived in London all his life. His eyes warmed as he gave me another nod, which worried me a bit.

Fortunately, Cynthia had already marched away and Paul had run off, neither noticing the exchange.

Turning my back, I hurried after Cynthia, catching up to her as she strode down the street. She halted after a time at the door of what looked to be a very old inn. The narrow building rose straight from the street for five stories, the facade only wide enough for a large door on the ground floor and a single window glinting on each floor above that. The glass in these windows was thick, as though surviving from the last century.

Cynthia sailed in through the front door, and I

went in after her. We found ourselves in a wide hall, the entrance to the taproom across from us and a staircase beside that. Cynthia went up the stairs without hesitation, and I followed, hastening to keep up with her.

The landing on the third floor led to a room that was more like a fashionable club's drawing room than a tavern's snug. Long tables with upholstered chairs around them filled the carpeted floor, a large fireplace with a carved walnut mantelpiece took up most of one wall, and bookcases overflowing with books lined the remaining walls. The wide window let in plenty of light from outside; that is, what could filter through the clouds and smoke.

I was relieved to see other ladies here, well-heeled women in subdued ensembles speaking earnestly with the ladies and gentlemen they were with. *Bluestockings,* I thought silently. Ladies who were more intellectual than was fashionable, who read books and journals on science and medicine and other topics women's brains were supposed to be too small and delicate to compre-hend. A nonsensical idea, I always believed. Women, in my experience, could understand complicated ideas quite well, sometimes better than a man could. Cooking, I'd decided, was only a form of what the chemical scientists did with their concoctions, only mine smelled much better.

Mr. Thanos rose from a table near the window,

where he had been holding up a book to catch the light. He dropped the book and made his way to us, bumping into the other chairs along the way. He looked so delighted to see us that my heart warmed. Mr. Thanos was a truly genial young man.

"Lady Cynthia, Mrs. Holloway," he said. "You honor me."

He came at us with arms outstretched, as though planning to embrace us, but at the last minute he seemed to come to his senses and shook Lady Cynthia's hand. Then he took mine in a firm grip.

"Please, come. Sit." He waved us at the table where he'd been. "They do a passable tea here, or coffee. Unless, er, you'd like something stronger, Lady Cynthia?"

All eyes in the room were on us. They'd know Mr. Thanos, if he was a regular here, and must have at least heard of Lady Cynthia Shires. Their stares were for me, I presumed. In this room, I was the oddity.

Mr. Thanos escorted us to his table and told the waiter who hovered to bring us a repast. We'd have everything—tea, coffee, and whiskey for himself.

"Have you told her?" Mr. Thanos asked Cynthia when the waiter had gone, Mr. Thanos's dark eyes wide and eager.

"Told me what?" I asked.

"Not had a chance," Cynthia said briskly. "The

house was in an uproar this morning, and by the time my aunt had finished pestering me and I was free, Mrs. Holloway had gone."

"It is my half day out," I said, feeling the need to explain.

"Not blaming you," Cynthia said. "Only saying why we haven't chatted. Anyway, Mrs. Holloway, last night after I went out, I ran into Mr. Thanos in Leicester Square, at a club there. Bobby was quickly drunk, so Mr. Thanos suggested we retire to a quiet room. There we did some thinking. When I needed to take Bobby home, we decided to meet up here today and continue the discussion."

I ought to be shocked. A lady and a gentleman—never mind she dressed herself so like a gentleman that the tipsy patrons of last night's club hadn't realized she was female—alone in a room together would mar Cynthia's reputation still more than it already was. I should scold her, warn her of peril.

Instead, I leaned forward, excitement building. "What did you conclude from this thinking?"

"Consider," Mr. Thanos said. "Antiquities are going missing from the British Museum." He fluttered his fingers in its general direction. "Possibly they have been for some time, only no one noticed until recently, as they are from obscure storage rooms. Now, collectors known to have large numbers of Roman, Egyptian, and Greek antiquities are having their houses burgled."

"Including Clemmie's next-door neighbor, Lord Chalminster," Cynthia put in. "You remember him—the odious Minty's father. Well, Chalminster's mad for relics of the ancient world. He had two small vases from Athens, and a Roman-era sculpture that was uncovered at Delphi—Emperor Hadrian's boy lover or some such. The vases are gone. The statue of the beautiful young man, untouched."

Again, I ought to be shocked that an unmarried lady made casual mention of a Roman emperor's proclivities, but in truth, I found it refreshing that we could speak of such things without embarrassment.

Lord Chalminster's name was familiar to me. His son, who went by the deplorable nickname of Minty, had, with his chums, once beaten Daniel down in front of Euston Station. Daniel told me later that Minty had invested money in Fenian plots—whether he'd done so from a desire to overthrow the government or because he was foolish and excitable, I never learned. The latter, I suspected.

Daniel had not spoken of the matter since, and I wondered if he'd promised Lord Chalminster to cover up his son's perfidy. I also wondered if these thefts had any connection to our adventure in Saltash, though I did not see how at the moment.

Mr. Thanos nodded at Cynthia's tale. "All this

tells me these thieves are the most interested in ancient Greece," he said. "The Roman statuary being found all over Greece is still valuable, but the true artifacts from the Athenian era—the time of Pericles, Socrates, and that ilk—are quite priceless. Especially if one is Greek."

He sent me a significant look I could not interpret. Did Mr. Thanos mean they were important to him because of his Greek heritage? From what Daniel had told me, Elgin's grand-father had been raised in Constantinople, rarely setting foot in Greece itself, but that did not mean his family could not be sentimental about Greece's ancient past.

Cynthia frowned at him. "You're being impos-sibly vague, Thanos. What he means, Mrs. H., is that these days, many archaeologists digging up the ancient world have begun stating that the antiquities should stay in the country in which they are found and not be carted off to museums in London, Paris, and New York. Nor should they be sold to collectors who hoard the bits they purchase in their mansions in Mayfair or Manhattan."

"Ah." I caught on. "You believe the thief or thieves are fanatical about returning the objects to their respective countries?"

"Greece in particular," Cynthia said, while Elgin nodded. "That is why we were discussing the Parthenon Marbles at supper. Greece repeatedly calls for their return, and repeatedly, Britain refuses."

"Because they know that if they return the marbles, they open the way for Egypt to request the return of the Rosetta Stone," Mr. Thanos said. "The Rosetta Stone is a stele that was found in Egypt, Mrs. Holloway, by Napoleon's army, and turned out to be the key to deciphering Egyptian hieroglyphs. You see, the stone had one text, but in three different writings . . ."

"Never mind about all that now," Lady Cynthia broken in.

"I have heard of the Rosetta Stone, Mr. Thanos," I said at the same time, though I was interested to know what the three scripts were. I would have to quiz him about it on another occasion.

"The point is," Cynthia went on, "perhaps thieves are nicking the things to take back to Greece themselves, never mind what the governments squabble about."

I recalled my encounter with Mr. Varley this afternoon and thought about his cryptic discussion with Daniel in the pawnbrokers shop. I remembered also the hands of the thug on the table at the morgue, with his blunt and callused fingers that had performed hard labor. Those two men were no more Greek than I was, and I doubted they cared much about what antiquities moved where.

I voiced the opinion as soon as I formed it.

"These are men who worry only how much money they obtain for their crime," I finished.

"True," Mr. Thanos said, undaunted. "But the fanatics might have hired them."

That was so. I wondered whether Daniel had drawn the conclusion Mr. Thanos and Cynthia had, or if he had other ideas.

"I believe this is precisely why Daniel—I mean Mr. McAdam—agreed we should suggest, Mr. Thanos, that you attend a few of the soirees and suppers in Park Lane and see what you can see. Lady Cynthia with you, of course. To discover whether a guest is taking the things, or whether a gang of thieves is using the gatherings to distract the household while they purloin the objects."

I paused as the pair of them stared at me, and I wondered if I'd offended them by suggesting that one of their class could steal. The idea that criminal tendencies happen only among the lower classes was nonsense, but one must choose one's words with care when speaking to a member of the family one works for.

As I opened my mouth to apologize, Mr. Thanos exclaimed, "When the devil did you see McAdam?" He flushed. "Oh, pardon my language, Mrs. Holloway, Lady Cynthia."

"An apt question," Cynthia said. "When the devil *did* you see Mr. McAdam? We haven't found hide nor hair of him."

"He found me." I lowered my voice and

explained about encountering him in the scullery stairwell the night before, and his wish to meet with Mr. Thanos in this very pub tomorrow evening.

"Damn and blast," Mr. Thanos said heatedly. "Ah, beg pardon again, Mrs. Holloway, Lady Cynthia. But I wish he'd let a fellow know he's alive and well."

"Possibly he feared that those who wish him harm are watching your rooms," I said to Mr. Thanos. "And he could not risk it. As he has no connection to me, he perhaps felt that contacting me would be safer, knowing I'd pass on messages to you."

Mr. Thanos nodded as though my speculation made good sense, but Cynthia eyed me sharply.

"No connection to you?" she demanded. "The man stayed with you in Cornwall after sending the two of us scurrying back to London. How can you say *no connection?*"

"I will thank you to not proclaim that in public, my lady," I said, leaning to her and speaking in a low, rapid voice. "Yes, I stayed in Cornwall, but quite separately from Mr. McAdam, to ensure that he came to no harm. He is apt not to take care. His son arrived, and of course I had to look after him as well."

"Of course," Mr. Thanos said without surprise. He saw a thing for what it was, another trait I admired in him.

Lady Cynthia's gaze grew sharper. "I beg your pardon, Mrs. H. I did not mean to impugn your good name. But it is a connection, mark my words."

"McAdam must believe no one knows of the connection," Mr. Thanos said reasonably. "Except his closest friends."

I said nothing, and mercifully, Lady Cynthia ceased her interrogation. Her eyes held interest, however, and I knew I'd not heard the last of it.

"I'm glad to hear he's all right," she said. "He has a good idea. I'd be delighted to go to my friends' homes and nose about. A stack of invitations arrives every day—I say no to most, but I'll shoot off a late reply to the ones who have antiquities, and we'll storm battlements."

She stuck out her hand to Mr. Thanos. He flushed but took the offered hand and shook it. He looked a bit bewildered but also happy.

I kept my speculations about *their* connection to myself.

Lady Cynthia insisted I accompany her home in the coach. I started to refuse her offer to ride inside with her, recalling what Mrs. Bywater had said about being too familiar, but changed my mind and accepted. If I were to ride on the outside, I'd have to sit on the box with the coachman, who was giving me a too-ready smile. Riding inside with Cynthia would be the much safer choice.

As the landau rolled west to Mayfair, Cynthia mused on what she'd wear to these soirees and what she'd say to whom, looking forward to confounding people. Thankfully, she did not mention Daniel, except to express her hope that he was well and we'd see him soon.

"Oh, he'll turn up when he is good and ready," I said. "With a cheery wave, as though nothing much has gone wrong."

"I believe you." Cynthia spoke lightly but gave me another look that made me uneasy.

The coachman turned from Oxford Street to Duke Street and Grosvenor Square and thence to Upper Brook Street. I asked Lady Cynthia to let me out on the corner of Park Street, so I could walk the rest of the way home.

Cynthia thought my request odd, but once she understood that I'd leap out of the coach whenever it might pause if she didn't comply, she knocked on the roof and called for Henry to stop.

Paul was kind enough to help me down. "I'll get on those invitations," Cynthia called to me before Paul shut the door. "Never was so excited to attend soirees before, I must say."

Henry nodded to me before he tapped the near horse with the whip. "See you at home, Mrs. Holloway."

"Indeed," I answered. As we were both going to the Mount Street house, it was inevitable.

Henry had to turn his attention to the other

vehicles, then the landau rolled on, and I walked on in peaceful solitude—that is, in as much solitude as one can have on a London street.

Because of my diversion to Bedford Square and the pub, I was returning later than usual, in spite of the relatively speedy journey in the landau. Six o'clock had come and gone. Fortunately, I was able to slip inside while the other servants were upstairs preparing the dining room or waiting on the master and mistress or Lady Cynthia just coming home. No one noticed as I ducked into the housekeeper's parlor to take off my coat and hat, tying on my apron as I emerged.

Only Tess fell upon me. "Mrs. H., I thought you'd never come," she said in a frenzy. "Whenever someone asked about you, I pretended you'd just popped outside or into another room for a moment. Mr. Davis is a nosy one, ain't he? But I smoothed the way for ya."

She beamed at me, confident I'd praise her for lying. I ought to explain to her that falsehoods for any reason were wrong, but as I had no wish to listen to Mr. Davis complain that I'd burdened him by being late, I did not scold her.

Tess had done well in my absence, I had to admit. She had the onions chopped and waiting in a bowl, carrots likewise, peas shelled, cauliflower heads removed from the stems and sliced. She was a dab hand with a knife, was Tess. I would advise her to begin saving money to buy a set of her own, as one could never depend on a kitchen to have good ones.

Sara came breezing in to tell us Lady Cynthia was going out, and so there would only be two for supper. I assumed Lady Cynthia was already beginning her task of wandering about her friends' homes to see what she could discover about the thefts.

It was a mercy this evening's meal could be simple. The scullery maid was cleaning a sole, which I'd fry and serve with butter and lemon. For meat I had mutton in a butter sauce, which would be sent up with a quantity of spring greens, the cauliflower with nutmeg and cream, and a light apricot soup. I'd made tarts this morning with rhubarb and fresh strawberries, and now Tess sliced strawberries to be strewn over the top.

I put aside thoughts of antiquities, thefts in Mayfair homes, Daniel skulking in the streets, and Mr. Varley frightening the wits out of me. At this moment, I was a cook, worried about her béchamel thickening, her lettuces remaining unwilted, and the cauliflower in cream sauce not curdling.

Mr. Davis strode in and out, setting down what wine I needed without a word. He'd learned to leave me be when I was in the final throes of a meal; only dire circumstances made him interfere.

Tess and I sent up the dishes, breathed sighs of relief, and prepared a lighter meal for the staff. I retreated to the housekeeper's parlor to eat mine and invited Tess to join me.

Tess seated herself at the table, bouncing a little on the wooden chair's cushioned seat, and took up her fork. "Well, ain't I a great lady?" She gave me a wide smile. "It's decent of ya, Mrs. Holloway, that ye share your table with the likes of me."

"The likes of you is a cook's assistant in a respectable house," I told her as I enjoyed a bite of the cauliflower. The cream was silky, the nutmeg pungent. The dish had turned out well. "Mr. McAdam would not have sent you to me if you were a bad 'un, as we say."

"Mr. McAdam is a wonderful man," Tess said with conviction. "I hope he's all right."

"He is," I said, deciding that Tess did not need to worry over him. "I have spoken to him." I had wanted to tell James the good news that Daniel was alive as well, but I had not seen him about, nor did I know where his boardinghouse was. I could only hope Daniel had sought him out and assured him he was well.

Tess blinked at me. "Did ya? When was this? When you were out today? Where is he? What happened to him?"

I doubted Tess wished any harm to Daniel, but I thought I should keep most of his secrets. "He does not want his location known at this time. But he is well."

"Oh good." Tess let out a breath. "Poor man."

Her eyes began to twinkle. "I think he's sweet on ya, Mrs. H."

I firmly changed the subject. "Tell me about yourself, Tess. Do you have family?"

Her face darkened. "You don't need to know about me family, Mrs. Holloway. You know I'm from the backstreets of London, and me mum and dad weren't no good. I'm putting that all behind me now."

"Very commendable. But you should tell *me*. I'll not impart anything of your past to others if you do not wish it. For instance, how did you come to be arrested? I know you were innocent— Daniel would not have helped you otherwise."

Tess avoided my gaze. "Weren't nothin'. Cove thought I picked his pocket. I didn't. But he seized hold of me and dragged me off to the magistrate."

I imagined Tess had not gone willingly, which had likely not helped her case. "Did you explain to the magistrate that the cove had it wrong?"

"Didn't I just?" Tess flashed me an indignant look that told me on this point she was speaking the truth. "Magistrate had the constable box me ears, and then I was off to Newgate." She shivered, her gaze dropping to her half-empty dinner plate.

I too had spent time in Newgate's common cell, a place full of desperation, rage, and fear. Young Tess would have been terrified, in spite of her defiance.

I reached across the table and took her hand.

"Well, that's all over," I said. "Daniel stood up for you and got you free." As he had done for me. "How did he know to save you?" I asked as I released her. "Were you already acquainted?"

Tess shook her head vigorously. "No, I didn't know him. He was there at the Old Bailey—I don't know why—when I was in the dock. He stood up and said he'd seen the whole thing, that a boy had picked the man's pocket and I happened to be behind him. Then he went on about my character being honest and other things, which was a huge lie. He'd never met me before. But the judge and jury liked him, and here I am."

Tess spoke quickly, her words evenly paced, as though the speech was rehearsed. I knew there was more to Tess's story than she let on, but I'd have to learn it another time.

"Yes, here you are," I said. "Safe and sound and not likely to be arrested again."

Tess released a ragged breath. "I hope not."

"Not while you work for me," I said stoutly. "I will look out for you, never you worry."

My heart constricted as I said the words. I'd promised my last assistant I'd look out for her, in almost those very words, and she'd turned up dead. I swallowed, trying to tamp down my feeling of foreboding. Sinead had died because of her connection to another person, who was also now dead. There should be no more danger in this house.

So I told myself as we finished our meal and made preparations for the next morning. I sent Tess up to bed, made my notes, and finally decided to retire for the night. I toyed with the idea of waiting up for Lady Cynthia to ask her what she discovered, but Mayfair gatherings could go on into the small hours of the morning; no telling when she'd return.

I ducked into the scullery before I went up and saw that the bolt across the outside door was firmly in place. Mr. Davis must have seen to it himself.

No more danger, I said to myself in my bedchamber as I washed my face and combed out my hair. I braided my long, thick hair into a single plait and climbed into bed, wishing I could rid myself of the disquiet that had come over me as I'd comforted Tess.

In the morning, my presentiments proved to be justified. As I entered the kitchen, I found Charlie there, his box of blacking, brushes, and cloths dangling in his hand as he stared fearfully into the scullery.

I looked past him to see that again the door was wide open, the iron strap that had held the bolt to the wall on the floor, a stiff breeze blowing down the stairs to wash over us.

15

Mr. Davis, grim faced, reported the incident above stairs. He came down to the kitchen as Tess and I were finishing up the usual breakfast of eggs, bacon, toast, and potatoes.

"They're sure I can't know the difference between bolting a door and not bolting it," Mr. Davis said in a bad temper. "I checked it to make bleedin' sure. I'm to fetch someone to fix the latch at once. I would have done it yesterday, but the mistress was trying to find someone from our stables to do the job to save the expense. I could have told her that those lads are expert at brushing horses or mending harness, but ironmongery is beyond them. Cheeseparing, bloody . . ." He trailed off as he stormed out again.

Tess was pulling pieces of buttered toast from the rack that had been on the fire, piling them on a plate and dribbling them with more butter. She didn't look up as Mr. Davis spoke, but I caught sight of her face, which was pale with fear.

"It's a faulty bolt and latch, Tess," I said, trying to reassure her. "Easy to mend."

"Ain't right," Tess said, her voice scratchy. "I don't like this."

I too did not know what to make of a back door opening but nothing in the house going missing—at least nothing we'd found. I scooped the bacon and potatoes onto the silver serving dishes, closing their domed lids to keep the heat in. Then, on impulse, I stepped to the larder.

Thieves in London weren't always after silver and Greek antiquities. The poor souls I fed scraps to were desperate, some of them so far gone in hunger or so drunk on gin that they'd think nothing of creeping into a house and taking food and drink.

Mr. Davis kept the wine cellar locked—he and I had the only keys. If that had been broken into, Mr. Davis would have said so at once.

The larder, however, was my domain, and I knew it like the back of my hand.

What I found missing wasn't obvious at first. There were a few apples gone from a basket, carrots jumbled into a heap to make the pile seem larger than it was, paper stuffed into the bottom of the strawberry basket to conceal the fact that only one layer was left. The missing cooked and salted beef had been harder to hide—its covered plate had been pushed to the back of a cupboard.

The larder was neat and clean, the floor swept. No telltale footprints on the flagstones, nothing out of place. The thief had known exactly where to look and how to conceal his crime.

Troubling thoughts filled my head. I dismissed the idea that Daniel had been there. Even if Daniel had decided to creep in and take provisions to keep himself fed, he would have found some way to leave money for what he stole, and more than that, he would never have left the back door open. If Daniel had done this, we'd never have known anyone had been in at all.

The only person new to the household was Tess, who had demonstrated that she'd been nearly starved before coming here. But she'd been well fed since, and why wouldn't she have simply asked for the extra food if she'd been hungry? She must know by now I'd give it to her.

Then again, she might be smuggling it out to someone—a lover? Or perhaps a parent. She'd snarled that her family was no good, but they might be coercing her to feed them.

Even so, Tess was intelligent enough not to announce that she'd been out by leaving the back door wide open. She'd have had no need to tamper with the bolt—she'd simply have opened the door, handed out the food, and closed it up again.

Curiouser and curiouser, as Mr. Carroll's Alice would say.

My interest in this problem took another leap after I finished preparing the midday meal some hours later and sent it up, and the man came to fix the latch. I saw Mr. Davis lead him down from the street and inside to point out the problem.

I wiped my hands and stepped to the scullery just as the man said, "Not to worry, Mr. Davis. I'll have this done quick as a wink."

The repairman in question had dark hair under a cloth cap, a rumpled homespun suit, thick-soled boots, blue eyes, a cheerful voice, and a ready smile.

"All right then, Mrs. Holloway?" Daniel asked me as I steadied myself on the kitchen doorframe. "I hope you have some of those ever-so-tasty scones baking."

Daniel was whole and well, as carefree as ever, his face clean and shaved. He looked fed and comfortable, as though he'd had a night in a soft bed and a hearty breakfast. Blast the man.

He set down the box of tools he'd carried with him and crouched to examine the lock and latch. Mr. Davis watched him a moment, arms folded, then he glanced at me.

"You might as well feed him, Mrs. Holloway. McAdam was the only one I could find in a pinch who knew anything about locks. Luckily for me, he'd popped in to visit the head groom."

Luck, was it? Had it been a coincidence that Daniel decided to hang about in the mews behind the Mount Street house just when Mr. Davis needed a handyman? Or had Daniel heard that Mrs. Bywater was looking for a chap to work on the door and made sure no one but himself answered the summons? I had no idea how he might do that, but Daniel seemed to be acquainted with everyone in London. If he'd put out word that no locksmith was to go to Lord

Rankin's home in Mount Street, I had no doubt that word would be obeyed. I imagined that when Mr. Davis heard Daniel was in the stables, he'd hastened to him, realizing he could hire him for a fraction of the cost of a true locksmith. Mrs. Bywater would be pleased.

"What do you know about locks?" I asked Daniel sharply.

Daniel lifted the iron strap from the floor and peered at it. "A good many things, Mrs. H.," he answered. "Had a misspent youth, didn't I?"

Mr. Davis rolled his eyes and stalked back into the kitchen.

I ought to return to the kitchen as well, shaking my head at Daniel's impertinence, and get on with my baking for the day. Instead, I lingered, watching as Daniel lifted a long, thin tool from his box and poked at the lock's mechanism with it.

"You truly are a jack-of-all-trades," I observed.

"I am." Daniel kept his eyes on the tool. "I would say *master of none,* but that's not quite true. I've mastered a few things."

"Like locks?"

Daniel chuckled. "Locks were my first area of mastery. The other things, like carpentry, horse grooming, and carriage repair, I had to learn from painstaking study. Locks are second nature to me."

"I see. So, if you had decided to pick your way

inside to steal food from the larder, you could have."

Daniel looked up at me. "Yes, but I did not. Is that what happened here?"

"That is what you need to discover. The door was bolted—I saw it. And locked. Mr. Davis was adamant about that. Except, it seems they broke the bolt." I indicated the iron strap, which used to be screwed into the wall but now lay on the flagstone floor.

Daniel set down his tool and carefully lifted the strap, scrutinizing it. "I can see where you were deceived into thinking the door bolted," he said after a time. "The screws that held this into the wall have been replaced by much shorter ones." He set the strap in the place it was supposed to rest on the doorframe, closed the door, and slid the bolt carefully into it. "It's a housebreaker's trick. So that when a person outside pushes at the door . . ."

He demonstrated, giving the door a yank, letting the tongue of the bolt shove the strap out of its place. He caught the strap as it fell.

I stared at the iron piece on his gloved palm in growing horror. "Only someone inside the house could have replaced those screws."

Daniel nodded. "Or a worker called in to repair something. Or a deliveryman, or some such. Did any stranger come down here yesterday? Left alone long enough to tamper with the bolt?"

And move the food around the larder so what

was stolen wouldn't be missed right away? "That explanation does not answer the question as to why the door was left open," I said. "Why take the trouble to enter so covertly, and then announce you've been inside by not closing the door when you go?"

Daniel frowned as he thought. "Maybe the thief heard someone coming and ran?"

"Perhaps—but two days in a row?"

Daniel blinked. "*Two* days? Why didn't you have someone fix the bolt yesterday?"

I felt my cheeks heat. "It was not broken yesterday. The thief had no need." I leaned to him and spoke in a whisper. "I had left it open for Lady Cynthia night before last."

Daniel nodded, understanding, not censuring. "But the thief—or thieves—could not count on you leaving the bolt undone a second time. And so they replaced the screws." He stared at the strap unhappily for a moment. "I'm sorry to say it, but you'd better ask Tess about this."

"Tess?" I glanced into the kitchen, but for the moment, it was deserted. "Why? She told me you kept her from being condemned for thieving—you would not have if she weren't innocent. Why are you now saying she's involved in a housebreaking?"

Daniel shook his head. "She *was* innocent. A bloke on the street had his pocket picked and shouted for a constable. Tess was nearby. When the constable approached her, believing her only a witness, she kicked up such a fuss that the victim of the crime decided to accuse her and even started to beat on her. The constable took her in, more to get her away from the enraged victim than anything else. While she protested her innocence to the magistrate, she did it in such a way that he was convinced she was lying. And so—Newgate and a trial."

"How did you know all this?" I asked. "She told me she hadn't known of you until you stood up in court and defended her. Were you masquerading as a barrister? Wig and all?"

Daniel's smile flashed. "Nothing so droll. One of the sergeants at Bow Street is a friend. He knew Tess from her prior run-ins with the law, and knew she hadn't done this crime—not her style, apparently. He told me what happened, as did the constable who'd arrested her, the sergeant knowing I'm always interested in unusual incidents. I went to Tess's trial and watched her in the dock—she was terrified but determined not to give way. I concluded she was covering up for someone. Her fit when the constable came to her in the street likely gave whoever it was time to get away. She protested to the magistrate, not very convincingly, so that the police would bang her up for the crime and give up the search for the true culprit." He let out a sigh. "I am so very sorry, Kat. I hoped that having her work here would take the villain out of her life, whoever he is, but she might still be helping him."

"I see." I had an ache in my heart—I liked Tess, I truly did. "I suppose I will have to put it to her."

"That's best, or this won't cease. Tell her we will help, not condemn."

"So we are reformers now, are we?" I asked glumly.

"She needs someone like you. A kind, good woman who will steer her right."

Or a complete fool, I thought. "I am pleased you wish to help her, but I must ask—why? What made you look at poor Tess in the dock and decide to set her life on the straight and narrow? Why *her* and not all the other poor souls who move through the Old Bailey?"

Daniel shrugged. "A feeling." He pulled several long screws from his toolbox and tested each in the holes on the iron strap until he found one that fit. "Perhaps more than that. I suppose she reminded me of myself at that age. Tess is very smart—she talked rings around the prosecuting barrister, to the great delight of the courtroom. He didn't understand half her jokes and grew incensed at all the laughter."

Daniel drew out three more screws of the same thickness and set the strap and the first screw into the doorframe. He balanced this while he fished out a screwdriver and fit it to the groove in the screw.

"Tess is at a crossroads," Daniel went on. "If she moves along the right path, she will be brilliant—she can do anything she likes. If she moves along the wrong one . . ." He began turning the screwdriver with harder strokes. "She'll hold out for a while but end up in a bad place. A very bad one."

I glanced behind us again, but still no one was in the kitchen. I was beginning to wonder where they'd all gone.

"You say you stood at these crossroads?" I asked.

"I did indeed. I could have ended up in great darkness, Kat, believe me."

"Why didn't you?" I leaned closer, wanting to lap up any secrets Daniel might impart.

Daniel gave the first screw a final twist and picked up a second one. "I met kind people. Like Thanos, and one of his professors. Others. They saw the potential good in me, not just the evil and villainy that so many did."

"Good heavens," I said in jest. "And I've let you into my kitchen."

"You would not have ten years ago, love," Daniel said with conviction. "That I assure you." He finished the second screw and began a third.

His revelation made me hunger for more information. Daniel was a good, intelligent, caring man. How could others have looked at him and declared him evil?

"I notice that you are no longer in hiding," I said, keeping my tone mild. "No more sores."

"As you see."

"Did you tell James?"

Daniel gave me a look of surprise. "Of course. He was the first person I went to as soon as it was safe."

Good. "And are you now safe?"

"Somewhat." Daniel set in the last screw. "At least, I am no longer in danger of being arrested. The constables caught—or believe they did—the man who killed the thug in the pawnbrokers. Chief Inspector Moss is letting me speak to him, which is where I'm off to after I finish here." He sent me an inquiring glance. "Would you like to come with me?"

16

I straightened up hastily. "Me? Whatever for?"

Daniel unhurriedly began to turn the last screw. "Because I respect your opinion. You see things others do not. I would like your assessment of this man." He finished and gave a final tightening to each screw in turn. "You may sit out of sight and listen if you don't wish to expose yourself to a villain, as we did when Varley came to the pawnbrokers."

Mr. Varley had seen me now, but he could hardly have known I was in the shop with Daniel. At least I sincerely hoped not.

"I will think on it," I said.

"Finish your cooking for the afternoon," Daniel said. "I'll be waiting, and we'll go if you like."

Daniel set down the screwdriver and began prodding the lock with his tools again, resuming his guise as efficient man-of-all-work. I'd get no more out of him, I concluded.

I returned to the kitchen, my thoughts unsettled. I had already grown fond of Tess, but if she was stealing from the house, even to help someone else, I could not condone it. I had no wish to turn her over to the constables, but she could not work here if she was thieving.

I wondered very much whom Tess wished to protect, so much so that she'd go to the dock for him. It was a *him,* I was certain. While Tess could very well be protecting a woman, I highly suspected she was not. She was at the age where romance made a woman do foolish things.

I heard Tess in the passage, speaking to Emma. Her voice was robust, her laughter lighthearted.

Would she sound so cheerful if guilty? Or have looked so frightened this morning about the open door until I reassured her? I hoped Daniel's idea was wrong, but I very much worried it was not.

I hadn't much liked my previous journey to the Metropolitan Police headquarters, but my curiosity rose as I finished a lemon tart and slid it into the oven. Who *had* killed the fellow in the pawnbrokers, and why? Had it anything to do with the antiquities' thefts? Or had it been simply a falling-out among thieves? I made up my mind to go with Daniel—if I waited for him to return and tell me about it, I might wait a long time and only learn what he chose to impart.

Tess came into the kitchen, half dancing, then stopped as she caught sight of me hanging up my apron and departing for the housekeeper's parlor to fetch my hat and coat.

"Take out the lemon tart in an hour's time," I said as she followed. "Do not let it burn. Then scrub the potatoes and put them in to parboil, about thirty minutes. When I come back, I'll teach you how to make an iced custard from tea and cream. Quite delicious."

"From tea?" Tess looked dubious. "Where are you off to?"

I shrugged on my coat and settled my hat. "Scotland Yard," I said.

Tess's cheerfulness dropped away, and her fear returned. "About the back door?"

"No, no. About the man who was killed at the pawnbrokers. Mr. McAdam wishes me to assess a suspect."

Tess relaxed, but she shivered, hugging her arms over her chest. "You watch yourself around criminals, Mrs. H. Dangerous lot. Me dad was one, God rest his rotten soul. Ye think there's really a hell? 'Cause he'll be in it." The anger in her voice was fierce.

"I believe God is more forgiving than people are," I said. "Remember the prodigal son? That parable tells us God welcomes even the worst of sinners into the kingdom of heaven."

Tess stared at me in puzzlement as though she'd never heard the story. "So you think me dad's up in heaven after all?" She gave another shiver. "Cor, then I don't want to go."

I patted her arm as I moved past her out the door. "Nothing to worry about. Souls in heaven are a different thing from people on earth."

"If you say so." Tess sounded doubtful. "Hope I never have to find out."

I left her, making my way down the passage to the kitchen and out through the scullery.

Tess's questions did raise a thought—if sinners went to heaven, then my husband would be there as well. As much as I'd comforted Tess by telling her we'd be different in heaven—apparently we'd all know how to fly and play the harp, for instance—I had no wish to encounter him again, in angelic form or otherwise. I couldn't blame Tess her reluctance to go if people who'd caused her grief awaited her there.

Daniel met me at the corner of South Audley Street and offered me his arm. We walked down this avenue as carriages and carts moved around us, past Grosvenor Chapel, where I'd spied him in the churchyard.

"It was kind of the vicar to help you," I said.

Daniel glanced at the chapel. "He is an old friend."

"I ought not to be surprised, I suppose."

His laughter warmed me. "You have lived in London all your life, have you not? I'll wager you know plenty of people. Cooks and house-keepers, fishmongers, stallholders, greengrocers, bakers, footmen, maids, butlers, majordomos—from Cheapside, Mayfair, and everywhere in between. I've lived in London as long. Stands to reason I have acquaintances everywhere."

"I suppose you have a point," I said. "But I don't know everyone from thieves to geniuses to chief inspectors to vicars."

"If you're friends with me long enough you will." Daniel pulled me a bit tighter against him, taking me out of the way of a wide landau, but he didn't ease the pressure on my arm after the carriage passed.

"Will you tell me more about your misspent youth?" I asked in a light voice.

Daniel gave me a sideways glance. "It's not a pretty story. I want you to like me, but I don't think you'd like the boy I was."

Now I was more intrigued. "I imagine you meant well. You simply fell in with the wrong people."

"I *did* fall in with the wrong people, as a matter of fact," Daniel said. "But the truth is, I was a horrible little mite, happy to help the villains who'd taken me in. My only defense is that I had no idea what a devil I was. I thought one of the villains was my father, you see." He shrugged. "He might have been. I'm still not certain, but why else would he have been so solicitous of me? He fed and clothed me and made certain I did not end up being used for what young boys often are."

"Chimney sweeps?" Sweeps liked very thin and small lads who could climb up into chimneys and knock out hard-to-reach lumps. Dangerous and cruel, I always thought. I made sure to give the sweep boys who came to the house scones or buns, which I had them eat out of sight of their masters, who would most likely take any food away from them. I also tucked pennies into the lads' pockets, whispering to them to keep them a secret.

Daniel sent me a dark look. "I mean as paramours for disgusting men. Many of those gentlemen live around these parts." He cast his gaze at the tall and elegant houses around us.

I did not like to think of such things. "Not all of them," I said quickly. "Not every person is evil, Daniel."

I found myself even tighter against his side in our next step. "Which is why I like you, Kat. You pull me back from despair."

This from a man who laughed more than any other I knew. "Well, I suppose you'd better cease disappearing then and come regular for my scones and tea."

His grin returned. "I will endeavor to do so, Mrs. Holloway."

We walked in silence the rest of the way to Curzon Street, where Daniel hailed a hansom. This took us through the lanes to Piccadilly and Haymarket, and past Trafalgar Square, where I'd stood debating yesterday, and to Whitehall.

Daniel did not walk in through the front door of the imposing building at Great Scotland Yard. Of course he did not. He took me down a noisome passage to a narrow space and rapped three times on a battered door there. It was opened

233

after about five minutes by a portly man in a sergeant's uniform, who admitted us to a tiny hall with peeling paint.

The stairs he led us up were confined into a smelly, dark stairwell, each step precipitous, and they had no handrail. I had no intention of putting my gloves on the dirty walls, so I went up slowly, holding my skirts from the dusty steps.

Daniel, behind me, steadied me in places with his hand on my elbow. The sergeant we followed strode quickly, his size not hampering him. Three flights up, he opened a door on a landing.

I stepped onto a floor that was a bit cleaner—at least someone swept here, even if the walls needed a scrubbing. But of course they were closing this building and moving, so I suppose they'd decided not to waste time and effort keeping things clean. Such is the logic of the male sex.

Daniel kept his hand on my elbow as we followed the sergeant down the hall. There was no need for him to guide me anymore, but I found that I did not mind him so close as we traversed the echoing hall.

The sergeant ushered us into a narrow anteroom at the end of the corridor. This had a door on its opposite side that opened as we entered, dis-gorging Chief Inspector Moss.

I glimpsed another small room behind him that held only a table and chairs. A man so large he seemed barely contained by the chair he sat in had been wedged between the table and the wall. He had shackles around his wrists, which were chained to the table, the table's edge pressing into his belly. He took up so much of the room that I pictured the wall behind him bursting with his weight, sending him down to the London street four stories below.

The man looked up. I caught a flash of blue eyes so cold they chilled me; a pockmarked, hard face; and a shock of red hair. The man exuded menace, filling every particle of air with it. Even Mr. Varley hadn't carried such a shroud of evil.

Chief Inspector Moss closed the door in the next moment, but I did not relax. The man might be shackled, but he was large and strong. Who could stop him if he chose to break his chains and escape?

The air of command I'd seen in Chief Inspector Moss was clear again as he faced me. His skin held London pallor, but its leathery look suggested it had once been heavily tanned, sometime before his hair and mustache had begun to go gray. He might have been a command sergeant major or perhaps an officer in a far-flung outpost of the Empire, one where unruly tribes objected to British rule. He had the bearing of one who'd seen brutal fighting—I doubted he'd spent his service behind a desk by day and at soirees with the regimental wives by night.

Moss's brows shot up when he saw me. "Why did you bring a lady here, McAdam? With *him?*" He gestured at the closed door.

"She is astute and knows about people," Daniel said before I could protest that I'd come here by my own choice. I had the inkling Chief Inspector Moss would wish me to be seen and not heard.

"This one's a true villain," Moss went on in a warning tone. "If we have to let him go, keep her out of his way."

"If you have to let him go?" Daniel repeated in surprise. "I thought it was certain he'd done it."

Moss scowled. "There's always uncertainty. Witnesses are never reliable. Mrs. Holloway, please, stand over here."

Chief Inspector Moss moved to a small panel set halfway up the wall. It opened to reveal a grill, beyond which was the room with the large man.

The man looked up when he heard the little door creak. Though many bars crisscrossed the opening, I was aware of being pinned by the eyes I'd glimpsed before, ones that said he was a crocodile and I was a foolish goat who'd strayed into his path.

"He can't see you," Daniel whispered into my ear. "The grill is too thick."

I was not reassured. The man stared right at me—or perhaps he could hear my frightened heartbeat.

I took a fortifying breath and gave Daniel a nod.

236

His returning nod told me he understood before he moved away and followed Chief Inspector Moss into the other room.

They closed the door and I heard the turn of a key in the lock. This did not relieve me as much as it might, because if that man attacked, I wasn't sure Daniel or the chief inspector could get the door open in time to save themselves. I could only hope the shackles were strong.

Chief Inspector Moss sat down facing the villain. Daniel took a seat at the end of the table, well out of reach of the big man's fists. I could see Daniel's face, but only the back of Moss's head.

The villain sniffled and jerked his chin at Daniel. "Who's 'e?"

"Never you mind," Moss said. "This here's Simon Pilcher," he said to Daniel. "Ever heard of him?"

Daniel shook his head while Mr. Pilcher looked Daniel up and down. "Ain't never 'eard of *'im* either," Pilcher said, his voice as large as his body.

"You know why you've been arrested, don't you?" Moss asked him.

"Accused of killing a bloke." Pilcher sniffled again, as though he were coming down with a cold. "I never."

"You can plead your case at the Old Bailey." Moss's voice was hard. "You've been in the dock before. The only reason you got off those times was because of luck and a good brief."

Pilcher shrugged. "'S'why I pay 'em."

So he was a criminal who could afford a barrister to stand up for him in court and plead his case. I did not like the sound of that. Such a man was likely in the employ of an even worse criminal who had plenty of money to keep his minions free of hanging or transportation.

"You were seen entering and leaving the pawnbrokers, with the murdered man found only an hour later," Moss said.

Pilcher scowled at him. "I were in that pawnbrokers on legitimate business. Bloke were already brown bread." *Brown bread—dead.*

"Can you prove that?" Moss asked.

"You know I can't." Pilcher's irritation rose. "Or coppers wouldn't have nabbed me and fit me up for it." His large hands moved restlessly, the chains clinking.

"What were you doing in the pawnbrokers?" Daniel asked quietly.

Pilcher snapped his gaze to him. "Why should I tell you?"

"You will if you want to keep your neck from the noose." Daniel's voice was smooth, no trace of South London in it.

Pilcher blinked. I saw him make up his mind that Daniel, despite his working man's clothes, might have come here to help him—perhaps he thought Daniel a solicitor. When Pilcher spoke again, his tone was calmer. "Paid to, weren't I?

Sent to fetch goods. I were going to *buy* them—nothing wrong about it."

Chief Inspector Moss huffed. "Where is the money you were given to buy these goods? Wasn't in your pocket when you were searched."

"Me boss had it. I take the goods to 'im, 'e pays. Not frew me. 'E knows better than to give *me* a bag o' cash." Pilcher chuckled, genuinely pleased he was so untrustworthy.

"Name your boss," Daniel said. "We'll ask him."

Pilcher let out another laugh. I did not like that he was so merry. "It's Naismith. Julius M. Naismith."

The name meant nothing to me, but I saw Daniel go very, very still. Chief Inspector Moss began to speak, but he caught sight of Daniel's expression and fell silent.

As I watched, Daniel's face went every bit as hard as Pilcher's, and a coldness entered his eyes, one that could have filmed the walls with ice. I'd never seen in Daniel the rage I glimpsed in him now, one that boiled up from somewhere deep inside, where he kept it hidden from all the world, including me.

I realized in that moment that the most dangerous person in the room was no longer the thuggish Mr. Pilcher, or the powerful Chief Inspector Moss, but Daniel McAdam.

17

"Where is he?" Daniel asked in a chilly voice.

Pilcher stared at Daniel for a time and then swallowed. His answer, "I dunno, do I?" was strangely quiet.

Chief Inspector Moss broke in. "If you don't know where your boss is, how will he give you an alibi? Or a reference for your character?"

Pilcher shrugged, having grown far less confident in the space of a few moments. "He mostly finds me."

"Well, he'd better find you quick, lad," Moss said. "You're for Newgate. If the trial is swift enough you might end up starting for a new life in Botany Bay before the next week is out, but only if the judge is lenient."

Pilcher had gone a sickly white. "Now hang on . . ."

"You might be *hanging* on," Moss said, liking his own joke, but Daniel held up a hand.

"Let him speak."

Pilcher's eyes flickered nervously to Daniel. "Mr. Naismith didn't have nothing to do with no killings, I swear to ya. 'E sent me to buy old bits he wanted—legitimate like. 'E had an understanding with the pawnbroker. 'E sends me or someone to carry the fings back to 'im, and pays if 'e likes the gewgaws."

"What did he send you to fetch this time?" Daniel asked him.

Pilcher shrugged. "Dunno what it was. I pick up packages and keep others from stealing 'em. I don't look at what's inside. Don't care. I get paid, don't matter what it is."

Chief Inspector Moss leaned forward. "Would it interest you to know we arrested that pawnbroker? He's cooling his heels in a lockup for receiving stolen goods. He'll be tried soon."

Pilcher shrugged again, trying to spread his arms, but was jerked back by the shackles. "Can't help that, can I? I was told to pick up a package, so I toddled along to pick it up. 'Cept, when I walk in, bloke is stone-cold dead on the floor."

"Did you know the bloke?" Daniel asked. "The dead man?"

"Never seen 'im." Pilcher balled his fists. "That's God's honest troof, guv. I didn't know 'im, didn't kill 'im. I turned around and walked out as fast as I could."

I believed him. Mr. Pilcher was quite frightened now, ready to loudly protest his innocence. Tess took the same tone whenever she was indignant about being wrongly accused.

"So you were unlucky," Moss said. "Is that what you are claiming?"

"'S'right."

"We'll let a judge and jury sort that out," Chief Inspector Moss said, sounding satisfied.

241

"Magistrate's already bound you over for the trial, so don't go ruining your chances by fighting your jailers. See you in the dock, old son."

"But I didn't do nuffink!" Pilcher wailed.

Moss rose and began to turn for the door, but Daniel's quiet voice had him pausing.

"Tell me where Naismith is," Daniel said to Pilcher, "and you might save yourself."

"I'm telling ye, I don't *know!*" Pilcher's eyes were wide. "Wish I did. 'E'd have me out of 'ere and you lot thrashed."

Daniel looked up at Chief Inspector Moss, the iciness in his eyes unnerving. "Let him go. On the condition that he tells Naismith to talk to us. To *me*."

Moss was shaking his head before Daniel finished. "I need someone to answer for this murder. Pilcher is a killer—he's done murders before but his brief got him off. He might have done this one; he might not. Whether he goes down for one he didn't do is all the same to me."

Pilcher's face was mottled red and white. "You can't do that. You're a copper."

"And you're a killer," Moss said. "I'm against those. And thieves that live the high life while their betters starve."

"Let him run back to his master," Daniel argued. "You'll catch him for something else sooner or later. As for this murder, I'll poke around, see

242

what I can find. Keep the local coppers off me, and I'll turn up your murderer."

"Listen to 'im," Pilcher said, gesturing to Daniel with a clank of shackles. "'E's a bloke what knows what 'e's talking about."

Moss smoothed his salt-and-pepper mustache. "Hmm. I'll think about it. Thank you for your time, Mr. Pilcher."

"Bleedin' 'ell." Pilcher lowered his great head to his hands.

Chief Inspector Moss opened the door and walked out, his step light. What he did not notice, and I did, was Daniel move to Pilcher, lower his head, and whisper into the big man's ear. Pilcher jerked up, looking at Daniel in a sudden mixture of hope and dismay.

Chief Inspector Moss saw nothing of this. He came to me and closed the grill in the wall, locking it, while he tamped down his impatience into something like deference. "I am sorry you had to hear that, Mrs. Holloway. I warned McAdam that he was filth."

I waited to speak until Daniel had left the room where Mr. Pilcher remained and closed and locked the door behind him.

"I don't believe Mr. Pilcher committed the murder," I said. "He might have had something to do with the stolen goods you sent Mr. McAdam to intercept, but he did not kill the man in the pawnbrokers. I'm certain of it."

Chief Inspector Moss nodded without hesitation. "I have the feeling you're right, ma'am. On the other hand, he's a villain. If I let him go, he'll only do more villainy."

"Have him followed," Daniel said. His cold look had faded, but he spoke determinedly. "He'll lead you to bigger fish."

Moss's brows rose. "You think this Naismith has something to do with the thefts? That could be true—from what I hear, he would deal in such things."

"It doesn't matter," Daniel said. "Naismith is an evil bastard. Use Pilcher to connect him with this murder—with anything—and you'll have a collar that will put your name in the history books."

Chief Inspector Moss shook his head, somewhat reluctantly. "If it has nothing to do with this case . . . You're being lent to me to find the stolen antiquities from the British Museum, not to chase every villain in London."

I broke in before Daniel could argue. "Put Detective Inspector McGregor to following Mr. Pilcher," I said quickly.

Moss turned to me, bewildered. "McGregor?"

"Yes. He seems in need of something exciting to do. Have him chase Mr. Pilcher, and he can arrest this Mr. Naismith too if need be."

Both men were staring at me, Daniel in something like admiration, Moss as though I were a dog that had just spoken English. I shrugged and pretended I didn't mind their scrutiny.

My reasoning was sound, though. If Inspector McGregor were chasing villains like Pilcher and his minder—who sounded even more dangerous than Pilcher himself—then McGregor would not be hounding perfectly respectable cooks in their kitchens. What's more, he'd leave Daniel alone.

"Another thing I will think on," Moss said. "Thank you for your time, McAdam."

He'd said the same thing to Pilcher. I didn't much like that.

"I'll find out who did the man in the pawn-brokers," Daniel said. "I promise you that. And keep trying to discover where the antiquities are disappearing to. I apologize for not being of much help thus far."

Moss straightened up, the demeanor of the commander returning. "Sometimes these things don't bear fruit. I wish they did. Men like Pilcher make me ill. Do you know a chief inspector who retired a few years ago—Turland? Did his job better than anyone, was given a commendation by the chief super. Last time I saw him, he was living with his sister in a tiny house in the East End, existing on boiled beans and cabbage. All the while Naismith and his henchmen dine on roast beef and fine wine. I'd love to see every one of them hanged, but not before they give their ill-gotten profits to people like Turland." The chief inspector ran out of breath and shook his head. "I am grateful for your help, McAdam, no matter what. Anything you turn up might be of use." He glanced at me again, trying to decide why Daniel had thought I could assist him, and then the glance dismissed me. "I'll have someone see you out."

"I know the way." Daniel sent him his usual good-natured smile, though the smile did not reach his eyes. "Shall we, Mrs. H.? How about a nice spot of tea before we take you home?"

I knew Daniel had no intention of doing anything so staid as to go out for tea. He took my elbow and guided me from the building, down the small passage, and back into the street.

It was not far to the Strand. We walked past Charing Cross Station and to the corner where the pawnbrokers stood.

The golden balls were no less tarnished, the windows no less grimy. Daniel produced a key from his pocket and opened the door. He ushered me inside then closed and locked the door, pulling the shades all the way down.

Very little sunlight filtered into the gloomy place. Daniel moved behind the counter, opening the back room to look inside, I suppose to make certain no intruders lurked. He returned without a word, so I assumed all was well.

He paused to light a kerosene lamp, which he set on the counter's wide surface. The lamp burned steadily behind its glass chimney, throwing a yellow-white glow over the small room and its dusty wares.

"I suppose we are here to discover who killed that poor man," I said.

Daniel came out from behind the counter. "Since he likely came here to kill *me,* I'm not sure I'd call him a 'poor man.' But yes, I want to know who struck him down. Not Pilcher—I agree with you about him. He's not guilty of this crime."

"Who is Mr. Naismith?" I asked abruptly.

The freezing anger had left Daniel's eyes, but a flicker of it returned at my question. "A name you should forget."

"I'm not likely to, am I?" I asked in reasonable tones. "You grew furious when Mr. Pilcher mentioned him." I gave him a small smile. "You ought to tell me, you know, to prevent me trying to find out on my own."

"Oh, Kat." Daniel took my hands, closing his strong ones over mine. "I shouldn't have brought you with me today. I was showing off. Clever Daniel will make a villain spill his secrets, while Mrs. Holloway observes. I had no idea he was keeping *that* one."

"Which you have yet to explain to me."

Daniel squeezed my hands, and for the first time, I felt a twinge of misgiving. I'd seen the power in the interrogation room shift from the murderer with reptilian eyes to the cold rage of Daniel. Mr. Pilcher, a very bad man indeed, had been afraid of him.

I was in a shop where a murder had been committed with no one noticing, with none but Daniel knowing where I was. Daniel himself could have killed the thug—though I reasoned that if he had, he'd not have come here to try to find clues. On the other hand, he might have come to make certain he'd covered up his perfidy.

I hoped I was being fanciful. Daniel had been plenty enraged and dangerous when he'd gone after the villains ready to kill the Queen, and on that occasion, he'd saved my life.

Daniel closed his eyes. When he opened them again, I saw resignation and a quiet resolve.

"Mr. Naismith might be the man who murdered the only father I ever knew," he said softly. "In twenty years, I've never been able to pin him down to prove it."

In the silence, the lamp hissed, and a muffled shout sounded outside as a man passed close to the door. His voice was lost in the hoofbeats and rumble of vehicles without.

"Twenty years ago, you must have been a child," I said.

"A lad of ten summers." Daniel's fingers firmed on mine. "Naismith's gang raided the house where I lived and murdered all within, hiding their crime by setting the place on fire. I hid behind the wood box in the kitchen, and they didn't see me. Either that or they didn't think me worth bothering about. I tried to revive my father, to get him out of the house, but in the end, I had to flee for my life, barely escaping before the entire edifice fell in. I didn't stop running for a long, long time."

Words rose in my throat and stopped there, forming a lump that halted my breath.

I imagined Daniel as a youth, thin and small, cowering in the darkness behind the barrier of the woodpile, watching as everyone he knew was butchered. Having to make the decision to abandon them to the fire and save himself. Alone, running through the night and the brutal London streets, nowhere to go. He'd been ten years old, the same age as Grace.

My eyes stung. Without speaking, I enfolded Daniel into my arms.

He started, as though not expecting my sudden pity, then he sank down into me, resting his head on my shoulder. His warm hair brushed my cheek, and I felt his breath lift in his chest.

We stood so for a few minutes, while uncaring traffic clattered by outside, and the gathering clouds let loose the first drops of rain on the city.

Daniel slowly straightened, and even more slowly drew my arms from around him. He kissed my palms through my gloves in turn and then said nothing for a time, only pressed my hands, his eyes downcast.

I understood now the terrible anger in Daniel when Pilcher had spoken the name. I'd been witnessing the despair of the boy, which had grown into the hardened resolve of the man.

Eventually, Daniel said in a low voice, "If Pilcher works for Naismith, I'll have him. Him and Naismith both."

"Are you certain Mr. Naismith was the one who ordered the raid on your father's house?" I asked.

Daniel shook his head. "No, because I was ten years old and terrified. But my father had been at odds with Naismith for a long time—a territory war. My dad was a villain, yes, but not a brute. He was cheery and even kind, even if he was a bloody thief. He ran most of South London—all the criminal families there answered to him. As I said, I don't know whether I was his natural son, but he treated me as such. He called me his heir apparent, and he took care of me. All that was gone in the space of an hour."

The words were uninflected, but I could sense the grip Daniel was keeping on his emotions. I longed to hold and comfort him again, but I was not certain he'd welcome such a thing. "What did you do?" I asked. "When you were so young a lad—who helped you?"

"No one, at first." Daniel shrugged. "I learned to survive. My dad had taught me well, both to find what I needed to stay alive, and how to be genuinely grateful to those who were kind."

"You learned to turn people up sweet," I said, understanding. "You became Daniel the charmer."

"If I had turned vicious, I would have died," he said, the conviction of that in his eyes. "I'd have been arrested for some crime or other, hanged or sent to hard labor. I had to choose."

He'd chosen to learn everything he could, including how to beguile. Twenty years had made him very practiced at it.

"Thank you for telling me," I said quietly. "I will keep your confidence."

Daniel only looked at me. "You are an uncommon woman, Kat Holloway."

My face warmed. "So you have said. I suppose we ought to be looking for clues."

Daniel gave me a nod and at last released my hands. I saw him take a sharp breath as he turned away to lift the lamp from the counter to examine the floor where I presumed the corpse had lain.

I moved aside, not wishing to step there, and gazed about the dross for sale in front of the counter.

I wondered, as I scanned the tables, whether the man who'd taken Daniel in had been his true father. Daniel had some doubt, I could tell. Daniel might have been the child of a friend, or an orphan, or a foundling, or had been simply wandering the streets. The man might have decided Daniel was ripe to be made into an apprentice thief.

The story explained how Daniel had learned to be so skilled at picking locks. If the man who'd raised him had been a thief, he'd have taught Daniel the art of lock picking, sneaking about, and keeping others from noticing him, things Daniel excelled at. His ability to groom horses, drive carts, do carpentry and plumbing, and coordinate packs of constables to save the monarch had come from his determination to survive.

Then again, Daniel might truly have been the man's son. Born out of wedlock, perhaps, as James had been. Daniel hadn't known about James for a long while, and this man might not have realized he'd sired Daniel.

"Was his name McAdam?" I asked as I browsed the wares. I lifted a particularly hideous little trinket box, the sort found on dressing tables. Cherubs, decently robed rather than naked, flitted about a garden with oversize roses, where several women with too-wide faces bared their teeth at one another over cups of tea. The box was edged round with curlicues of gold and silver gilt, glittering, useless, and awful.

"No," Daniel answered. "It was Carter. I took McAdam because I worried Naismith would come looking for anyone named Carter, to make certain he'd cleansed the lot of us."

Daniel had tried to join the police, he said, and they'd turned him away. Had he wanted to do so in order to hunt down this Naismith and arrest him?

"There must be any number of people in London called Carter," I remarked. I moved on from the box to a gilded picture frame containing a faded photo of a child with a toy horse. The gilt was flaking off, and the photo could barely be made out. "He could not go after them all."

"Perhaps, but I decided it was safer to be known as McAdam."

"So that is not your real name. What about Daniel?"

He did not answer, and I turned to find Daniel leaning against the counter. "I've always been called Daniel. Any other name, I do not know."

"I'm sorry," I said softly.

"It happened a long time ago. My name is now Daniel McAdam. I made it so officially when I came of age."

"It fits you." My heart beat in thick little pats. I'd only known him as Daniel McAdam, and now he was telling me even that was not true.

"I've made it fit." Daniel gave me a hint of a smile. "Well, I have found nothing here I did not expect to. The constables have been blundering about, likely trampling every boot print, every dropped handkerchief with the killer's name on it . . . They decided Pilcher was the man, and that was that."

"I am convinced he did not do it."

"As am I." Daniel gave one more glance about then blew out the lamp's flame. "Shall we return to Mount Street? This afternoon has made me hungry, and I believe I was promised scones."

He had closed in on himself once more, sending his good-naturedness beaming out like the lamp spilling brightness beyond its chimney, while the core of it remained untouchable.

Much of Daniel's good nature was his true character, I was sure—he had a kindness in him that I'd not mistaken. However, I'd learned today some of what he hid deep inside himself, and both he and I knew I'd never forget it.

When we reached Mount Street I went to the larder and retrieved scones I'd put back for Daniel. I wrapped his in a napkin and thrust it at him, shooing him out the back door.

Daniel thanked me, flashed his smile over everyone in the kitchen, and left with a wave, whistling his way up the stairs.

Tess shook her head as she watched him go. She'd flung herself at him when we'd come in, rhapsodizing about how glad she was to see him well. She'd hugged him hard then spun away, wiping her eyes. "Never know what he's going to do, do ya?"

No, I did not. I was both grateful Daniel had shared some of his story with me and troubled as well. Daniel's pain was true, though he'd learned to mask it, and I wondered what his suffering as a child had done to him. I also wondered if the fact that he'd shared a deep secret with me would change our friendship. He might regret what he'd told me and be too uncomfortable to go back to the way things had been. That would be a pity.

A great pity, something whispered inside me.

I could not think of it now. I had to make tea, then supper. Tess had prepared for both meals quite well, showing once again how quick she was to learn—very bright, Daniel had recognized, and I agreed with him.

Too bright, perhaps, to be a mere cook. But what choices would she have? A working-class young woman who'd already been arrested once in her life would not have many. She could only marry so high without ruining the man who chose her. Professions for women were very limited unless one was extremely wealthy or very eccentric— usually both.

I would teach her what I could, I decided. *And* discover what she knew about the back door.

I decided not to accuse her openly. If Tess were innocent, she'd take offense, and I truly did not want to hurt her. If she were guilty, she'd try to lie, and I did not want to watch her do that.

"Do you have a beau, Tess?" I asked the question as casually as I could. "It is all right if you do—I am only curious."

"*Me?* Have a man? Lord, no." Tess stared at me

in amazement. "Men ain't to be trusted, are they? All sweetness and light one minute; the next, you have a little one to raise, and they've disappeared into the blue. Seen it happen to too many of me pals to let it happen to me, Mrs. H., and that's a fact."

18

Tess finished with the adamancy of one who has found wisdom and pitied those who hadn't.

Her answer put paid to my theory that she'd robbed the larder for a lover. I'd seen Tess be adept with a lie, but when she had deep convictions, her words rang with truth.

I also realized she had a more prudent head on her shoulders than I'd had at her age. I had not been nearly so cautious when a man had come around offering *me* sweetness and light.

But then, if I'd been wise, I'd not have had Grace. I could not regret being mother to the most beautiful child in the world. Such are the complications of life—it is neither entirely one thing or the other.

I let the topic drop and showed Tess, as promised, how to make tea cream. I'd set pans of fresh milk to heat on the stove this morning, and now the cream was thick on top. I skimmed off the cream, boiled it in a clean pan, and added tea leaves that were still green—that is, they hadn't been rolled and dried, which is what makes tea black. I stirred in a bit of sugar and isinglass, which is a jellylike substance, to thicken it.

I scooped a little of this concoction onto a spoon and shoved it at Tess. She hesitantly tasted the cream then seized the spoon and ate the whole dollop. "That ain't bad," she said, licking her lips. "Those upstairs eat well with you in the kitchen, don't they?"

We sent up the tea with scones and the tea cream then turned to the labor of getting supper. Tess asked me what I had discovered at Scotland Yard, and I gave her a truncated version of the story, eliminating Daniel's reaction to Mr. Pilcher and his revelations to me.

"Hope they find the bloke what did the killing," Tess said darkly. "I worry for Mr. McAdam. He's a bit reckless, he is."

I could not disagree.

I taught Tess to make maître d'hôtel butter, which combined butter with parsley, salt, pepper, and a squeeze of lemon juice, mashed together with a wooden spoon. Tess asked why the butter was named after a gent who worked in a hotel, and I had to admit I did not know.

We served the butter with the fish I'd broiled, sending it up first thing when supper above stairs commenced.

Tess continued to ask about my outing as we turned to preparing the meat, a roast I'd finish off with potatoes and a salad topped with fresh mayonnaise. "Did you find out who's burgling all the houses in Park Lane?"

She spoke with an air of curiosity, nothing in her manner suggesting she knew anything about these crimes other than what I or Mr. Davis had mentioned.

"No, I have not," I said. "But I intend to."

Things had gone on long enough. Tonight, Daniel was to meet with Lady Cynthia and Mr. Thanos at the pub near Bedford Square and discuss what they'd discovered. I wanted to be there to listen to what they had to say, but I knew I was too busy tonight to hie off that far from home. If I left too often, Mr. Davis would grow incensed, and so he should, as he had as much work to do running the house. Also, Mrs. Bywater might give me the sack. Then she'd no doubt try to save money by promoting Tess to full cook, which would be a disaster.

"Ooh," Tess said, watching my face as she whipped the egg yolks for the mayonnaise. "What'cha up to, Mrs. H.?"

"I am up to cooking supper," I said coolly as I ladled the beef's juices over the potatoes that I'd thrown into the pan. "But tomorrow, I will introduce you to my colleagues in Mayfair kitchens. You need to know the right people if you're to make a name for yourself."

Tess did not look as though that pleased her, but she only nodded and kept whipping the yolks until I deemed them ready to receive the clear oil that would make them into mayonnaise.

And if I took Tess to the houses that had been burgled and then poked about, that was my busi-

259

ness. I trusted Lady Cynthia and Mr. Thanos to do their best, but none knew the workings and secrets of homes like their servants. It was high time I discovered things for myself.

I woke in the morning more buoyant than I had been in a few days. This was Wednesday, and I was always lighthearted on Wednesdays. Tomorrow was Thursday, which I whimsically called to myself my Day of Grace.

Tess and I prepared Mr. Bywater's rather staid breakfast, but I was more exotic in the staff's repast, layering eggs, wilted spinach, bacon, cream, and a bit of cheese in a piecrust and baking it until it was brown and bubbling. I served slices of this with potatoes and strawberries with fresh cream. I am pleased to say the staff ate every crumb without complaint.

After breakfast, I had Tess begin preparation for the midday meal while I made lists for the market. The luncheon repast was a cold one—mostly leftover roast and mutton from previous meals—and I left instructions for Mr. Davis to take it up to be served. Tess and I, I said, needed to do quite a lot of shopping to prepare for the coming week, and supper would be an easy affair, as the Bywaters were going out. Mr. Davis agreed, grudgingly, and I took up my shawl and hat, let Tess borrow my light spring coat, and out we went, baskets over our arms.

I would have to do something about Tess's clothes, I mused as we walked. She wore a black broadcloth that had belonged to one of the downstairs maids, hastily altered to fit Tess's thinner figure. She'd need cloth for her own frock, preferably gray, to set her apart from the other maids. The dress she'd worn when she arrived was hardly fit for working in, and she'd want it for her days out.

"Fridays," I said as we walked along Mount Street toward Park Lane.

"Eh?" Tess asked behind me. The street was too thronged for us to walk side by side. "What's that, Mrs. H.?"

"Would you like Friday as your day out?" I said over my shoulder. "You cannot have Thursday or Monday, as I leave then, and we cannot both be gone at the same time. On Wednesdays I have too much to do to prepare for Thursday, and on weekends, the family tend to have more visitors, larger suppers to prepare."

I heard only silence from Tess, which I found odd. I sidestepped a lad walking a dog and turned to find her staring at me in pure shock. "A day out?" she asked, wide-eyed. "You mean, leave work for a whole day, like you do?"

"Yes, of course," I answered. "Every member of the staff has a day out. This is England, not a country in the hinterlands where they work their servants to death."

Tess took a few hurried steps to catch my arm and press herself close to me as we walked around a clump of carts. "Aw, you are too good to me, Mrs. Holloway. I don't deserve it, I don't."

I wanted to be pleased with her gratitude, but I remained brisk. "It is not me being good; it is common practice. Now, shall it be Friday for you? Or Tuesday?"

"Friday, if ya don't mind, Mrs. H. That'd do very well for me."

"I have to ask Mr. Davis and Mrs. Bywater, of course," I said. "But I am certain they will agree to my way of thinking."

"They will." Tess rubbed her shoulder against mine. "You can bring anyone round, you can. You're a dab hand at it."

I warmed—Tess could be quite affectionate—but I reminded myself that I could not grow soft with her until I discovered whether she'd betrayed my trust. "Don't talk nonsense," I said.

We arrived at our first destination, a large house on Park Lane, a little south of the Sardinian Embassy, set back from the avenue behind a drive lined with elm trees. Tess looked about in awe as we approached it, and I felt a moment of disquiet. If Tess truly was a thief, I was showing her the way into private residences stuffed with things to steal.

On the other hand, I did believe that Lady Cynthia's and Mr. Thanos's idea was correct—the thieves were stealing very specific things rather than making a random grab of anything valuable. That was the key to the matter, I thought, and as I walked along with Tess at my side, my conviction grew.

I led Tess around to the back of the house, following a little path that was muddy from last night's rain. Down a short flight of stairs was the kitchen door.

I knocked on this, to have the door pulled open by a scullery maid who peered around it in suspicion. She brightened when she saw me and flung the door wide. "Come in, Mrs. Holloway, do. Mrs. Hemming needs some cheering."

I walked in through a kitchen that was three times the size of mine. Though the room was below the ground, it wasn't in as deep a cellar as the Mount Street house's, and had wide windows to let in abundant light.

The servants' hall was screened off from the kitchen by a wall filled with windows—in fact, all the rooms down here had half walls of glass, which did not do much for privacy, but lent a feeling of spaciousness. The wine cellar and larder were closed off, I knew from previous visits, but only because wine and some food do not benefit from sunlight.

Mrs. Hemming was not the cook; she was the housekeeper. She rose from the table in the servants' hall, where she had spread out mending, and came to greet me. The cook of this house did not much like me—she was an aging woman I often heard grumbling that I got above myself. She was not wrong, but she never had a good word to say, and never spoke to me directly.

Even now, the cook carried on a low-running mumble about servants what thought they were fine ladies, traipsing about of an afternoon when the respectable were working. Tess sent the woman a frown, but fortunately said nothing.

Mrs. Hemming, neatly attired in a high-necked black gown, a large bunch of keys dangling from her belt, was about forty, with rigidly tamed blond hair pulled back from a rather colorless face.

She'd been housekeeper in one of the first places I'd worked, before the widowed master, an aging marquess, had married a rather insipid young lady. Mrs. Hemming had given notice after clashing with said young lady at every encounter. I'd been more tolerant, feeling sorry for the chit thrust suddenly into running a wealthy home with no experience. But even I'd had enough when she began to ask for exotic meals such as dormice and ants, and then laughed in my face when I protested. The poor thing had gone into a decline not long after I'd departed, I'd heard. I believe the marquess took her to the warm climes of Italy and never brought her back. The best thing about that post had been Mrs. Hemming, who'd become a friend.

"Good morning, Mrs. Holloway," Mrs. Hemming said as she ushered me down the windowed hall to her parlor. "Always pleasant to see you."

"This is Tess Parsons," I said after we'd settled on the comfortable chairs within. "My new assistant. Tess, this is Mrs. Hemming, a wise and capable woman."

Mrs. Hemming looked pleased, a small amount of color coming into her cheeks. Her eyes were a deep blue, which helped mitigate her paleness. "I am glad to meet you, Tess. You are fortunate in your mentor. Mrs. Holloway is a most talented cook."

"Don't I know it," Tess gushed, then looked chagrined. "Oh, was I not supposed to answer? Don't know the rules yet, do I?"

Mrs. Hemming's brows climbed, and I cut in soothingly, "As this is a social visit, it is fine for you to participate in the conversation. Tess is a bit raw," I said to Mrs. Hemming, "but she is quick and soon will learn polish. I was the same at eighteen."

"As were we all." Mrs. Hemming gave Tess a reassuring nod. "Now, Mrs. Holloway, I had your note. What's it all about?"

I had written brief missives to the staff members I wanted to visit this morning—they would all be busy, and springing on them unexpectedly would be rude and might anger their employers.

"You've had a burglary here, haven't you?" I

asked. "Mr. Davis and I are trying to find ways to protect our house, so we thought we'd ask what happened."

Tess shot a glance at me, knowing jolly well Mr. Davis and I had discussed no such thing. But she kept her lips tightly together and remained silent.

Mrs. Hemming shuddered. "Horrible, it's been, Mrs. Holloway. The master sets such a store on his antiquities collection. He'd been out to Greece, you know, to Athens and other places where they are digging up old pots. Brought them so carefully home and put them in his glass cases. He invites his friends who are collectors over and they gaze at them for hours. No idea why dusty old bits of pottery are so fascinating."

"I believe I understand." I remembered my visit to the British Museum with Grace, the two of us gazing at a miniature Egyptian kitchen full of little clay people baking bread and making beer with great gusto. I'd been enthralled. "It's like people reaching out from the past, isn't it? Someone thousands of years ago made that piece, and you are seeing their handiwork."

"I suppose." Mrs. Hemming's shrug dismissed it—she'd never been romantic. "But what a to-do when some of it went missing. The master forbade any of the staff to leave the house— searched our rooms, if you please."

Her outrage was palpable. The balance between master and servant was one of trust—servants saw a household's most intimate secrets. Our masters trusted us to keep our silence, and we in turn were allowed to get on with our tasks unhindered. When that trust was breached, either way, it made for an uncomfortable, sometimes intolerable, place.

"But nothing was found," I said quickly.

"Of course not." Mrs. Hemming's chest lifted in indignation, the black buttons that closed her bodice to her chin sparkling. "Why would the footmen or maids steal his lordship's pottery? We wouldn't know what to take—what do we know about Greek vases? Except not to touch them, ever, not even to dust." She finished with a sniff.

A maid entered at this juncture, laden with a tray holding a steaming teapot, three cups, and a plate of cakes. Tess moved her hands under her legs as though keeping herself from snatching up the treats. Her eyes rounded in delight as Mrs. Hemming lifted the pot and served us tea, asking first me then Tess how much sugar and cream we took.

"Who does his lordship invite to view the collection?" I asked as we lifted our cups. Tess had a piece of sponge cake on her plate, which she carefully cut with her fork. She put the tiniest piece into her mouth and chewed and swallowed, smiling all the while. I wondered if she meant to show me she could eat like a lady and not a starving beggar.

"Quite a number of gentlemen," Mrs. Hemming said. "Lord Chalminster, who likes Egyptian things, including bits of mummies, if you can credit it. A bishop from Derbyshire—quite a gentleman *he* is. Old and kind, rather absent-minded. Oh yes, and the vicar of Grosvenor Chapel. He and the bishop are old friends. A few archaeological gentlemen his lordship spent time with in Greece come here often—he paid them money to work on a dig and give him the best of what they found. And Sir Evan Godfrey, who avidly collects antiquities but mourns he can't afford them now that he has a pretty young wife."

An interesting cross section of upstairs life, I mused. "Have any of them been burgled as well?"

"Oh yes. Lord Chalminster and the bishop both have, they say—Lord Chalminster lives next door to Sir Evan Godfrey. The bishop has had things go missing from his house in Derbyshire. I gather he has quite a massive collection from Greece, Egypt, and the Near East."

I took a bite of cake as Mrs. Hemming spoke, nothing as dainty as Tess's. The cake was dry, and the cook had put in too much vanilla, which I suppose she'd done to counteract all the lemon. A sponge cake ought to be light and full of bubbly holes—hence its name—which comes from separating the eggs and beating the whites until one's arm is stiff. This cake was dense—the cook had either not separated the eggs or she'd not whipped the whites long enough.

Mrs. Hemming continued. "Sir Evan Godfrey has had paintings stolen, but none of his antiquities. He is in less of a bother—I suppose a brilliant painting by an old master isn't as important to him as a bit of powdered mummy in a jar."

Tess wrinkled her nose as she took another tiny bite of cake. "Must have been a different thief, then."

"Perhaps." Mrs. Hemming returned to her earlier theme. "What I dislike is our master's suspicions of us when it is clear this is the work of a gang. Her ladyship, mercifully, put her foot down and halted the searching of our things. His lordship, however, is very upset."

"I imagine so," I said in sympathy. "How did the burglar get in? Through a window? The back door?"

Mrs. Hemming frowned over her teacup. "We don't know. That is why the master swore it was one of the staff. No broken windows, no forced doors. Lord Chalminster reported the same thing, as did the bishop."

"This thief knows his stuff," Tess said. "Must be an expert at lock picking."

"Indeed," I agreed. Or, as I thought before, they'd been let in through the front door as a guest, or the back door as a servant of the guest.

Lady Cynthia's speculation that the thieves were fanatics who wished to return antiquities to their native land went with this idea. The lord who lived in this house invited archaeologists into his private rooms, did he not? They could have secreted items away to smuggle back to their respective countries when they returned there to dig.

My own idea of what was happening was simpler. Collectors could be mad about their bits and pieces, enough for them to commit crimes for them. I'd worked in a house where the master had collected guns, uniforms, and drums and such from the Napoleonic Wars—French things, not British. He'd scour the markets and make trips to Paris, rejoicing in cheating other collectors out of things that they didn't realize were valuable, or selling them pieces he knew were fakes. He'd sit in his room with Napoleon's army's leavings about him for hours and hours, not eating, not sleeping, doing none of us knew what.

In my experience, collectors would go to any length to purchase a new item to display in their glass cases—would they stoop to stealing it from their fellow collectors? I thought perhaps they might.

I finished the cake, as did Tess, though the cook ought to be ashamed to let something like it be served, said a cordial good afternoon to Mrs. Hemming, and took Tess away.

"Lovely house," Tess said, walking backward to look at it as we traversed the path next to the drive. "Kitchen was nice. Much bigger than ours."

"It isn't the size of the kitchen but what comes out of it that's important," I said. "But yes, more room would be nice, wouldn't it?"

We continued along Park Lane, a cook and her assistant out to do whatever the wealthy of Mayfair thought we did. I gazed at the house that must be Chalminster's as we passed it, a grand white mansion towering above the rhododendrons that strove to hide it. He'd been implicated in the last mess I'd helped Daniel investigate—was he to blame for this one?

Lord Chalminster's was not my destination, however, but Cynthia's friend Clemmie's home. I made my way around the white house with its Indian-like domes and pointed arches—Tess staring openmouthed at the bizarre architecture— to the kitchen door. Mrs. Martin, the cook, had known I was coming, but when we entered, she was rushing about, her heavy tread loud on the flagstones, her assistant and several maids trying to help her and stay out of her way at the same time.

Pots boiled over on the stove, the oven had heated the large room to scorching, and the kitchen table was a disaster of flour, chopped vegetables, oil, cream, and spilled peppercorns.

271

Even when my roasted pig had come to grief, my kitchen had not been this chaotic.

"Mrs. Holloway!" Mrs. Martin paused in mid-stride, her eyes round with panic. "Please, if you ever called me friend—save me!"

19

"Good heavens, Mrs. Martin." I threw off my shawl and snapped my fingers at one of the hurrying maids, instructing her to find me an apron. "What has happened?"

"The mistress has decided to have a supper for forty, that's what." Mrs. Martin's white hair had escaped its bun to straggle down her face. "Decided not an hour ago. Came down here herself to tell us, if you please, saying she was enjoying being whimsical. Then she hurried off to send notes to all her friends." Mrs. Martin lowered her voice. "She's doing it to bother her husband, and we all know it. But it's mostly a bother to us, isn't it, Mrs. Holloway?"

"It is indeed, Mrs. Martin."

A wise woman had the foresight to see that upsetting her cook could have dire consequences on the tranquility of her life, but Clemmie must have decided she no longer cared for such things. I wondered if this sudden supper party was a volley at her husband for trying to push the blame for his underhandedness on her, a sign of her defiance. If so, I admired her audacity, but what Mrs. Martin said was true—the servants would pay for her pique more than her husband would.

"Come along, Tess," I said as she stood agape,

clutching her empty basket. "Fetch an apron and help me clear off this table."

Tess thumped the basket onto a chair and shrugged off her coat. "What about *our* supper, Mrs. H.? And the master's?"

"Mr. and Mrs. Bywater are going out to a subscription dinner tonight, for one of their charities. If I am right, Lady Cynthia will be coming here, as Lady Godfrey's guest. We won't be needed except for the staff, and we can prepare something quickly for them. It's much easier on me now, since you've come."

I hoped to please Tess with this compliment, but her face darkened, and she looked unhappy. Mrs. Martin began to wail, and I hurried away to help her inventory her larder and determine what we needed.

"Did the mistress not give you a menu?" I asked as I went through the shelves as well as the boxes of produce stacked on the floor. "Mrs. Bywater lets me have a free hand, but when she wants a particular dish for a supper gathering, she informs me."

Mrs. Martin shot me scowl. "Not that one. She's sweet as sugar, is the mistress, but no idea what it is to create a meal for so many on short notice. Comes from a family what waves its hand and all is done for them. At least the master is a wee bit more sensible. Hires extra men right and left for little jobs."

I noted that the fish course would be tricky. A good lobster sauce covered numerous sins of fish that were not the best. But there were no lobsters in the larder and no time to procure fresh ones— however, I found a bucket of shrimp in ice that could do for making a faux lobster sauce.

"What little jobs?" I asked. "This is a large house, but you have quite a number of servants, don't you?" At least twenty people worked here, I'd counted, inside and out, and there might be more in the stables.

Mrs. Martin pulled a pathetic dead fowl down from where it hung and gave it a look of despair. "Mary, pluck this!" she shouted at a maid and tossed it at the poor girl when she came running. "Moving furniture, repairing windows, knocking out a wall in one of the attic rooms, rebuilding a garden shed." She trailed off as she snatched up bunches of asparagus, one in each hand, and trundled herself back to the kitchen.

I wondered, as I worked, whether these extra workmen had been the ones helping Sir Evan smuggle his artwork out of the house to sell.

Tess and I worked like demons helping Mrs. Martin and her staff ready the supper. I always liked a challenge, but I did not let on to Mrs. Martin that I relished throwing together dishes that would please a king on a moment's notice.

The soups—a light asparagus with a touch of cream; oxtail in rich broth; and a cold cucumber with white wine—came out well. Heavenly, in fact. I tasted each, as did Mrs. Martin, and we sent them up without a qualm.

Next the fish—turbot with shrimp sauce, which was shrimp chopped up and simmered in butter with a bit of cayenne, poured over the poached turbot. We sent salmon up as well, a huge specimen sliced into filets in hopes there would be enough. This we dressed with a sauce of dill, butter, and mushrooms.

For the meats, I showed both Mrs. Martin and Tess a spice mixture that could be kept for a long time and used to season meats or rub fowl—a mixture of cloves, mace, cayenne, dried ginger, cinnamon, black and white peppercorns, and nutmeg. I had Tess grind all these with mortar and pestle until they were a fine powder. I sprinkled this over the beef chops as they came out of the frying pan, readying them to be sent up after the fish.

The crowning glory of the meal was the rib roast, a huge cut of beef, seasoned with my spice mixture, which came out of the oven as the fish was being removed and the chops served. This would be carried upstairs by the footmen and lovingly carved by the butler.

The butler himself was currently running up and down, bottles under his arms, cursing as roundly as Mr. Davis ever did at having to find so many choice wines on so short a notice. I would have to explain to Lady Cynthia what a strain Clemmie Godfrey had put on her staff for this supper.

With the roast, which mercifully stayed on its platter, went ham and a pie of veal, and then vegetables—more asparagus; early cabbage sprinkled with lemon juice; a salad of parsley dressed with lemon and oil, salt and pepper; and a dish of stewed mushrooms.

At last we sent up the puddings—rhubarb tart, a few cheesecakes, iced cream, and simple bread and butter pudding. After all this went cheese and sliced fruit, and then we were finished.

Mrs. Martin collapsed into a chair as the dumb-waiter creaked upward for the last time. "This has ended me," she said. "I'll be off to live with me sister in the Lake District, you mark my words. I'm much too old for this sort of nonsense. Mrs. Holloway, you aren't looking for a new place, are you?"

Mrs. Martin gave me a hopeful look, but I shook my head. "I am happy where I am for now." Mrs. Bywater might be a bit tightfisted but she was not unreasonable. Cynthia was there to mitigate for me, and I had my days out. I didn't mind a quiet household.

It was nine o'clock, dark now. Whenever the door at the top of the stairs opened to the main house, we heard waves of merriment from the guests. At least they were enjoying themselves.

Lady Cynthia had indeed come—I knew because I asked one of the footmen who was running back and forth from dining room to kitchen to tell me if she was there. Mr. Thanos had been invited too, a fact that I found quite interesting.

Tess was elated by our success. "We did it!" she cried. She embraced me, and I did not stop her. I rather enjoyed her youthful enthusiasm, her warm body crashing into mine as Grace's did. Tess, like Grace, didn't do anything by halves.

We left Mrs. Martin recovering and the rest of the staff busily eating anything leftover. As we walked from the house, Tess's basket now full of rhubarb pie, asparagus, parsley salad, and a small jar of my spice mixture, she breathed a sigh.

"It's for nothing though, ain't it?" she asked. "We did all that work, and we won't get paid for any of it. A few comestibles to take home ain't much—we made all this ourselves anyway."

"Not for nothing," I told her. "We helped a fellow body in need, and Mrs. Martin won't forget it. When the guests praise the cooking, and all learn that Mrs. Holloway and her assistant, Tess, were there to lend a hand, our reputations will gain a boost. And Mrs. Martin will be grateful and help us in return whenever we might need it—whether that is with her hands in our kitchen or recommending you when you're ready to venture out as a cook in your own right. Sharing skills and time is never a waste. It's putting the Golden Rule to practical use."

"Golden Rule . . . Which one is that?"

I hid a sigh. Reformers and temperance women roved up and down London admonishing girls like Tess, but did they pause to give them the simplest of lessons? And these ladies called themselves religious—they ought to be ashamed.

"The Golden Rule is, more or less, 'Do unto others as you would have them do unto you,'" I said. "It is a good saying to live by, no matter if you never go to church."

Tess considered my words. "You mean if I want people to be kind to me, I have to be kind to them first?"

"Of course. We must help one another in this world, because it is a difficult place. Too difficult for us all to be selfish. It is also fine to ask for help—we should not be too proud to admit when we need it."

I emphasized my last words, hoping Tess would break down and tell me for whom she was stealing food from my larder. If Tess were indeed stealing it, I reminded myself. Charlie, for instance, was always the first one down in the mornings, would have time alone in the larder, and he was a bright little chap. He'd likely be able to hide his misdeeds.

There was also the possibility that the open door and the food gone from the larder had nothing to do with each other. I tamped down my impatience. I so hated not knowing the answer to a puzzlement.

Thinking of puzzlements, I also wished I'd been able to speak to Lady Cynthia about what she, Mr. Thanos, and Daniel had discussed at the Bedford Square pub last night, but our busy day and evening had precluded it. I'd have to corner her discreetly tomorrow and ask, making sure Mrs. Bywater did not spy us speaking too familiarly, of course.

Tess didn't seem to notice my hint that she tell me all. She only looked up at the dark sky as though she could see stars, a rare occurrence in cloudy, foggy, smoky London. She said nothing at all as she followed me along Park Lane to Mount Street, and so home.

I was awakened a few hours later from a sound sleep in pitch darkness by a thumping on my bedchamber door. I blinked a moment, coming out of a dream in which Daniel, James, and my daughter were laughing about something. The vision was sweet, and I did not want to let it go.

The dream died to chill darkness and more pounding. Without bothering to fumble for a candle, I rolled out of bed, snatched my flannel dressing gown from the chair, thrust my feet into slippers, and shuffled to the door.

I expected Tess or one of the maids, but I found Lady Cynthia, clad in an evening dress of gray silk with a black beaded shawl over her bare arms. The beautiful gown was a sharp contrast to her face, lit by the candle she held, which was drawn and almost green, her eyes full of fear.

When I opened the door, Cynthia pushed me into the room. I caught myself before I stumbled, and shut the door behind her.

"What is it?" I asked in a whisper. "What's happened?"

Cynthia's eyes were wide, their light blue nearly swallowed by the black of her pupils.

"Oh, Mrs. H., it's awful," she said, her voice a croak. "A man is dead, Clemmie is ill, and so is Mr. Thanos. At Sir Evan's. The police have come, and Mrs. Martin might face the noose for it."

20

"What on earth are you talking about?" I took the chamber stick from Lady Cynthia's shaking hand and set it on my bedside table. "Sit down. Tell me."

"We can't linger," Cynthia argued, even as she collapsed into my chair as though her legs would no longer support her. "It might take Mr. Thanos off too. And Clemmie."

"What might? A fever?" I touched my hand to Lady Cynthia's forehead. Fevers could come on suddenly, and people died, and no one quite knew why. Cynthia felt normal, but contagion did not obey neat patterns.

Cynthia brushed my hand aside. "No, not a fever," she said impatiently. "The mushrooms."

I drew back, confusion replacing my fears. "Mushrooms? What mushrooms?"

"The ones Mrs. Martin served for Clemmie's supper. We all ate them—well, I didn't . . . I don't much care for them. Clemmie enjoyed a jolly good helping, as did Mr. Thanos, and no one ate more than Mr. Harmon. And now he's dead."

"Harmon?" I asked. "Who is Mr.—?" I vaguely remembered Clemmie mentioning him on our visit to her. "Sir Evan's man of business?"

"Yes, yes," Cynthia said. "That's the chap.

Sir Evan confessed to Clemmie that he sold the paintings at Mr. Harmon's request, she told me tonight. Apparently, he owed Harmon a powerful lot of money for business transactions Harmon conducted in his name."

"And now Mr. Harmon is dead." Very convenient. My indignation at Sir Evan grew, along with my fears.

"I'm so very worried about Mr. Thanos," Cynthia said, clenching her hands. "You must know about poisonous food—can you help him?"

"There was nothing at all wrong with those mushrooms," I declared. "I prepared them myself."

Cynthia regarded me with confusion in her red-rimmed eyes. "Yourself? *You* cooked for Clemmie's supper party?"

"I was downstairs in her kitchen, helping Mrs. Martin, because your friend Lady Godfrey expected the poor woman to throw together a meal for two score of people in a few hours. I made the stewed mushrooms, and I know there wasn't a wrong one in the pan. Good heavens, they want to arrest Mrs. Martin for it?"

I flung open the chest at the foot of the bed and rummaged for clean combinations, stockings, and my corset. I thrust my legs into the lower half of the combinations, turning my back to throw off my nightgown and slide the top of the combinations on over my shoulders. My corset went over this.

"Will you lace me? Or shall I call Tess?"

"I'm no prude." Cynthia was on her feet with her usual restlessness, grabbing my laces and threading them through the holes with skill. "I have to lace my fellow ladies when they are done being gentlemen and before they toddle home to their husbands or fathers or brothers. Some daren't even tell their maids, and so Bobby and I have learned to be quite the abigails." She jerked the laces tight, and I gasped a breath, but Cynthia finished and let me go.

Cynthia paced as I tied on my petticoat and then my skirt, finally buttoning my bodice overall. My hair was a mess, but I wound my braid around my head and pinned it the best I could.

Lady Cynthia snatched up the candle and was flying out of the room so rapidly once I had my shoes on and fastened that she nearly caught her clothes on fire with the flame. I firmly took the candle away from her and herded her before me.

We climbed down the back stairs the many flights to the main hall, then through the green baize door and on down to a dark and silent kitchen. I fetched my coat and bonnet, and then we were outside in the cool spring night. I worried for Cynthia, who had no wraps but the thin shawl suited for a heated parlor, but she only hurried down the street on foot, heading for Park Lane.

She must have run all the way home, I realized. No hansom cab was in sight, nor was the town coach. Cynthia planned to run all the way back, it seemed. I jogged to keep up with her.

The roads were quieter than in daytime but people still roamed—beggars looking for kitchen scraps, pickpockets watching for the unwary, ladies bold enough to walk through respectable neighborhoods. I'm certain other villains lurked in the shadows as well. We moved so swiftly that I doubted any villain would be able to catch us.

Sir Evan's house was lit from top to bottom. Carriages lined the drive, and constables were trying to shepherd the ladies and gentlemen milling about the grounds back into the house. Those ladies and gentlemen wanted to leave, and protested loudly.

Cynthia ignored them all, ducking past the constables and through the house's front door.

Inside was pandemonium. More constables swarmed in and out of the dining room, and a maid sat on a side chair there, weeping. The door to the back stairs slammed open to disgorge a harried footman, and I heard raised voices below, querulous and panicked.

I knew I needed to go down to Mrs. Martin, but I was more worried about Mr. Thanos. Lady Cynthia rushed up the main stairs ahead of me, her skirts bunched in her hands to show an unladylike amount of calf.

I followed Cynthia to the second floor and then along a gallery that wrapped around the lower floors. Halfway around this she opened the door to a bedroom with a lofty ceiling and windows that looked out to the front drive.

Mr. Thanos lay in a bed the size of a small barge. The head and footboards were heavily carved, matching the night tables on either side of the bed and the clothes cupboard against the wall. Mr. Thanos was propped up on pillows and covered in quilts, his face as pale as the sheets. From his white face, his dark eyes burned, and his unshaved whiskers stood out in black shadow.

"I've brought Mrs. Holloway," Lady Cynthia said in a tone of forced cheer.

Mr. Thanos struggled to sit up, but I went straight to him and prevented him with an admonishing hand. "You stay right where you are, Mr. Thanos. What have they given you as an antidote?"

Elgin blinked, his eyes unfocused without his spectacles. "A doctor fellow fed me ipecac. It was disgusting." He sank back with a groan. "But possibly saved my life."

"Well, they must decide what noxious substance you ingested before they give you anything else," I said. "They are blaming the mushrooms, but I assure you . . ."

"Nothing wrong with the mushrooms," Mr. Thanos said in a wheezing voice. "Very tasty."

"Taste is no assurance," I said. "I have heard that death caps are quite delicious. What happened?"

Lady Cynthia answered before Mr. Thanos could draw another labored breath. "Nothing," she said. "One moment, everyone was right as rain, the next, they were dropping. We'd finished supper hours before, and were playing ridiculous parlor games—at least some of us were. I was trying to have an intelligent conversation with Mr. Thanos and a professor, and several of the younger people were sneaking out to the garden for a bit of spooning."

Elgin nodded. "I was discussing Maxwell's ideas on electromagnetism with a fellow—we were arguing about the necessitation of the luminiferous aether. I think there is a good chance Maxwell is wrong about it, though he has advanced the understanding of light and waves in a monumental fashion . . ."

"Never mind about all that," Cynthia said impatiently. "Tell her how you became sick."

"Oh yes. Well, I began to have the most awful cramps in my stomach. I downed a glass of brandy, hoping to mitigate them, but they only grew worse. I was trying to explain that if the aether existed, surely we could see or feel it in some way, at least by some scientific means, and the other fellow said that was nonsense—a wave needs some medium to travel through, doesn't it? Even if we can't perceive it . . ."

"Elgin," Cynthia said, and Mr. Thanos coughed then flushed.

"I do beg your pardon," he said breathlessly.

He seemed not to note that Cynthia had called him by his Christian name, something no lady would do with a gentleman before they were engaged or at least had the understanding of one. Cynthia did not seem to note it either, so I said nothing.

I confess I was pleased to hear Mr. Thanos go off on his tangents, chasing whatever thought interested him. If Mr. Thanos had been terribly ill, he would have lain in a stupor, not grown animated at arguments about the aether.

"What happened then, Mr. Thanos?" I asked as gently as I could.

"I became very dizzy from the pain and had to sit down. At the same time, I heard a shout, and a gentleman was trying to hold up Lady Godfrey. And then that Mr. Harmon—an unctuous gentleman, I must say—fell to the ground. He had the most awful convulsions and started to vomit right there on the carpet. Ladies were screaming, Sir Evan shouting for his servants, his language unfortunate. And then Mr. Harmon expired. I was terrified I would too. But Lady Cynthia had me by the elbow and ordered a couple of footmen to get me to a bed. The butler rushed out for a doctor. And here I am."

Mr. Thanos trailed off, his voice weak. His hands moved restlessly on the quilt, the loose nightshirt someone had put on him too large for him.

"We will get you better," I said, trying to sound reassuring.

I doubted very much anything had been wrong with the mushrooms, though I knew that if there had been, mushroom poisoning was no joke. A person could be perfectly fine after eating poisonous mushrooms, even seem to recover, only to fall dead in a few days' time. A cook had to be very careful when choosing them.

But I knew in my bones the mushrooms had been all right. In that case, I needed to discover exactly what had poisoned Mr. Thanos so we could get him better.

A commotion rose in the gallery, and the imperious voice of the housekeeper came to us: "What do you think you're about? You leave this house at once before I have a constable take you to jail. No, you may *not* go in there . . ."

The door to Elgin's bedchamber swung abruptly open, and Daniel strode inside, his expression thunderous. The housekeeper rushed in after him but halted when she saw Lady Cynthia. "I beg your pardon, my lady," she said, flushed and flustered. "I do not know how this person got past the police . . ."

Elgin again tried to sit up. "No cause for alarm, dear lady. McAdam is a friend. How are you, old chap?"

The housekeeper's outrage did not fade. She glanced at Lady Cynthia for confirmation, who sent her a reassuring nod. The woman regarded us disapprovingly but departed.

I could not blame the housekeeper for being outraged—the poor woman must be at her wits' end with all this mess. If the food was blamed, the housekeeper might be held liable as well as the cook, as it was her job to see that the correct produce was purchased.

"How am *I?*" Daniel asked Elgin in his robust voice as Elgin reached for and wrung Daniel's hand. "How are *you?* What the devil happened?"

"Well." Elgin cleared his throat. "I was discussing Maxwell's theories of electromagnetism, and how his equations might be simplified . . ."

"Good Lord," Cynthia muttered.

"Fascinating," Daniel said, keeping hold of Elgin's hand. "If anyone can shed light on that, it's you. But I'm more interested in *your* inner workings, lad."

"Oh yes. Well, as I was telling the ladies . . ."

As Elgin launched into the story again, I pulled Cynthia aside. "I'm off to the kitchens to make sense of this. Please do not let any of the policemen arrest Mrs. Martin—I'm sure she is not to blame. How is Lady Godfrey?"

"About the same as Mr. Thanos," Cynthia said. "Taken ill, given a purge by the doctor, and weak as a kitten."

"Keep an eye on her," I advised in a low voice. "Poisoning is no light matter. I will stake my reputation that there was nothing wrong with the food. That means, don't you see, that the poison was administered above stairs. Perhaps when the food was served at table, or slipped into the wine, or some such thing."

"Good Lord." Cynthia's eyes went wide. "That means any of us could have dropped dead."

"Exactly. Eat or drink nothing, and make sure no one gives Lady Godfrey anything that I have not looked at. It might have been Lady Godfrey who was the intended victim."

Cynthia's astonishment turned quickly to anger. "You mean Evan, that little toad, might have tried to kill her? I see. If she falls ill and dies, she can cause no scandal for him—the world will have more sympathy for him too. The ass."

"Yes—look after her."

Rage sparkled in Cynthia's eyes. "Right." She rushed past me, her silk skirts rustling as she headed down the gallery. "You there," she called out to a maid. "Are you taking that to Lady Godfrey? Stop, I say."

Elgin was speaking rapidly and earnestly to Daniel at the bed, and Daniel nodded at him—I hoped some of Elgin's words were about the incident. I knew I left him in safe hands, so I hurried after Lady Cynthia.

Cynthia had halted a startled maid before she could enter Lady Godfrey's chamber with a tray holding water and brandy. I sniffed both the brandy and the water, and tasted a little of each on the tip of my finger. When I nodded that all was well, Lady Cynthia took the tray herself and carried it into her friend's bedchamber. Leaving her to it, I hastened to the back stairs and thence to the kitchen.

I found Mrs. Martin in hysterics, as I knew I would. She sat on a kitchen chair, her face buried in her apron, her wails filling the room. The rest of the staff who were present had drawn away from her and the man facing her, none other than Detective Inspector McGregor from Scotland Yard.

McGregor's yellow mustache quivered and his hazel eyes sparkled in triumph. "Mistakes are made, Mrs. Martin," he said in a hard voice, "and you must answer for them."

"I never." Those were the only coherent words from behind Mrs. Martin's apron. "Never."

I strode forward, noting as I did so that Tess, dressed with my shawl over her rumpled gown, stood with the house's servants near the door leading outside. I wondered why she'd followed me, but questioning her would have to wait.

"Stop this at once," I shouted at McGregor, the only way to be heard over Mrs. Martin. "She did nothing. The meal was not to blame."

Detective McGregor jerked his attention to me, and the look of pure fury he shot me made me take a step back. This was a dangerous man, I realized, and ruthless, ready to let nothing stop him.

"How do you know that, Mrs. Holloway?" he demanded.

"Because I was here." Might as well stick my head into the lion's mouth. "I made most of the meal in question, and there was no harm in it. You should be looking for the culprit *above* stairs, not below."

21

I thought Inspector McGregor would arrest me on the spot. His eyes blazed, and his mouth tightened.

Then I watched a new expression come over him. Determination did not leave him, but I saw him decide to be careful, to not be led by his anger. I had to commend him for that as much as it meant he now chose to direct his intensity toward me.

"Sit there, Mrs. Holloway." He pointed a blunt finger at a ladder-backed chair. "Tell me exactly how you can be so certain the food at last night's supper did not kill one man and send two other people to their beds."

Out of the corner of my eye, I saw Tess approach. She looked worried but more angry than afraid.

"Because I am a very conscientious cook," I answered McGregor. "And have quite a lot of experience. I know how to tell a bad bit of fish from good, when cream is beginning to turn, and when vegetables are past saving. And I would certainly never send a pan full of poisonous mushrooms to a table. If I did it out of carelessness, I would lose my post and never gain another. If I did it on purpose—well, suspicion falls first on the cook, doesn't it? That would hardly be discreet of me."

McGregor studied me as he had when he'd interrogated me in the Mount Street house—as though surprised I could form a cogent argument. He would no doubt be stunned that I knew the word *cogent*.

"The fact of the matter, Mrs. Holloway," he said in a hard voice, "is that the guests ate, and the guests took sick."

"And I am telling *you,* Inspector McGregor, that they did not take sick from the food. It was thoroughly cooked, or as in the case of the parsley salad, thoroughly washed. I picked over those mushrooms myself."

"I saw her." Tess chose that moment to step next to me, her head high. "I watched her do it. She threw out a few. I asked her why. She said they were too shriveled to be pretty in the dish."

"Oh yes?" McGregor fixed a fierce gaze on Tess. "And what did she do with these discarded few?"

"She didn't do nothing with 'em," Tess said stoutly. "I did."

The inspector's scrutiny sharpened. "And what did *you* do, my girl?"

"Et 'em, didn't I?" Tess looked him in the eye. "And there's nofink wrong with me, is there? In fact, I helped myself to a spoonful of everything that went up." She flashed me a guilty glance. "I know it weren't right, Mrs. H., but I was powerful hungry, and I guessed we wouldn't be going home for hours."

"Tess," I said in quiet admonishment, but relief crept through me. I'd seen her sneaking a few mouthfuls here and there, but I'd not realized she'd eaten of every dish.

She had McGregor's full attention now. "Did you?" he snarled. "Would you be prepared to swear to that in court?"

Tess jumped and her face lost color, but she stuck out her chin. "Don't never want to see the inside of a courtroom, that's a fact. But yeah, I'd swear to it. A Bible oath. Weren't just me doing the tasting. Mrs. Holloway had a nip of things, and so did Mrs. Martin. And I saw plenty of the staff nabbing bits. Stands to reason—all that food around and us having to wait for our supper. 'Course we're going to take some."

I broke firmly through her babbling. "She makes a good point. All cooks and assistants taste dishes to make sure they turned out well. If we put salt in the crumble instead of sugar, we would want to know before it goes to table. Has anyone from below stairs taken sick?" I made a show of scanning the staff who stood inside the kitchen. "They all look right as rain to me."

McGregor growled. The sound rumbled up through his throat, beginning under his lopsided waistcoat. Small wonder he had no woman in his life if he made those appalling noises.

"No one told me the food had been eaten below stairs."

Anger and frustration poured from him. Mrs. Martin lifted her tearstained face and sniffled. "They didn't ask, sir."

McGregor ignored her. It occurred to me that he was not referring to the staff when he said *no one,* but to his colleagues. He'd been sent down to interview the servants without any preparation, it seemed, which I agreed was hardly fair.

My speculation was confirmed when a much younger man in a plain suit scuttled into the room and bent to McGregor. I'm certain he meant to keep his voice down, but we all heard his words.

"You're wanted upstairs, sir. And he ain't happy."

McGregor's cheeks went an interesting shade of pink, but his reply was steady. "All right, Detective Constable. Stay here and take statements, will you?"

The constable gulped, unhappy. "Yes, sir."

McGregor, without a word to the rest of us, rose from his seat and trundled out. I whispered to Tess, "Stay here. Tell me what happens," and went quickly up the stairs after Inspector McGregor.

The upper rooms were filled with people. Ladies in finery, gentlemen in black suits, all restless, all annoyed. A few had sat down to a game of cards, as though determined to enjoy themselves if they were forced to stay. The others paced, sat and complained to one another, or clustered around a tall man with graying hair and mustache who had clearly just arrived.

I recognized Chief Inspector Moss. He was trying to soothe the feathers of the aristocrats, who were very angry that they'd been detained. When he saw McGregor, Moss scowled and made his way to him, beckoning McGregor to follow him into an anteroom, where they could speak out of earshot of the ladies and gentlemen. Neither noticed me lingering to listen.

"These people aren't rabble in the streets," Chief Inspector Moss said sharply. "Let them go home, and we'll send you and your sergeant around to take their statements tomorrow. They had nothing to do with their friends' illnesses."

"Beg pardon, sir, but we don't know that," McGregor answered. "Those in the kitchen say it couldn't be the meal. Which means we need to look at the wine, or any way the dishes or glasses could be tampered with after they were sent up. That means the butler, the footmen who served, or the guests. Any of them could have a vial of poison on them, sweet as you please, and you're about to let the culprit walk away and throw it down his cistern."

Moss's scowl deepened. "You have a lot to learn, McGregor, about how you treat the upper classes. They're likely best mates with the commissioners; their fathers are probably firmly ensconced in the Home Office. You are jeopardizing your job—and mine. Let them go. If one's a poisoner, he'll give himself away eventually, and we'll have him. But penning them all up and interrogating them isn't done. You have to be wise about it, handle them with kid gloves."

Moss turned away, a dismissal, and put on an air of conciliation as he made his way back to the parlor.

McGregor's expression turned to one of pure hatred as he watched Moss go. Rage so dark I feared McGregor would find a weapon and have at him.

I scurried into another room as McGregor stormed from the anteroom, not wanting him to direct all that anger toward *me*. He strode past the doorway through which I'd ducked, the breeze of his passage touching me, but he didn't notice me. He growled at the constables in his path, barking orders to find the coats and wraps of the guests and search them.

I hardly thought they'd find anything—any guest who'd brought in poison wouldn't have had the opportunity to stow the now-empty bottle in his greatcoat, which would have been taken away by maids for safekeeping below stairs. If *I'd* smuggled in poison, I'd have left the bottle or vial or box somewhere it wouldn't be noticed, like on the rubbish heap, or I'd have already dropped it down Sir Evan's cistern.

I avoided constables and guests by heading up the back stairs. I went not to Mr. Thanos's room but to Clemmie's boudoir and bedchamber, where I'd spoken to her on my visit to the house last week.

The room was empty of all but Lady Cynthia, who sat in a chair beside Clemmie's bed. Clemmie appeared much as Mr. Thanos did, her face waxen and a bit yellow, her breathing shallow, her hand pressing her stomach whenever a cramp took her.

Cynthia bathed Clemmie's cheeks and forehead with a damp cloth, pity in her eyes.

"How is she?" I asked softly as I approached the bed.

"Not well, poor thing." Cynthia's tone was absent its usual cynicism. "If Evan did this, I'll kill him."

"I don't think she was meant to take ill," I said. "Or Mr. Thanos. They were innocent bystanders, I believe."

"Humph, well, her husband isn't in here holding her hand, is he? No, he's down trying to keep the crowd from lynching the policemen. His reputation and hospitality are more important than his wife."

To be fair, he and his wife had recently become estranged, Clemmie finding refuge in a lover.

Where was this lover? I wondered. Or did he even know his beloved was ill? I did not at all approve of husbands and wives who betrayed their marriage vows, but I was wise enough to know that the heart does what the heart does. I would have to find out who this gentleman was and send him word. Perhaps he truly loved Clemmie and would help her get away from her monster of a husband. It would ruin her, but I did not believe in imprisoning a wife with a husband who made her miserable.

"Poor little thing." Cynthia dabbed Clemmie's forehead. "I should have run Evan down with my rig when he first proposed to her. Saved her a lot of bother."

"Hurting people is not always the best answer," I pointed out.

Cynthia rose to rinse the cloth in the basin. I gave Clemmie's limp hand a gentle squeeze then joined Cynthia. The washbasin was an elegant piece of furniture, tall on graceful legs, with a porcelain bowl fitted into a round opening, and a mirror above it. The mirror was fixed between two posts so it could be swiveled up and down. The dressing table next to the washbasin had the same tapered legs and burnished wood, the mirror's frame carved with flowers and leaves.

"A hearty smack is what Evan needs," Cynthia said decidedly. "Most men do. You wouldn't be quite so gentle if you knew what they get up to when they're not around ladies. Bobby can pass easily for a man, but I can only sneak into clubs where the gentlemen are so drunk they don't notice they're sitting next to a woman. They see trousers and a waistcoat and don't bother to look into my face or under my hat. What they say about women when they're in that state, especially their own wives, is disgusting. They see women as nothing more than places to stick their wicks, if you'll pardon my frankness. Put on this earth to spread our legs to give men pleasure or heirs, whichever they want. Otherwise, we are to keep quiet and out of sight until we're called for. Any woman who denies a man deserves what she gets, they state. Bobby laughs at them and goes along with it, but it's all I can do to keep still so I won't give the show away. They all need a kick up the backside, I vow to you."

I did not disagree. Gentlemen had been given far too much power in this world of ours, and it had quite gone to their heads. But I had also learned that while this was true, all people, women and men both, had individual personalities, and it wasn't fair to lump any under one description.

"Not all gents are horrible," I said. "You see the ones who band together in these appalling clubs, where they feel free to drink themselves insensible. Perhaps many of them, like Bobby, simply go along with what their friends say. I have never heard Mr. Thanos speak a bad word about a lady."

"True," Cynthia acknowledged. She wrung out

the cloth, spattering her silk gown with dark droplets. "Not that I've ever seen him in his cups. McAdam is deferential enough as well, but again, when he's inebriated, he might spin a different tale."

I could not disagree—I'd never seen Daniel drunk. He'd grown up rough, but . . .

My thoughts trailed off as I caught sight of several items on the dressing table. One was a hair receiver—a round box where strands of hair from a lady's hairbrush were stored so they could be used to pad out the hair when styled. Next to that was a powder box. Respectable ladies didn't use powder or any sort of cosmetics—but only in theory. In reality, a pale complexion was much desired, and ladies resorted to all sorts of trickery.

It was not the sight of these symbols of vanity that caught my eye, but the style of the boxes. Fat cherubs in gauzy robes danced around a too-blue sky, while ladies below enjoyed tea, their smiles too wide and tooth filled. The boxes both had curlicues with gold and silver gilding on the rims and handles.

I stared at them in shock, knowing I'd seen a box that exactly matched this set not very long ago.

Cynthia caught my gaze. "Hideous, aren't they? But expensive. Ridiculously so."

"Where did Lady Godfrey obtain them?" I asked, my heart beating faster.

"Shop in the Burlington Arcade. They had much more tasteful pieces, but Clemmie wanted these—an artist she likes painted them. Seems to me there was another box." Cynthia glanced about the table then shrugged. "She must have put it somewhere else or already broken the thing."

"A box about this big?" I asked, holding my hands in the approximation of a foot in length and then six inches wide.

"Yes. How the devil did you know that?"

"I saw it somewhere." I bit the inside of my mouth to keep from blurting out my speculations. Finding a similar box in a pawnbrokers did not mean Clemmie's had ended up there. The shop in the Burlington Arcade might have sold many of them, and perhaps one had made its way to the pawnbrokers in the Strand. Or Clemmie might have pawned hers, or had a maid do it for her, in her search for money to pay her gambling debts.

I doubted, however, that the box would have brought in enough to pay the thousands a lady could lose at whist. Clemmie had always gone to her husband for assistance with her debts, and then when he refused her, she'd turned to her lover. Cynthia had never indicated she'd tried to sell anything herself, and a lady would most likely pawn her jewelry, not a curio box.

So how had the box ended up at the table in Daniel's pawnbrokers shop?

"Will you excuse me, my lady?" I asked, not waiting for her answer before I headed to the door.

"Of course," Cynthia said behind me. "Provided you come back and tell me what is going on in that head of yours. You've had an idea, haven't you?"

I turned back. "I am not certain. But do guard Lady Godfrey. If she wakes up, she might be in danger."

As could Mr. Thanos be. I slipped away while Cynthia sent me a worried look, and I hastened through the house to the spare bedchamber where Mr. Thanos lay.

I let out a breath of relief when I saw Daniel still with him. Daniel sat beside the bed, his feet in their scarred work boots planted firmly on the carpet. He had his elbows on his knees and his head resting on his fists, every line of his body betraying both concern and self-chastisement.

I knew he believed it his fault Mr. Thanos lay here in a near stupor. But if I was right, Mr. Thanos's poisoning had nothing to do with guests stealing objects from collections of antiquities during the supper parties in Park Lane. Guests hadn't committed those thefts. I'd been correct all along that the answer to *that* particular puzzle lay below stairs.

I closed the door softly and moved to the bed. Mr. Thanos appeared to be asleep, his pallor as wan as Clemmie's.

"Daniel," I whispered.

He didn't start—he'd have heard me come in. Daniel was a man ever aware of his surroundings.

He lifted his head. "I'd like you to go home, Kat," he said, eyes somber. "It isn't safe here."

For answer, I dragged a chair next to his and sat down. "I am certainly not going to eat or drink anything in this house until we discover how the poison was administered. But I believe I am safe for now. It is Sir Evan's wife I fear for. She knows too many of her husband's secrets."

Daniel gave me a level look. "You think Sir Evan is the poisoner?"

"I do. He owed much to the man who died. Very convenient, is it not?"

"That does not mean Sir Evan no longer owes the money," Daniel pointed out. "Someone will inherit the debt, or Sir Evan will still owe the firm Mr. Harmon worked for."

"Sir Evan might not have thought of that," I said, undeterred. "I believe all of this happened because Sir Evan Godfrey is a mad collector who ran out of money, or at least of enough money for his passion."

Daniel listened, mystified, but he nodded. "You might be right. My thoughts were running along a different line, but that is not to say you are wrong."

"What line? You ought to tell me all you're thinking, Daniel, so we are not at cross purposes."

Daniel's smile flickered, his grim and guilty expression fading. "Stealing to order. Someone wants something, he summons a thief, and it is obtained."

"Not fanatics who wish antiquities returned to Greece?"

Daniel glanced at Elgin. "Thanos told me the idea he and Lady Cynthia came up with when we met up in the pub. They might not be wrong either—but I am thinking that a group of fanatics is simply but one of many customers."

"Of a gang, you mean."

"I mean just that. I think we can haul in the henchmen if I can put my hands on Varley or this fellow Pilcher, but it's the ringleader we'll want."

I listened quietly. "You want it to be this Mr. Naismith, don't you?"

Daniel's eyes held a determined light. "It is exactly the sort of thing he would do."

"This man of business, Mr. Harmon, might very well have been the leader, you know. And Sir Evan murdered him to keep from having to pay him. You should have Sir Evan arrested and questioned."

"The very thought has occurred to me." Daniel's grin flashed. "But one must be careful arresting a prominent man like Sir Evan, who has many high-placed friends."

"Have Chief Inspector Moss do it," I said. "Mr. McGregor will only get into trouble."

"Sage advice."

I studied the sparkle in his eyes, which covered a hard anger. "You have already decided to do so, I see," I said in irritation. "You ought to tell me these things before you laugh at me. I—"

Mr. Thanos woke with a gasp. His eyes flew open, too dark in his overly pale face. He gazed at us sitting at his bedside, parted his cracked lips, and croaked, "Mummy!"

Daniel's hand went to Elgin's restless one. "Easy, my dear chap. It's Kat. As lovely as she is, she's not your mum."

Elgin studied Daniel in confusion that quickly dissolved to scorn. "Not that sort of mummy, you dolt. An actual one. Or the essence of. Curative properties. That's what's poisoned us. Bloody hell, how asinine am I? Oh . . . beg your pardon, Mrs. Holloway. As I say, my language can be so very unfortunate."

22

Daniel leaned to him. "Thanos, cease your babbling and tell us what the devil you mean."

Mr. Thanos had run out of breath. He lay back, wheezing, waving his hand as Daniel offered to fetch him water.

"No, no. Good Lord." Elgin coughed, swallowed, and coughed again. "I was a fool. Serves me right." He pressed his stomach, eyes closing. "No, I did not anticipate this. Nor did I deserve it, really. Arsenical salts, I believe."

"From your color and your symptoms, I agree," Daniel said. "That is why I sent a footman running for charcoal."

"That doesn't always work, you know," Elgin said weakly.

"I don't give a damn," Daniel growled. "I will take the chance and pump it down you as well as various other liquids. How much did you ingest?"

I was on my feet, hurrying to the washbasin, as the two debated behind me.

"Very little," Elgin said. "I only had a taste, you see, as did Lady Godfrey. Harmon downed a whole dose, which is why he's already dead, poor chap."

I rinsed out a cloth and returned with it to dab Elgin's sweating face. "Do you mean to tell me you tasted *arsenic?*" I demanded. "Why? For the fun of it?"

Elgin relaxed under my touch, his breathing easing. "Good heavens, no, dear lady. I had no idea it was arsenic. I thought it was mummy powder."

"Mummy powder," I repeated. I remembered something Mrs. Hemming, my friend the house-keeper, had said about Sir Evan . . . *a brilliant painting by an old master isn't as important to him as a bit of powdered mummy in a jar.*

"Sir Evan gave it to you?" I asked. "Whatever for?"

"It's a remedy," Elgin said. "A loathsome one, but people have long believed that the ground bones of mummies from the tombs of ancient Egyptians have curative powers. It's all nonsense of course, but I've read many a tome that pre-scribes a bit of ground skull to ease headache. Sympathetic medicine, you know."

"It ought to be harmless," Daniel said.

"Harmless?" I cried. "Rather disgusting, I'd think. Are you saying, Mr. Thanos, that Sir Evan mixed arsenic with the mummy powder and fed it to you and Mr. Harmon?"

"*Someone* did," Elgin said, his voice a scratch. "I'll give Sir Evan the benefit of the doubt and say he may know nothing about it. We were in his collection room, looking over his antiquities—ushabtis, pots, beads, even gold collars and marble statuary—and Mr. Harmon complained

310

of a headache and congestion. No wonder— we'd been out in the garden and all the flowers had made him sneeze. Sir Evan, in jest, said he believed in the mummy remedy and showed him a ceramic jar full of the stuff. Lady Godfrey laughed and said she took a pinch now and then for fun, good for the humors. She took a tiny bit into her mouth, I suppose to show Mr. Harmon it was all right. Mr. Harmon said—why not? And took a jolly large dose with a glass of water. And I, as I am insatiably curious . . ."

"Oh, Mr. Thanos." I pressed the cool cloth to his forehead. "Can't you be curious about noxious substances without *tasting* them?"

"The scientists I know taste their chemical concoctions," Elgin argued. "To see what they've got."

"A very foolish practice," I said with force. "A wonder any of them are still alive."

Elgin let his eyes drift closed. "Ah well. McAdam, if I do not revive, my library is yours. The little funds I have in my accounts can go to James. Do not argue. Mrs. Holloway may take a small legacy for herself. Tell Lady Cynthia . . ." He trailed off and wet his lips. "No, dash it, tell her nothing. Except good-bye."

"Do not be so maudlin, my friend." Daniel stood over him, taking his hand. "I am not about to let you die. Kat, stay with him while I locate this infamous jar of mummy powder."

"No, indeed." I thrust the cloth at Daniel. "I

311

can move through the house less conspicuously than you—I am only the cook come to help Mrs. Martin. The housekeeper has already shouted that she will have *you* arrested if she finds you about. I will fetch the jar, never you worry."

Daniel did not like this, but he had to concede I had a point. Daniel was more likely than I was to be ejected by the constables, but the servants knew me and would explain my presence if any of the police asked.

I leaned down to press a kiss to Mr. Thanos's forehead. He looked as though he needed some affection, poor lad.

"You will get well," I told him. "We will make certain of it. Now, have yourself a good sleep."

I straightened the quilt over him then took myself out of the room before Daniel could change his mind and stop me.

When I reached the ground floor, I saw that Chief Inspector Moss's wishes had prevailed. The guests were leaving. Carriages moved up the drive, and ladies and gentlemen gathered in the front hall, waiting for theirs to appear.

No one paid any attention as I made my way toward the back of the house. Instead of heading for the servants' stairs, I veered into the parlor where Clemmie had showed me where the missing paintings had hung and through to a library beyond, searching for the room where Sir Evan stored his collection.

I found it in a room tucked behind the library, a square box of a chamber whose far doors opened to a conservatory. Dawn light filtered through the conservatory's palm trees, giving me just enough illumination to see what was in the room.

I walked along the shelves and cases, trying not to be distracted by their contents. Sir Evan had labeled his pieces carefully, and I peered at the gold bracelets of an Egyptian princess, red pots with strange but beautiful black figures painted on them from Athens, a tablet with square-looking writing from Asia Minor.

My greatest fear was that Sir Evan had already disposed of the mummy powder. Clemmie and Elgin might realize, when they recovered, that only the two of them and Mr. Harmon had partaken of it last night, and I would think he'd want to rid himself of the evidence.

However, I wondered if Sir Evan had assumed his wayward wife and the eager Mr. Thanos would die as well last night, thus giving him plenty of time to steer the blame from himself. If not for me rushing in and convincing Inspector McGregor to the contrary, Sir Evan could continue to point to the mushrooms as the cause and dispose of the powder at his leisure.

On a shelf near a window, I found several jars of white alabaster, their lids carved into fantastic shapes. One was a monkey, one a cat, and one the mask of an Egyptian man. The label on the last read, *Powder of mummified remains. Obtained in bazaar, Constantinople, March 1869.*

I reached for the jar.

"What are you doing in here, Mrs. Holloway?"

I jumped and whirled around. Inspector McGregor stood just inside the doorway of the conservatory, his arms folded, his eyes glittering in the dim light.

Inspector McGregor—the one person in the house who most certainly would believe I was up to no good. Before he could admonish me, accuse me, or banish me, I snatched up the jar with the powdered mummy and thrust it at him.

"Test this," I said. "The poison that killed Mr. Harmon is most likely in here. Take it!"

McGregor's eyes narrowed even as he wrapped his hands around the jar.

He could have accused me of putting the poison into it myself, but he said nothing. Inspector McGregor only watched me closely as I turned from him and hurried back through the library to the main hall.

I breathed a sigh of relief when I reached the back stairs to climb up to check again on the patients.

Lady Cynthia resolutely stationed herself in Clemmie's chamber and vowed she'd stay until she was better and Sir Evan arrested. So far, Sir Evan had not been taken by the police; in fact,

I hadn't seen him downstairs when I'd gone to search for the powder.

I offered to send for a change of clothes for Cynthia, but she told me not to bother. She'd already ruined the silk gown with water from the cloth she'd wet to wipe Clemmie's face, as well as a few tears she must have obtained in the night's adventures. I had the feeling she'd like to see the beautiful gown on the rag heap.

"I'll fend off Sir Evan," Cynthia said. "See to Mr. Thanos. I am angry that he's come to harm because of my horrible friends—please tell him I shall make it up to him." Cynthia's words were brusque, but the consternation in her eyes was acute.

She was not terribly surprised when I told her about the mummy powder.

"Ha!" she exclaimed. "Clemmie will swallow any potion she thinks will make her complexion better. I'm surprised Sir Evan hasn't attempted to poison her before this. Which makes me conclude she *wasn't* the intended victim, just in the wrong place. Not that Sir Evan tried to stop her or Mr. Thanos taking it, the blasted weasel."

"I suppose he was so determined to kill off Mr. Harmon that he persuaded himself it didn't matter," I said, my anger at Sir Evan surging anew. "You are right that Sir Evan is a bad man, and your friend is better off away from him, never mind the scandal her leaving him will cause."

"Hang the scandal," Cynthia said brightly. "And hang Sir Evan. Clemmie *is* better off without him."

There were places in the world, I had heard, where divorce brought no stigma, but Britain wasn't one of them. Both Clemmie and Sir Evan would be socially marked by divorce, which could harm Sir Evan's career and prevent Clemmie being accepted among polite society or into a new marriage.

I wished it weren't so. A woman should not be made a prisoner in her own household, socially condemned if she escaped her jailor and torturer. There had to be a better lot for us.

I left Cynthia guarding Clemmie and returned to Daniel and Mr. Thanos. I entered the bedchamber to see Daniel and a strapping footman bundling Mr. Thanos into a bath chair—Daniel quickly told me he had made arrangements for Mr. Thanos to be taken to Daniel's rooms, where both he and his landlady could watch over him.

I am certain Lady Cynthia could have asked her uncle to make room for Mr. Thanos in the Mount Street house, as Mr. Bywater seemed taken with him, but I did not suggest it. I wanted Mr. Thanos well away from Mayfair and out of the reach of Sir Evan Godfrey.

Distance from Mayfair hadn't helped the thug who'd been struck down in the pawnbrokers on the Strand, I remembered, but I had other ideas about who'd done that and why.

Daniel himself pushed Elgin in the chair to the head of the staircase, then the footman and Daniel, with me helping, got Elgin and the bath chair downstairs. Daniel sought out and spoke to no one as we went, not McGregor, not Chief Inspector Moss. Outside, Daniel and the footman trundled Elgin into a hansom, the cabbie on the driver's perch one of Daniel's friends. The bath chair remained behind, looking forlorn and empty in the morning sunlight.

Before Daniel climbed in beside Elgin, he leaned down and whispered into my ear.

"Did you find it?"

"Indeed I did," I whispered back. "I gave it to Inspector McGregor."

Daniel started. "McGregor?" I feared for a moment I had made a great blunder, but then his smile blazed out. "Good lass."

Without explaining why he was so pleased with me, Daniel touched his cap and swung into the hansom with Elgin.

The cabbie, Lewis, nodded down at me in greeting and then chirruped to the horses. The hansom darted away, skidding a little on the mud in the drive, then was gone, swallowed in the mists that enshrouded the London morning.

I fetched Tess, and we went home. The police were finished, Mrs. Martin was safe from them, at least for the moment, and I was exhausted.

Tess drooped on the walk to Mount Street, but she held up, not collapsing until we'd reached the kitchen.

"Whew," she exclaimed as she threw herself into a chair. "What a ding-dong. I thought we'd all be in the dock before we knew what was what."

"It was clever of you to tell the inspector you'd tasted all the dishes," I said. "Your robust health has cleared the kitchen of any conspiracy. But it was bad of you to help yourself without asking leave. We always keep food back for the staff's meals—you know that by now."

As I spoke, I rid myself of my outer wraps and tied on my apron. I'd start breakfast and also prepare a basket to take to poor Mr. Thanos. I had no doubt that if anyone could cure him, it would be Daniel, but Elgin would need to regain his strength, and very good food was key.

I worried far more for Clemmie, still in the house with her murdering husband. I had no doubt that Cynthia would guard her like a dragon, but I would feel better when McGregor made his tests on the jar and went back to cart Sir Evan off to Newgate.

"We wasn't in our own kitchen," Tess argued as I fetched a bowl of eggs and side of bacon from the larder. I dropped the bacon to the table and filled a pan of water to set on the stove. "How was I to know whether old Ma Martin would feed us after all the work we did for her? 'Ere." She slid out of the chair and moved in front of me as I took my chef's knife from the drawer. "Are we cooking breakfast *now?* After our night? I was thinking of doing some sleeping first."

"The household is rising, and they will expect their morning repast," I returned calmly. "After which I will do some preparation for the rest of the meals, and then I'm off. It is my day out. You'll be able to have a nap between dinner and supper, and then I'll be back. I can likely manage supper on my own tonight if you want to go up to bed early."

Tess gaped at me, her color rising. "You're still having your day out? Leaving me to it? I have to work while you hole up and sleep?"

"I will not be sleeping, and you will not have much to do," I said as I dodged past her to the table. I began to slice the bacon, its smoky odor filming the air. "We will keep dinner and supper simple—no guests are expected, and with any luck, the master and mistress will decide to go out. Lady Cynthia will remain at her friend's home for a time. I never miss my day out, Tess. That you must learn. Recall that tomorrow is yours. I will guard that time for you as staunchly as I guard mine. We work together, my girl, not against each other. Always remember that."

Tess only stared at me, her brows drawn on her tired face, but at last she nodded, and lifted the bowl of eggs to ladle them carefully into the boiling water.

I was enormously tired, but Tess and I finished the breakfast for the household and the staff and made preparations for the midday meal. Tess ceased complaining and meekly assisted me, though she did not hide her yawns.

As soon as I could, I washed my face and hands, changed my dress, put on my coat and best hat, and went downstairs and out through the scullery. I left Tess regaling Mr. Davis with our adventures of the middle of the night, but I did not linger to put in any word.

I climbed aboard an omnibus in Piccadilly, nodding off as we made our way eastward. The conductor had to nudge me awake when I needed to descend in St. Martin's Lane and change for the Strand.

We rolled past the pawnbrokers, still shut and dark, on past Southampton Street, where Daniel had rooms and had presumably had taken Mr. Thanos, past the bulk of Somerset House and St. Mary le Strand on its little island in the middle of the road, and around the next island of St. Clement Danes.

Again, I had to be prodded to leave my seat at St. Paul's Churchyard, but the tiny naps had refreshed me, as had journeying ever closer to my daughter.

I was fully restored by the time I reached the Millburns' home, and Grace was throwing her arms around me. Her warmth, her kisses on my cheek, her voice flowed through me and took away all the hurt.

I spent a wonderful day with Grace, walking, talking, joining in games and singing with Mrs. Millburn and her four children, culminating with Grace and I having our tea in a shop.

I reluctantly said good-bye, my heart burning with the need to be with my daughter always, though I told myself it was only three and a half days until I could see her again.

I decided to leave the omnibus where Southampton Street intersected the Strand, to walk to Daniel's rooms and visit Mr. Thanos. I hoped to see him improved, but when I knocked on the outer door of the boardinghouse, the landlady, Mrs. Williams, told me she hadn't seen a thing of Daniel for weeks.

I stepped back, stunned, then covered my expression and hastily said I'd taken the chance to look him up. I disliked to ask her where else Daniel might be staying, because if Daniel hadn't told me, Mrs. Williams would conclude he did not wish me to know.

I returned to the Strand to find another omnibus, too tired from my night to walk the rest of the way to Mayfair. Once aboard, I clenched my hands over my reticule and moved from anger to worry back to anger.

I tried to be reasonable—Daniel hadn't said *exactly* where he'd be taking Mr. Thanos, as there had been too many ears close by. He'd only said to his "rooms," and I'd inferred he meant his boardinghouse in Southampton Street. But, I reasoned, others must know of this boardinghouse, and Daniel wished to conceal Elgin to keep him safe. Therefore, Daniel would have taken him elsewhere, to lodgings I did not know about. I remembered visiting Daniel in Southampton Street and reflecting that he had nothing personal in his rooms. I'd concluded that he kept anything personal in another place—I only wished I knew where.

The one person who must know was Lewis the cabbie. Daniel hadn't given him a direction before they started off, so either Lewis had already known where to go, or Daniel had told him once they were out of earshot of Sir Evan's house.

I began to keep my eye out for Lewis as I went, but the chance of me finding one cabbie among the myriad hansoms flowing through London was slim.

My legs were wobbly by the time I left my final omnibus of the day and walked up South Audley Street toward home. I hoped the Bywaters truly would go out so I'd only need to throw together a meal for the staff. I'd go up to bed early—Tess knew by now how to make preparations for the next morning, and I'd let her take her day out as soon as she woke tomorrow.

Shadows were lengthening as I rounded the corner to Mount Street. In one of those shadows, I saw Tess.

She was not alone. She spoke earnestly to a taller man, who was as slim and freckled as she was, his hair the same shade. Tess leaned to him as though admonishing him, at the same time she shoved a cloth-covered basket into his middle.

"Tess!" I called, striding forward.

Tess saw me. Her eyes widening in alarm, she bodily turned the tall man away and gave him a push. "Run!" she shouted at him.

The man sent her a frightened glance and began to shuffle away. Tess whirled around and threw out her arms, blocking my path.

"Let him go, Mrs. H.," she pleaded with me. "He ain't doing anyone no harm."

23

I stood quietly, making no move to go around Tess as the large young man vanished into the crowd.

Passersby halted when Tess cried out, Londoners always ready to round up and sit on a thief. But seeing the two of us facing each other and no one in hot pursuit of a culprit, they hesitated, allowing him to slip away. One passerby in particular, a youth with reddish hair and Daniel's smile, sent me an inquiring glance, but I gave him a minute shake of my head.

"Who was that?" I asked Tess. "Your brother?"

Tess lowered her arms and eyed me uncertainly. "I suppose we look enough alike. He ain't no harm, Mrs. Holloway. He's only hungry."

"So are many. He's old enough to work, isn't he?" The lad wasn't a youth—older than Tess, I guessed.

Tess swallowed, her eyes moist. "He's not much good at it. No one will hire him."

I pulled Tess out of the way of traffic to the railings that separated our house's scullery stairs from the street. "He's the one you were protecting when you made the fuss and got arrested, isn't he? You were willing to stand in the dock for him. Why didn't he come forward? Surely your own brother would have tried to save you."

Tess's eyes were full of pain. "Because they'd hang him, and he knew it. He don't mean to be bad, Mrs. H. But no one understands him."

"You took food from our larder to give to him, so he wouldn't steal it himself," I said, laying out the series of events in my head. "You unbolted the door for him, and I'd guess unlocked it too, unless he picked the lock. After the door was discovered open the first time, we were more careful about the bolt, so you came down and replaced the screws so the bolt would simply fall out." I stepped against the railing as a cart rumbled by too close. "But why would he leave the door open? It announced his presence— shouted that someone had been inside."

Tears beaded on Tess's lashes, and she blinked them away. "Because he's simple. He don't know. He don't steal because he's bad—he steals because he don't understand. I look after him. I'd have come down here and made sure the door was shut, but I was never sure when he'd come, and I never been in beds so soft and warm before. I sleep so hard, no matter how much I try to keep awake or come down early . . ."

"Tess," I began.

"He didn't go through no one's things, I promise. Didn't even come far into the house. I'd leave the basket inside the scullery, under the sink, and he'd come in and fetch it. I didn't want to leave it outside, because then any beggar would have snatched it away, or the cats would get it. He'd pick up the basket and be off. He does what he's told if I tell him right."

"Tess—"

"I'll go. You can take everything I gave him out of me wages. You don't have to give me any wages at all. I'll just go. I'll—"

"Tess, for heaven's sake, cease interrupting me." I had to take a breath when Tess halted mid-flow. "You are not going anywhere. You could have avoided all these dramatics if you'd simply told me your brother needed help. I would have found a way to provide it. You did not tell Daniel about him either, did you? Daniel suspected you were protecting someone, but he never learned who. Whyever didn't you explain, child?"

Tess wiped her nose with the back of her glove. "And have him carted to a workhouse or Bedlam or some other horrible place? No, thank you. He does well enough on his own—only he can't hold a job more than a few days. He gets restless and has to move on. Sometimes whoever hires him gets angry and don't pay him, and so he's done all the work for nothing. The worst is he never notices. He comes to me, and I help him. He knows he can always come to me."

Tears trickled down Tess's cheeks, and her lips trembled.

Without a word, I took her by the arm and

guided her down the steps and into the house.

Below stairs was full of the usual comings and goings of maids and footmen fetching tea or hot water or extra coal. Mr. Davis strode through the passage, admonishing a footman who'd not cleaned a piece of silver up to his standards, but stopped when he saw me.

"I hope you had a fine day out, Mrs. Holloway," he said cheerfully. "The master is at his club tonight, Lady Cynthia is still sitting with her ill friend, and the mistress is off to visit her cronies in an hour or so. House to ourselves tonight. Ain't it grand? Looking forward to tucking into one of your pies, Mrs. H."

"You presume I have rushed home to cook for you, Mr. Davis," I said, keeping my tone light. "You might have to do with a cold supper."

"Cold pie or hot, it will be delicious." Undeterred, Mr. Davis continued on to the butler's pantry, whistling.

I ushered Tess, who was trying to hide her weeping from the others, into the housekeeper's parlor. "Sit," I said, pointing to the Belter chair.

Tess plopped herself down. I shut the door and sat in a chair beside her.

"You should never be afraid to come to me, my dear, no matter what. I gather scraps for the beggars every night—I can keep something back for your brother, which you can hand to him without him having to pick locks or you breaking the bolt. You will have to pay back the equivalent of what you stole, because I can't have a thief in my kitchen, but you can work it off and promise you will never do it again. I do understand, Tess. It is a difficult thing when a woman has to be the head of the family and take care of everyone in it. Trust me to comprehend this."

I wondered whether some of Tess's rage at her father and mother had come from them being cruel to her brother for his slowness. She'd ended up with the burden of taking care of him far too early in her life.

"What is his name?" I asked in gentle voice.

"Robbie." Tess took a handkerchief from her pocket and blew her nose, her hands shaking. "Poor lad."

"I want you to tell Daniel about him," I said. "He'll know what to do."

Tess's eyes widened, and she shook her head. "Oh no. I'm not having me brother locked up in a madhouse. He'd die in there. Don't tell 'im, please, Mrs. Holloway. I'm begging you on my knees."

She did slide from her chair and land with a bang at my feet, desperately clutching at my skirt.

"Don't be so silly," I admonished. "Daniel will do no such thing. I would think that by now you'd realize Daniel is a different sort of man than the usual reformer. He knows what's best for people, and how to help them. He sent you to me, didn't he?"

"I learned never to trust nobody," Tess said darkly.

"Well, you need to make a start. Daniel is the best person to begin with. And me, of course."

Tess stared up at me, clearly astonished by my words, and then a flicker of hope shone in her eyes. I saw that hope turn to belief the moment before she launched herself up and at me, her arms flying around me in a wild embrace.

"Mrs. Holloway, you are the best, best, best woman in the entire born world. I wish you'd been me mum. Maybe I'd not turned out so bad."

Tess cried, hugged me tighter, kissed my cheek. I gathered her to me as tears stung my eyes—the poor child had been starved, not only of food but of true affection and friendship.

"Now, now, enough hysterics." I patted her as I untangled myself. "We will work all of this out. For now, we must pull ourselves together and make a meal for the staff. I do not wish to hear them complaining all night."

The last made Tess smile a little, and I convinced her to dry her tears. We went to the kitchen, washed up in the sink, and turned to cooking a simple meal of meat pies and mash.

The servants ate it with gusto, including Mr. Davis, who waxed eloquent on the lightness of the pastry. True to my word, I put together a basket of the leftovers for Tess to take to her brother if she could find him. As I went out the back door with her, performing my nightly task of handing out food to the beggars, I beckoned to the youth I knew would be hanging about as well.

"Do you know where your father is?" I asked him.

James nodded readily. "Want him, Mrs. H.?"

I considered but gave my head a shake. "Not just now." I did not want some villain following James and springing upon Daniel and the weakened Mr. Thanos. "Tell the coachman I said you could sleep in the mews tonight. Be on hand if I need you to run to your dad—can you do that?"

James grinned. "I'm your man, Mrs. H."

"Be on your guard," I warned. "There are villains about."

"This is London. Always are. Good night."

James swung away and ran off down the street, heading for the mews behind Mount Street where the horses and carriages were housed. He'd be safe there—the head groom and the stable lads knew him and would look after him.

I returned to the house. Tess came running back a half hour later, with gratitude and an empty basket. She'd told her brother, at my suggestion, to see if he could find a bed with the vicar at Grosvenor Chapel, as Daniel had done. Daniel trusted the vicar, and therefore, I did as well.

I left the rest of the cleaning up and preparing for the morning in Tess's charge and took my weary bones to bed.

I was annoyed with myself for tossing and turning instead of sleeping when I was so exhausted, but too many things knocked at my brain for me to succumb to slumber.

The garish boxes in Clemmie's bedroom and the matching one at the pawnbrokers danced through my head, their gaudy colors swirling. I saw again the dead man in the morgue, with his work-worn hands and broken nails, Mr. Varley staring down at me in dark suspicion, and Mr. Pilcher with his huge body and cold eyes. I thought of Sir Evan Godfrey feeding poison to his guests and wife without qualm, and Daniel spiriting Mr. Thanos out of his reach. The fact that Daniel hadn't taken Mr. Thanos to Southampton Street meant he feared someone who knew exactly where those lodgings were.

In the small hours, I finally found sleep and woke sandy eyed and groggy. I washed, dressed, went downstairs, and fetched my bowl of dough from the larder, only to find Lady Cynthia waiting for me at the kitchen table.

She'd obviously returned home some hours ago, for she'd divested herself of her lovely gown and now lounged in trousers, an ivory waistcoat, and a finely tailored black coat. When she saw me, she came to her feet, her face somber.

"Is Lady Godfrey well?" I asked, fearing what her expression meant.

Cynthia nodded. "Yes, she'll pull through. She has the best doctors looking after her, and her mother arrived too. Her mum doesn't like me much, so I decided to come home. And to tell you the news. Sir Evan took sick in the night, and now he's dead too."

24

My bowl thumped onto the kitchen table as the breath rushed out of me. "Sir Evan is *dead?* But I thought . . . We thought . . ."

"That Evan poisoned Mr. Harmon, his wife, and Mr. Thanos," Cynthia finished for me. "I still do believe that. Evan must have had a fit of remorse and took a dose himself."

I wondered. I wondered very much.

I dropped into a chair, never mind that Cynthia was still standing. "Perhaps we were wrong and someone else did this dreadful thing," I said. "I am very glad Daniel has hidden Mr. Thanos away."

"Well, it wasn't Clemmie who killed Evan," Cynthia said, resuming her seat. "She was insensible most of the night, and I was right beside her. Do you think she's still in danger?"

I rested my limp hands on the table. "I do not know. She is rather an innocent bystander in all this. If Lady Godfrey is surrounded by people who will protect her, she'll likely be all right."

"Well, she's a widow now," Cynthia said. "Free of her oik of a husband. I know it sounds horrible to say it, but it's true. As a widow, she'll have respect, whatever money he provided for her, and the freedom to marry whom she wishes. Being a widow is much better than being a spinster, in my opinion, or even a wife."

"One must be a wife before one is a widow," I reminded her, but I spoke absently, my thoughts elsewhere.

Sir Evan might not have known there was poison in the powder he gave Mr. Harmon, Clemmie, and Mr. Thanos. When Sir Evan realized what had happened, perhaps the murderer killed him before he could report how the poison had been administered, or perhaps Sir Evan guessed who had dosed the bottle.

But then, Elgin had told Daniel and me that the powdered mummy had been poisoned, and no one had crept here in the night attempting to kill *me*. No, I held firm to my belief Sir Evan had deliberately killed Mr. Harmon to rid himself of a man to whom he owed money.

Still, I glanced uneasily at my bowl of dough, which had sat all night in the larder. It would be easy to poison every bit of food in this house—I did not believe anyone had done such a thing, but the thought put me off wanting my breakfast.

Poison was sadly easy to obtain. Anyone could go to a chemists and purchase a bottle of arsenic with which to kill vermin. Arsenic was also used in the making of common things like glass, wallpaper, and paint. A thief who knew what he was looking for could take arsenic from a manufacturer, though I would hope they kept such dangerous chemicals under lock and key.

Sir Evan had been killed—that was a fact. I did not believe for one moment that he'd done it himself in a fit of remorse. He'd known too much, and so the murderer had decided to add one more body to the heap.

This killer must be stopped.

"I will have to go to the shops," I announced abruptly. "The dough is spoiled, and I'll have to purchase our bread."

Cynthia blinked in surprise before her eyes narrowed. "Are you thinking a murderer came in here in the night and sprinkled arsenic everywhere? The front door was fastened like the portal to a fortress. I had to bang on it before anyone opened up. Back door locked today too. I doubt anyone's been in here."

"Even so." I was already on my feet, heading for the housekeeper's parlor. "Tell Tess to throw away the dough and wait until I return to begin breakfast. She'll start her day out after that."

"Have someone else tell her," Cynthia said, slamming herself up. "I'm going with you, wherever you're off to."

Mr. Davis came out of his pantry as I fetched my bonnet and coat and headed for the scullery, Lady Cynthia at my heels. "Going out *again,* Mrs. Holloway?" he asked in amazement.

"To the shops," I called over my shoulder. "Tell Tess to wait for me."

"A footman can run to the shops," Mr. Davis tried to protest.

Cynthia shouted back at him, "Very important. Just hold breakfast until we return. *Do* it, Davis."

"Yes, my lady." Davis's chill deference spoke volumes. I heard him muttering to himself as he closed the door.

I led Lady Cynthia around to the mews, she striding easily beside me. James was just coming out of the stables, clapping two currycombs together to beat off the dust and horsehair.

"Mrs. H.," he said in surprise, then made a little bow. "My lady."

"Please find your father," I said without preliminary. "And make bloody certain no one follows you. Tell him to meet me at the pawnbrokers in the Strand. If he argues, explain that I am already off there, so he'd jolly well better come."

"Right you are." James tossed the brushes at another stable lad, touched his cap, and took off at a run.

"The pawnbrokers where that chap died?" Lady Cynthia asked even as we hurried to the street. "What are you thinking?"

I wasn't certain what the thoughts whirling in my head meant. I was certain I understood the sequence of events, but I wasn't certain who the head villain was. I thought I knew, but it was a very bad thought.

Cynthia whistled sharply for a hansom on Park

Street. A cabbie halted, looking askance at Cynthia's suit and bare head, but he said nothing as we climbed aboard.

The hansom veered into traffic, and then halted abruptly amid shouts and curses as a slim figure darted from among the horses and wagons and sprang into the cab. She landed next to me in a flurry of skirts, making the vehicle list dreadfully.

"You ain't going off and leaving me, Mrs. H.," Tess said breathlessly. "If you're hunting murderers, I'm coming with you."

"How do you know I'm hunting murderers?" I asked as the hansom moved forward after a snarl from the cabbie.

"Mr. Davis said you and her ladyship flew out the door and told me not to leave until you came back. Why would you unless you were off to track down villains? Stands to reason. Besides, it's my day out, and I can go where I please, you said. So I choose to follow you."

"Fair enough," I said, in too much of a hurry to argue.

The hansom wove its way out of Mayfair and along Piccadilly to Haymarket, and down to Charing Cross and past the railway station to the Strand. I called out for the cabbie to stop when we reached the pawnbrokers, and we climbed out. Lady Cynthia handed the man the fare and a generous tip, and he clopped away, his snarls lessening.

The door to the pawnbrokers was unlocked, opening easily to my touch. I hesitated, peering into the dim interior, but Lady Cynthia pushed past me and strode inside, every inch an aristocratic lady.

"Shop!" she bellowed, the standard cry that meant she was ready to be waited on. "Anyone here?"

No one appeared to be. I entered more cautiously, Tess right behind me, so close she nearly trod on my skirts.

I made my way immediately to the table where I'd seen the trinket box. It was still there, to my relief. Had the killer not thought anyone would notice it? Or perhaps he'd known it would be too risky to try to return it to Sir Evan's house.

"That's Clemmie's," Cynthia said in surprise as I snatched it up.

"Indeed. A thief trying to make extra money on the side brought it here, and he paid with his life. So did Mr. Harmon, and, I believe, Sir Evan."

Tess blinked. "For stealing an ugly old box? That's a bit hard, ain't it?"

Footsteps sounded without, and we all swung around, but it was Daniel. Behind him came Chief Inspector Moss, who I was not as happy to see, but I supposed we'd need the police if I was right.

James had come as well, though he lingered outside the shop, likely instructed by Daniel to keep watch. I saw James through the window, leaning against the wall near the door, his foot propped behind him as he gazed at the passersby.

"What do you have there, Mrs. Holloway?" Chief Inspector Moss peered interestedly at what my hands hid.

I held it out. "A keepsake box. Originally found on Lady Godfrey's dressing table. It is part of a set."

"Ugly, ain't it?" Tess shook her head. "What the upper classes think is lovely, I don't understand. Oh, sorry, me lady."

"I agree with you, Tess," Cynthia said without offense. "It's completely awful—Clemmie has no taste at all. Are you saying a thief grabbed it from her dressing table and decided to sell it at a pawnbrokers? It's gilded and expensive—I suppose he must have realized its value."

Daniel nodded. "A professional thief would."

I moved a step closer to Daniel, my worry rising. "How is Mr. Thanos?"

"Much better," Daniel said, his relief unmistakable. "He is stubborn, and I believe he'll mend."

I let out a breath. "Thank heavens for that."

"Indeed," Cynthia said. She turned her back and touched her finger to her eyes, as though rubbing dust from them.

Tess was gazing at the box, still mystified. "Explain it to me, Mrs. H. Why would someone get himself killed for stealing this hideous box?"

"Perhaps you should give that to me, Mrs. Holloway." Chief Inspector Moss held out his hand. "Mr. McAdam will tell me all about it at the Yard. This is no place for ladies."

He must have been of the opinion that women ought to bury themselves in domestic affairs and not come out of their houses. But this *was* a domestic affair, I'd realized, one that had run headlong into professional crime.

I held on to the box. Daniel made no move to take it from me; he merely folded his arms as Chief Inspector Moss lowered his hand, frowning in impatience.

"As I say," I began, "the man who was killed here stole this box from Lady Godfrey's bedchamber. Which raises the question—why was he in the Godfreys' house at all?"

"Robbing the place," Tess said. "He looked a right thug."

"Yes, but Lady Godfrey told Lady Cynthia and me that no break-ins had taken place—no broken windows, no forced locks. Therefore, the man must have been invited into the house. But for what reason would such a villainous-looking man be admitted? I wondered until Mrs. Martin—Sir Evan's cook—told me that Sir Evan had been hiring extra help for things like moving furniture, and doing work in the attic and on a garden shed. All sorts of men hire on as laborers

340

for the cash. What an excellent excuse to have a man on hand to take away the paintings Sir Evan wanted to sell in secret, or to deliver to Sir Evan the antiquities he coveted. While the thief was in the house either coming or going, he sneaked into Lady Godfrey's room and helped himself to a small item he reasoned probably wouldn't be missed. He took it to the pawnbrokers, thinking to make himself a few extra bob on the side. His mistake was to bring it to *this* pawnbrokers." I sent Daniel a significant look.

Daniel's interest rose as I spoke. "Because his coming *here* would connect stolen antiquities from the British Museum and other collections with Sir Evan Godfrey and his purchase of said antiquities."

"Mr. Harmon must have been the go-between," I went on. "Lady Godfrey told us that Mr. Harmon conducted business transactions for Sir Evan. Mr. Harmon hunted up the antiquities, and Sir Evan paid him. When Sir Evan ran out of money, he gave or sold Mr. Harmon the paintings. I imagine the choicest pieces from archaeological digs are very expensive, especially now that many archeologists are advocating for not taking the items out of their respective countries. That can only make the price of the antiquities rise. More of a risk to smuggle them away—fewer antiquities in England at all."

"Well thought," Daniel said. "The antiquities

were brought to this shop by a network of thieves, and then sold from here to shady collectors or men like Mr. Harmon, who had buyers. A neat market."

"Stealing to order, as you speculated," I said. "Mr. Harmon promised collectors like Sir Evan that he could get them specific pieces, and then hired men, like Mr. Varley and the man who died here, to do the thieving. I imagine the former pawnbroker paid the thieves regularly, which is why Mr. Varley was happy to tell Daniel he'd bring in things—he believed Daniel would be his new paymaster. Mr. Harmon would take the things, or have the thieves deliver them to their new homes. Collectors, I've observed, can be quite insane for their bits and bobs, and I imagine some didn't care where the antiquities came from as long as they could have them. Mr. Harmon would have to be careful, as many collectors know one another, to not sell them one another's things."

"Thus, the basement storage at the museum began to be raided," Daniel said, his eyes gleaming in growing excitement. "Those were pieces no one had seen before, and Mr. Harmon likely told his clients that they were fresh from digs. Setting *me* up as the pawnbroker was a way to halt the thefts—I'd simply take what I was given to the police." He paused with a flash of irritation. "I ought to have pretended I was a collector, not the pawnbroker, and nabbed Mr. Harmon when he brought me the stolen things. He was the biggest villain of all. If I had done so, Mr. Harmon might still be alive, though in gaol, of course."

"Yes," Chief Inspector Moss said darkly. "But not for long. I'd have seen him on the gallows."

I shook my head. "I believe it would have been difficult even for *you,* Daniel, to pretend you were crazed enough to do anything to acquire antiquities. Mr. Harmon likely would have smelled a rat and offered you nothing. In any case, if you *had* arrested him, he could tell many a tale, such as who he was working for. His life was already forfeit before you even started your investigation."

Moss looked puzzled, as did Cynthia and Tess. "Wasn't Mr. Harmon working for himself?" the chief inspector asked. "If I understand your speculations, Mr. Harmon was the leader of this gang. He killed his thief when the man nearly gave the show away by stealing Lady Godfrey's box and pawning it in this shop. If Lady Godfrey had reported the theft and the box was found here, the pawnbrokers would be investigated and all might come out."

"Hang on," Lady Cynthia said, frowning. "Why didn't Mr. Harmon simply take the box back, leave it somewhere in the house so Clemmie would think a maid had moved it, and give his

343

thief a severe ticking off? Bashing in his head was a bit extreme, was it not? And if Mr. Harmon had been the source of the antiquities, I have to revise my opinion that Sir Evan killed him, even if he owed Harmon money. Evan would have found a way to pay to keep his antiquities coming, even if he had to pawn Clemmie's jewelry. He was that sort."

"I think I understand," Tess said decidedly. "This Mr. Harmon knew too much about everything—rich coves buying stolen antiquities, his hired thief helping himself in Sir Evan's house, Sir Evan selling off his paintings and pretending they were stolen. Maybe Mr. Harmon was having a fit of conscience and threatened to go to the police. Or was angry at someone else in the gang and threatened to expose him. Or made a blunder when he killed the thief what took the box. Gangs don't like it when one of their number takes too many risks."

"And now Harmon is dead," Cynthia finished. "And can tell no tales."

Chief Inspector Moss listened, brows raised, but his stance told me he was manifestly uncomfortable with Lady Cynthia. He cleared his throat. "McAdam, perhaps we could adjourn and discuss this."

I took a step closer to Daniel. On no account was I going to let him go off alone with Chief Inspector Moss.

"This is as good a place as any," Daniel said with his usual affability. "I've invited another to join us—ah, there he is." He waved through the window at James, who nodded and opened the door.

The man who came in was Mr. Varley. I stepped even closer to Daniel—Varley was large and brutish, and I did not like the way he glared at us. He might have a knife or worse, a pistol. A man did not have to get very close to his victim to shoot him.

Varley took in Tess and Lady Cynthia, who'd drawn together, then me. I saw him look puzzled but then dismiss us ladies. He looked over Chief Inspector Moss, but instead of being worried that a policeman, especially a high-ranking one, was present, he only shot Daniel an annoyed glance.

"Tom," Varley greeted Daniel—I remembered Varley had thought this was Daniel's name. "What's 'e doin' 'ere?" He indicated Moss with a flick of his thumb.

Moss gave him a hard look. "I'm afraid the game is up, Varley."

"What game?" Varley asked in unfeigned astonishment. "What you goin' on about?"

"Selling stolen goods," Moss said in clipped tones. "Antiquities, paintings, whatever you brought through here, you name it."

"But—" Varley swung back to Daniel. "You're havin' me on. I agreed that if anyone was to go down, it were Pilcher. Magistrate would want to bang *'im* up for any number of fings."

Daniel apparently hadn't heard this. He went still, his good-natured expression vanishing as he turned to Chief Inspector Moss. "Pilcher?"

"Yeah, that were the agreement, right?" Varley looked at Moss. "That's why you brung in a villain like 'im. *And* to scare off any poachers on our business."

"You hired Pilcher?" Daniel asked Moss, his voice dangerously quiet. "To do what, kill anyone who might talk? Clean up the mess?"

I thought of the overly large, granite-faced man in the interview room at Scotland Yard, how the shackles had barely fit his fists. He was terrifying—Mr. Varley looked harmless in contrast, and I knew Mr. Varley was a long way from harmless.

"How horrible," I said softly, unable to stop myself.

Lady Cynthia and Tess had gone very quiet, no doubt realizing the situation had drastically changed. Instead of simply telling a policeman about the thefts at Clemmie's, we now stood in the presence of killers.

Moss looked me up and down. "What is this woman to you, McAdam? I was persuaded to take you on because you were unconnected. Are you married to her?"

Daniel didn't answer, but I noticed he'd edged

sideways so that his left shoulder was in front of me.

"Why the devil did you allow me to be set up in *here?*" Daniel demanded of Moss. "Did you think me too stupid to twig to what was going on? My guvnor wouldn't have sent an inexperienced underling to clear up a museum theft, one possibly tied to nationalist fanatics, but I suppose you didn't understand that. You've let me learn who all the members of your gang are. I don't care so much about them—they're blokes trying to make a living. But Pilcher is the last straw, Moss."

"Why would I mind if you learned about villains?" Moss asked impatiently. "They deserve nothing more than the noose."

"'Ere," Varley began, affronted.

I said to Daniel, "He set you up here because Varley and the other thieves would bring *you* the stolen goods. And you would collect them and take them straight to Chief Inspector Moss. If anything went wrong, Moss could blame you."

"Oh, I know I would have been the scapegoat if it all went wrong," Daniel said without heat. "Once Chief Inspector Moss had the antiquities, he could return them to Harmon, and I and my guvnor wouldn't be the wiser. Weren't you worried I'd get wind of that and report you?" he asked Moss.

"That is why I brought in Pilcher." Moss

shrugged then turned abruptly to Varley. "Albert Varley, I am arresting you on suspicion of theft and for murdering one John Waters, a known thief; Mr. William Harmon; and Sir Evan Godfrey. Better not to fight, Varley. You won't win."

"You wha'?" Varley's mouth dropped open, showing his brown teeth. "I never went near Sir Evan Godfrey. He was a mark, wasn't 'e? Never had much to do with Mr. 'Armon neither. I brought gear to the pawnbroker, who was a mate. That's all."

"I suspect Lady Cynthia and I were right in the first place that Sir Evan killed Mr. Harmon," I broke in. "Though evidence or a witness will have to be found to prove it conclusively. But that explanation fits. Sir Evan owed Mr. Harmon much money, and probably Mr. Harmon threatened to tell the world Sir Evan was selling his paintings to buy stolen antiquities. Sir Evan valued his reputation very highly." I thought of the haughty photos of Sir Evan in India, the pride and arrogance, every inch, as Lady Cynthia had called him, the pukka sahib. "You are correct that Sir Evan would not have wanted to cut off the flow of antiquities, my lady, but sadly I believe he would have found another source without too much trouble. But then Daniel and I learned about the mummy powder, and I gave it to Detective Inspector McGregor, a conscientious man. Sir

Evan might be arrested for murder, which would be a disaster for the gang and its leadership."

I remember Daniel saying to me *Good lass,* in a hearty tone, when I'd told him I'd given the bottle to McGregor, not Chief Inspector Moss.

"And what a tale Sir Evan would tell to the magistrate," Daniel finished. "So his wine or whisky or bedtime tonic was doctored."

"Chief Inspector Moss was in the house," I pointed out, "most of the day."

"Good Lord," Cynthia whispered.

Varley looked bewildered. "What are you telling me, Tom?" he asked Daniel. "That you're a copper? If you're working for *'im,* what does it matter? There's no call to arrest me. I didn't do nuffink."

"Mr. Varley is correct," I put in. "Apart from stealing things, of course. Mr. Varley brought all sorts of items to this pawnshop, I am guessing, from what I heard the night he visited you. But he murdered no one."

"I don't remember *you* being 'ere that night, missus." Varley glared at me but then shrugged. "Don't matter none. No one will listen to the likes of you."

"Very likely not," I said. But they'd listen to Daniel.

"I don't work for Chief Inspector Moss," Daniel told Varley. "I answer to another. You, Varley, it is true, didn't actually do anything in this

349

case. You and I chatted a number of times, but I never bought anything from you, and you never showed me any stolen items. I only needed you here today to confirm my suspicions about Chief Inspector Moss. I'd leave, were I you. Perhaps you should run a long way from London."

"Bleedin' 'ell," Varley said.

He wasn't a stupid man—slow perhaps, but no fool. Varley drew a breath, said, "Right you are, guv," spun around, and headed for door.

"No!" Moss went after him. Varley doubled his speed, making the street before Moss did.

Varley nearly ran into a man larger than himself, the cold-eyed walking danger that was Mr. Pilcher. Pilcher grabbed at Varley, but Varley slid from his grasp and dodged into the crowd on the Strand, moving rapidly out of sight.

James shot Daniel a questioning glance through the open door, but Daniel shook his head the slightest bit. Varley disappeared and was gone.

Mr. Pilcher blocked the way out for the rest of us. "I also invited a friend to this gathering," Chief Inspector Moss said smoothly. "Come in, Mr. Pilcher."

Pilcher's bulk threw a shadow as he filled the doorway, then he was inside, the door shut. He drew a thick knife from the pocket of his coat.

"Which one you want done?" he asked, directing the question to Chief Inspector Moss. His glance fell on me before moving to Tess.

"Cor, that's a nice morsel," he said, staring at Tess. "Can I 'ave 'er?"

"Certainly not," Moss answered, indignant. "But none of the women can leave here. You may make it look as though they were robbed, or toss them into the river—I don't mind which you choose. But nothing that leads back to me. *I'll* take care of McAdam."

25

Daniel didn't move. Though my heart was in my throat, Daniel, blast him, didn't look either surprised or worried.

"There would be plenty of inquiries about my death," he said to Chief Inspector Moss, his tone deceptively mild. "From men far more frightening than Pilcher."

"I will say you were killed in the line of duty," Moss answered, unconcerned. "You'll be given a hero's funeral. You went up against dangerous men, after all."

Pilcher was staring at Lady Cynthia, who had her arm around Tess, her chin up. "'S'truth, that's not a bloke," he said in amazement. "It's a lass in trousers. Who'd 'ave thought? Can I 'ave *'er?*"

"Only if you want to be drawn and quartered," Moss returned sternly. "She is the Earl of Clifford's daughter, and he is a war hero. If you touch her, you'll be roasted alive. So make sure she is still a virgin when she's found."

"Huh," Pilcher said. He kept staring at Cynthia, who gazed steadily back at him, her cheeks flushed.

"Enough," Daniel said firmly. "Give up, Moss. It's over. I don't know what your colleagues at the Yard will do to you, and I don't much care.

I only want Pilcher for a while. I'll hand him in when I'm done."

I'd never heard Daniel speak so. He behaved as though he had the upper hand in the room, never mind Chief Inspector Moss, who was not denying he was up to his neck in the stolen antiquities scheme, and never mind Pilcher. The cool way Daniel studied Pilcher as he stated his intentions made me shiver.

"Just let me kill 'im," Pilcher said, impatient. "I didn't like the way he talked to me before, and I don't like 'im now."

Chief Inspector Moss sighed. "Oh, very well, go ahead." He reached into his coat pocket and withdrew a pistol.

My throat closed up and I had the sudden desire to run, hide, dive over the counter—be anywhere but in front of the black barrel of that gun.

The chief inspector did not immediately hand the gun to Pilcher. "You are correct about Sir Evan, Mrs. Holloway," he told me. "He pretended the death of Mr. Harmon was an accident, but I knew he did it. He sent one of *my* workmen, if you please, to purchase poison for him, saying they needed to rid the garden shed they were working on of rats. My man did it and then reported it to me offhand, stupid geezer. Mr. Harmon had become a worry to Sir Evan. McAdam here is too perceptive, and it was my misfortune that one of the men Sir Evan poisoned turned out to be McAdam's best mate. I reasoned McAdam would find some way to have Sir Evan arrested or at least questioned about the deaths, and I knew Sir Evan would give me up. And so . . ." The chief inspector spread his hands. "I had the run of the house, and you are correct that it was easy to put a dose into the bottle of whisky Sir Evan kept in his bedside table."

It chilled me the way he explained so calmly, the soldier outlining what must be done to win the battle.

"Why on earth should you?" I asked before I could stop myself. "You are a chief inspector, a respected man with a long career." Two careers if I was right about his army background. "You've done your duty well. Why spoil it now?"

Chief Inspector Moss regarded me with pity. "Duty? What has my duty got me? You are young—you believe that if you drudge all your life for people who'd rather spit on you than give you a moment's kindness you'll somehow be rewarded. You will learn. Policemen, like domestics and tradesmen, are not allowed in the front door. Remember what I told you about Chief Inspector Turland? Worked his way up through the ranks, was lauded all around, and ended up a bitter old man eating tasteless food in his sister's hovel. I'm not about to let that happen to me—in fact, I'm doing this to have something to give Turland and men like him. We arrest villains who steal far more in a day than any of us earn in a year. Why should they have what I can only dream of? Oh, wait a moment, you told me. I sacrifice it for my *duty.*"

"And self-respect," I said softly.

I understood what he meant, however. I lived every day in opulent homes owned by people who had every privilege granted them. Meanwhile, I slaved for a pittance and was shouted at if I did not do it quickly enough.

I could very well steal from these people, carefully so they would not know. I could hoard my spoils until I had enough to buy or hire the house I dreamed of to live in with Grace, or begin the shop we planned.

But then I'd have to explain to Grace where I'd obtained the money, and I'd be ashamed. Not all the people in the glittering houses of Mayfair were horrible—Lady Cynthia, for instance—and not all of the privileged were wealthy and powerful—for example, Mr. Thanos. Some were beastly, of course, but this was why I chose my situations with care.

Chief Inspector Moss had been rubbing elbows with criminals for so long—arresting them and interrogating them in small rooms like the one in which he'd had Pilcher at Scotland Yard—that he'd forgotten the difference between right and wrong.

I hadn't, and with Grace's help, I would continue to remember.

"Pilcher works for Naismith," Daniel broke

in. "Is he a part of this too? I doubt he'd have truck with helping a policeman, even if you are committing villainy. Naismith hates coppers more than he hates other villains on his patch."

Chief Inspector Moss's eyes were flinty. "He lent Mr. Pilcher to me. We have an understanding."

"Which means you'll go light on him," Daniel finished for him. "You'll inform him if any are coming after him—like me." A coldness entered Daniel's voice, the same one he'd taken on when Mr. Pilcher had first mentioned the name *Naismith*. "And for that, I'll make sure you pay and pay and pay."

Moss gave Daniel a dismissive look, finished with his confessions. With the same chilling calmness, he turned to Mr. Pilcher. "Do the women when you are finished with McAdam. As I say, let *nothing* be traced back to me."

Daniel stepped all the way in front of me. "Kat, get them behind the counter," he said swiftly.

If he was ordering me to take Lady Cynthia and Tess into the back, he must know the door to it was unlocked, else he would not have suggested it. I thought about how the front door had been easily opened, which now led me to believe he'd already prepared the ground before we'd arrived.

These conclusions flitted in my head, and I was about to shove Tess and Cynthia toward the counter, when I saw James.

He was peering through one of the windows,

his hands cupped around his face so he could see through the grimy glass. He caught sight of Moss training a gun on Daniel, and his eyes went wide. I shook my head at him, but James gave a wild shout and burst in through the door.

Moss started, and in that moment, Daniel was on him. Pilcher swung around to meet the threat of James, who barreled into him. Pilcher, used to fighting, brought his knife hand up, but he met me and the pewter candlestick I'd caught up from one of the tables. I brought that instrument down hard on his arm, preventing the knife from going straight into James.

James had enough sense to jump aside, and then he too grabbed a candlestick from the wares, a turned wooden one, and batted at Pilcher with it. Cynthia and Tess, instead of being rational and running into the street to summon constables, chose weapons of their own and laid into Pilcher. He batted and flailed, growling that it was like being attacked by flies. But enough flies can drive away a predator.

I turned to the more frightening threat of Moss. If he shot Daniel . . .

Daniel grappled with Moss, holding Moss's arm and neck in a wrestling lock. Moss fought like the soldier he was, reaching his other hand into a pocket, probably groping for another weapon. Before I could rush forward with my candlestick, Daniel let go on a sudden and crashed his fist into

Moss's face. Then he grabbed Moss's pistol arm and dug his fingers hard into his wrist.

Moss's hand opened under Daniel's pressure, and the pistol fell to the ground. It was a black thing, a revolver, its handle decorated with mother-of-pearl inlay that glistened softly in the shop's dim light. I had always been intrigued by the fact that knives and pistols, instruments of destruction, could also be items of intricate beauty.

I picked up the pistol.

I would not shoot it, because I knew I had as much chance of hitting Daniel as I did Moss, and holding it made me feel a bit queasy.

Moss looked at me in terror. "Put that down!" he commanded.

Instead of obeying, I pointed the gun shakily at him. He froze, which gave Daniel the opportunity to hit him again. Moss's head snapped back, but he jerked himself upright, and a blade flashed in his hand, slim and long, a stiletto.

As I shouted at Daniel to take care, the room suddenly filled with constables. They came in through the front and surrounded Moss and Pilcher, who was still fighting, while a single man strode out from the back.

This man had a fair mustache, rumpled clothing, and towering fury in his eyes. He moved to where Daniel and Moss struggled, clamped his hand on the back of Moss's head, and yanked the man upright.

"I beg your pardon, sir," Detective Inspector

McGregor said in a hard voice. "But I'm arresting you for theft, dealing in stolen goods, murder, fraud, and corruption. I'm sure I'll think of more charges as we go. Constable, put cuffs on him, if you please."

A junior constable, looking both grim and fearful, clapped an iron manacle around the wrist McGregor had already pulled behind Moss's back. The constable caught the other wrist and clicked a second cuff closed.

Moss jerked around, off balance, and roared, "I'll have your badges, all of you! You've ruined your career, McGregor."

"No, sir." McGregor's head was up, his eyes sparkling. "I'd say you've ruined yours."

A strong hand, Daniel's, closed over mine and took the revolver out of it. Daniel popped the chamber open and let the bullets slide out into his hand.

Tess, Lady Cynthia, and James were panting, wild-eyed, as the constables surrounded Pilcher. Daniel made his way toward the large man, white patches about Daniel's eyes and lips.

He stepped close to Pilcher and said clearly, "I want Naismith. How about we pay him a visit? Right now."

Pilcher stared at Daniel and the gun in his hand, and his ruddy face paled. He must have seen Daniel unload the pistol, but Daniel's eyes were cold and hard, and the pistol and bullets were ready to hand.

Pilcher snarled like an animal. He flung off the constables as though they were sparrows trying to hold him down, and bolted out of the door.

Daniel charged after him. "No, you don't!"

I ran out behind them both.

The Strand this afternoon was a crush of cabs; private carriages; wagons delivering beer, produce, ice, and dry goods; and carts carrying lumber, machinery, livestock—all manner of things. Pilcher dove between wheels and horses' hooves, twisting and turning as he sprinted desperately away from Daniel.

Daniel pounded after him. I jumped back to the walkway a second before I could be clipped by a carriage wheel, and decided to stay put.

"Dad!" James was past me in a second, his lithe body moving through the traffic with ease. "I'll get 'im!"

Pilcher ran down the middle of the street, earning curses and yells, but the man was obviously used to navigating the arteries of London. Daniel was hampered by a large wagon that drove into a relatively empty space between cabs, but James, with his youthful energy and slimness, sprinted after Pilcher.

Pilcher gained the other side of the road near the Adelphi, and James plunged after him, Daniel not far behind. I hurried down my side of the road, struggling to keep them all in sight. I heard Tess panting after me, calling my name.

Daniel reached the other side of the street a way down from Pilcher and resumed his chase. James ducked and dodged through traffic, his youthful stride rapid.

I was not certain how it happened. One moment, James's cloth-capped head was bobbing along between the carts, the next, it disappeared completely.

Shouts and cries sounded, carts and carriages halted abruptly, and horses danced aside, sparks showering from hooves on the cobbles. I saw Daniel stop, horror on his face, his mouth opening in a yell I heard even over the traffic.

"James!"

A carter stood up on his bench. "Bloody hell!" he yelled, wide-eyed. "He ran right under me wheels!"

Pilcher disappeared around a corner, gone. Daniel didn't even mark his passage. He left the relative safety of the walkway and plunged into the road, heading straight for James.

I lifted my skirts and dodged and wove through the traffic, Tess behind me.

I reached the cart, the driver on the ground now, holding the nervous horses. Daniel knelt on the pavement, lifting James. The lad's face was creased with dirt and blood, his eyes closed.

Daniel gathered James close, holding his son against his chest, rocking him.

I dropped beside them, hand on James's shoulder. "Daniel . . ."

Daniel's eyes burned as he looked over James's head at me. I saw fear, self-loathing, and terrible rage. I also saw grief. In that moment, I knew what Daniel's son meant to him—the same as my daughter meant to me. No matter how casual he might seem regarding James, no matter how much he let James roam, Daniel loved the boy with a ferocity he let on to no one. Daniel had already lost so much, but I abruptly understood that if he lost James, he'd believe that everything he had done in life would count for nothing.

I ran my hands along James's shoulder to his throat, feeling the flutter of his pulse. "We must get him to a doctor," I said. "Daniel—"

Daniel stared at me without seeing me before clarity returned to his eyes and he gave a curt nod. I started to help him up, and then Tess was beside us, her hands going to James to assist in lifting him.

"You," I said to the carter. "Make room in your wagon. We need to get him through this crush to a doctor."

The carter was near to tears. "I never saw him. He popped out o' nowhere."

"I know, I saw. Now help me fix a place where he can lie down. At once."

My command, delivered with just the right amount of sharpness, galvanized him. The carter hurried to the back of his wagon and shoved bags of produce this way and that until there was space to lay James.

Others had stopped to assist, holding the horses and wagon steady, directing vehicles out of the way. Daniel carried his son and laid him down, his movements gentle. He climbed up beside him then reached a hand for me.

"Kat," he said. "Please."

Tess pushed me up before I could speak, though I had every intention of going with him. "Go on, Mrs. H.," Tess said. "I'll get Lady Cynthia home and the breakfast made and everything. Take care of the poor mite. He's a good lad."

"Yes, thank you, Tess."

She gave me an encouraging smile, this kind-hearted young woman who had already proved an asset to me.

The cart began with a jerk, the carter determined to bull his way through the halted vehicles. "I know where is a doctor not far," he said. "I'll get ya there."

I gave Tess a wave of thanks as we bumped away, just as James fluttered open his eyes and croaked, "Dad? Did we get 'im?"

"No, son," Daniel said, leaning over James and stroking his hair. "But I've got you."

James gave him a confused look. I took James's hand, holding on to him and balancing on the lumpy bags of new potatoes and parsnips, as we jolted along the Strand to save James's life.

26

The doctor in question had a house in St. Martin's Lane. The surgery was on the ground floor, with a stair that led to the doctor's living quarters opening from the front hall.

The woman in a gray frock with a starched apron who admitted us was not pleased at our arrival, but when the doctor saw Daniel carry in James in his arms like a baby, he was solicitousness itself.

He helped Daniel take James into a small back room, and I watched from the doorway as Daniel laid James on a bed. Then the assistant or nurse or doctor's wife, or whoever she was, blocked my view and pushed the door closed.

"I'll fetch you a cup of tea," she said in a sharp tone. "Sit there." She pointed at a hard chair near the front window.

I sank down, barely noticing the chair's discomfort. After a time, the woman brought me a pot of lukewarm and overly steeped tea and a slice of stale sponge cake before disappearing out another door.

I sipped the tea, trying to ignore its acrid taste, but gave up on the cake after one nibble. Food should comfort, but this food could only lead to despair.

I sat for a very long time as the clock above the doctor's desk ticked, each passing minute like an hour. I knew I ought to leave—I had duties, a kitchen to return to, responsibilities.

But I could not abandon Daniel. If James died, I could not let him face that alone.

The clock had struck eight, sunshine leaking through the dusty windows, before Daniel emerged. He trudged heavily to a chair next to mine and collapsed into it.

"James," I said, not daring to voice anything more.

Daniel shook his head and let out a ponderous breath. "He'll live. He has some broken bones and a broken arm, and his head is concussed. He'll have to stay still for several weeks." His lips twitched and fond exasperation filled his eyes. "I don't believe the doctor knows what he is asking."

My body unclenched as relief poured through me, and tears filled my eyes. Safe. James was safe.

"You'll stay with him?" I asked when I could speak again. "Live with him, I mean? Take care of him? Your rooms in Southampton Street won't be large enough, not for the pair of you, and Mrs. Williams might not like a youth about the place—"

"Peace, Kat." Daniel slid his hand over mine, stilling my tumbling words. "I will move James

365

into my rooms in Kensington. Plenty of space there."

"Kensington," I repeated. "So that is where your elusive lodgings are. Do you have Mr. Thanos there?"

"I do," Daniel said with a nod. "I apologize for not explaining to you, but there were too many listeners around us at the time, and I wanted you to be innocently ignorant if Moss or anyone else tried to question you. Thanos does not know how to keep quiet—he'd babble all his theories about how he was poisoned and by whom to anyone who would listen, and then he'd be next on the list."

"You are good to take care of Mr. Thanos," I said warmly.

Daniel's hand tightened on mine. "Once upon a time, Elgin Thanos took care of me. When I was young, angry, and tore into everyone around me, Thanos took me under his wing. He talked to *me,* man-to-man, not as gentleman's son to a boy from the gutter. He genuinely sees no difference between us."

"I noticed that," I said. "He speaks to me the same way. And to Lady Cynthia."

"He doesn't even know he's doing it." Daniel's tone was admiring. "I've been talked at plenty by reformers who say they want to help the downtrodden, but they still make you know you are one of those downtrodden and will never rise above your situation. Used to infuriate me."

"I understand," I said with sympathy. "I've met such people."

"Thanos would never dream of being so condescending. If he calls you friend, you know he is sincere." Daniel brushed his thumb over the backs of my fingers. "You are another who sees a person for who he or she is. It's one reason I treasure you, Kat."

My heart squeezed, but I gave him an admonishing look. "You must be feeling better. Else you'd not revert to base flattery."

"It is only truth, Mrs. Holloway," he said, no teasing in his voice.

We sat in silence for a moment. I did not withdraw my hand, letting Daniel's strength come to me. The clock ticked away, the sound quiet and serene.

"But for God's sake, Kat," Daniel admonished after a few moments. "You must cease your inclination to charge after armed men. This is the second time you've rushed *toward* a villainous man instead of away from him."

I frowned. "I told you—if I see you or anyone I care for in danger, I will not stand aside and wring my hands. I will sail in and set about said villains."

"I know." Daniel's words were a groan. "What am I to do with you?"

"You may begin by telling me all. How did you know Chief Inspector Moss was in on the plot?"

Daniel let out a breath. "I didn't. Not at first. He seemed genuinely interested in capturing these culprits. The thing is, if he'd stuck to simply robbing other collectors, he'd never have encountered me. It was only when the museum started having things go missing that I was called in. Certain men feared what Thanos concluded—that nationalists were trying to return antiquities to their home countries."

"When I first met Chief Inspector Moss, I thought *he* was your employer." I gave Daniel an inquiring look, hoping he'd impart who he truly worked for, but Daniel didn't seem to notice.

"It was Moss who suggested I replace the pawnbroker and wait to be offered the antiquities. Thinking it through, I suppose Moss thought it would do no harm. I'd trot to him with any antiquities they brought me, and if I had the thieves arrested, he'd bang them up and bring in new ones. Moss hates criminals, that is the truth, no matter how much he says he envies them and their easy wealth. He sees them as useful tools, and I have no doubt that in the end, they'd have paid for the thefts. They could sing in the dock that Chief Inspector Moss himself had commanded them, but would they be believed? From my conversations with Varley, I gathered that Harmon did most of the hiring—Moss only paved the way and of course collected the money." Daniel shook his head. "As

Moss said, the problem with being a policeman for a long time is that you see boxes and boxes of evidence from crimes brought in—paintings, valuables, so many things stolen, so much of it never recovered. Why should a policeman live in cramped rooms barely earning a living when one item from those boxes could set him up for life? Eventually, men like Moss forget why they became coppers in the first place."

"The temptation grows too much for them," I finished.

"I suppose I can't really blame them," Daniel said. "Policing can be a thankless job. You have to have a core of certainty inside you, a firm belief that what you're doing is right. And that belief has to be enough for you."

"I gather that Chief Inspector Moss does not have that certainty," I said with conviction. "But Inspector McGregor does. He is fierce about weeding out corrupt men from the police. *He* suspected Moss from the beginning."

"Yes." Daniel let out a sigh. "I will have to apologize to McGregor for not coming to him sooner and thank him at the same time. I'm not certain he'll get a promotion for his actions, unfortunately. As much as the Yard hates corruption, they also don't like a grass who goes against one of their own. A fine line to walk."

"That is hardly fair," I said in indignation. "McGregor is right, and Moss is a bad 'un. Moss was a soldier, wasn't he? I would think he'd have learned honor in his regiment."

"Yes, he was a sergeant major," Daniel answered, confirming one of my guesses. "In Africa, fighting against the southern tribes. Soldiering is not always an honorable game, I'm sorry to say. Moss said he learned to fight dirty to win, because winning was what mattered in the end. He said it proudly. Makes me glad I never tried to be a soldier."

If he had, he'd have been sent to the front lines, which was where most lads from the streets ended up. Although, I thought with feeble humor, knowing Daniel, he'd have worked his way to general by now.

"You hid McGregor in the back room of the pawnbrokers before we arrived," I said with conviction.

"Of course I did. I had been on my way to . . . well, a place nearby to Scotland Yard, when James came running to tell me you were heading to the pawnbrokers without delay. While that alarmed me to no end"—Daniel paused to send me a glare—"I sought McGregor and told him I could hand him all the culprits if he hid there with a contingent of men, and *then* I went to Moss and convinced him to come with me. McGregor was sufficiently suspicious of Moss that he summoned trusted constables and hid them nearby. I never would have let you into that shop without some way to to protect you." Daniel lifted my hand and kissed it, but the look he sent over it was one of exasperation. "You'll turn my hair gray, Kat."

I glanced at his very thick hair, which was quite dark, no danger of it becoming gray for some years. "I went to the pawnbrokers because I wanted to be certain before I put my theories before you," I said primly. "I did send for you instead of simply going myself. And I brought Lady Cynthia for corroboration, since she'd have recognized Clemmie's things. Tess, on the other hand, invited herself along and I had no time to send her home."

Daniel's gaze was thoughtful as he listened. "Your friends are valiant, I have to say," he said. "At least they will not let you run headlong into danger alone. But what made *you* begin to suspect Moss?"

He asked with true interest. I liked that Daniel wanted to know my opinions and didn't dismiss them. A rare thing in a male, in my experience, and another reason I was grateful for our friendship.

"I'm not certain," I began. "To tell the truth, I never thought much about Chief Inspector Moss until I realized you hadn't taken Mr. Thanos to your rooms on Southampton Street. I wondered who you worried about finding him there. I doubt Sir Evan knew where your lodgings were— or even who you were at all. Lady Cynthia has never been to your Southampton Street rooms, and I have never told her about them, as far as I can remember. So, she wouldn't have talked about them with Clemmie, and Clemmie couldn't have imparted such information to Sir Evan. Therefore, you weren't worried about *Sir Evan* finding Mr. Thanos—which meant you were worried about someone entirely different. The fact that you did not tell *me* where you were taking Mr. Thanos in front of others meant that the person you wanted to evade was in Sir Evan's house at the time. Mr. Harmon was already dead, and the only people left to suspect were Sir Evan, Clemmie, and Chief Inspector Moss. Clemmie was a victim herself, Sir Evan passed away that night, and so Chief Inspector Moss was left." I spread my hands, as though the solution had been simple. "I asked to meet you at the pawnbrokers because I wanted to show you the box and explain why I thought the thief had been killed."

"You could not have simply sought me out beforehand?" Daniel asked sternly. "And told me all this? Instead of rushing straight into danger as usual?"

I flushed. "I wanted to find the box first, as I said. And, truth to tell, I knew if I told James to bring you to the pawnbrokers, you'd be more certain to come."

Daniel's gaze was penetrating. I found myself wanting to look away, and because I did, I forced myself to stare straight into his eyes.

372

It was Daniel who blinked first. "You might have been right," he said. "But know this, Kat—I will always come to you if you need me. You don't need to trick me."

My face warmed further. "I wasn't sure I could draw you out of hiding, and I didn't want to unless I had evidence."

"Which you found. Bless you." Daniel stopped and studied his boots. "What I did not expect was Pilcher."

I remembered my cold fear when Pilcher had walked in, the chilling way he'd calmly discussed with Chief Inspector Moss how he might dispatch us. Moss had been ready to let Pilcher kill three women and drop their bodies into the Thames, damn and blast him. Any sympathy I'd had for Moss had evaporated at that moment.

"You still believe Pilcher can lead you to the man who killed your dad?" I asked Daniel.

He nodded, old pain in his eyes. "I certainly want to find out."

"I ought to have kept James from running after him," I said in remorse. "I am so sorry."

Daniel shot me a look of amazement. "How could you have? I've never been able to stop James doing precisely what he wants, and I'm his father. You would have had to throw a net over him and had half the constables sit on him before James would stay put." Daniel leaned back, resting his head on the whitewashed wall behind him, his face drawn. "I'll never forgive myself if he takes sick from this. I was so zealous to nab Pilcher and bend him to my will that I paid no attention to my own son. I ought to have known James would want to help. He always wants to help me, though God knows I don't deserve it." He trailed off bitterly.

"You let Pilcher go," I reminded him. "You let him go without a word and turned back for James. That tells me what sort of man you are."

"There was no choice. When I saw James go down, Pilcher suddenly didn't matter, and neither did Naismith, or my need for vengeance. Nothing mattered at that moment except James. I also realized in that instant that my single-minded stupidity might have killed him." He shivered.

I wrapped my hands around both of his, holding on tight. "James is a sturdy lad, and he'll mend quickly. You'll have him living with you now, so you can look after him, like a proper dad."

"The reason I have him stay elsewhere is to keep him safe. I know insalubrious people, men and women both. I don't want them near him."

"Stop telling those insalubrious people where you live, and it will not be a problem," I said. "Although I concede that I can speak with such loftiness because I have Grace in a house where she *is* safe. I would lock her in there until she's sixty if I thought it would prevent any terrible thing from happening to her."

Daniel sat up straight as he chuckled, the rumble of his laughter vibrating me. "Together we will wrap cotton wool around our children and keep them from harm."

I sighed. "If only it could be done."

Daniel touched my face. His fingertips were streaked with dirt, grime from the road, and blood, and I did not mind in the slightest.

"We will do it," he said. "We'll help each other keep them safe. Agreed?"

"Agreed," I said, and smiled.

His lips were close to mine, his eyes warm. Instead of waiting for him to take a liberty, I leaned forward and kissed him myself.

Daniel started, and then he slid an arm around me, drawing me close as he gently returned the kiss.

Daniel's lips were warm, but the touch of them was light, as though he feared I'd leap up and run away if he kissed me harder. I could have told him that nothing short of a hurricane could make me leave at this moment, and then it would be only to seek shelter with him where we might carry on kissing.

I tugged him closer and let my lips play upon his, my body heating. I knew in my heart I could let myself be seduced by this man, and rush willingly all the way to my ruin.

We would not have the chance for this today, however. As I rested my hand on his shoulder, liking the steely hardness of it as we continued the kiss, the nurse, or whoever she was, walked briskly into the room.

Her heels clicked on the hard floor, and she sniffed. "Well, *really.*"

As Daniel and I sprang apart, my fingers going to my tingling lips, we found ourselves bathed in her chill glare of disapproval. "The lad is ready to be taken home," she said coldly. "That is, if there is anyplace decent for him to go."

Daniel rose to his feet, his smile ready, his good-natured persona sliding onto him like a glove. "Indeed, ma'am. The lodgings I'll carry him to are of the utmost respectability, and there he'll be tutored by one of the best scholars from Cambridge." Daniel clasped my hands and raised me to my feet. "Shall we take him home, Mrs. Holloway?"

"Of course, Mr. McAdam," I said with all the dignity I could muster.

"Humph," the woman said, and she disappeared into the back room.

Daniel and I waited until the door closed, and then we laughed until we had to hang on to each other to keep from collapsing. We laughed for relief that James was well, for the headiness of our stolen moment, and for hope of what the future might bring.

27

Daniel hired a carriage to take us home. I walked out beside him as he carried James with careful tenderness, James half asleep with the opiate the doctor had given him.

I rode with them as far as South Audley Street, where Daniel helped me down and said good-bye. As we were in a public road, I concluded our farewell with a nod, and then Daniel climbed back into the carriage, which rolled westward along Piccadilly toward Kensington.

I walked on to Mount Street, my steps tired. My worry for James was mitigated somewhat, but the adventure, which had followed hard upon my restless night, had worn me out. The long way up South Audley Street, past Grosvenor Chapel to Mount Street, nearly did me in.

But I was a cook, not mistress of my own household, and so I could not retire to bed and loll there. I'd had my day out yesterday, and now it was time to labor.

When I plodded into the kitchen, the fire was roaring in the stove and a pot was bubbling, a layer of eggs dancing in it. Bacon sizzled in a pan, and a pile of toast warmed on the stove, butter dripping down the stack. Another sauté pan held potatoes and sausage, and two loaves of shaped dough rested on a wooden board on the table, Tess just covering them with a cloth.

"Here you are!" Tess sang out when she saw me. "Lady Cynthia and I came home all right, and I told you I'd start in. Sit yourself down, Mrs. H. I'll pour you a cuppa."

She waved her hand proudly, indicating the breakfast preparations, including the oval covered dishes in a row, waiting for the cooking food. Mr. Davis strode in, his butler's kit neat, his hairpiece straight, his movements lively.

"Good morning, Mrs. Holloway. Tess told us about James. Poor lad. Is he all right?"

I wondered exactly what Tess had told him, but her face remained blank and innocent.

"He will be," I said. "He is receiving good care."

"I am glad," Mr. Davis said, sounding genuinely relieved. He was a warmhearted man, I'd come to know. Mr. Davis might be a stickler for household protocol and all of us doing our jobs correctly, but he'd proved to be a reasonable fellow, and I'd begun to count him as a friend.

Tess poured tea—clear, smooth-tasting oolong— and set buttered toast in front of me. I fell upon it hungrily. The bread was toasted to perfection, the butter hot and melted through.

"Well done, Tess," I said as I chewed. "My services might no longer be needed here."

Tess shot me a petrified look. "No fear of that. I'm off. It's me day out. Let nothing stand in the way of a day out, you told me."

"So I did. I was teasing you. You have done beautifully, and it is kind of you to let me rest a moment."

Her grin returned. "That's all right, then. I'm glad James will be well. He's in good hands with his dad."

"He is indeed." I finished the breakfast and helped Tess transfer the rest of the food to the platters, which she sent up to the dining room.

I then made my way to the larder, returning with a small basket. "You take this," I said to Tess, pushing it into her hands. "You have someone to care for, and I told you, you'll always have help here."

Tess stared at me in shock. "But you can't nick food from her ladyship's kitchen."

I gave her an indignant look. "I'm not nicking it. These are goods I bought with my own money. I always choose something for myself from the market, a treat after a hard day. But I want you to take this to your brother. Has he got anything decent to wear?"

Tess nodded. "He'll do."

"I'm sure we can find a castoff in his size around here, if he needs it. Just make certain he has someplace to sleep at night, someplace safe."

"We have a room I let for him," Tess said, and then her voice broke. "You're too good to me, Mrs. H."

I held up my hands in alarm. "Please do not fly

at me weeping again, my dear. I have had a long morning."

Tess's sunny smile beamed as she clutched the basket. "Right you are, Mrs. Holloway. I did preparations for dinner already, so you rest as much as you like. I'll be back to help you make supper."

I knew she would be. I was well aware that Tess could take the basket I'd just given her and disappear forever, but I knew she'd return. This house was not ours in the strictest sense, but that did not mean we hadn't found a home here, at least for now.

I gave Tess a kiss on the cheek as I sent her off. She went, dashing up the outside stairs with enviable energy.

Mr. Davis returned to the kitchen after breakfast, at the same time the empty platters creaked down the dumbwaiter. The scullery maid and Charlie carried the dishes to the sink to clean while I sat and had another cup of tea. An efficient assistant was a fine thing to have.

"Lady Cynthia got a right ticking off for running about the streets all morning in her trousers," Mr. Davis told me. "Her aunt and uncle are too hard on her, in my mind. Considering what some young ladies get up to these days—eloping with rakes, gambling themselves into penury, even drinking spirits—Lady Cynthia wearing trousers should be the least of their worries."

I quite agreed. But then, Mr. and Mrs. Bywater

were trying their best to marry off Cynthia and be done with her. The more eccentric she chose to be, the more difficult their task.

I remembered what Cynthia had said about the widowed state as the best one for a woman. The restrictions society put on unmarried and even married ladies made that true. It was a wonder all wives didn't poison their husbands once they'd secured a good jointure, I thought, taking another sip of the delicious tea.

Mr. Davis closed his mouth as Lady Cynthia herself tripped lightly down the back stairs.

This morning she wore a suit of soot black with a light gray waistcoat, and she carried gray kid gloves and a tall hat. "Davis," she said rather stiffly. "Sorry you had to listen to that scene in the dining room. My aunt hasn't yet caught on to the fact that butlers and footmen are actual people."

Mr. Davis gave her a formal bow. "Not at all, Lady Cynthia. I take it as a compliment that I am in the family's confidence. I assure you, nothing said goes beyond these walls."

Within these walls, however, Mr. Davis felt it his right to discuss anything the family said ad nauseam, but I kept this observation to myself.

Cynthia huffed a laugh. "You're a good man, Davis. Mrs. Holloway, may I borrow you a moment?"

Davis walked away, back to his duties, breaking

381

into humming as he made his way to the butler's pantry. Cynthia lingered, fingering her hat.

"Do you think Mr. Thanos is up to seeing visitors?" she asked. "I'd like to look in on him—and young James, of course. See if they are well. They're heroes, rather."

I rose. "Indeed, I believe visiting Mr. Thanos and James is an excellent idea. Might I accompany you? Tess has managed things so well I won't be needed for a few hours."

Cynthia raised her brows. "I meant for you to accompany me. Didn't I say? Wouldn't be proper, would it—me visiting an unmarried gentleman without a chaperone, never mind he's in his sick bed? Good Lord, the house might fall down."

I gave her an amused nod. "Well, we can't have that."

I filled a basket with fresh bread, seedcake, sponge cake, apples, gooseberries, and a pot of my lemon curd as well as one of clotted cream to take to Mr. Thanos and James. Sometimes the best medicine is a bit of good cooking. Cynthia enjoyed helping me choose the comestibles, telling me to take whatever I wanted—she'd see it right with Aunt Isobel.

I donned my coat and bonnet, and we went out, Cynthia clapping the tall hat on her head and settling her gloves as any man might do.

She'd already hired a coach, as she neither wanted to take her brother-in-law's stately landau or squash herself in a hansom all the way to Kensington. We climbed inside. I had pried the specific address of Daniel's rooms from him as we'd ridden from the doctor's, and I directed the driver to let us off at a house in Campden Hill Road.

The house was a modest affair, three floors high in a row of similar houses, all of them with brown brick on the upper floors and whitewashed brick on the lower. Two square windows marked each floor, the facade narrow enough that I suspected the house was only one room wide. A green painted front door with a polished knocker reposed next to outside stairs that led down to the basement level.

My instinct was to go down these stairs to the kitchen below, but Lady Cynthia stepped up to the front door and banged on it with the knocker.

Daniel himself pulled open the door. He was dressed in plain broadcloth trousers and a linen shirt with no waistcoat, these topped with an unbuttoned frock coat he must have pulled on as he hurried to the door. This ensemble was neither his working clothes nor his City gent's suit, and I wondered if this was what he wore when he didn't need to be anyone but himself.

Daniel seemed to have the run of the entire house. I'd expected that he rented only a few rooms here, but he ducked into the parlor to neaten newspapers he'd been reading and then led us up to the first floor to the two bedchambers there—one in front, and one in the rear.

The rear one held James. The lad was sleeping, one arm bandaged and in a sling, the other thrown across the pillow next to him. His face had regained color around his bruises, and he let out a soft snore.

The whole of myself relaxed when I saw him. He was young and strong, and had Daniel to look after him. Seeing him struck down in the street had sent profound fear through my soul, but he would be well, I knew it.

Mr. Thanos, in the front bedroom, was wide awake. He sat up in the bed against a pile of pillows, wearing a dressing gown of a deep shade of purple. He was surrounded by books, newspapers, and notebooks, all open and strewn across the covers and the bedside tables, some spilling onto the floor. He dropped a large tome onto his lap as Daniel opened the door, and he looked at us with joy in his eyes.

"Thank God," Elgin cried. "Do tell him to let me out of this bed, ladies. I am perfectly well, but McAdam has turned nursemaid on me. We are within shouting distance of both Kensington Palace Gardens and Holland Park, but will he let me stroll and absorb the wonders of botany? Not a bit of it. I shall die here, I know it."

Elgin's color was high, his eyes sparkling, and he did look well, but I remained cautious.

"Poisoning is no light matter," I said to him. "Especially by arsenic. It can linger in the system for some time. We must make certain it dissipates and does not cause you sickness because you rise too quickly."

Elgin's eager hope died into glumness. Cynthia drew a chair close to the bed, sat down, leaned the chair back, and propped her boots on the coverlet. "Not to worry, Mr. Thanos. I've come to cheer you up. My uncle hopes you're feeling better and says he'll be ready for your museum outing whenever you recover."

"Ah well," Elgin said, looking a bit mollified. He peered at me. "Jove, I didn't realize you knew all about poisons, Mrs. Holloway."

"I am a cook," I answered. "I make it my policy to know about everything a body can ingest. Arsenic is unfortunately prevalent in many aspects of life."

"That's heartening," Cynthia remarked. She took the basket from me, set it on the bed, and began rummaging through it. "We've brought you some jolly nice cakes, Mr. Thanos, and Mrs. Holloway's excellent lemon curd. We'll chew through these in a trice as you tell me what you are working on."

Elgin brightened. "Ah—it is a new model of the known universe. I am not certain whether the bright but nebulous objects seen through the strongest telescopes are gas clouds within our

385

own galaxy, or something beyond it. Proving they are the latter is the devil, though. I have calculated . . ."

He sifted through papers, shoving them at Cynthia, who plucked them up and peered at them as though she had any idea what they meant.

Daniel and I left them to it. I kept the bed-chamber door open as I went, of course—I would be lax in my duties as a chaperone if I did not.

After we took another peep at the sleeping James, Daniel led me back down the narrow staircase to the parlor. The room was comfortable if small and a bit cluttered—this was most definitely a bachelor's house.

"Sorry I didn't lay on any tea," Daniel said as he waved me to a sofa that was free of newspapers. "I didn't realize you would come so soon."

"Of course we would come," I said as I seated myself. "Lady Cynthia and I are naturally worried about our friends." Sunlight poured through the front window, brightening the room. "I do hope you have a cook or housekeeper to look after you."

Daniel shrugged. "I have a woman come in the mornings to get us breakfast." He sat down on the sofa next to me. "Otherwise, I fend for myself. There's a decent inn up the road, and I fetch food from there."

"It is a fine house," I said, glancing about. "If a bit far from things. Why haven't you brought

James here to live before this? There's plenty of room."

Cozy, I thought. Two rooms on each floor, a bit of garden in the back, leafy trees on the street.

"I only hired it a few weeks ago," Daniel said with the beginnings of a smile. "I hadn't realized it would become a convalescent home."

"You are good to Mr. Thanos," I said with conviction. "And your son."

"Do *you* like it, Kat?"

The change in his voice made my senses sharpen. "It is not a bad place," I said, trying to sound offhand. "I will have to inspect the kitchen and see if it passes muster, but otherwise . . ." I gave him a nod. "I approve."

His full smile shone out. "Thank heavens for that. Perhaps you will deign to visit me once in a while?" The question was hopeful.

"While Mr. Thanos and James are recovering, certainly," I said. "Otherwise, it would be improper."

Daniel's eyes sparkled. "I'll find us a chaperone, then. I promise that you will never have to worry about your reputation with me, Mrs. Holloway."

"I should certainly hope not," I said. It was what I was supposed to say.

Can I be blamed if I felt a frisson of disappointment? A lady doesn't truly want to let herself be seduced and ruined, of course, but sometimes she would like to think she has the choice.

"What will you do now?" I asked quickly. "Now that the mystery of the stolen antiquities is solved and the villains taken? Pursue Mr. Pilcher?"

Daniel sobered. "I don't know. Is it worth it, raking up the past? But then I remember . . . It was so horrible, Kat. They killed everyone in that house. No caring, no remorse. Can I let men like that get away?"

"It was a long time ago," I reminded him.

"The passing of years doesn't make their crime any less." Daniel shook his head. "It has driven my life. Turning a corner, taking a different direction . . ." His eyes held a flicker of something I couldn't read, but I thought perhaps it was fear. "I don't know if I'm able."

"You have James now." I reached over and took his hand. "And me."

Daniel's focus moved to me, all amusement gone. "Do I?"

"Of course," I said. "I am loyal to my friends. The true ones."

Daniel said nothing. He held my hand and studied me, emotions dancing into and out of his eyes faster than I could decipher them.

"I'm not certain if what is around the corner is an easy path or a sudden cliff." Daniel swallowed and tightened his grip. "It terrifies me."

I heard the truth in his words, saw his uncertainty. I understood—when I'd heard of my husband's death and then found out I was not a widow but an unmarried woman with an illegitimate child, an abyss had yawned before me. I'd held on to Grace and skirted the edge, barely making it back to firmer ground.

I squeezed Daniel's hand. "We will find out together," I told him. "I promise."

Daniel abruptly leaned to me and kissed me. He closed his eyes as he did so, hiding all that was in them.

The kiss was quicker and quieter than the one in the doctor's house, and also full of gratitude and hope.

"God bless you, Kat Holloway," Daniel whispered.

For answer, I pressed my hand to his cheek, feeling the prickle of his unshaved whiskers.

Boots thumped on the stairs, and Cynthia's frantic voice called down. "Do help me. The bloody man's ready to go up on the roof and build himself an observatory."

Daniel was on his feet in an instant, and he pulled me up with him, still holding my hand as we made for the hall.

"Damnation," Daniel shouted up the stairs. "Do I have to strap you down, Thanos?"

Elgin's voice answered weakly. I could not help laughing as I ran up with Daniel, ready to assist, my good fortune at having such friends surrounding me with happiness.

Jennifer Ashley is the *New York Times* and *USA Today* bestselling author of the Below Stairs Mysteries, including *Death Below Stairs*, and winner of a Romance Writers of America RITA Award. She also writes as national bestselling and award-winning author Allyson James and bestselling author Ashley Gardner. She lives in the Southwest with her husband and cats, and spends most of her time in the wonderful worlds of her stories.

You can contact her online at
jenniferashley.com

and visit her at
facebook.com/JenniferAshleyAllyson
JamesAshleyGardner

and twitter.com/JennAllyson.

Center Point Large Print
600 Brooks Road / PO Box 1
Thorndike, ME 04986-0001 USA

(207) 568-3717

US & Canada:
1 800 929-9108
www.centerpointlargeprint.com